Dedicated to:

Peter Kougasian

I stole from him more than he taught me.

TABLE OF CONTENTS

PREFACE

This volume is like a bride's trousseau. Something, old, something new, something borrowed, and, *definitely,* something blue. Skip the short stories that have already appeared elsewhere. Many of the tales in the title piece are old and worn, so you might as well skip those, as well. Basically, all the new or unfamiliar parts should take about twenty minutes to get through. Thanks for buying it anyway.

Andrew Smith --- February 2018

I WASN'T MY FIRST CHOICE

It hasn't been easy, my life. Well, okay, actually, it's been *pretty* easy-*ish*. But *adjusting* to it hasn't been a walk in the park. I've always been on the outside looking in. Nobody ever described me as normal. Nobody ever said, "Hey, let's go hang out with that guy. He's normal". What they said, instead, was, "Hey, let's go fuck with that guy because he'll do anything." Yeah, I was the guy in third grade who would run into a wall to get a laugh. I was the one who put the tack on the teacher's chair and got caught doing it. I killed birds and tortured small animals. I'm not proud of it, but I *am* proud that I had the balls to do some stuff. I didn't fantasize. Maybe, I *was* the fantasy. I did it. *Somebody* had to do it. *Somebody* had to be crazy enough. Otherwise *nobody* would have any stories.

My problem was that the stories continued on throughout my life. Stories. There were always stories to tell. A tale. "You'll never guess what happened," I would begin. Or, "This actually happened." I was never at a loss for words. I found out early on in life that telling the truth was easier than making it up because nobody believes you anyway. And telling the truth helps with the delivery. If you tell the truth, you're a comedian. If you make it up, you're bullshit.

So, most of my forays into the fantastic were in the service of a story to tell. Or vice versa. I can't tell which. But crazy things *did* happen to me, I think, more than to other people. It's as if I was a lightning rod for "whacky". I was "God's sitcom". But why me? What was I doing? What was I after? Was I all story and no pay off? The problem was that the big payoff in life proved highly elusive or missing altogether. I was left with only the outrageous. All bits and no legitimacy.

But is that what's in store for all kids who run into walls for laughs? Should I feel sorry for myself? Of course I do, but I don't advertise it. It's considered a pejorative. But is it? Why can't you truly feel sorry for yourself and *still* have everyone applaud you for being inappropriate? Like the psychiatrist in the joke who says, "You don't have an inferiority complex. You *are* inferior," I'm okay with that.

* * *

I tested my Depends recently. They work! June Allyson lives! I feel like an astronaut for the first time in my life. But be forewarned. The issue with Depends is not that they work, but that, afterwards, taking them off is like emptying a septic tank in your pants.

But why am I wearing Depends? Because, like some women on those "special days", I spot. And why am I spotting? I don't know. But getting undressed these days is like administering a Rorschach test to yourself. It's all part of the process, I suppose. A life examined turns out to be what's left in your underpants. Yeah. *Now,* I get the answers. *After* the test. Thanks a lot. That's a *great* help.

* * *

Elmore Leonard's best writing advice is to leave out all the parts that readers tend to skip. Apply that to life, and what do you get? The best life is the one with the least skipping, I guess. But what do you do if you're actually *in* your life, and you say, "I think I'd like to skip this part." What do you do? Just skip it? Did Nike get it wrong? Is life like a bad movie you can walk out of at any time? I used to think that. My default position was "exit." Now it's something else. Sort of, "in your face" existentialism.

But, you see, mere existence isn't enough, either. You have to exist *as* something. A friend once told me, when I was trying to decide whether to go on a college road trip or stay on campus, that the choice was really between something and nothing. If I stayed on campus, I would do nothing; if I went on the road trip, I would at least be doing *something*. And something was infinitely more productive than nothing. So I learned a lot. But not in school.

Most lives are boring and tedious. Too many parts that would be better off skipped. Maybe that's where I come in. There used to be an ad on television that offered classical music records "with all the unfamiliar parts left out". They would announce it proudly as if *that's* what we'd been looking for all our lives. All the boring parts left out. Nothing unfamiliar. You could go to sleep on that. It must have struck a chord with everyone because the ad persisted for years and always with the same semi-class pitch guy. I think he even had a waxed moustache, so you *knew* he was the real McCoy. "All the unfamiliar parts left out", indeed. On the other hand, maybe "the unfamiliar parts" are what we want.

I remember an eccentric friend once turned to the person next to him at a small gathering and said, flatly, without affect, "Do I look unfamiliar to you?" It always struck me as the greatest opening line of all time. "Do I look unfamiliar to you?" The listener must prove the negative by saying, "Yes, I recognize that you are unfamiliar. That you look like nothing or no one I have ever seen." But, then, that renders the unfamiliar one eminently unique, memorable, and, henceforth, familiar. Or, if the answer is "No, you do not look unfamiliar to me", then the questioner looks familiar, but may *still* be unrecognizable and unidentifiable to the listener. The polite answer, I suppose, is, "No," because it places the questioner, at least, within the realm of possibility; but then that comes across as a harsh rejection nevertheless. These are the double negatives of cocktail parties.

* * *

The question is often asked, "Do other species experience life the same way humans do?" In other words, do animals feel emotion, love, loyalty, friendship, art, and charity as humans pride themselves as exclusively experiencing those qualities? Or are these "higher" emotions unique to the human experience? Often there follows examples of animals *apparently* demonstrating some of these virtues. Animals befriending each other or experiencing loss. Somehow, this "unity of life" is supposed to make us feel better. Animals are just like us. Sort of. Except when we eat them. Or enslave them, or make them to do stupid shit for food. But there is *one* quality that animals definitely do *not* share: stuttering. Animals do not stutter. Only man does of all the living things on earth. Have you ever heard a dog go, "B-b-b-b-b-bow w-w-w-w-w-wow? Or a bird say, "T-t-t-t-t-t-tweet? No. The truth is, stuttering, unlike love and loyalty, is ours alone.

I once worked in a bar in Iowa City. What I was doing in a state I could not say properly, I do not know. The bar was called "The Airliner." The Airliner was owned by a woman named "Astrid." My name began with an

"A". There was trouble every time I picked up the phone. Even in my twenties, I stuttered badly on words with initial vowels and, *especially*, on anything that began with the letter "A". The University of Iowa had a world-famous speech pathology school. After a few telephone grotesqueries at the bar, the owners insisted I pay a visit to the University speech department.

Walking into the University of Iowa School of Speech Pathology and Audiology was like a stutterer's bad dream. Everyone in the joint either stuttered or was a reformed stutterer trying to pass. But stutterers can clock a fellow language mangler no matter how well they've strategized themselves around the problem in the way that drunks can instantly spot a dry alcoholic.

The trouble started right away at the desk.

"C-c-c-c-can I-I-I-I h-h-h-h-h-help y-y-y-you?" the girl said.

You have to understand that any encounter with another stutterer tends to make the first stutterer an immediate Demosthenes. Otherwise, they think you're making fun of them.

"Yeah, I'd like to talk to someone about a program."

"R-r-r-r-right t-t-t-this w-w-w-w-w-way."

I stopped in my tracks and would not follow her. You rarely meet female stutterers. It seems to be a male affliction and, most often, the sons of lawyers. But that's when I looked around and saw that the place was crawling with stutterers. I had to get out of there. I begged off and said I would be back later.

"Y'all c-c-c-c-come b-b-b-b-back a-a-a-and s-s-s-see u-u-u-us r-r-r-real s-s-s-s-soon," she said.

I stopped answering the phone at the Airliner.

I have never seen an *old* stutterer. There are no speech impediments in old age homes, I think, because stuttering is a disease of intimidation, and, at some point in life, the stutterer decides he just doesn't give a fuck. Either that or you get real smart about not answering the phone. Mel Tillis, who made a career out of stuttering, told me that as soon as he started making money and became successful, the stuttering faded away. He was faking it from then on.

But, of course, stuttering didn't stop me from taking "Public Speaking 101" in college which was the equivalent of a blind man taking "Art Appreciation". I dared them to punish me for my disability and ended up with a "B". Mission accomplished.

Religion courses filled out the rest of my curriculum because as a good Catholic I already knew more religion than most of the frustrated minister-type professors. Thus, I would pay a visit to my religion professor each semester to inform him that I had had a "conversion experience" as a result of his class. That always worked since it served as the ultimate compliment. And I think they loved the idea of "rescuing" a Catholic who was contemplating the priesthood.

The priesthood flirtation was actually real. In those days, because of the Hollywood and Irish glorification of "men of the collar", Catholic priests seemed to be more like cowboys than religious leaders. They were magically smarter; they could go anywhere; everyone loved them; they could work small miracles; and, if they played the piano, everyone applauded and considered them brilliant. Priests also got a *lot* more laughs than they deserved as well.

But the specific problem with having a late vocation at a secular college, in *my* case, at least, was that the very same road that led to a Carmelite monastery outside of town, and where I would go for counsel and confession, was also the same one that led to the locally infamous woman named "Rita the Heater". I had to literally pass the latter in order to get to the former. As my bumpy college years passed, it became easier and easier to turn into Rita's place rather than to continue on to the monastery. "Rita the Heater" was a blousy Marilyn Monroe-type blonde from New York. Her husband was on the run from Proctor and Gamble, or something, and ran the local liquor store. Consequently, Rita was well-stocked as well as well-stacked. As my trips to the monastery succumbed more frequently to Rita's turn-off (or, "turn-on"), my vocation fell by the wayside. Or should I say, "roadside"---meaning Rita's place on the way to the monastery. It was like one of those cautionary fairy tales. But with a *very* happy ending.

* * *

I read my menus very carefully. And I believe them. I read restaurant menus as if they are literally true and contain vital information to help me make my dining decisions. I can't help it. Why would they lie? I mean, wouldn't I rather have a "succulent" pork chop than the simple a "rotisserie-roasted" chicken? And, by the way, whenever I read it, I also think I probably deserve it, too. "Freshly picked greens" are better for me than the simple "house" salad. And gimme "farm-fresh" every time. When I see "freshly caught wild Salmon", I picture the chef with a pole standing next to a Grizzly on a rock next to a river in Alaska fighting with him for my dinner. I'm sorry, but "tasty" means something to me when I see it. And "slow- cooked" means just that. No hurry. Thanks for taking the time to cook it slow. I like "*au jus*" almost as much as "succulent". And I choose a certain bag of nuts over another bag simply because those nuts happened to have been "*gently* roasted" as opposed to just "roasted." I will never be fooled again.

I am a married man. I had a dream the other night that a very attractive woman was interested in me; and, in the dream, I decided to take her up on it. So I, very charmingly, asked her for her number. Then I took out a pen and paper to write it down, but the pen didn't work. I asked her to wait while I looked around for another pen. I found another pen, but that one didn't work, either. I kept trying pens but couldn't, for the life of me, find a pen that worked. They kept running out of ink and not being able to write at all. I could only write part of the woman's number down before each pen became useless. WHAT DOES IT ALL MEAN!? The only good thing about the dream was that the woman was very patient and didn't mind waiting for me to find a pen. She's still waiting. I woke up before I found a good one.

* * *

I knew all about the Ho Chi Minh trail long before anyone else did. In fact, I knew about it when it first came out. It was in the National Geographic in the winter of 1961. I was home reading magazines while on sabbatical from college. I had made the mistake of not going to class for an entire semester. Who knew that that could lead to reading magazines at home for a year? So I read about the Ho Chi Minh Trail and how North Vietnam was infiltrating the South on that goddamn trail. Okay. Then, at about the same time, President Kennedy invented the Special Forces. Just the thing to inspire a twenty-year-old who had never so much as camped out in the back yard. I liked the idea that the Special Forces guys could do special things, like make a radio out of a bar of soap, or something, or go places undetected. I think it was the undetected part that inspired me the most.

My first stop was at the U.S. Army recruiting station in Bridgeport, Connecticut. The recruiter was a Special Forces guy. I never asked him what the hell he was doing wearing a Green Beret in Bridgeport, Connecticut and not on the Ho Chi Minh Trail. It was none of my business. Maybe he was being undetected. I spent a lot of time visiting that recruiting station with the result that, ultimately, I think I was somewhat "over-recruited" when the time came for me to actually sign up for duty. There's only so much Green Beret bullshit a twenty-year-old can take without becoming saturated. At the time, I was under the simultaneous care of a psychiatrist and the Jesuits ---both of which, I considered, good training for commando work. The shrink's name was Dr. Kloth (conveniently), and his office was over the local meat market. Both good omens, I thought. (The office later became an after-hours Irish drinking club, but don't tell Dr. Kloth)

But being over-recruited had its drawbacks. Sure, you were more likely to think that free-falling out of a helicopter in the middle of the night into a rice paddy in a strange country was a good thing; but you were also more likely to assume that the draft board exam, itself, was a test of your "Special Forces-grade" mettle and, very possibly, a clever trick to separate the Green Berets from the wimps.

So it was that I found myself in the Army induction center in New Haven with my pants off, surrounded by draft inductees who were ready to ship out to Fort Dix that afternoon. It was during the Berlin Wall crisis; and President Kennedy had said that if you were married, you didn't have to go. Consequently, there were fiancées literally pulling guys out of line saying, "Okay, I'll marry you," as we all moved forward. But then, *I* got pulled out of line, but not by a fiancée. I got pulled out by a staff sergeant.

It seems I had answered one too many questions on my medical history exam. As a result, the United States Army did not want to take the chance of having me stand in line with the other recruits with my pants off any longer. They had sprung into action. But I was sure this was all part of the Special Forces selection process. "The Few, the Proud, the Continent".

My specific problem turned out to be my unique "Special Forces-type" interpretation of how that tricky little medical history form had been worded. It had *said,* "Do you have now, or have you *ever* had....." A trick question if I ever saw one. A Special Forces candidate guy, like myself, could spot that a mile away. The recruiter had told me, in no uncertain terms, that truthfulness and forthrightness were the hallmarks of the proud wearer of a Green Beret. I was way ahead of these jokers.

Consequently, not to dissemble in any way, I had checked every disease I *thought* I might have had, just to be completely transparent. Diphtheria, whooping cough, pellagra...*everything*...*anything*. I was sure I had touches of most of them even though it might not have been full-blown at the time. "Menstrual cramps and excessive bleeding" were another story. As a kid I had had a chronic intestinal blockage which had expressed itself as cramps. Okay, maybe it wasn't *exactly* menstrual, but it was cramps all right. And bleeding? *Fugeddabowdit.* I've picked enough scabs to know about bleeding.

They were clever, these Army medics, but I was way ahead of them. They didn't know that I had been diagnosed as "over-scrupulous" by a prep school priest who had grown tired of my overly-detailed, and lengthy, confessions. Today it would be called "moral OCD". The problem in trying to be free of sin in those days was that I knew *exactly* what I had done wrong; but, goddammit, I was man enough to confess it completely if that's what it took to gain eternal redemption and salvation.

"Do you have now, or have you *ever* had?...." "Bed wetting." The form asked that right next to a little box. "Check!" *Please*! Do not try to trip up a Special Forces candidate with such a simple ruse. The right answer is, obviously, "Yes!" Of *course*! Hasn't *everyone*? As a child? So, I checked "Bed wetting." Then, there were a few more like "Depression", "Problems with sleep", and "Headaches." All, "Check". They weren't going to fool me or be able to say I tried to hide anything. By the time I was finished, my medical history had more checks than a Slovakian unity rally.

"Grab the one with the still-dry underpants and get him out of line," they probably ordered. "Trouble". "Red alert"."May Day". "No wonder there are no fiancées around who want to marry that guy." Of course, I thought it was because I was being singled out for, perhaps, a beret fitting or something, in a private room. As it turned out, it was closer to a straitjacket fitting in the Army headshrinker's office.

When I realized that I was being sent to see an army psychiatrist, I thought it was about the funniest thing that had ever happened to me. I literally began singing the lyrics to, "Officer Krupke" from West Side Story. This was *funny*.

So, I sat down with some pencil-necked Yalie who was working as an army headshrinker for that day, and I chuckled to myself unabashedly. I thought the whole thing was ridiculous and hysterical. "Officer Krupke, you're really a square; this boy don't need a judge, he needs an analyst's care....."

I continued to laugh and chuckle as I sat down opposite the psychiatrist at a small table in a side room in the induction center. I thought he would find this ridiculous, also. But he was all business. He wanted to know if I was seeing a psychiatrist. I told him about Dr. Kloth. He wanted to know if I ever heard voices. I told him that, actually, I often thought I heard my father calling me to do some chore or else summoning me for some disciplinary reason. He asked me if I ever talked to myself. I said I did as a way of reassurance. He wanted to know if I ever got excited. I told him sure, on Christmas mornings, and, actually, I had even been excited to come down there that day to the induction center. He asked if I slept soundly. I told him I usually had to get up in the middle of the night to go to the bathroom (Oh-oh). At that point, he then looked at me, turned my file over and said he thought I should go home.

I stood up immediately and angrily.

"Whaddya mean 'go home?'" I said loudly. "Whaddya talkin' about?"

"See?" He said quietly. "You're getting excited."

I sat down. Then, while he wrote his report, he said, "The army's not for you. You should go home."

At that point I thought I should let him know that I was actually there for Special Forces. He wasn't impressed. He just looked at me.

"I don't think so," he said. And that was it. It was over.

Years later I went to the Selective Service archives in Bridgeport and looked up my records in order to see exactly what he written about me. And what follows is what kept me out of Vietnam and, most certainly, kept me alive to tell this tale:

"The inductee is a twenty-year-old, former college student, who is currently under psychiatric care. He smiles and laughs disassociatvely and admits to freely communicating with himself. He experiences auditory hallucinations which indicate a schizophrenic reaction. Recommendation: Deferred."

That was it. "4-F, Section 8." I was classified with homosexuals (the Army thought they were crazy in those days) and outright lunatics. I was forbidden to go to Vietnam and too crazy for the Ho Chi Minh Trail.

I went home and told my mother that I would not be shipping out to Fort Dix that day and, therefore, would be home for supper. She was glad, but she hadn't known that I had been about to enlist in the Army and join the Special Forces.

The next day I went *back* to the induction center in New Haven and tried to gain access. I was stopped at the door by a large, imposing sergeant in an Army uniform. (no Green Beret). I promptly informed him that I had been there the day before and that I had received a classification of "4-F, Section 8", which was a *huge* mistake and that I had returned to appeal that decision. He took one long look at me and replied, "Get the fuck outa here." He would not let me enter. So, now, I was banned from Vietnam, the Ho Chi Minh Trail, *and* the Army induction center.

My family did not seem to mind or even register that I had been classified as a military punch line. And it wasn't until I applied for a job with the C.I.A. years later after returning to college that it became a problem. The C.I.A had come up to the school to recruit on campus because the son of the C.I.A. Director, at the time, was a student there.

When I saw the announcement for C.I.A interviews my senior year, I immediately signed up. Thoughts of the civilian equivalent of the Green Berets flooded my consciousness. When I walked into the Placement Bureau office for the interview, the first thing the C.I.A. guy did was stand up and pull down the window shades without saying a word. I remember thinking, "Wow! These guys are *serious!* This is real *spy* shit.

The C.I. A. recruiter then sat back down at his desk.

"What is your draft status?" He asked without any preliminaries.

"4-F Section 8," I told him somewhat proudly.

At that point, the C.I.A. guy stood up and raised the window shades back up again. Then, he sat down and leaned in toward me.

"I don't think you could get a job with the Agriculture Department," he said.

I told him how it was all a huge mistake. He didn't believe me, of course, but he was nice enough to say, "Then, if I were you, I'd get it fixed. *Immediately.*"

And that was the end of my C.I.A. interview. About two minutes.

It was then that I realized I was never going to work for the government of the United States of America. I never *did* get my classification fixed or changed, or even tried to. Actually, in the end, I decided the Army head-shrinker had been right for the wrong reasons. If I *had* ever gone into the military, I most likely would have ended up either dead or in the brig.

* * *

As it was, the closest I ever came to uniformed service was when I enlisted as an NBC page after college. At that point, I think I was the oldest page to ever be on active duty at NBC. It was during the height of the Vietnam War by then, so I would wear my uniform to church just to make my mother proud. The uniform was dark blue and had the same sort of gold epaulets and braid on the shoulders except that, instead of a bald eagle on my hat, there was a peacock. But, as it turned out, I was unfit for the Page Corps as well. I was fired shortly before the end of my 13-month tour of duty for dropping my pants in an elevator at 30 Rock. That's when I was *sure* the Army induction center had known something that I didn't.

For a college graduate, being a uniformed usher with a paper collar is not exactly the most demanding of occupations. Even the kids doing it part-time while they were in school were bored. The pages would entertain themselves during the day with various games and pastimes. One of my colleagues sold dried banana skins to Johnny Carson because it had been rumored that if you smoked a banana joint, it would make you high. This was during a time when everyone on the "Tonight Show" wore turtlenecks because Carson did.

Most of the pranks were usually aimed at the tour guides whom we always considered to be of lower status on the "buddy-fuck" ladder at NBC Guest Relations. We would hijack studio tours of sightseers when the guides weren't looking and lead the unsuspecting tourists into electrical closets or dead-end hallways and leave them there looking at walls.

But what got me fired wasn't any of those shenanigans or the heinous crime of standing with my hands in my pockets since the pockets on all our uniforms had been sewn shut to prevent just such a breach. No, my sin was that whenever I found myself in an elevator with strangers, once the doors closed, I considered it an opportunity for a command performance in front of a captive audience. Specifically, on my last afternoon as an employee of the NBC Guest Relations Staff, I was doing an imitation of Ed Sullivan getting a blow job from his wife, Sylvia. "Right here in my crotch. A *really, really* big erection" ("erection" is a great Ed Sullivan word---like, "Italy"). I had learned my "Sullivan" impression from the trombone player in the Tonight Show Band. The only problem on *that* afternoon was that the wife of the president of the network happened to be riding in the elevator along with the tour. Thus, she became an unwitting, and unwilling, member of my captive audience.

I was fired by the time we reached the 8th floor. My semi-military service had, once again, been cancelled ignominiously and without appeal.

* * *

I've basically been fired from every job I've ever had. One termination was from a position where, for the first time, my boss was not only an attractive woman, but much younger than me as well. I was so taken by that concept that I thought it would be droll if I announced to everyone that I had fallen in love with my boss. I even sent her flowers. She sent me home.

Then, another time, in New York, our offices happened to be directly across from a construction job that was happening on, approximately, the same floor in a building across the street. It was springtime. During lunch, I would open the large windows in our office and shout at the construction workers across the way who were also having lunch and relaxing in their hardhats. At first, I just waved and yelled benign greetings.

"Hello," or "How's it going?" I would yell to the workers across the street between us.

But then I got more personal.

"I want to suck your cock!" I would shout.

This sort of thing tends to get the attention of construction workers. But then I added choice epithets, lewd invitations, and personal insults. And, of course, I didn't stop. I continued to taunt them about their gender and their sexual preferences. And then, I made sure to brazenly identify myself in an equally loud and challenging fashion. Except the name I used was not mine, of course. It was my boss' name. I would then challenge them to do something about it, like *men*. I figured that, in-between their "dinosaur takes" (when you actually get a construction worker's attention he tends to raise his head up like a brontosaurus feeding in a primeval swamp), they would determine exactly where our offices were in our building and come across the street. The scenario I envisioned was that a delegation of enraged construction workers would arrive abruptly at our offices, demand to see the man (my boss) who had been taunting them, and then proceed to beat the shit out of him even though he would insist it wasn't him.

But this is what I *didn't* calculate. For some reason, I forgot that *my* window was only several windows down from where my boss's window was. And, it being a fine spring day, *his* window was open, too. Thus, he was actually fully aware of my performance and the misuse of his name and my construction worker homosexual taunts in his name. He was not amused. Mainly because, at a previous venue in his career, there had been some rumors. My inadvertent re-visiting of this issue did not sit well. I was fired.

* * *

The concept of random insults had always fascinated me. In my own twisted brain, I did not know why a person would consider an unprovoked and unrelated, random insult, from a complete stranger, actionable. In other words, if I gave the finger, for no reason, to someone driving a car on a highway, why should he feel personally threatened and obliged to respond in kind? Wouldn't the correct reaction be merely to shrug and ignore it?

The variations in response tended to run along ethnic, racial, and gender lines. Thus, if an African-American man saw an average white guy give him the finger on the highway, for no reason, he would just chuckle to himself the way a sleepy lion might do if, say, a gazelle had stuck its tongue out at him. But an Italian male? Well, *now* you're talkin' major brouhaha. Italian males take that random shit *very* personally.

For some reason, Italian men of a certain age and economic status, respond to all insults, perceived or otherwise, while on the road as if they knew you and you knew them. I have tested this out extensively. Thus, a random finger, flashed innocently and for no reason to an Italian male, drives him *crazy*! Try it. Everyone else that you might give the finger to just shrugs it off because they think *you're* crazy. But, for an Italian male, it's war. At the very least, they get all involved in the insult and give you the finger back, *con brio*! But, at the worst, as happened to me once, they will swerve their car over to yours and try to kill you. And then they will follow you off the highway, to where you live, and even into your driveway. When this happened to me, being the coward that I am, I went into the house and didn't come out while the Italian gentleman revved his engine menacingly before finally going away. I may be a crazy white asshole; but, seriously, folks, as Rodney King would say, can't we all just get along?

Older white people will respond guiltily if you merely shake your finger at them admonishingly. They think they've done something wrong but can't, for the life of them, figure out what it is. Of course, this is best done in pantomime through closed windows at 60 miles per hour. This is how I used to entertain myself when I had to sit in the back seat. Especially if we were in slow moving traffic. Then, at some point, my driver would say, "What's the matter with that guy in the next car? He keeps looking at me like I'm crazy."

* * *

Another time, when I got fired, I was completely blind-sided by the abrupt termination. But that didn't prevent me from going down on one knee while taking my pulse and apparently becoming disoriented. I knew I had a chronic irregular heartbeat going for me anyway, so I wasn't *entirely* faking it; and I figured why should I let these bastards off easily? As it turned out, I was, at that moment, half-way through writing a novel based on this particular job. The opening scene of the fiction piece was one in which the hero gets fired and fakes a heart attack in the executive producer's office. Thus, when it actually happened in real time, it was like following a script. I knew exactly what to do.

The boss called the in-house paramedics and then an ambulance, and I left the office feet first. But get this. No one called the hospital where they took me and where the emergency room doctors wanted to admit me as a heart patient. The boss had absolutely no guilt, no fear of me dying, nor any sense of responsibility for sending me to the hospital by firing me. Finally, I rose up, Lazarus-like, from my hospital stretcher after several hours of emergency nonsense and heart monitoring and went back to the office after hours and cleaned out my desk. But I still liked the fact that I left the job in an ambulance. It was a good lesson: pay your union dues. They're the only ones who will stand by you in the end.

* * *

I was once fired by the husband of a comedienne for writing too many bra jokes for her. He was semi-English, and I think *he* was offended. Of course, the comedienne was famous for making placenta jokes, for crissakes, so you would think jokes about "D" cups and underwires would be a step *up*. The husband was her manager and the titular producer of the show, but his main job, by his own design, was to stand by the studio coffee table to check to see if people from other studios were coming in and drinking *his* coffee. He ended up committing suicide while the comedienne was having liposuction. If he'd had a neck he would have hanged himself, but I think he took pills instead.

* * *

The first real job I had I was fired from because they didn't really want to hire me in the first place. I could tell they weren't really serious about me working there because my office was in the coat closet. I had done free-lance work for them, *sub rosa*; so maybe they felt obligated when I got fired from the job I was hired to do. But not *that* obligated. They moved a desk into the coat room for me. People used to come in and hang up their coats over my desk while I worked. I got to know everyone there real fast.

But it didn't last long. I think my office mates complained. They thought I was disrespecting their hats and coats or something, and I was fired within three months. Besides, it was winter. They needed the closet more than they needed me.

* * *

When Screamin' Jay Hawkins, the legendary black rock 'n roll icon, died, his obit said he had fathered fifty-seven children. Somebody even set up a website in order to find and locate all of them. Naturally, I signed up immediately. When the website people contacted me, I told them my mother had been a talent coordinator for a New York late night talk show, and she had had an affair with Jay when he was on the show and had gotten pregnant by him. Hence, me. It all seemed to make sense to the interviewer, and they wanted to meet me. I told them I was too shy to actually meet them. My mother was dead, and I was trying to put the whole story of my sordid parentage behind me. But they persisted.

Then a British documentary team got on the case, and they started calling me. I was working in Daytime for a network at the time, so maybe that gave me some legitimacy. But I remained steadfastly shy and elusive, knowing that were I ever to actually show up, the gambit would be over. In fact, there actually *was* a time when I was in Los Angeles, and the documentary people were there interviewing other "Jay's Kids". We happened to be staying in the same hotel. The producer tracked me down, and I told the guy I would meet him at the hotel bar, but I never showed up. I think this "cat and mouse" routine just added to the verisimilitude.

Finally, a British film crew arrived in New York, and they were extremely aggressive about finally meeting me and getting me on tape to talk about my mother and Screamin' Jay. At the same time, "Prime Time Live", the ABC News Magazine, got wind of the "Jay's Kids" story, and *they* were preparing a segment for *their* show. All of a sudden, I got a call from the producer of "Prime Time Live". The request for my services was now coming from inside the company and from the Network News Division to boot. They wanted me to come over to the News Department and see them immediately. Fearing for my job in Daytime, I reluctantly confessed to the producer that it was all just a bit, and I wasn't *really* one of Jay's Kids. But I told him he should think twice about getting ABC and Prime Time Live involved in such nonsense because I had determined that the whole thing was a scam to try to get part of Screamin's supposed estate. The producer was not happy and hung up abruptly. But I was still employed. I had not been fired.....yet.

But that didn't deter the British film crew that was in town. They were buying all of it and wanted, now, an *exclusive* interview. So I enlisted my friend, Joe, a legendary Democratic ward heeler and Irish contract guy of indeterminate income stream and even *more* indeterminate credentials, to act as my lawyer. I did this because I knew Joe maintained an office on Fifth Avenue through one of his many enterprises, and it would provide a necessary buffer zone.

A meeting was set up in the conference room of his Fifth Avenue offices between Joe, myself, and the English documentary producer. We all met and shook hands. Joe then began to regale us with tales of my sainted mother as a young Irish girl in Greenwich Village who had been known, then, to be of "easy virtue" and, also, have a soft spot in her heart for the *mulignan* ("blacks"). The British producer was intrigued. Joe went on and on about how my mother was the neighborhood slut, and that he remembered the whole affair with Screamin' Jay. He was really into it, and I remember thinking that, maybe, my letting my sainted mother be so extensively maligned wasn't such a great idea, even for a few laughs.

My friend, Joe, had a look about him that I always described as that of a "spoilt priest". Thus, he had certain verisimilitude about him; but, at the same time, he also projected a certain sense that he might *just possibly* have another agenda. After Joe had gone on for half an hour about what a harlot my mother was, the British producer finally stopped him. At that point, the Brit stood up and requested a private meeting with Joe. They asked me to leave the room. I obliged.

Apparently, after I left, the outraged British producer, who had come all the way to America with his film crew to interview me, pounded on the table and demanded an explanation.

"Sir," he declared. "This man isn't even the slightest bit black!"

My friend Joe could do high dudgeon and mock outrage better than anyone else. Consequently, he was "Shocked, *shocked*!" that the producer would raise such an sensitive issue. The meeting was over, and the producer and film crew left and went back to England.

I was released from the ruse once and for all.

* * *

Joe and I once tried to charter a 165' WWII Mine Sweeper called the "USCGC Mohawk" docked in Wilmington, Delaware and sail it up to New York Harbor for the Statue of Liberty centennial. But, then, Joe also wanted to scuttle the ship in the middle of the harbor after the ceremony to collect the insurance. I didn't know about the scuttling plans until we were well into the scam which was also done under the auspices of my recently incorporated Catholic Boat Owners of America.

I had planned to make a fortune selling t-shirts, hats, and hoodies with the CBOA emblem on the front. (St Brendan's bark ---the Irish discoverer of America--- and the motto, "Cling to the Rigging" on some and "World's Greatest Semen (sic)" on others). But even though I built a website (www.catholicboatowners.com) which still exists, I failed to sell even one T-shirt or hat. So much for our mission to promote "good Christian boating" to the masses where we asked the question, "What would Jesus sail?"

Joe felt it was only fitting that this proud warship, the Mohawk, which had been involved in D-Day and the Battle of the Atlantic, should die nobly at sea instead of being consigned to the scrapyard. But the deal fell through because we couldn't get Coast Guard certification for "ocean navigation" in order to bring the Mohawk from Wilmington to New York; and, also, because Naval Intelligence got wind of Joe's claim of bribery on the bridge during our inspection tour which turned out to be merely his purchase of a "Mohawk" hat. But the "bribery" case eventually involved several federal agencies, including the F.B.I., before it was dropped. The ship was subsequently was sold to an immigrant machinist from Jersey City whom we continued to harass by claiming ownership. That guy finally sold the ship to someone in Florida, and it ended up there.

Joe had not been far off with his plan. Twenty-five years later, the Mohawk was intentionally sunk off Sanibel Island in Florida to form an artificial reef that was dedicated to all WWII Veterans.

* * *

Joe also taught me the value of "charitable donations." When a girlfriend's landlord tried to repossess his refrigerator, Joe reported that the refrigerator had been donated to the "Blind Negro Sea Scouts" who reportedly were using it on their frigate, the "S.S. Louis B. Armstrong", as a live bait box. The Sea Scouts were thrilled. The landlord, one of the most powerful attorneys in Los Angeles, decided not to press the issue even after we offered to deliver the refrigerator directly to his Century City office as soon as the "Armstrong" returned to port.

A mistakenly delivered IBM laptop was immediately "donated" to a leper colony on Molokai, and it could have still been reclaimed from the lepers if IBM had insisted. They didn't want to touch it. Then an unreturned Samsung S-7 cell phone had been "given" to my "sister" who worked in the Catholic Missions in Hong Kong who needed it for their refugee camp. But even *that* could be still retrieved if Verizon had really wanted it.

* * *

I wrote a pilot script for CBS Television based on Joe and his unique life and times. The pilot episode centered around an actual situation of his where he had rented a desk in a multi-desk office suite in the Pan Am Building. But then, through one means or another, he had ended up subletting, and, then, re-renting, all the *other* desks in the space, making him the de-facto landlord of the office much to the dismay of the original executive on the lease who was paying the bills.

The TV pilot concerned one of Joe's enterprises called "New Careers for the Religious" which was an actual 501(c) corporation dedicated the raising of funds for the rehabilitation of nuns who had renounced their vows in favor of secular life; but, then, had no idea of how to put on make-up or do their hair. The show never got picked up because the network powers on the West Coast claimed it was too far-fetched and unbelievable even though Joe did a screen test as himself and explained everything. And the 501(c) (3) corporation and New Careers for the Religious were absolutely real.

* * *

Everything for Joe was either a "deal' or a "scam". Whenever I would report that someone we knew had died, or, as Joe would put it, "Gone to God"; and, especially, if it was an untimely death, Joe would pause respectfully and then ask with his signature, inquisitive twinkle, "Was there a will?"

By this he meant that if no will was in existence, Joe might just *possibly* be able to supply one. Since, now, Joe has "Gone to God", and the statute of limitations has run, I can report that a certain inheritance was secured when Joe searched a deceased widow's apartment with a police officer from the "death detail"; and miraculously found a signed and notarized will directing that the widow's assets be paid directly to a *very* "close" beneficiary.

Joe had told me about how the Police Department's "death detail", or whatever it was called, was a highly sought-after assignment because the cops from that squad were the first ones sent to investigate a "smell" coming from an apartment or a tenant who had not been seen recently. Being the first on the scene had its advantages, and there was always a certain amount of "miscellaneous loss" accompanied by their arrival depending on how much the officers could grab before the coroner arrived.

Of course, Joe learned of all this from his friend, Tommy, a former desk sergeant in the "4-1"----that is, "Fort Apache", in the South Bronx---who had retired shortly before the Knapp Commission got to him. This particular ex-cop (Joe always corrected me by saying it's an "*ex*-con, but a *former* nun") was famous for running a "pad" in that very bad neighborhood of the "4-1" by which he would even demand $.50 a day from even the Good Humor ice cream man on the corner.

Tommy was a large, "hale fellow" sort of man who loved the finer things in life. He loved to go to the Boat Show in New York and sign up for million dollar yachts to be delivered to his "dock" in Florida. Accordingly, he always demanded and received the best service and attention from the yacht brokers at the show.

When he "went to God", the priest read a letter from Tommy to all those who might have come to his funeral. In the letter, he left a signed check so that all his friends might have a drink and a bite to eat, on him. However, in typical Broadway fashion (he had once worked the Theater District and always considered himself part of show business as a result.) he went on to ask that the priest "please hold the check for, at least, two weeks before cashing it so that proper funds might be made available." When the priest read this final request, the congregation erupted in laughter. It was the best send-off imaginable. This was the same ex-police officer who once told me that he wanted to start a "scam newsletter" that would come out once a week and announce the various scams that were available to all who might be interested. It was never published.

Tommy lived alone but rented his couches out to Joe and an itinerant bartender friend of ours. The three of them would fight over the individual couch assignments and, more vigorously, over any food left in the refrigerator. Joe would report to me how he had to sleep with one eye open because of our ex-cop friend's habit of going through Joe's pants in the middle of the night for any loose change or bills.

* * *

Joe was responsible for some of the more colorful turns of phrase I had ever heard. When he said, "You could go to sleep on it," it signaled a sure thing beyond a shadow of a doubt. "He'd steal a hot stove," was how he would describe an inveterate thief. "One Thousand Percent" was a certainly way beyond 100%. And "We were poor but never *that* poor," described a person's somewhat dubious circumstances or origins. Anyone, or anything, that was truly extraordinary was, "Like a breath of fresh air." A "rascal" was a person of questionable background or intent. Some moments were so special, "It could bring a tear to a glass eye." The only profits Joe ever sought were, "Just the crumbs," or "Whatever falls off the table." When asked how he felt on any particular day, Joe would say, "Not bad for a guy born in this country." When asked about anything pertaining to homosexuality, Joe would state confidentially, "You know what they say. There's a little lavender in *all* the Irish." And if pressed as to someone's sexual preference, Joe would proclaim, "Hey, I was born and raised in Greenwich Village. If I'd grown up in Hershey, Pennsylvania, I could tell you what a chocolate bar was." If someone was particularly good and generous, Joe would say, "Just give us an article of your clothing so we can cut it up into little pieces and sell as relics after you die."

I have appropriated his entire canon.

He would sarcastically refer to any enterprise not his own as, "Some sort of *nonsense*" in a dismissive tone of faux indignation as if whatever it might be was far beneath him. He got that term from a high-minded attorney friend of his who would say it in earnest about the 18-B (court appointed) cases he was forced to take in order to "make a dollar". When approaching the bench, this nattily dressed attorney would always walk a step or two ahead of his court-appointed charges of dubious moral turpitude, and refer to them disdainfully as "my (roll of the eyes) *clients*".

But, for Joe, "making a dollar" was always on his mind. He never forgot what his self-imposed mission was in this world. But this didn't necessarily involve actually having a *job,* although he did have many. At one time or another he was a "Parkie" (Parks Department), director of a federally funded summer lunch program, and zoo consultant. But, typically, his first priority upon entering any situation was, "How're we going to make a dollar here?"

Joe formed "United Catholic Parents", which consisted of him and his wife, in order to secure federal funding for a summer lunch program that the Archdiocese of New York didn't want any part of. By the end of the summer he was providing over 50,000 box lunches to school-age children throughout New York, including a few Mob guys in front of social clubs on Sullivan Street. But let the record show that some of his mob-influenced purveyors, like "Billy The Butcher", would often exceed designated portion guideline so that the "kids could have a decent meal" (Billy the Butcher was famous for having been called by the authorities to pick up and dispose of a dead, escaped gorilla that had been found on the West Side Highway. Those “in the know” tended to avoid any of Billy’s meat products from then on.)

After the success of the lunch program, (which only ran for one summer) Joe was then able to sell the endorsement of the “United Catholic Parents”, complete with a suitable press conference and announcement, to any political candidate with a checkbook.

It was Joe who told me when my mother died, “That’s when you know the world’s a piece of shit---when your mother dies.” And that was the extent of his grieving. I have used that line many times since in similar situations.

* * *

There was a guy at P.J. Clarke’s who was known as “Five Dollar Frankie”. Frankie was short, no more than five feet tall and probably less; but he was the *de facto* maître d’ of Clarke’s, and many people thought he was, in fact, P.J. Clarke incarnate from the way he conducted himself around the joint. Unfortunately, he was neither the maître d’ *nor* the owner of the place. He was completely freelance. Apparently, he had wandered into the bar one day and just started seating people in the back room. If you talked to him, he would tell you he was, somehow, part of the antique business upstairs that was run out of the second floor by Danny Levezzo, the, then, owner of P.J. Clarkes. Danny, himself was rarely seen at the establishment owing to the fact that he liked to play the horses. There was even a race horse named after him, I think. But Danny got into a little gambling trouble with some "wise guys" in Jersey and had to "take it on the lam" for a number of years. As a result, you thought twice about asking what was in the hamburger.

Frankie would regale you about the great deals he had made turning over antique furniture and Tiffany lamps. But I never saw him do anything more than write names down on the back of an envelope and look over people's heads to see if there were any *bigger* celebrities coming through the door.

Five Dollar Frankie was Italian *and* short. Maybe that had something to do with the fact that the regular Irish waiters and bartenders at Clarke's, who had been there for years, even *before* Frankie had arrived, all vehemently hated him. I mean, they *really* hated him. This was because he was never on the payroll but always acted like he owned the place. His money came solely from his tips for getting tables in the back for the likes of Bobby Kennedy or Aristotle Onassis. His favorite trick was to make heavyweight celebs wait in line along the wall between the front and back rooms. The bartenders made him run a tab even though he would "buy" patrons rounds of drinks "on the house." But that didn't stop Frankie from acting like he was P.J. Clarke incarnate. He would boss the waiters around and shout commands to the bartenders all for the benefit of his high roller "customers". Then one day he got philosophical with me.

"Do you realize that I have been here for over 35 years?" Frankie announced to me one night, apropos of nothing. So, I congratulated him on that. "But, you wanna know something?" He continued, and then he brought his knuckles down on the table like he was announcing the winning bid on an antique door knocker. "But you wanna know something?" He said again. "I'm lookin' to make a change," he announced grandly.

I congratulated him on that, too. But I remember thinking, "*Now,* after 35 years of saying, 'How many are you?' *Now,* you're lookin' to make a change?"

Anyway, very shortly after that moment of clarity, the "change" Frankie thought he was "lookin' to make" turned out to be a massive stroke. He was hospitalized, and he survived. But he was severely impaired. He was forced to go into a rehab facility afterwards. It was at that point that Joe and I decided we should start a rumor. We told the longest standing waiter at Clarke's, who hated Frankie the most, that when Frank had his stroke he was alone in his apartment. But when the police were finally called, the cops who broke into the place *vouchered* over $30,000.00 in $5.00 bills. And this didn't count what the cops were able to grab for themselves.

The rumor went through Clarke's like bad chili on an off night. Everyone believed it immediately; and, best of all, no one attributed the rumor to us. Shortly thereafter Joe and I had occasion to call Frankie in rehab to inquire how he was doing. Frank was not doing well. His speech had been affected by the stroke. He could only blurt a few words out at a time and had to spell (for some reason) anything important. He was not a happy man. News of the rumor had reached him, and he was livid. Perhaps, we thought, because the amount of $5.00 bills had only been put at $30,000.00 and not more. But, over the phone, he spit out his denial that there had been any cash lying around. Then he spelled out the word "C-O-C-K-S-U-C-K-E-R-S" to describe the waiters at Clarke's who he was sure had spread the vicious rumor.

I don't think he ever made it out of rehab. He died a short time after we spoke to him. But he was never able to dispel the notion that his apartment had been filled with five dollar bills when they found him, or that he had amassed a small fortune from his job as the unofficial, but hated, Maître d' of P.J. Clarke's. It was still a great story and a shame he couldn't have appreciated it.

Joe's father had been, himself, a legendary Irish politico and was famous for being Mayor Gentleman Jimmy Walker's personal piano player. Joe had originally been a stutterer which may have been why we were so close. He told me he actually had gone to a speech therapist as a young boy in Greenwich Village, but only once. When the bill from the speech therapist arrived at their modest Greenwich Village apartment, his father had exploded and raised such hell in the household that Joe was instantly cured.

As crazy and unconventional as Joe was, he was a visionary, and I always thought it behooved one to listen to all his wild schemes as a portent of the future. He had identified the looming fiscal crisis in the Catholic Church in America, but he knew, at the same time, that the church would have a hard time divesting itself of property and assets that had been donated by the faithful. In order to shield the Church and justify the sale of so much of its vast holdings, he had wanted to set up an organization with a religious enough sounding name (like "The St. Clement's Society," or something), which would act as suitable holding company between the church and the realized profits from sale of donated property.

Being from Greenwich Village, he saw the viability of a Gay Museum long before the LGBT movement made one actually feasible. I remember one time, when he was outlining a fund raising campaign for the museum that he foresaw, I, facetiously, chimed in and asked, "But Joe, will there be anything left over from all those donations that could possibly be used for administrative expenses?" To which he replied with one of his classic lines.

"Just the crumbs," he said, "Just the crumbs. That's all we want."

I remember he used to say to me, as an aside, when we were engaged in some *nonsense,* "They don't understand our 'mission.' They don't know we have a 'mission,' and they don't understand what we're all about."

The "mission", of course, was some sort of undefined "higher calling". This was always said with appropriate reverence for the "mission" and with the back of his hand to the side of his mouth, as if the existence of the "mission" was strictly *entre nous*. And *definitely* "on the Q.T."

He loved to tell the story of the *real* Stonewall riots which had been started, originally, by local mobsters who were pushing back at police and city pressure on their mob-run gay bars. The Stonewall Inn was a famous gay bar that had been run by the Genovese crime family for years. The mob had installed a married man, who had a wife and five kids, to run the place. That was fine until the mobbed-up married guy turned gay and started dating the patrons. Around the same time, certain "protections" broke down as a result, and the place was summarily raided by the New York Police.

The Village boss at the time decided to turn the raid into a case of police brutality, and mobsters quickly organized a demonstration outside the Stonewall. What has been forgotten in the history of the riots was that the first demonstrators were all mob guys carrying placards. They were quickly joined by the gay community who then made the Stonewall demonstrations and subsequent riots one of the landmarks of gay rights in America. But Joe always maintained, which has been confirmed by others, that the mob was, initially, behind the whole thing as an attempt to take the heat off one of their very profitable gay bars. The LGBT movement conveniently forgets that.

* * *

My default mental state, in those days, was mostly "depressed"; and I would often complain to Joe that it seemed everyone around us was doing better than we were and had more money and power than we did. But Joe taught me an important lesson in addition to his generous gift of his inimitable New York Irish style, lexicon, and unique turn of phrase.

Whenever I would complain to him about the apparent good fortune of others, he would squeeze my forearm as only he, the consummate Irish contract guy could do, and draw me close to him while never actually looking at me---as if what he was about to impart was "strictly on the Q.T."

"That may be true," he would say to me. "But just remember one thing: They don't have the *fun* we do." And that was the end of the discussion. "They don't have the fun."

* * *

There was a great comedy writer that I knew in Los Angeles who, one day, was sitting with another writer at a restaurant there. As they ate, the other writer became fixated on a very good looking woman at the next table who, perhaps knowing that the writer was looking at her, kept flicking her long blonde hair back over her shoulder. First on one side, and then on the other. Somehow, the implied sexuality of her behavior finally became too much for this writer who, like all Hollywood writers, felt deprived on all fronts.

Finally, he couldn't take it anymore. She was driving him crazy with her flicking and her beauty. He grabbed my friend's arm and looked at him wild-eyed.

"That woman over there is driving me nuts with her hair," he said to my friend maniacally. "First she does this, and then she does that, and then she does this again, and then that," he said, imitating her. "You know what I'd like to do with that hair?"

"What," my friend said.

"I'd like to take her hair and shove it up my ass."

My friend had to turn around to understand what he was talking about. The woman saw them both looking at her and stopped flicking her hair.

In real terms, what my friend's companion had said made no sense at all, either sexually or anatomically. But, at the same time, it spoke to an unrequited sexual tension that men often feel when confronted with an attractive, but unattainable, woman who flaunts her advantage. Even though the "taking of another person's hair and shoving it up one's ass" is an impossible task on many levels, it *does*, somehow, convey a specific and familiar male emotion. It speaks to the ache of sexual tension, the anger of implied rejection, and the frustration of longing. I don't think women understand that. Of course, were a woman to actually *hear* this man's strange desire spoken out loud; and if a woman were to actually take that threat literally, I suppose it'd be a felony in most states. Men, on the other hand, understand its existential meaning immediately. Anytime I, myself, have said it, in *situ,* of course, to express my *own* impossible frustration/attraction, other men have understood the metaphor instantly. It becomes, almost, a political statement.

* * *

In college, when I was a senior about to graduate, I convinced my roommate to help me secretly paint the top of the "Gargoyle Fence" in the middle of the night before the annual Gargoyle Honor Society initiation ceremony. As a result of our 3:00 A.M. paint job, none of the junior class candidates dared to sit on the flat part of the fence during the tapping ritual the next day for fear of getting wet paint on themselves. Instead, they had to stand. It meant that any "tapping" had to be done on the selectees' shoulders or heads, or simply a hearty handshake, instead of the traditional thigh slap. Oh, the hi-jinks!

* * *

I had a job, once, on the 17th floor of a midtown skyscraper. It was an old building, so the windows opened all the way up. The cleaning lady on the floor was afraid to come into my office because the previous occupant had set up a free-basing lab in there, and it had terrified her. But *my* problem was that the men's room was not even close to our offices. It was at the very farthest end of the floor that we were on, and it was a maddeningly long journey when in distress. As a remedy, I simply pissed out the window. I figured any urine released from the 17th floor would dissipate into random drops of mist by the time it reached the street. But, of course, I never checked *that* out. My impromptu urinal saved a lot of time and trouble. But, now, whenever I walk around Manhattan and occasionally feel a random drop of something wet from above, I *do* wonder.

* * *

At that same job, there was a wonderful man who worked with us as our assistant. He was very comfortably gay, and we would talk and joke about that freely. I would chase him down the hall shouting, "I love you," as a joke. He was one of the nicest, hardest-working coworkers I have ever experienced. He had a funny sounding last name that sounded like either some exotic Italian seafood dish or a dreaded skin disease.

Since I was in a position of semi-management, I thought we should honor this fellow and, also, thank him. But, mostly, it was an excuse to have a party in the office. I organized a dinner in his honor that was to be in the form of a telethon using his last name as the, so-called, dreaded disease we were pretending to raise money for. This was at the height of the Jerry Lewis MDA marathons which had become high camp even then.

Everybody was into it. We all got up and spoke about this wonderful man and his dreaded disease. The whole evening, celebrated in our 17th floor office, was performed in the self-serving style of bleeding heart celebrities on telethons. It was an incredibly fun evening, and everyone rose to the occasion, including this fine gentleman who played his part as "victim" and honoree to the hilt.

Shortly thereafter, I got fired (natch) and subsequently left those 17th floor offices. Shortly after *that*, this wonderful man came down with AIDS which, at that point in time, was still being confused with AYDS, the diet candy. He ended up dying a terrible death of an incurable, dreaded disease after all. In the end, he didn't want to see anyone because he was so sick. I never saw him again. It's a great lesson about black humor, I suppose. Sometimes the darkness wins.

* * *

When the internet arrived, the idea of speaking intimately to strangers was an incredible breakthrough. I discovered chat rooms. But I mean the *first* chat rooms, when they first came out. One was called, "The Dungeon," where you had to be either a "sub" or a "dom"---as in "submissive" or "dominate". Fortunately, I had learned to type with one hand when I used to write pornography for five cents a word. But the sub/dom scene was something I had never encountered before. And, although it was a "chat" room, it was all done through instant messaging.

I learned that "The Dungeon" would schedule occasional "fly-ins" where all the subs and doms would fly to an agreed-upon airport, go to an airport motel, fuck their brains out for a weekend, and then fly back home. There were strict rules of engagement, of course. I never did it. I mean, for me, not having to leave home was why I loved internet sex in the first place.

I learned a lot about rural and suburban America in those early internet days. One was that Middle America really gets its freak on, make no mistake about it. I was told tales about life around army bases outside of St. Louis where they would have Saturday neighborhood barbecues. Then, while the kids would play badminton on the lawn, the adults would go down into the host's basement and have "sub" and "dom" games. What??? This went/goes on all over America. I was in deepest, darkest New York City; but I was appalled at the extent of sexual perversity in Middle America. These were housewives, nurses, and army personnel. Regular people. They just wanted to have fun.

But that was in the early, *early* days of the internet. We're talkin' DOS, my friend. I think, now, you must have to go to the "dark web" or something for your sub/

dom games these days. Who knows? Maybe it was hotter when you had to type everything out. For that brief moment in the history of America, a good writer could be a real sex object. No more.

* * *

I had been trying to get a humor piece published in the "Shouts and Murmurs" section of The New Yorker magazine for years. The current editor of that department was a young woman, a recent graduate of Yale, whom I had researched thoroughly and had attempted, unsuccessfully, to make some sort of contact with. She had never responded to my e-mails or my written letters, much less to any of the actual submissions I had made to the magazine. I had tried everything. I even self-published all the failed pieces in a book and sent *that* to the young editor to demonstrate my seriousness. I had just about given up all hope of ever breaking through. The New Yorker, and its young female editor were, to me, impenetrable.

Then, one day, I went my eye doctor for an appointment. At his office, there was a sign-in sheet on the receptionist's desk in the waiting room. When I signed in, I saw that the name just above mine was that of the very same editor at The New Yorker to whom I had been submitting and with whom I'd been trying to make contact. God had brought us together in a strange and wonderful way.

I immediately called out her name in the waiting room, and she happily identified herself. I sat down next to her and told her who I was. She seemed pleasantly charmed by our meeting although I don't think there was a lot of name recognition. I told her this was like a scene out of a movie. I even told her that, by chance, I actually had her name and contact information with me on that very day. I showed her one of my 3X5 cards in my pocket with her name on it as proof. I kept mentioning how magical it was that we were actually meeting like this after all these years. I reminded her of the serendipity of it all. I chatted with her and made her laugh and expressed my delight that we were, finally, actually talking. I reminded her that this was, truly, a magic moment in my life. We laughed and chatted about writing in general, our tastes in humor, and the arduous submission process at The New Yorker. It all seemed wonderfully normal and predestined.

When I was finished with the doctor's appointment, I said goodbye to the editor and told her that I would definitely be in touch now that we'd made this special contact. She seemed intrigued and receptive. The next day I e-mailed her at The New Yorker to remind her who I was; and, at the same time, to submit my newly penned "Shouts and Murmurs" piece for her consideration.

Nothing.

She never responded. Never. Nothing. Not even to tell me to stop trying to contact her.

I told the eye doctor about the crazy, chance meeting with his patient in his waiting room. He responded by immediately retiring the sign-in sheet because it violated all HIPAA guidelines and regulations since I had read her name and, then, made contact with her as a result. The next time I went to the doctor, there was no sign-in sheet. Then he stopped being my doctor.

There is no moral to this story. There is no story.

* * *

I used to write a column for a sub-teen magazine called, "Ingenue", which probably was a felony in most states at the time. I wrote sort of a "Man to Virgin" column for them under the name of "Justin Thurston" or something like that. They supplied the name because they thought it sounded preppy and non-threatening.

I discussed topics like "Kissing with your mouth open" and "Tongues are for shoes". Stuff like that. Then, the editors finally met me. I was promptly fired.

* * *

I think I suffer from severe "Shower Amnesia." Whenever I take a shower, I can't remember the parts of my body that I've already washed. I'm thinking of using "Post-its".

* * *

I have to admit that if I ever had a first date with a totally blind woman, the first thing I would do is look up her dress.

* * *

My eldest son came out of his bath one Sunday night when he was about 4 or 5 years old. His hair was wet and slicked back in a way I hadn't seen before. He was nude and happy and ran into the living room in our New York apartment. It was such a startling and uncommon look for him that I immediately told him to wait and grabbed my Rolleiflex camera, figuring that this would be a shot for the ages.

I told him to stand in the hall doorway and then, for some unknown reason, I told him to stand at attention thinking that this would give the resulting photograph some "attitude" and raise it above a mere family snapshot. I took two shots---one of him facing me and one of him turned around, facing away. But both at "attention" with his hands smartly at his side, heels together. Then he lost his concentration, and the moment vanished as most special moments with kids do. Little did I know that I had just entered the "Sally Mann Zone".

I had the roll of T-Max 400 developed downtown and a proof sheet made. From that, I cropped the two shots of my son and ordered two fancy 11X14 fiber prints, matte. No problem. When I got the prints back I took them out to Connecticut to get them framed. Nothing fancy. A narrow, black frame with a 2 inch mat. Piece of cake.

About two weeks after I had left them at the framer, I got a call from a detective at the local police department. The detective wanted to talk to me about my photographs. Apparently, when I was getting them framed, a woman had spotted the shots over my shoulder and had turned me in as a child pornographer. The case had gone all the way to the Connecticut State's Attorney's office who, after some consideration, had decided not to bring formal charges but suggested the local police interview me justto make sure. It was a Saturday, and they wanted me to come down to the station immediately. I called a lawyer.

The only local lawyer I knew was the husband of an old girlfriend. I figured this would justify the way things had turned out in our respective lives.----The lawyer and his wife were living in a beautiful country home and practiced law together, and I was a child pornographer. I think it's why he insisted, under the circumstances, that I *not* come to his house. He picked me up in his car and drove me downtown to the police station. On the way, he fantasized about how this would put him on the map as a famous First Amendment champion. He had visions of himself arguing my case before the Supreme Court. I was not as enthusiastic.

At the police station, we were ushered upstairs to the detectives' room. There, on the table, were my photographs. I was immediately proud of them all over again.

After I acknowledged that I was, indeed, the photographer and that the nude boy was my son, I couldn't help but fish for a compliment.

"Look," I said, "Regardless of the issue here, you have to admit, these are pretty great images."

The burley detective took one dubious look at me and then glanced back down at the nude shots of my son standing at attention.

"They are not to my taste," the detective said succinctly.

My lawyer then suggested I remain where I was and stop talking while he and the detectives went into another room to talk. They were gone for a substantial amount of time. When they emerged the matter had been settled. I was not going to be arrested, and I was free to go home. But they weren't going to give me back my photographs, either. The police would keep them on file. They seemed somewhat disappointed that the State's Attorney had declined to prosecute, but they wanted a record. Their problem, besides the obviously documented nudity, was that, son or no son, the kid looked coerced, like he was being forced to have his picture taken. Of course, they weren't entirely wrong. But no candy was involved in the taking of those pictures. I was prepared to testify to that.

That should have been the end of it. But several years later I took *another* set of photos of my wife, nude with a towel on her head, and our second son, also nude, on her lap both looking into a mirror over dressing table in our bathroom. Now, *these* shots seemed totally innocent as they were classic "mother and child" portraits. I decided to have a triptych framed of three of the shots which seemed to go together and match a similar set of photographs of son number one and his mother. I went to a *different* framer this time in an entirely *different* part of town. These were mere snapshots as opposed to the earlier black and white gallery photographs.

A uniformed police officer came to the front door of my house this time. He was armed.

Again I called the ex-girlfriend's husband. This time he said he would try to handle it without me. I was neither a good witness nor a helpful client. I brought the earlier matching shots of my oldest son and his mother to his office. Those photographs had been locally framed without incident, and I thought that would help. But that turned out to be just more nudity and more evidence, and it was not helpful for my defense. He suggested I take the older photos back home. The lawyer was able to get me off again. But the police department informed him that they would, again, keep all the photographs in case there was, yet again, *another* reoccurrence.

The only consoling part of this whole tale is that, as of this moment, the only retrospective of my life's photographic work resides to this day in the files of my local police department. I think it is part of their permanent collection. I have stopped framing my photos.

* * *

I was once able to score a date, for no logical reason, with a fairly famous actress by merely calling up the hotel where she was staying and asking her out. I had read in the newspaper that this formerly famous nymphet was in town to make an independent movie and was staying nearby. I cheekily called her up and asked her out to dinner. What I *didn't* know, at the time, was that this fading sex kitten was also a notorious eccentric and an impulsive (some might say, "perverse") bohemian. She took my call and accepted my invitation immediately because she was, at that moment, bored and hungry. Or maybe, *cheap* and hungry. I never knew which. And, oh yeah, she wanted to bring along her six-year-old daughter because she was bored and hungry also. Anyway, the date went nervously well. She got her free dinner, and she got her kid fed on time. And I got the thrill of feeding a celebrity.

That was the end of it. She then got busy with her movie and left New York shortly thereafter. I may have even asked her out again. But her perverse impulse had passed, and her daughter had gone back to California with the nanny. I remember she laughed mockingly at the notion of actually seeing me again and declined my invitation.

But then, when I moved to California, I called her again (hope springs eternal). As it was, I was still working, and she was the only woman I knew in California. But, in the interim, she had gained a large amount of weight as was her wont between movies. She was receptive again, but this time she said I had to come directly to a house she was staying in in Malibu. Her own Malibu house had tragically burned to the ground in one of those famous California wild fires, and she had lost everything. Absolutely everything. On top of that, because of her weight gain, she didn't go out in public anymore.

Fat or not fat, she was still an actress, a celebrity, and incredibly beautiful. And God knows, now, there was even *more* of her to look at. We started an affair --- I, because I was working and had nowhere to go, and she because she was a shut-in, and bored, and because I *did* have a job which meant I wouldn't bother her during the day.

It was a great score and a great way to be in California--- working *and* sleeping with a semi-famous actress. But the problem was I couldn't prove it. We never left her house and never went out in public. It was like some sort of pipe dream that I would insist was true, but I couldn't verify. But when you're making love to a famous actress, even one who is overweight, it's a little like being in the movies.

At one point, my family came to town, and I was able to introduce her to my father. Suddenly, *he* wanted to be in the movies, too. He fell in love with her at dinner and announced that he had never been in love with another woman other than his wife until he had met her. I think the dinner merely confirmed her rule about never leaving the house.

The little daughter tolerated me marginally but would randomly announce loudly, "Nothing's funny!" referring to, I assumed, nothing more than my presence. But, basically, the kid knew the drill better than I did, and she made it a point not to get close to any of "Mommy's friends." In the end, the actress got thin again and left me for a German actor who played Nazi's and U-boat captains in Hollywood movies and who was in town for the Academy Awards. He didn't get an Oscar, but he got her instead.

When I complained about my dismissal to the nanny, I remember she shrugged and said something in Spanish which, when translated, meant, "When you wash the pussy, it is new again." Or something like that. She knew the drill better than the daughter.

After the German actor left town, the actress---who by now was almost down to her playing weight---heard some prowlers or stalkers outside her bedroom window one night. She called me up. I lived a short distance away in a bungalow guest house. I figured this was how I would get back with her again. I raced over to her house in the middle of the night like a super hero. But by the time I arrived, the intruder had either left or been invited inside. Now, *I* was the intruder, and I was asked to leave. That's how you know when it's *really* over with a semi-famous actress. Your "Gate Pass" gets lifted. People with autograph books in their hands have better access and are more welcomed than you are. Soon, I was without a girlfriend *and* out of work. That's when it's time to go back to New York. So I did.

* * *

Years later, the actress ended up moving back to New York also. At that point we had an arm's length relationship through mutual friends that she felt *much* more comfortable with than me. But one day, she called me up looking for a moving company to move her from one apartment to another in the city. Famous actresses do that. Theirs is a world of agents, managers, lawyer, make-up people, and personal assistants who are poised to fulfill any whim from the mundane to the outlandish. This was a mundane one, far beneath her consciousness level, and I, apparently, was the one in her extended life who was positioned to fulfill it.

I called my friend Joe, the Irish contract guy, to ask if he might recommend someone competent and discreet. (She *was* a semi-famous actress, after all) He immediately recommended "Greenwich Village Movers" which I took to be a firm he knew from his early days in the Village. I relayed this information to the actress who immediately announced that they were hired and, then, authorized me to handle the move.

I called Joe back and asked whom I should talk to at Greenwich Village Movers, and he said, "You're talkin' to him." These were the days when he was still renting a couch from Tommy, the ex-cop. "Greenwich Village Movers" turned out to be Joe and Tommy in the Tommy's un-repossessed ten-year-old Cadillac. "Greenwich Village Movers", indeed. The ex-cop was only too happy to call on the ex-actress and get the particulars of the job. He played his part to the hilt. After all, he *had* been known as "Broadway Tommy" due to that, one-time, theater district assignment. A date was set for the move. I was not part of "Greenwich Village Movers".

The actress was not home when the move occurred which enabled Tommy to make a thorough investigation of her personal records and financial statements. He ended up knowing more about her than her accountant, business manager, and lawyer combined. The actual move consisted of more than thirty-five trips in the Cadillac with furniture and belongings inside and on top of the car. At one point, the actress came home, which prompted Joe to proceed immediately to the window to yell down for the driver to, "Take the truck around the corner," lest they get a ticket for blocking traffic. The shouted orders to the "phantom truck" would continue until the actress left the premises. She never suspected anything nor noticed that there never *was* a truck on the street outside her apartment but only a somewhat distressed Cadillac.

At the end of the move, Joe and the ex-cop presented her with their bill which included such extra charges as "electrical disconnect" which, when I asked Joe exactly what "electrical disconnect" meant, I was told "pulling plugs out of the wall"----tricky, but dangerous, work. Then came the *pièce de résistance* of the job. The actress made the mistake of asking "Greenwich Village Movers" if, by any chance, their company provided "storage" as well since she couldn't fit all of her belongings into her new apartment.

"Storage?" Joe said, affecting mild surprised. "Storage? Why it's half our business. 'Storage' is our middle name. We're officially, 'Gotham Storage *and* Moving'." A quick call to the "home office", and it was established that, yes, there was a unit available at a *very* reasonable price.

So it was that several television sets belonging to the actress, along with a Hi-Fi, couch, and some other items ended up in Tommy's living room. He was more than happy to have a piece of furniture that paid for itself without having Joe or the itinerant bartender sleeping on them. The items remained there until the actress called years later looking for the items. It "turned out" that those very things that she sought had been lost in a warehouse fire and were "unavailable". The only *good* news was that that "loss" prompted a call to me from the ex-actress/ex-girlfriend complaining about "those shady Greenwich Village Movers" that I had recommended and who had absconded with her possessions. She wanted Joe's number so she could sue him. I couldn't come up with either the number *or* an explanation. But it was great to hear her liquid, honey voice again on the phone even *with* the expletives.

*   *   *

I should have known better than to have fallen for an actress. I remember a renowned audio engineer and famous New York eccentric who lived as a self-imposed shut-in and had, literally, not left his West Side apartment in 40 years by choice told me, in no uncertain terms when I visited him, "Never date an actress." I think he attributed his agoraphobia to his own unfortunate dalliance. He was a genius who had worked with Marshall McLuhan, so I believed him. But, obviously, I didn't follow his advice.

The problem was that actresses tended to be better looking than normal people, so it was a tradeoff. When you dated an actress, you had to understand that the highest you would ever get on her list of important people in her life was, maybe, sixth. Tops. Ahead of you were her manager, her co-star, her scene partner, her agent, her producer, and, if she was a star, her make-up person. The trouble was, you don't know any of that when she said, "I love you", and you lived a life of unreal expectations.

A show business psychiatrist once told me that, in his clinical experience, all actresses were insane; and that they acted out their insanity for as long as they were actresses. When they evolved into something else (director, producer, etc.), it was a sign of their growing mental health and rehabilitation. I have never seen such elephantine-size tears shed than from an actress/girlfriend who had just lost a part or blown an audition. I remember telling her that I hoped she shed such tears when her mother dies.

* * *

My favorite psychiatrist was a man who had been born and raised in Germany but ended up practicing in Beverly Hills. He had been trained by Sigmund Freud, himself, in Berlin; so, I figured, how bad could he be? He was recommended to me by a holocaust survivor internist who made a fortune doing prostate exams on Canon Drive. The doctor was also a sculptor and sculpted my head in-between prostate exams which I still have, cast in bronze, to this day. (My head, not my prostate) In those days, every sculpted head in bronze looked like JFK, so I was pretty pleased.

But the psychiatrist had married a Jewish female doctor back in Berlin and, thus, had to flee Germany before the war like so many other German psychoanalysts who saw what was coming. He ended up in Beverly Hills and became the go-to shrink to the stars. He never tried to modify his thick, almost "stage Nazi" accent which, in fact, became the model for Danny Kaye's comic German character, "Dr. Schickelhoopeer".

Interestingly enough, once in this country, the German doctor joined the U.S. Army as part of the war effort and went to work as an Army psychiatrist. I often wondered what the effect was when a soldier, suffering from battle fatigue, suddenly found himself being counseled by *Das Fuhrer* himself. My doctor told me of treating one patient who had been brought to him claiming that he worked on a "top secret" project that was a single bomb that could destroy an entire city. One single bomb. Then, the deranged patient claimed that whoever had this new bomb could, then, rule the world! My good doctor told me he immediately diagnosed the man as a hopeless paranoid schizophrenic and had him committed to an insane asylum forthwith. It turned out the poor guy had been working on the Manhattan Project. He was probably not released until after Hiroshima.

The psychiatrist also told me that, back in Berlin, he took his, then young, son to the Reichstag in Berlin for a private tour. As the good doctor and son were being shown around, the young boy explored some of the desks and lecterns. He located a specially designated button that, when activated, in case of a fire, was supposed sound an alarm and release a torrent of water stored in a tank on the roof. Basically, it was the Reichstag sprinkler system. But when my psychiatrist's son pushed the button, to the horror of the guides and Reichstag personnel, nothing happened. Guards and officials rushed to get the boy away from the alarm, but, strangely, neither the alarm nor the water had been activated. Everyone breathed a sigh of relief, but then they wondered why the alarm had not gone off. The tour continued without further incident. But shortly thereafter, the famous Reichstag Fire occurred which destroyed the German Parliament building which was immediately blamed on the Communists by the Nazi's which, then, hastened their ascendancy. But my doctor, who subsequently became the "shrink to the stars" in Hollywood, always knew that the alarm had actually been disabled days beforehand. That was how he knew it was time to get out of Germany.

I was with the good doctor when he closed up his office and officially retired as shrink. He had pioneered psycho analysis and group therapy; and, as he stood in his, soon to be empty, office, he pointed to each of the chairs there as if they were patients.

"I can't help the homosexual; I can't help the schizophrenic; I can't help the alcoholic; I can't help the adulterer. Their treatment only benefits *me*, the therapist. *I* become an enlightened student of human nature, but they learn nothing. I can't help them."

I remember thinking, "Geez, I wish you'd told me that before I put your kid thorough college. I could've saved a fortune."

A few years later he wrote a paper called, "The Day I Got Old", in which he described the feeling when old age had come upon him all at once, as if a switch had been thrown. Years after that, as he lay dying, curled up on his couch in a fetal position, I went to visit him. I remember him saying, "Keep talking. Because as long as I can hear your voice, I know I am still alive." That was the last time I saw him. He didn't charge me.

The good doctor was right. He *couldn't* help me, although, God knows, he tried. He told me that the completion of my rehabilitated sanity would be the crown jewel of his practice. But the *good* news was he wasn't big on confidentiality, and he freely "consulted" with me on his other patients with tales of his celebrity practice and the various foibles, exploits, and failings of the Hollywood stars he treated. Now, *that* helped a lot.

* * *

I once picked up a girl who was working as a cashier at a resort in Port St. Lucie, Florida when I was visiting my parents there one spring. I met the girl after she had finished her dinner service and invited her out for a drink. No sooner had she gotten into my car than she started telling me that she had finally decided, that night, to kill herself. But she was real happy that I was the person she was going to spend her last night on earth with. This was slightly more than I had bargained for that evening. I told her I thought we were just going for drinks. She said, no, there was no time for that, but she *did* want to go to a church to pray for forgiveness before she killed herself. I must admit, it is an indication of how desperate young men are for the company of attractive, blousy blondes that I automatically figured, "Whatever," and drove her to a church.

We found an open Catholic Church (It was Easter time), and I knelt with her as she cried and prayed for forgiveness for what she was about to do. I *still* thought that, eventually, this would lead a more normal date of liquor and sex. But I remember being somewhat unnerved by it all. Consequently, as an act of noble selflessness, and seeking forgiveness for *myself,* I decided right then and there to throw away the condoms I had bought for the occasion.

She became quite hysterical after we left the church, and I remember being so unnerved that I drove South in the North lane of the Florida Turnpike for several exits while she wailed and cried about her life. It was that distracting. She was a southern girl, so it all sounded even more dramatic than what she was actually upset about. In other words, maybe her life wasn't so great, but it wasn't *that* desperate. After all, I was going to pay for dinner.

Finally, she had had enough of our driving around and asked to be taken home. I drove her to a little bungalow where she lived. She immediately bolted out of the car and ran straight into the house. At first, I was relieved that I had, at last, deposited her home in one piece. I was about to drive back to my parents' condo; but, then, I thought, maybe, just *maybe,* I should, *maybe,* check on her just to make sure she was all right.

I got out of the car and walked up the sidewalk to the front door. It was wide open. She had run into the house in tears and straight into the bathroom which was directly across the living room from where I stood. The bathroom door was open; and, as I looked, I could see her crying and slashing her wrists at the same time in front of the mirror. I knew immediately this was not a good thing and entered the house without being asked. I got to the bathroom just as she was slashing her second wrist. The evening, apparently, had not gone very well at all. Right then and there, I said to myself, "No more pick-ups."

I grabbed her (for the first time that night) and held her wrists together in one hand like a newborn baby's ankles and raised the slashed wrists up over her head to reduce the bleeding. This caused the blood to flow down into her blonde hair which made the whole scene look even *more* dramatic. With the other hand, I reached for the phone and called 911 for an ambulance.

The ambulance came and took her, and I followed them to the hospital. At the hospital, I stayed in the emergency room area while they took care of her. I noticed that the first thing they did was check to see if she had been raped even before they had bandaged her wrists. I thought that was strange. Then, the police arrived and asked me to come with them to the station to fill out some forms.

I said goodbye to my date and went to the police station figuring I was going to get, maybe, a commendation or something. But, instead, I was immediately arrested and booked, and put into a holding cell. I remember thinking this is no way to treat a hero---someone who had just saved a stranger's life. They fingerprinted me and told me I could make things a lot easier on myself if I would only confess. I told them I had nothing I could think of to confess about. (I didn't tell them about the condoms.) I remember the graffiti on the walls of the holding cell consisted mainly of prayers, petitions to God, and famous quotes about freedom. It was like a movie. I almost started humming, "Nobody Knows the Trouble I've Seen."

The police kept urging me to confess. They said that they knew who I was, and that it would be a lot easier if I *did* confess because they already had a mug shot of me. I asked to see it. When they showed it to me, and I took a good look at the photo, I had to admit that the guy *did*, in fact, look just like me. I mean, it *wasn't* me, but it *looked* like me.

Finally, after a long time, (it was close to morning, now) and after my fingerprints didn't match the guy's in the picture, (they had to wake up the fingerprint guy), they let me go. Besides, I think the girl finally vouched for me as just an innocent bystander who had nothing to do with her departure from Texas where she was from. I guess it was lucky for me that she was a cashier because, I guess, she had, at least, *some* sense of fiduciary responsibility.

Then they put *her* in jail. It turned out she had run away from her husband in Texas. He would lock her up in the basement when he went to work; and then, when he came home, he would let her out an beat her up for not having his dinner ready. And I thought *my* life was rough. Apparently, she finally broke out of the basement and hitchhiked from Texas to Florida with the guy who looked like me. But he, it turned out, was also wanted in several states for passing bad checks in *addition to,* I guess, now, kidnapping the guy's wife. (The husband had filed charges after he had come home, and couldn't find his wife *or* his dinner.) *I* could have told the authorities that the bad check guy she left with didn't have to exactly *kidnap* her in order to get her to leave with him. After all, she let *me* pick her up.

I visited the girl a few times in jail and brought her some shampoo. She didn't look as good as an inmate as she did as a cashier. She told me the guards had made her strip all the time and abused her. I didn't know what to say or do. My biggest problem was that it was the end of Spring Vacation, and I had to go back to college.

That should have been the end of the adventure. But many years later, I was living in New York; and, one day, I was in the process of buying something from the Horchow Collection catalogue on the phone. The Horchow catalogue just happens to be headquartered in Dallas, Texas. But when I gave my information to the guy on the phone, the guy on the phone turned out to be an old fraternity brother of mine from college. He recognized my name and said "hello." But then he disappeared off the phone. Instead of coming back, he then put on a woman who turned out to be my suicide date from all those years before. Incredible.

She was all cheery and upbeat as if *we* had gone to college together ourselves. She had remembered where I had told her I was in school back then, and she had made the connection with my fraternity brother who turned out to be her boss. (Maybe *he* had picked her up, too.) Then she told me that I had saved her life. But, to tell you the truth, it sounded like she was, now, having a much better one than I was at the moment, so I had mixed emotions. I wondered how much she had told my friend, her boss, about her life and how we met. Maybe they were dating now. I didn't ask. I didn't want to blow her cover again.

* * *

Vincent "The Chin" Gigante, the *capo di tutti capi* of the Genovese crime family, used to hang out in a social club on Sullivan Street in Greenwich Village. I knew his brother, Father Louie, who was the pastor of St. Athanasius in the South Bronx and a former

Georgetown basketball star. The Chin had a German shepherd named "Slugs" that he was devoted to and who would stay with him in the social club while he played cards and ran things. By all accounts, Slugs was the meanest, most vicious dog anyone had ever come in contact with. But "Chin" loved him, and so the dog stayed in the club. Chin would make his underlings take the dog out for walks during the day. But the dog was so vicious that he would growl and bite people. He especially liked biting black, homeless men. But because it was Chin's neighborhood, and Chin's dog, they didn't complain much or else were told not to.

Consequently, Slugs got away, for the most part, with biting homeless black men; but then one day, while being walked around Washington Square Park, he bit the wife of an editor of the New York Times. This was, now, a "bite too far"; and Slugs was immediately arrested, muzzled, and incarcerated by the police as a three-time loser. They put the dog in the main ASPCA headquarters and municipal pound on the Upper East Side of Manhattan.

Chin was desolate. "Get the dog," he told his minions without any elaboration. "Get the dog."

This meant that, somehow, Slugs had to be sprung from the confines of the ASPCA kennel and the clutches of the law before his hearing. According to legend, Slug's case was referred to a young Barry Slotnik, the, now, famous mob lawyer. But this was Slotnik's *first* mob case. Slotnik's job was to have Slugs "walk" as if he were a "connected" mug up on a murder rap. There was to be a hearing on the fate of the vicious animal, and Barry was assigned to represent him.

In typical mob fashion, Gigante's people secured the services of a certain German shepherd from New Jersey who resembled Slugs and who "agreed" to take the fall. Then, a couple of Chin's mugs showed up late one night at the ASPCA and asked to visit Slugs because they missed him so much. These were mob guys and hit men who, supposedly, became weepy at the thought of their beloved pooch being incarcerated. All they wanted to do was visit with Slugs and take him for a walk around the block. Money exchanged hands. The city pound night watchman reluctantly agreed to spring Slugs for a midnight walk. It was during the walk that the dog from New Jersey took Slugs' place, and Slugs was sequestered in a parked car. The Jersey shepherd was then returned to the pound with profuse thanks to the kennel guard and more cash.

At the hearing, not only did the Times' editor's wife testify as to the viciousness of the animal, but there was even testimony from several of the abused African American homeless men as to Slug's unwarranted attacks. The homeless men were in on the scam and were only too happy to finger the bogus dog as a favor to Chin. Finally, the magistrate ruled that Slugs was, indeed, a menace to society and beyond rehabilitation. He had to be destroyed.

Chin's people and Barry Slotnik left the courtroom "devastated". The Jersey Sheppard was, in fact, put down; and Slugs was moved to an undisclosed farm in upstate New York where Chin would visit him regularly. But Slotnik had his first "win" which cemented (to use an unfortunate term) his reputation as a stand-up guy and the go-to lawyer for mobsters.

* * *

Two women have sung to me in cars but never a man. But, then I think, cars make women crazier then they make men. One woman, who rode in a borrowed Mercedes Coupe with me, insisted on swimming in every swimming pool we passed when we drove across the country together. She swam in, probably, fifty swimming pools between San Francisco and New York. And she wasn't that good a swimmer, either.

The *second* woman who sang to me in a car was in Los Angeles. She even brought a tape along with her to use as a backup track to accompany herself. I foolishly thought we were going to have some form of sex when she had abruptly insisted we pull off the road and into an empty parking lot of a supermarket late one night.

But, no! Instead, she put the backup tape into the car's tape deck and started singing. It was some sort of half-assed song of her own composition, I think. But she sang, not like a civilian would sing along with the radio; she *performed* her song right there in the front seat of my car as if she was doing the second show of her nightclub act. That's when I knew we were definitely *not* going to have sex in the parking lot. She was way too far into her music to get hot.

When she finished singing, she popped the tape out of the player and turned to me.

"Whaddya think?" she said.

"It's good," I said. "*You 're* good." Then I asked, "Now what?" thinking, perhaps, *now,* the blowjob.

"I want to go on television," she said.

"Great. But this is Ralph's, not CBS," I pointed out. "You need an agent."

Everyone is in show business in L.A. Even the people who aren't, are. The concert was over, so I put the car in gear and drove my front seat singer back to her car. On the way, she told me that she used to go out with Don Henley, the rock star; and, also, that a comedian from Alaska had given her crabs. I remember thinking, "Alaskan crabs. Very rough." But at least she didn't try to sing again.

The *first* woman to sing to me in my car was my college girlfriend during my freshman year in college. I remember driving all the way up to the top of the local mountain, in the dark, hoping that the altitude and the achievement would inspire her to take off her bra.

When we got to the top, I turned to her expectantly, full of nothing but love and accomplishment. We had made it to the top of the mountain. That's when she started to sing.

She sang "When I Fall in Love", *a cappella*. Full-throated and serious, like she was auditioning and without a hint of self-consciousness. She was obviously not the least bit embarrassed to be doing something she had never done before. (She was not a singer). I felt like Snooky Lansing on the old "Your Hit Parade " television show when he would have to stand there and smile while Dorothy Collins sang the number one love song that week in his face. Even then I thought it was weird that the poor guy had to smile and react silently as if she was actually saying something meaningful to him.

I remember my girlfriend sang the whole song, slowly and carefully, including all the verses and, then, a reprieve. I didn't know what to do. So I nodded now and then as if the lyrics were part of our conversation.

"When I give my heart, it will be forever," she sang.

I know, I know, I nodded silently, as if answering her. *That is so true.*

She was really into it, I couldn't stop her. I wanted to say, "Hey, c'mon. Whaddya doin? I thought we were gonna neck."

She sang the song all the way through. Then, when she was finally finished, she stopped and bowed her head as if in prayer, and folded her hands quietly in her lap.

"I think we should go back down," she said.

I know for sure that Martin Luther King had a better time when he went to *his* mountaintop.

* * *

Sometimes I entertain myself by crying profusely when talking to tech support or customer service. I believe I get better service that way. It's anonymous anyhow, so even if I have to occasionally listen to the operator tell me to "Take a deep breath" or "Get a hold of yourself. It's just a cable bill", or "Get a glass of water" it's worth it. I also like to say that I'm afraid that the police are going to arrest me and put me in jail. Once, when I was doing "extreme elderly", the police and EMS arrived at my door having been called by the customer support lady who thought I was dying. I once told a telemarketer that he had just called into a crime scene where a dead body had just been discovered. I identified myself as a police officer and called for the detective since the caller was, now, considered a material witness or friend of the victim. I ordered him to stay on the line until I got the Lieutenant. He kept trying to explain to me that he was just a telemarketer and had nothing to do with the murder. I didn't listen. That's what they all say.

All this comes from working alone at home when the phone literally doesn't ring for days at a time. I call it, "The Silence". For these reasons, there is never such a thing as an "unwanted call".

* * *

I got on a train at Penn Station to go to Philadelphia to see my best friend. As I entered the train, I saw an incredibly beautiful young girl, with long blond hair, trying to put her suitcase up on the rack. I offered to help. Then, since it was still a free country, I thought, "I have an unreserved ticket. I think I'll sit right down opposite the beautiful young girl." It was my lucky day. I had no idea how lucky.

I took the seat across from the beautiful girl and immediately started chatting her up. She was smart and agreeable (as opposed to calling a cop). I had always prided myself in my ability to pick up women in public places. But as brilliant as I considered myself on the street and in the subway; I was, at the same time, a total loser in bars where you're *supposed* to pick up women. I picked up a homeless girl once. (But I guess that's not *that* much of an achievement, is it?) One has to accept one's limitations. Luckily, this was on an Amtrak train on the way to Philadelphia, so at least I was in my element.

The woman was suitably younger but not *so* young as to generate litigation or an arrest. We talked and laughed and shared. It was like a "meet cute" moment in a movie. I think I even cited that trope in our conversation. As we rumbled through Trenton, I realized that our relationship was about to come to an end, so I invited her to come with me to Philadelphia where we would join my friend at his home on the Main Line. She declined. She was on her way to her home in Virginia.

When we arrived in North Philadelphia, I knew we had precious time left together. That's when I made my "modest proposal". I would travel with her all the way to Washington and continue our wonderful encounter if, upon our arrival, we would get a hotel room and have sex. I told her we would only have this one chance, this one time, to do something as reckless as what I was proposing. One can only decide to have sex on the first date once. You only get one opportunity to do that with each person you meet. This was our unique opportunity to have immediate sex on a chance encounter.

By the time we passed the Philadelphia zoo, she had agreed. Thirtieth Street Station came and went. We were on our way.

When we passed Elkton, Maryland, I remember mentioning that Elkton was famous in the old days for being the first place a couple from up north could elope to and get married the same day. I asked her if she wanted to get off there. She declined.

We arrived at Union Station in Washington. She was still game and up for the bargain. She had a large suitcase which I helped her carry to a nearby hotel where I explained to the disinterested desk clerk that we were between trains and needed a place to relax and freshen up. It was more information than he required. We went up to the room.

The actual assignation was sweet and, surprisingly, loving, given that we had just met. Passionate without being startling. She was on her way to rural Virginia where she lived, but I forget how she was going to get there. The next thing I knew I was back on the train and on my way back up to Philadelphia.

It would be poetic if that was the start of a long and torrid affair. But it wasn't. We saw each other briefly again, but neutrally, shortly afterwards in New York. And then, after that, we spoke only on the phone several times; but we never slept together again. We lost touch. Ultimately, I think it dawned on us how crazy it was to have done what we actually had done. It transmogrified into a story, but not much of one, because I think we both felt we had dodged a headline in the Post about how our train ride had turned into "A TICKET TO DEATH" or some variation of a "strangers on a train" calamity. I think we were both relieved and chagrinned at the life-altering possibilities that we had flirted with but, luckily, had avoided.

Fade out. Fade in: (as they say). Thirty-eight years later (or something like that) I got a letter from the fantasy "train girl" out of the blue. She re-introduced herself and said she was coming to New York and thought it would be fun to catch up. "Catch *up*?" I thought. "This smells like trouble." At that point, I was married. And she told me, in the letter, she was married, also. But, now, all of a sudden, *now*, she wanted to "catch up."

She came to New York, and we arranged to meet in a cocktail lounge at her hotel. But it was not without a certain amount of hesitation on my part. This is what I thought. I figured I had gotten her pregnant during that one time in Washington, and she had, then, given birth to the baby and raised it by herself without telling me.

Once we sat down, I figured it would be only a matter of time before my thirty-six-year-old son would walk into that cocktail lounge and give me a hug. I thought about asking her point blank, but I was afraid. I figured, the longer I went without asking her, the longer she would continue to keep the secret she had kept all these years.

When we finally met in the cocktail lounge, I was nervous and tentative. She was warm and effusive and looked great. But she didn't say anything. We talked and reminisced about the train ride, and she *still* didn't say anything. And I didn't ask. We ended the drink with hugs and appropriate kisses but no revelations. Then a year went by. We e-mailed back and forth a lot. She re-entered my life. But there was still no mention of the kid.

We met again the next year. (It became like "Same Time, Next Year"). I was still not convinced she wasn't keeping the "big secret." We e-mailed and shared stories and projects. Then, every year she would come to New York, and we would meet for dinner. And every year I thought she was going to say, "This is what I never told you. I want you to meet your son, Biff." (It never occurred to me that it might be a daughter.) But, still, there was no revelation. She even told me that she and her husband had no children; but, in my mind, that just reinforced what I had been thinking all along. This went on for seven years.

Finally, in year six, we talked about that train ride once again. I mentioned how dangerous the whole thing had been and how foolhardy it was. Besides all that, I opined, she could've easily gotten pregnant. That's when she told me, flat out, that she did *not* get pregnant. Suddenly, At last, I believed her. And I finally accepted the reality that she was not going to whip out a photograph of "Junior."

But, then, I remember thinking, "Am I sad?"

* * *

I used to have this mistaken idea that, when you bought a musical instrument, the talent to play it came along with it. Of course, it then followed that the more you *paid* for the instrument, the more talent you got, and the easier it was to play. Or something like that. You get the idea. Or, as my youngest son used to inform me, as he banged away on the keyboard I bought him, "God is my teacher."

I have had experience as a musician with the piano, several ukuleles, a banjo, a trumpet, the drums, cornet, flute, trombone, a baritone sax, the vibraphone, the double bass, and six tubas. I have never fully learned how to play any of them. And I'm not being, as people might assume, "modest." Just ask the real musicians who have played with me. I could make rudimentary sounds and scales on most of the instruments I owned, but I have never approached anything that could remotely be described as "ability," much less, "talent". But I have never let something as minor as *that* thwart my dream of being an accomplished musician.

I've played in numerous jazz groups and have been the leader of three bands. I was fired from my last band by the very musicians I had hired who refused to play if I remained. And I was their *leader*! A ragtag street band of homeless drunks from the Lower East Side who called themselves "The 3rd Street Stompers", told me to go home. And they were *homeless*! Once when playing tuba in a band at a party at Cornell, the trumpet player stole a slide from my tuba while we were on break and threw it into the woods in order to render my instrument mercifully silent. I was forced to leave that gig early. Then, later, I successfully stole a replacement slide from a similar tuba I'd found at "Styne on Vine" in Hollywood, run by Jules Stein's brother, Maury. I stole it in order to pursue my "career". Maury would have understood.

"Jazz is my life," I was fond of saying in those days. But there were those who hoped it would be a short one. Yet, I still think of myself as having had a long and wonderful life in music and have enjoyed the camaraderie of many great musicians. Desire trumps reality, I think.

My best friend is an accomplished jazz pianist. I met him in college. Our first encounter was when I saw him wearing a leopard skin and hanging off the back of a convertible on the school's main drag. I knew he would be my best friend because he taught me how to approximately play the bass fiddle while we were in a fraternity together. He was endlessly encouraging, despite my obvious lack of natural music ability. Our only breach came when I started "playing" the tuba. He hated the tuba, but we're much closer now that I don't play it anymore.

Design has always been more important to me than music. I bought my upright bass fiddle because of its size, elegance, and apparent simplicity. Four strings in an indistinct lower register. What could go wrong? My piano friend would write all the changes for various tunes on 3X5 cards which I would then stick onto the back of the bass and play them by pure rote. Serendipitously, the contortion of my body from such an arrangement made me look like more of a serious musician than I obviously was. Instead of being "lost in the music", I was only trying to read the changes on the back of the bass. That instrument is long gone, but the 3X5 cards have endured as a ubiquitous notebook in my back pocket. What was pretty much of a total loss, musically, has become an endless collection of "notes to self".

My friend taught me to play the bass so he would have an ever-ready accompanist when entertaining college friends and stray women at the fraternity. He was also the leader of a notable and famous college jazz band that was scheduled to go to Bermuda for spring break one year and, of which, I was, obviously, not a member. Touring with a jazz band seemed to be about the best thing in the world that could happen to a "musical wannabe" such as me, so my friend generously encouraged me to go and start my own group. Consequently, I made a lot of calls to Bermuda that winter.

When negotiations over first class plane fare and their exurbanite demands for luxury accommodations broke the bank for my friend's legitimate college jazz band, the sponsoring hotel pulled out of the deal and declined to subsidize their spring vacation. Suddenly, the legitimately famous college jazz band was out of luck and out of work, and nobody was going to Bermuda that year for spring break. But, as it turned out, I had made contact with a small, half-assed hotel that wanted to get into the Ivy League college business and thought that a preppy jazz band would be just the ticket. Hence, in short order, *I* had an all-expense-paid engagement in Bermuda, and my best friend and mentor had nothing. The only problem was that, along with any discernible musical talent, I didn't have a band, either.

The mythical band that I said I was the leader of, and whose name I had commandeered, was a defunct college dance band called, "The Purple Knights". Fortunately, the gig I had secured was an iron-clad, three-week engagement, all expenses paid. It was at a place called "Harmony Hall" (The "Hall" obviously hadn't heard *me* try to play in tune.) The well-known college jazz band that my best friend was the leader of had dispersed as soon as they didn't secure their classy spring break gig. Consequently, my best friend, the piano player, agreed to assist me in putting together the newly legendary, world-famous, "Purple Knights", whoever they might be.

It is important to understand that the managers of Harmony Hall were under the impression that they were hiring a reputable, semi-famous, preppy, Ivy League college Dixieland band. In other words, young men in Lacoste shirts, playing happy jazz. What I was able to assemble, between getting the gig in late February and our departure date the following month, was slightly to the left of that.

To begin with, there was me, a less than semi-proficient bass player and titular leader of the band. Then there was my friend, the jazz pianist, who was, certainly, the musical leader of the group, but who had recently retired from the logistics of leadership.

But after me and him, the band roster went slightly askew. The rest of the group was comprised of three musicians of questionable Ivy League pedigree. The drummer was a counter-culture, long haired scion of a famously wealthy family currently living in abject poverty with his drum set and a diminutive girlfriend in an abandoned grocery store on the Lower East Side of New York that still had a "Salada Tea" decal on the front window.

Next was a Greenwich Village jazz flutist, cartoonist, and LSD aficionado who had grown up in Greenwich Village and had never been north of 14th Street, it seemed. Rounding out the front line was a sullen, sallow tenor player who was from a weird, progressive institution in Vermont who was doing his thesis on "Loneliness". He wore dark glasses 24 hours a day as "research."

The only kind of music my group agreed to play was "hard bop" jazz---Coltrane and beyond. Ivy League we were not. We were about as far away from a "good-time" college band as you could possibly get. Junkies and low-lifes would have called us "too far out."

In fact, the band had never actually met each other before we all got on the same plane to go to Bermuda. It also happened to be my first commercial airplane ride; so, I think, I dropped my pants in celebration of that fact in response to the stewardess' "fasten your seat belt" directive. I also knew that I probably never would have been able to book the actual gig had it not been for the fact that the promoter of "College Week" in Bermuda that year was a proper Englishman who was currently dying of leukemia. As a result, he had a certain amount of fatalism about the whole thing which came in handy. Very handy.

Harmony Hall was not exactly on the Bermuda "College Week" circuit in the way that the Elbow Beach Club (referred to as, "Elmo Beach", by our hippie flute player) or the Coral Beach clubs were. Hence, the craziness of our engagement in the first place. Harmony Hall was an "also ran" resort which was far off the radar of any college revelers. It was a modest hotel with modest claims of semi-luxury and very little "Bermuda Charm". And, rest assured, any "Bermuda Charm" that *might* have been gleaned from the surrounding pink sand was dispelled upon our arrival that first night.

The flute player decided he needed to immediately test the acoustics of the room we would be playing in.

He was a flute prodigy who had recently discovered the microphone and P.A. system as adjuncts to his, otherwise, modest instrument. He had learned to play jazz by improvising on John Phillips Sousa at the rear of the marching band at the High School of Music and Art in New York. Whereas most flute players in marching bands were regulated to the back of the band to provide obbligato on whatever the horns up front were playing, our particular flute player was on the vanguard of modern jazz flutists who had discovered the soaring solo flights of amplified flute music. He was one of the first, and, according to him, the best jazz flutist in the world. I was not about to deny him.

In short order, after unpacking our bags and instruments, and after rescuing my bass from the top of the taxi where it had been secured and then run under the hotel *porte cochere* leaving a sizable notch in it, our flutist started playing, solo, in the empty hotel night club. He was fond of, no less than, thirty-five minute long solos ---riffing on an opening theme---and this was no exception. It didn't matter that he didn't have a band behind him at the time and that it was after 10:00 PM in a resort hotel. He had fired up the sound system and taken flight with his heavily amplified jazz flute. If you have never experienced it, you probably still have your hearing intact.

The impromptu jazz concert immediately introduced us to our host, the German manager of Harmony Hall, who was subsequently exposed as an escaped Nazi war-criminal on the run. He was ultimately either arrested or thrown out of Bermuda, but we could have ratted the guy out right then and there after our first encounter with him on that first night. He was not pleased with what he had heard. Nor were the other guests in the hotel. Finally, the flute player mercifully stopped, and there was peace and "harmony" in the Hall.

The gig went well. But I wasn't accustomed to playing the bass so consistently and for that long each night. Consequently, my hands became quite raw. As a remedy, I decided to purposely urinate on my hands every chance I got in order to make the skin on my fingers tougher. Someone had told me that's what *real* musicians did to form *their* calluses. It's an old wives' tale, I think, because it didn't work. It just made my hands smell like shit, and I wasn't able to shake hands with anyone for three weeks. Everyone thought I was just being "standoffish". But I remember thinking there was probably a mental disorder connected to what I was doing ten times a day in Bermuda, and it could've gotten me committed had anyone found out about it.

We alternated with a local, dance band lead by "Big Al", a native Bermudian who referred to us, alternately, as the "Purple Hats" or "Purple Hearts", depending on what he was drinking (He never got our name right) The musical problem that became abundantly clear was that, as soon as we started playing hard bop *avant-garde* modern jazz, the college kids avoided us like the plague. But they were quickly replaced by every drug dealer and low-life on the island. We were playing *their* kind of music. The Nazi war criminal manager was not happy. He berated me daily on our playlist and style of music. He claimed we were trying to be like "*Schtann* Getz" (sic) instead of something more benign and more compatible with preppy college kids. But I had little control over my own group. One reason was that I was placed so far back on the bandstand with the bass that I looked as if I was playing solo at another venue. The "Purple Knights" were not about to play "Moonlight in Vermont" instead of extended versions of some hard bop classic, like Horace Silver's, "Sister Sadie", or our flute player's endless, piercing solos on a two-chord Miles Davis atonal riff called, "So What?"

On top of that, my mentor and best friend was otherwise engaged by having an affair with the daughter of the owner of one of the island's leading hotels. And my drummer would disappear before the gig in order to practice "trading 4's" with his miniscule girlfriend who had made the trip to Bermuda as part of his "drum kit" and who actually slept in the closet of our hotel accommodations.

Things quickly went from bad to *really* bad. The drug people were thrilled, of course. And the next thing you know they approached me to buy some drugs for the band. No doubt because of the way I looked when I played my instrument and my distinctly *modern* atonality. I was shocked, *shocked* that someone would mistake the Purple Knights for a drug-addled jazz band. This was before "The Sixties" had really taken hold as a life style.

Thus, except for the flute player and his ever present LSD tabs, none of us knew very much about any drugs beyond aspirin.

But when I told our Greenwich Village flutist how much the drug dealers were charging for their marijuana, he was outraged. He said he could get a better deal and better dope on Bleecker Street in New York. He suggested we bust them just for their avarice alone. Thus, I became, not only a band leader, but a Bermuda "narc" as well.

Of course, I was about as proficient as a double agent as I was as a double bass player. We set up a late-night rendezvous, but neither the police nor the drug dealers showed up. I was practically arrested for loitering.

Then, simultaneously with the half-assed sting operation, our flute player, who had never driven a car much less a motor bike, had a major motor bike accident and cracked his skull from ear to ear. He would survive the coma eventually, but his face was left partially paralyzed. (He ultimately resumed his very successful musical career with, at first, a prosthesis in his mouth when he played to compensate for the partial paralysis. One side of his face was left completely expressionless. But, in the end, he made that work as part of his mystique and his "cred" as a musical genius.)

The accident happened close to our last day in Bermuda. The flute player, who had endeared himself to the college girls on the island by drawing elaborate cartoons on their bodies with his Rapidograph pen, was shipped back to New York. The putative drug bust never really happened. Nobody, including the Bermuda CID, had watched as much "Peter Gunn" on television as I had, so none of the players knew how to act in such a situation, or exactly what to do.

Finally, we got off the island with the help of a friendly airline ground hostess from one of the local "40 Thieves" families whom we had dated and who happily forged our tickets.

* * *

The Tuba business wasn't much better. The tuba is an interesting instrument. Usually, only fat assholes are the ones who play them; and, even *then,* they only do it because they feel they have to. I wasn't fat, but I guess I made up for it with the other attribute. I remember seeing an incredibly massive tuba for sale at an audio recording studio in the old Paramount Hotel. Like I said, for me it was all about design. I bought it more as a piece of sculpture than as a musical instrument. But it led me into a friendship with my tuba partner, a kid from Long Island who worked there. We formed the "Tubas R Us" business where we would dress in long lab coats and hawk our wares at music instrument conventions. At one point, I think, we were the largest second-hand tuba dealers in the country. Our specialty was separating tubas from the widows of dead tuba players. The widows, of course, were more than happy to get rid of the stupid (to them) horns, but the transactions *did* take a certain amount of finesse to pull off.

One purchase got me fired from a job by a boss who overheard me negotiating on the phone with the recent widow of a tuba player in Poughkeepsie where I was claiming that the only photograph I had of my late father was a picture of him holding the exact same tuba as her dead husband owned. And I would do *anything* to purchase it in order to honor my father and help me remember him. But, at a fair price, of course.

The producer, upon hearing my side of this phone exchange, immediately designated me a sociopath and then promptly fired me for taking advantage of a grieving widow. It was a superb horn, so it was almost worth it. Of course, the star of the show he was producing was famous for masturbating into a towel *twice* just before "air" and then handing the semen-laden towel to the make-up girl while the stage manager was "counting down". The code for that little pre-show ritual was, supposedly, "I have to put my contacts in." And, yet, that same producer termed *me* a sociopath because of my tuba negotiations.

The tuba business is not one for longevity. Even the sound guy who sold me that first tuba (a massive Conn "C" that had been stretched to a "B" flat) eventually stopped playing tubas and closed his recording studio. Apparently, he grew tired of playing on all the porno soundtracks that were dubbed in his studio. (The tuba, apparently, is a porn staple). It finally dawned on the tuba player and his wife that they could easily produce and shoot the same pornographic drivel that he had been playing for all those years. Consequently, the sound guy traded in his tubas for K-Y Jelly, and they went into the porn film business. They made a fortune. The wife directed.

The bottom dropped out of the second-hand tuba business when the Eastern Europeans discovered the Middle School horn market in America. They proceeded to flood the US with fancy, new, rotary valve tubas. Suddenly, vintage tubas like The Navy Kings, Conns, and Martins that we dealt in were shunned for brand new shiny Czechoslovakian models. (The same thing happened with women and Donald Trump). I still have my "Tubas R Us" coat. My wonderfully talented partner has his own store now, but I think he spends most of his time collecting engravings on tubas and other brass instruments rather than selling the horns themselves. He's going to do a book.

The best thing that ever happened to me with the tuba was that I carried one of my horns out to the Belmont Racetrack for the Belmont Stakes one year and was immediately admitted into the track and the clubhouse free of charge. No one stops somebody with a tuba. You look like you belong.

I didn't see the big race that day. The drummer in my best friend's jazz band decided to break up with his girlfriend shortly after they had arrived at the track for their gig. She promptly O.D.'d and was taken down to the Belmont infirmary deep within the clubhouse. I was dispatched to attend to the woman while the band played

"The Sidewalks of New York" when the horses came out of the paddock. I think I was down there with the, now, ex-girlfriend mainly to relieve me of my tuba and dispel any chance that I might sit in. But I had learned my lesson in Ithaca, and out of respect for the integrity of that particular tuba, I didn't even try. The ex-girlfriend was a cute Asian woman who was even cuter when delirious.

* * *

A friend of mine, who became a famous singer and who, years earlier, had married an ex-semi-girlfriend of mine was chosen to perform for the halftime show at the Super Bowl. He was kind enough to invite me to be part of his entourage which amounted to a large busload of friends and family.

It was out in California, at the Rose Bowl, and the weather was perfect as usual. Since we were the famous singer's guests, we had great seats, about midway up on the fifty yard line. It was definitely one of those "It's *good* to be king" moments.

I had decided to bring just about every camera I owned to the event since this was a once in a lifetime opportunity. And, because I was going to be part of a large group and not traveling on my own, I thought it would be best to wear all the cameras, on straps, around my neck.

I'm not a big football fan, but the spectacle of a Super Bowl was definitely something I wanted to experience. I walked around the stadium a lot; and, at one point, I remember, I ran into Rudy Giuliani as he was coming up the stairs toward where we were sitting. Rudy and I spoke briefly, and I asked him about *another* girlfriend of mine who, at that time, was working for him in New York.

"I *love* her," he said. (I guess that made two of us.)

The game had not started when I walked back down the stadium steps again (after the Giuliani encounter). All my cameras and lenses were still around my neck. All of a sudden, a security guard at the bottom of the steps, on the field level, motioned for me to come all the way down to him. I obeyed his invitation. When I got there, the security guy automatically opened the gate at the bottom of the aisle and admitted me onto the actual playing field of the Rose Bowl. Naturally, I proceeded as if I had expected him to do so. He, apparently, had mistaken me for an official game photographer because of all the cameras, and he wanted to be accommodating to the press.

The next thing I knew I was standing on the actual sidelines of the Super Bowl football field at about the 40 yard line when the big game began. This is what I learned from being able to watch a Super Bowl football game from the sidelines. I was closer to the action than even the football players who were sitting on the bench just to my right. What I learned that day was that NFL football is, really, all about television. The most alarming thing about being on the sidelines of the playing field was the silence. The silence of the game. I couldn't even hear the crowd. Nothing. All I could hear were the officials' whistles and the random grunts, collisions, and heavy breathing of the players. And when a play would veer toward to me at the sidelines, it was terrifying. It was like being in the way of a runaway freight train.

But the lasting impression was mainly the silence. Without commentators, the stadium perspective of the television camera, the reactions of the crowd, and the televised replays----it was like not being at a football game at all. I was simply too close to it to enjoy it. There was a deadness to it all. There were no shouts from the players (other than the quarterback calling signals), or yells, or screams. Nothing. Just a lot of thuds.

But I *did* get great pictures. Incredible photographs. These were once in a lifetime images. Then, at some point in the fourth quarter, somebody figured out that I didn't belong there, and they told me to go back into the stands. They weren't mad or anything; they just couldn't let me stand on the sidelines for the Super Bowl without proper credentials anymore. I think one of the real photographers had busted me because I didn't look right and the camera combo hanging around my neck was lame and amateurish. They didn't like that I was crowding their field position either.

I wasn't upset at being thrown off the field even though that particular Super Bowl game was the greatest single comeback effort in NFL history. The truth of the matter was that the contest, from where I stood, was unexciting, mundane, and confusing. It would have been better to have been home watching television.

But I *was* able to sell the Super Bowl photos to a Hollywood personal manager who wanted to thank our host in a special way. And the famous singer actually used some of my shots in his own promotional materials. So it wasn't a total waste of time. But the silence. The silence on the field was the most incredible thing about the Super Bowl for me that day. In the end, it all just seemed like a lot of large, ugly men running around aimlessly with no purpose. Like back in Hollywood.

* * *

I like to talk "gorilla talk" which is a series of grunts much like the apes did at the beginning of "2001, A Space Odyssey". But my children find it boring and tedious. So it is hard to find someone who will spend a full weekend with me speaking nothing but "gorilla". Perhaps it's the kind of thing you can only do when you're single, and there's a real possibility of "gorilla sex" as a result. Married life is different. "(Grunt!)"

* * *

I was acting in a commercial once, and they had me dressed in some god-awful wool outfit complete with a broad-brimmed hat. I looked like a cartoon of a pimp in a new suit. We were shooting the commercial down at the old Gleason's Gym on 30th Street and Eighth Avenue in the middle of the Manhattan fur district. It was the boxing gym of choice at the time because of its proximity to Madison Square Garden.

While they were setting up the shot, I walked out to the corner of 30th and 8th in what could only be described as the the Wool Council's unwitting pimp outfit. I stood there for some time acting like I was waiting for something and gesturing to the cars going up 8th Avenue. Presently, a very young police officer, whose hat was *definitely* too big for him, came up to me and wanted to see some identification.

"What for?" I said.

"I have been observing you for some time," the police officer said. "You look like you are up to no good."

"And that's a crime?" I said.

"Identification," the officer persisted.

I didn't have any identification on me. I was in *costume* for crissakes. The cop was about to arrest me when I called the assistant director over to explain the situation to him. The AD thought it was some kind of joke, but it wasn't. The cop was really going to arrest me because I looked like I was up to no good from the way I was dressed and the way I was acting on the street corner. Finally, the *actual* director, then, had to come over and explain. Then the cop was embarrassed because he suddenly looked like the green rookie that he was. He almost arrested me for *that*. He told me to get in off the street and go about my business, which I did.

But the experience introduced me to Gleason's Gym and the world of professional boxing. I had never been in a place like Gleason's. It was like walking into a gladiator's holding pen at the Coliseum in ancient Rome. I met Bobby Gleason who was then in his eighties but could still go several rounds with young fighters while correcting their boxing flaws as he did. He told me about how he used to fight on the barges down at the seaport when he was a kid.

I decided to learn how to box and started training at Gleason's because I figured it was an interesting way to get in shape, and I would actually learning something. It introduced me to an alternate lifestyle that I was totally unfamiliar with. I met trainers, fighters, pugs, and promoters. Gleason's operated like a community center of sorts, and famous and infamous characters would come and go at various times during the day. I saw Miles Davis in there once. He spoke in a low, raspy whisper.

I sparred very sparingly since I could tell, early on, that most African-American fighters only had two speeds: "Stop and kill". The golden age of average Irish guys was long gone. There was one black fighter I became boxing friends with who was named after the restaurant whose owner managed him. He longed to get a shot at me in the ring, but I would never give him the pleasure. Mostly, I just worked on the bags and skipped rope while watching the likes of Eddie "The Flame Gregory and Saul "Sweets" Mamby get ready for their fights.

There were strict rules at Gleason's. "No Spitting" and "No Talking to Other Fighters" were emblazoned on big signs all around the twin rings. I found a trainer who was a nattily dressed black man who looked like Uncle Ben. The joke around the gym was that he was a "credit to his rice". He was patient with me and extremely kind; and, I think, protected me from the likes of "The Undertaker"---a promoter who was always looking for "tomato cans" as opponents to put on cards in Portland, Maine. My mentor didn't think I should spar either. His assistant was a hotheaded, younger guy who was always mad at somebody. He went on to train a world champion heavyweight.

Of course, being the true phony that I was, the first thing I did was choose a "boxing" name for myself. I came up with "Kid Natural" because I thought it sounded young and proficient---of which, I was neither. I had t-shirts made up which was fairly cheeky of me. Then a friend suggested I should, more appropriately, call myself, "Kid Elderly", which I also emblazoned on t-shirts. But the joke was lost at Gleason's; and I remained "Kid Natural".

While I was training, I got to know the people who televised the fights as well as promoted them. It was through them that I eventually signed to have my first professional fight in Wheeling, West Virginia. But even the prospect of a professional fight didn't induce me to spar. As my boxing mentor---a man who billed himself as the "quintessential opponent" and boasted that he'd been knocked out on five continents---said "Why get hit when you're not getting paid?" I trained hard for about a month and then flew down to Wheeling for my professional boxing debut.

I was scheduled for a preliminary fight on a card that featured a famous Canadian fighter who later became the light heavyweight champion of the world. By the time I made my debut, I was too old to be a contender for anything but assisted living. I remember, once, telling another fighter, sarcastically, that I was thinking of "goin' for a shot at the title." (In my best "Waterfront" Brando) When he heard how old I was, he said "No fuckin' way. Not at *your* age". But I was complimented that he thought there might even be a possibility.

There was some issue with the boxing trunks before the fight, and my opponent and I exchanged trunks. It was then that I realized that, like gladiators, the enemy is not your opponent but the crowd who wants to see you get hurt. Fortunately, I had joined a merry band of fighters who traveled the towns of the Midwest fighting, sometimes, twice a week; but always losing to the local hero. This was before computers ruined this unique livelihood for such "journeyman fighters". Fortunately, the "journeymen fighters" told me that local women preferred losers to the victors in most of those matches, so losing regularly wasn't *entirely* altruistic.

All I can say is that my opponent was "highly motivated", and I survived two rounds in a three round match to emerge the winner by technical knockout (three knockdowns). I like to tell people that I grew up on the "Mean Streets" of Southport, Connecticut where the only way out was the fight game or in a Volvo. After my victory, I promptly retired, but they said that if I could get two more officially sanctioned fights, I would be in the record book for all time. By then the merry band of fighters had moved on, and I was never able to induce any of them to fight under my name, much less actually win. God knows, I wasn't going into the ring again *myself.* My opponent, who used to wrestle alligators in Florida, went on to marry a woman who owned a driving range. He retired also.

* * *

I'm afraid of the dark. There, I said it. When I get up very early, and it's still dark out, I don't feel comfortable until the sun comes up. At least, a little. The night is not my friend. I don't even wear dark glasses. I figure I'm depressed enough anyway, so why add to the problem. I don't need to look at the world in black and white on purpose. Every time I put on a pair of dark glasses I think, "Why do people find these so comforting? This depresses the shit out of me. I've got enough problems without wearing something that makes things look worse."

Once I was really depressed in L.A., (Note: Don't get depressed in California. They report that.) I mean, *really* depressed. I happened to stop by Junior's, a fast food joint on La Brea. I waited in line and, then, paid for my sandwich. But after the kid gave me my burger and I thanked him, he said, "Jesus loves you, and I love you." I almost cried. Really. The funny thing was he didn't say it to anyone else. Only to me. Out of the blue. It must have been the look on my face. I thought, only in LA can you find redemption at a fast food joint. I was stunned by his remark and wanted to embrace him and talk further, but there was a line of hungry, fast food-type people behind me. I think I said "Thank you." or maybe nothing at all. Then I turned and walked away. It changed my life. Well, that day, anyway.

The other sweet thing that happened to me in L.A. was that I used to live in a shack on the side of the hill in Laurel Canyon. I lived there alone. The place really was a shack, and it was mostly wide open. But every day a pack of dogs would come by and visit me. They'd come straight into the house and run throughout the place, barking and slobbering, like a band of canine party revelers. That's the only way to describe them.

They were a mangy group of dogs despite their extreme friendliness. One was a large, brown, boxer mix. He was the leader. The other was small terrier type, with shaggy white fur. They were obviously friends, but I don't know where they came from or where they went after they left. Sometimes they would bring other dogs with them. But I never saw them around the neighborhood. Only when they would burst through the door to visit me. I didn't give them food or anything although I was always very happy to see them, and I would pet them. They would clamor into my place like a bunch of footballs fans whose team had just won the championship, and they'd run all over the little shack with great joy and excitement. I would greet them happily; but then, just as suddenly, they would turn and leave. And that was that. Every day. I don't think the two main dogs lived with each other. I always had the feeling the big one picked up the smaller one on the way, and then they would come over to my place. I could never figure out where they were from, or whose dogs they were, if anyone's. Maybe they were wild and lived in the canyon wilderness above me. It was one of the nicest things that ever happened in L.A.

* * *

I went out with a girl, once, who announced to me, beforehand, that she was severely dyslexic. Not just normally dyslexic, her dyslexia was so severe that even architecture and, especially, interior walls and floors didn't appear straight or make any sense to her inside her brain. *That* dyslexic. Other than that she was a great girl and a lot of fun.

But when we went back to her place, and I walked into her apartment, I was met with a thick cloud of hot steam. She explained that all the hot water outlets in the place were broken and that nothing could be turned off. She was fighting with the landlord over it, but the result was that steaming hot water from the bathroom and kitchen faucets ran 100% of the time. Hence, the thick fog in the place.

It made her apartment a steam bath. There was steam and hot mist in every room. Sheets of condensed moisture cascaded off every wall and surface. She told me she had been living like this for some time, months in fact; so she had gotten used to it; but she was determined to outlast her stand-off with the landlord. It was an incredibly desperate situation, and the living conditions were extreme, to say the least. On the other hand, there wasn't as much as one wrinkle in any of her clothes.

I spent the night there nevertheless. It was like dating a girl from the tropics. Sex in a rain forest. Everything was wet, *including* the girl. The next morning, I got up and left the apartment. I have to admit that I never went back and never asked her out again. Too hot, too steamy; and vaguely unhealthy. The apartment, I mean.

* * *

I met Paula Jones, the woman that President Clinton wanted to have sex with in a hotel room when he was Governor of Arkansas. I spent the day with her in Little Rock because I believed her story; and, at one point, I owned the rights to it. I wanted to make a movie about her and the incident. Unfortunately, nobody else wanted to get into business with Paula Jones, or have anything to do with her. So the project never got off the ground.

The only good thing that came out of that meeting (besides lunch) was that she showed me, with her finger, how the President's cock had a very definite and distinctive curve in it, to the left. It made the whole trip worth it.

* * *

I got into a cab once and noticed, by the driver's name and accent, that he was an Irishman. Being Irish myself, I immediately struck up a conversation with him. He was a diminutive and cheerful man who said he was from County Roscommon.

"My mother's from Roscommon," I told him. "But she says nothing good ever came out of Roscommon"

"Well, she's got a point right there, she has," he replied. "And I'm livin' proof of the puddin'. Just got released from jail, meself."

"What were you in for?" I asked.

"Kidnappin' and extortion. Maybe you heard about it? "'Twas a famous case in New York and twas in all the papers."

I could tell this was not going to be an ordinary cab ride. The driver then explained to me that he had done an excessive amount of jail time as the unwitting driver in a very famous kidnapping case. He explained that he had done more time than anyone else who was convicted because he was the only one who refused to swear that the very famous kid who had been "kidnapped" and the good looking Irish fireman who had, supposedly, "kidnapped" him were not gay lovers as they actually were. The whole case had fallen apart when it was discovered the boys had signed a lease together on an apartment on the upper West Side of Manhattan.

He told me that he had been working as a chauffeur when his friend, a fireman, asked him to drive him up to Westchester to the huge estate of a famously rich family where the fireman's boyfriend lived. Once they were parked on the street outside the estate, the boy, who lived in the mansion, would sneak out of his house and climb over the fence and join the fireman in the back seat of the cab driver's limo. Then my new Irish friend would drive them around Westchester while the two lovers would kiss ("Just like a man and a woman, they were," he told me in his Irish lilt) and would have sex in the back seat. Then my driver would take the boy back to the his mansion and the fireman back to his firehouse.

That was all well and good, but then the Irish cab driver made the mistake of driving the limo when the boys staged their "kidnapping" scheme to get a few million dollars out of the boy's rich family. They were all arrested, but the high-powered lawyers, hired by the prominent family to deflect the scandal, got the kidnapping charges dropped in favor of a charge of extortion. Everyone eventually got off except my poor guy, the driver. He told me he simply couldn't tell a lie and testify that the fireman and the rich kid weren't gay. And that's what kept him in jail. They kept coming to him and asking him to sign an affidavit to that effect while the fireman and the others got on with their lives.

So, now he was driving a yellow cab instead of "chauffeurin.'" I believed his story. I told him I was on my way to a party with friends at the San Remo on the Central Park West. He took me there, and I invited him up to the apartment. After I introduced him to the group, he was the hit of the party and had a fine time including dinner. I guess he thought there might be a movie in it for him at some point because my friends were all Hollywood types. But no one offered. In the end, I gave him a big tip. After all, he'd just gotten out of jail. And he *was* from Roscommon, just like my mother.

* * *

My father used to claim that my mother was part Passamaquoddy Indian, owing to the fact that there was a Passamaquoddy Indian Reservation just outside of Eastport, Maine where she grew up. He figured the odds were that someone in her gene pool had co-mingled. It became a family legend.

When I found myself working at a desk job that gave me a lot of time on my hands, I started calling the Passamaquoddy tribal office at Pleasant Point, Maine. I became quite friendly with the head of the Tribal Census Department there. I figured no one had ever paid much attention to the Passamaquoddys (the name means "plenty of Pollock"), and there was no possibility of a casino in that remote area of Maine, so they might be open to the idea of a new recruit or two. I applied for membership. I wanted to be the only legitimate Native American in our family.

Unfortunately, it turned out to be slightly more complicated than filling out an application form. They wanted *proof*! I told them that my grandfather's mother was a Passamaquoddy which would make me one eighth Native American. This was actually unwittingly shrewd because only tribal members who are one quarter Native American, or greater, have voting rights. Therefore, there was no threat of me upsetting the teepee by my inclusion. I found a picture of Mary Selmore in my grandfather's effects and sent that in as my proof of my lineage. I claimed that Mary was, obviously, my grandfather's mother. They were initially impressed. Mary Selmore had been known as "Big Mary" and was somewhat famous in the Eastport area for being a Passamaquoddy *Catholic.* Perfect. I figured I was on my way. I assumed it was only a matter of time before my kids would be able to go to Dartmouth for free.

But then, after talking to the Tribal Census people for more than 20 years and pleading with them for some sort of certification, (After all, didn't I produce a picture of Mary Selmore, my great grandmother? What *more* did they want?) The tribal office finally suggested I get my DNA tested at Ancestry.com. My dear brothers and sisters of the Passamaquoddy Nation had gone digital. I stopped asking for certification, but I still called. After all, the census lady was my friend, now. We're, like, *family*.

* * *

Not being one to rest on mere official certification, I was so sure that I could talk my way into being a Passamaquoddy that I started listing myself as a Native American on various application and identification forms. After all, it had worked for Elizabeth Warren, and she got a job at Harvard and a Senate seat out of it. This quickly led to my classification as an Alumnus of Color at my alma mater. What bothered me about *that* was the seemingly out-sized organizational structure I discovered that existed at my old college to service the "Alumni of Color".

I considered this somewhat counter-productive to what I thought the whole college experience was supposed to be in the first place. I thought, once we got to college, we were all supposed to be *in*clusive not *ex*clusive. We were all supposed to be the same at that point. No more fraternities, or secret societies, or exclusions. We were all just college people. But, by the amount of mail and announcements of events that I received as an "Alumnus of Color", I realized the fraternity system was, in fact, alive and well. Except that, now, it was called the "diversity system". And I became truly offended by the exclusiveness of it all *and* the *de facto* segregation it implied.

On the other hand, I *liked* being an "Alumnus of Color" and did nothing to dissuade my fellow graduates or Alumni Association handlers that I was anything but. I mean, a person can only take so much! But then I came to know that there were classifications of alumni that I had, hitherto, never been aware of. "Latino Alumni", "Asian Alumni, "BiGLATA" Alumni", "Women Alumni". In fact, there seemed to be much more segregation and exclusion *after* college than during those blissful, utopian, "we are one" years. Who knew?

The last announcement I received from my college was an invitation for a weekend celebrating "Alumni *Men* of Color". So, now, after fifty years of our institution turning co-ed, *now* I had to be offended as a feminist, as well. I still filled out every form for every invitation for special alumni group events. I communicated freely with the Director of Diversity. (a position I had never known ever existed) And I fully expected to have been "outed" at every turn. But it didn't happen. Of course, they *did* turn my son down for admission. I hoped it wasn't due to a race issue, but I *did* have my doubts. I was sorry I wouldn't have the opportunity to challenge the diversity people by saying, "What? Am I the *wrong* color?"

* * *

The nicest stranger in New York City, a Hispanic gentleman, motioned for me to roll down the passenger side window on my car. I was at 93rd Street and Third Avenue, in the middle lane.

"Do you speak Spanish?" he said in perfect, unaccented English.

"No," I said.

Then he pointed in the general direction of my right front tire. "You have smoke coming out of your car," he said pleasantly and calmly. "You should do something."

I thanked him profusely for going out of his way to help a fellow driver and to alert me about a problem of which I had not been aware. I looked around for an opportunity to pull off to the curb. I saw an open spot on the northeast corner of 93rd Street just behind a truck which was in the process of unloading.

"You can pull in ahead of me," the Saint of Third Avenue kindly said. "It's okay."

I pulled in front of him and into the empty space behind the truck on the corner of 93rd Street and Third Avenue. I knew this was an emergency because average citizens were volunteering to help me. There happened to be a black man standing on the corner who I thought was involved in the unloading of the truck. He was big and wore dirty blue overalls that had a company name on a white patch on his chest.

"Oh, yeah. You got trouble," the large, black man said immediately. "Smoke. You hit a pothole, and musta knocked the pins out. Turn off your engine."

I was on my way out of the city in my Subaru Outback. I had an appointment in Connecticut. This was not what I needed. But, suddenly, it seemed as though the whole street corner was there to help me through my personal emergency. My car problem had been caught in the nick of time.

The large black guy seemed to know immediately what the trouble was and how to solve it. I was grateful for this outpouring of New York neighborhood help. He kept repeating that I had "hit a pot hole and knocked the pins out." That seemed reasonable although I didn't remember hitting any potholes and had never heard of any vulnerable pins. But on the mean streets of New York, you never know.

I got out of the car and stood in front of the hood with my new best friend. I didn't see any smoke or steam, but I didn't go around to right side of the car, either. I assumed it was there; but, now, it was subdued because I had turned off the engine as instructed.

"Open the hood," the black guy said. "I work on these cars all day long. I'm a mechanic. That's what I do. I work at a garage in Brooklyn."

I didn't dispute this, but I also realized that I didn't know how to open the hood of my own car.

"I don't know how to do this," I said fumbling around looking for a latch in the front that I assumed was there. I sounded meek, white, and suburban.

"There's a latch inside," the guy said pointing to the front seat.

I opened the front door of the car and felt around where I thought the latch might be, but I still couldn't find it.

"Underneath," my Good Samaritan said.

I felt under the dashboard and located a latch and pulled it. The hood of the Subaru popped up. I went outside but still couldn't raise it. But my new African-American best friend found the safety latch and raised the hood. We stood there together and looked at the engine. There was no smoke.

"Yep. That's what it is. The pins," he said. "See?" He pointed down to the pan beneath the engine. It was definitely wet. I could see a puddle of water underneath the engine block. "You musta a hit a pot hole and knocked the pins out. I can fix that right now."

"Huh?" I said.

Suddenly, everything was happening very fast and was very confusing. I knew I was in the middle of New York, and in unfamiliar territory. And I knew my car was in trouble. But I thought, perhaps, this was one of those easy, nonprofessional-type fixes--- like removing a small branch caught under the car.

"This is what I do. All day long. See?" He pointed to the garage name, or whatever it was, on his overalls. "I'm a mechanic. I do this all day long. Lemme call my boss."

The next thing I knew he was on his cell phone talking to, presumably, his boss at the repair place in Brooklyn. I was, sort of, looking around, trying to figure out what to do. This was "Bonfire of the Vanities" territory, and I felt every inch of it. I was confused, addled, and unsure. On one hand, whatever was wrong was being described as an easy fix, and I would be on my way in a second. On the other hand, I had never heard of any "pins" ever being "knocked out" causing the car's cooling system to drain and make smoke come out of my car.

The large, friendly, black guy was on the phone.

"That's right. It's the pins," he said. "I can do it. How much?" There was a pause. "A hundred and eighty dollars. Okay. That's it? Okay. A hundred and eighty." He hung up and put the phone back in his pocket. "My boss says it'll cost $180.00. That's what he says. A hundred and eighty dollars to put the pins back in. I'm on the job. I don't have a choice in this. That's what my boss says. I don't get anything out of this. That's just the price. But he wants me to get back to the garage right away. So what'll it be?"

"Huh?" I said.

I looked at him. He was a pleasant enough looking man and certainly friendly and helpful to a stranger like me. His lower teeth were bad on one side of his mouth, but that just added to his overall aura of folk wisdom and simple goodness. The scene had the feeling of one of those quaint "New York stories" unfolding, something out of the Times' "New York Diary".

"A hundred and eighty?" I said.

"I don't make anything," he said. "That's just what my boss charges. That's what they charge for this job in the garage. I don't get any of it."

"Oh," I said. I could feel things lurching out of control.

"Come on. I gotta get back to Brooklyn. I'm late. Whaddya wanna do?" he said, still smiling and being very friendly and helpful.

"I don't know," I said. "I guess I've got to get it fixed. I'm on my way to Connecticut."

"Then lemme do it. It'll only take a second. I know exactly what the problem is."

"Well, all right," I said somewhat reluctantly. I wasn't quite sure exactly what I had agreed to. I think I thought that $180.00 was the standard garage price, but he was going to do it for a tip because he was such a nice guy. I think I thought I was agreeing that he would fix it right there, unofficially, and not tell his boss. And then I would give him a tip that he would, at first, refuse like The Good Samaritan he was. Or something like that.

"Okay, let's fix it." I said although I don't remember *actually* saying it. But I think I *indicated* something along those lines.

Suddenly it was like one of those "birthing a baby" scenes in the movies.

"Okay, now I'm gonna need a gallon of water and one of your mats."

"My what?"

"I need a gallon on water. You got any water?" He barked, gesturing toward the car.

"No," I said.

"Then, go into the CVS, right here, and buy a gallon of water," he ordered.

"Huh?"

"Right there," he said, pointing to a large Duane Reade drug store that occupied the entire block between 93rd and 94th Streets. "Go in there and get me a gallon of water. Right now."

His urgency galvanized me. I took a couple of steps toward the Duane Reade, even though he kept calling it a CVS. Maybe that should've been a tip-off.

"Right," I said, feeling like I was part of a team now. Part of the "hood".

"And I need a mat," he said.

I was momentarily confused. How was a mat connected to fixing a smoking car? I asked him what he meant.

"One of your floor mats," he said. "From the car."

"Ohhhhh, right. A *floor* mat. Right." I said and turned back to the car.

I couldn't pull the driver's floor mat out in the front, so I opened the back door and easily removed the smaller back seat floor mat. I still wasn't exactly sure what the mat was for; but, at least, we were making progress and the repair was happening. I handed him the mat as he stood in front of the car, facing the hood. He took it approvingly. I was relieved that it was the right mat and, hopefully, exactly what he needed for the job.

"Now go in there and get me a gallon of water. I'll take care of the pins," he said like a soldier in combat.

Then he threw the mat on the ground in front of the car, and, I realized he wanted it to lie on. I remember thinking how dainty, sort of, it was for this guy in the dirty overalls to not want to lie directly on the ground. But then I figured it was some sort of professional mechanic's protocol. You don't go under a car without a mat.

"Now, go get the water while I fix your car," he said.

I had been dispatched, and I wanted to perform my duty like a good soldier. I tried to get into the Duane Reade, through several of the doors closest to us, but they were locked. Then, some lady told me I had to go all the way around to the front on 94th Street. I looked back and saw that the big guy was, now, actually lying on the mat and apparently about to go under the car.

I ran into the Duane Reade like it was an emergency. Like a "birthing baby scene", and somebody had called for boiling water. Fortunately, in this instance, I just had to get plain, room temperature water. I ran up to the lady behind the counter. She was Indian, or Pakistani, or something and was just checking someone out. I broke into the transaction at the counter. This was an *emergency*!

"Do you have any water?" I said with the urgency of a man dying of thirst. "I need a gallon of water."

The lady was not impressed. Maybe she had heard this request before. She pointed to the back of the store.

"In the back," she said.

I ran to the back of the giant, block long Duane Reade afraid that I wouldn't be able to locate the water section and would have to come back to her for directions. There was no time to waste. Fortunately, her casual pointing to the back was on the mark, and I ended up in front of a large bottled water section. *Really* large. "What goes on here?" I thought. "Why is there this incredible amount of water for sale here." Then, I was afraid I was going to have to settle for only two little individual bottles and that it might hurt, or delay, the repair. But then I saw a shelf of only gallon sizes. A whole rack. I was in luck. I grabbed one and returned to the lady clerk who, thankfully, had not engaged another customer.

"How much?" I said breathlessly.

"One-ninety," she said.

There was no time for a credit card. I reached into my pocket and found two dollars and handed them to her. She rang it up and gave me a receipt and a dime in change. I thanked her and ran out of the store. When I came around the corner the nice black mechanic was, now, standing by the front of the car with the mat in his hand.

"I got the pins in," he said, handing me the mat.

"Great," I said, and took the mat and ran to the back door of the car to replace it. "How did you do that?" I asked when I returned.

"I just did it," he said. "I just put the pins back in."

I was confused. I thought the pins had fallen out. Where did he get new pins out of nowhere? But, then, I figured maybe the pins were somehow attached and all they required was to be re-inserted.

"Okay. Now, gimme the water," he ordered.

I handed him the gallon of water. He raised the hood up again and pointed to the coolant reservoir which was approximately where the radiator would have been on a 1952 Ford. I don't think modern automobiles have radiators, as such, any more. He popped the cap off on the plastic coolant tank which looked at first, to me, like it was for windshield washer liquid, and I almost stopped him to correct him. The tank was made of white, milky plastic and didn't look "official" or serious enough to be part of the actual engine. But then I saw, embossed on the top, the "coolant" designation. What I *didn't* see, at the time, was the "See technician" stamped there also. He popped the plastic cap off, grabbed the gallon jug of water, and proceeded to pour in a small amount in order to top off whatever was missing in the coolant tank. I could see that the level of coolant was down slightly, but it wasn't *that* depleted.

Then he handed the gallon of water back to me and put the red, plastic cap back on the coolant tank.

"Here. Keep this in the car," he said. I thought he meant that this was only temporary fix and that I would have to re-fill the tank as I drove. But then he added, "You should always have a gallon of water in the car. Carry one with you all the time," he advised.

I thanked him for the good advice, and I think I apologized for being so stupid as to not have a gallon of water in my car in the first place.

"Now you gotta get my a hundred and eighty dollars," he said.

"Oh," I said.

"You got a credit card?" he asked. At first, I thought he was actually going to take a credit card. I was momentarily relieved because it made the whole thing seemed legitimate. "You gotta go to a cash machine. An ATM," he said. "I need a hundred and eighty dollars for my boss. I don't get any of it. It's for my boss for lettin' me do this on the job."

"Right," I said. "You want cash." I looked around. "But I don't see any Citibank around here. I don't know how..." I said. I was confused as to how to proceed. I really didn't know how I was going find a cash machine that wasn't in a Citi Bank, and I didn't see one nearby.

"No. Go into the CVS. They got an ATM in there," he said as if this was no problem.

I was still confused. "What?"

"Go to the ATM in the CVS," he repeated. I was struck by how he knew that there even *was* an ATM in there. I was not convinced, and I expressed this to him.

"It's a *drug* store," I said.

"They got an ATM. You can get the cash in there," he said with assurance.

I ran back into the Duane Reade (now, even *I* thought it was a CVS). The Indian lady was still behind the counter.

"You got an ATM in here?" I said with the urgency of someone who needed cash fast.

She pointed again in the same general direction as the water department as if she had done this before. I ran back and was confused as to exactly what I was looking for. The only cash machines I ever used were the official ones along the wall of the Citibank branches. I was worried that if I used a privately run ATM, I was going to be charged an arm and a leg for the transaction. And I considered *that* a scam. But then I spotted, thank you Jesus, an actual free-standing Citibank cash machine on the other side of the store. I ran over to it and put my banking card in. This particular machine would only let me take out $80.00 at a time. So I tried to make up the difference from the cash I already had in my wallet. But there wasn't enough. So I had to go *back* to the machine and wait while another customer got cash in order to get a *second* $80.00. Then I stepped to the side and emptied my wallet out onto a chair, counted out exactly $180.00, and then put everything back into my pocket.

Fortunately, the large, benign, black man was standing patiently by the car. I ran out of the store with the $180 in my hand.

"Here," I said triumphantly as if this was a perfectly normal transaction.

He took the money without looking and was about to put it in his pocket. This where, what I would call, my "Bourgeois guilt" kicked in. I wanted him to know that I wasn't going to haggle or argue and that I was straight-up about our informal relationship.

"Aren't you going to count it?" I asked. I wanted credit for being honest and giving him the exact amount.

I wanted his approval. Reluctantly, he stopped and counted it out.

"Five, six, seven, eight, nine," he said as he counted out the twenty dollar bills and somewhat impatiently shuffled the bills as he did it. "One hundred and eighty."

"Okay," I said. As if I had done something terrific. He could see that I wasn't leaving.

"I'll send you a receipt," he said. "What's your e-mail?"

This actually relaxed me because it confirmed to me that he had been telling the truth, and that this was all done under the auspices of his home garage in Brooklyn. I carefully spelled out my e-mail, making sure he wrote it correctly, which he did, but not the "@AOL" part as if that was too much trouble. I was about to remind him; but, then, I figured he already knew. He didn't *need* no fucking "@AOL"

"Now, is the car okay to drive? I have to go out to Connecticut, " I said. "Will I be able to get there?"

"Yeah. Just drive the car," he said dismissively.

"But do I have to be careful? Is everything okay?"

"Go to Connecticut. Go on," he said like it was an order.

I thought he was being slightly abrupt. As if he was urging me to get out of there. I, on the other hand, wanted to make sure the car was "safe". But, then, I decided he was *that* confident in his work and the success of his repair job, that it was a foregone conclusion. He wanted me to just proceed normally. Everything had been fixed, perfectly.

"Just go to Connecticut," he repeated. "Now!"

"Okay, thanks," I said, not wanting to argue, and got into the car.

I turned the engine on. All the gauges seemed normal. The temperature gauge was right in the middle between blue and red which I thought was sufficient (I had never checked it before). Then I thought I saw a whiff of steam or smoke float up from the front grill, but everything seemed okay.

My Good Samaritan (with my $180 bucks) crossed to the other side of Third Avenue. I watched him go. I thought he was going to get into a truck or something, but he didn't. He just kept walking. He saw me watching him as he walked north toward 94th Street and gave me one final wave--- a sort of good natured, brotherly "farewell". The light changed and I drove off.

I actually felt I had dodged a bullet. I figured that, although it had cost me a fast $180.00, my pins were intact, and I was on the road. The whole thing had taken less than twenty minutes. It was probably worth it. I felt hip and very "New York" for being able to adapt on the fly and use the city with all its native resources.

The next day, I took the car into my Subaru dealer thinking I'd better have those "pins" checked out just to be on the safe side. After I told my story of the breakdown, the service manager called in the head technician who informed me he didn't know about any pins, and he couldn't find anything wrong with the car after testing all the systems. The only problem was that the cooling system would have to be flushed and cleaned and refilled with only coolant because I had put water into it. That would be an additional $225.00. But other than that, the car was in great shape. "Pins" or no "pins".

I had to take to my bed. I was devastated. I had been hustled for $180.00 cash and a repair bill. How could I be so stupid and naive? What was I *thinking*. After all I'm a "*Plus*" member of Triple A. I felt violated like one does when you come home and find your house has been robbed. It isn't the missing items that bother you, it's the violation, the intrusion, and the feeling of being nothing but a demeaned punk that, ultimately, hobbles you to the core.

But then I figured this. Somewhere in Brooklyn, this same story was being told by the large African-American man and his Hispanic co-hort. I figured they were all part of a team. Part of my willingness to go along with the repair was the seemingly legitimate corroboration of the "perfect stranger"—the mild-mannered Hispanic gentleman who thought I was Latino.

But what consoled me the most was that somewhere in Brooklyn, this same story was being told with great glee and laughter, not humiliation. With raucous laughs, and howls, and "high fives". That made me feel better---sort of. Okay, not really. In fact, not at all. I take that all back. It didn't assuage my feelings of abject shame in the least. But it *is* true---you can't always be the winner, the one with the story. And the other thing I kept telling myself was, "nobody died."

* * *

I was working on a talk show where the young, female host, on camera one day, expounded on something she called, "Necktitude". "Necktitude" was the neighborhood "neck jive" thing that, mainly, Latino women do to emphasize their disdain for the person they're talking to, or about, and to underline the seriousness of their "dis". The young host of the show then demonstrated, for the audience, how dismissive anything one said with "Necktitude" would be, and how it totally destroyed the person on the receiving end of "Necktitude". The audience loved it.

The next guest on the show was Vice President Joe Biden. I thought it would be good talk show fun if he would continue the "Necktitude" discussion. I told him he should come out for his segment and give the young host some of his own "Necktitude". The Vice President then proceeded to come on the show for his segment. But, instead of doing "Necktiude" with the young host, The Vice President of the United States launched into a discussion some very sensitive United States foreign policy issues terms of "Necktitude". He said the Palestinians had given the Israelis a lot of "Necktitude" over the settlements issue. Then he went on to talk about negotiations with countries like North Korea. He said the United States didn't like getting Necktitude from Kim

Jong Un. He thought the United States should give Kim Jong Un a lot of Necktitude back just to teach him a lesson. It was amusing, and I was glad that the Vice president had "gone with it"; even though it wasn't exactly what I had had in mind.

Suddenly The Vice President's staff was frantically running around backstage looking for people. They were looking for me and the producer of the show. It turned out that the staff understood "Necktitude " better than the Vice President. Biden's performance was in danger of precipitating an international incident if we did not cut all the "Necktitude" statements from the segment. Fortunately, the show was on tape that day so the damage could be rectified.

Nothing ultimately came of the incident, but the idea of the Vice President breeching foreign policy in the service of a bit tickled me. I don't think he ever fully understood "Necktitude ". He didn't get the fact that it was a negative statement and a "put down." He never realized how close he had steered the United States Government into an international incident with Kim Jong Un because of the Vice President's "Necktitude" toward the dictator. On the other hand, it *was* fun and great television. I mean, what's a nuclear holocaust compared to *that*?

* * *

Whenever I make reservations at a restaurant, I always ask if they have a defibrillator. The person on the phone is always taken back aback by my question. Sometimes they admit they don't, in fact, have a defibrillator. But other times, I get a detailed description of the establishment's emergency equipment and their procedures. I think I get a better table as a result. Close to an exit. To help the paramedics.

*   *   *

I befriended a young prostitute once, but I was never a client, although she did spend one or two nights in my apartment when she was hiding out from a "bad guy" or an abusive football player or something. She was incredibly attractive and sweet.

I met her at the bachelor party for the son of a famous actor where I thought, at first, that she was another guest and had started chatting her up as if it was a college "mixer". She looked like a coed from The University of Wisconsin. But then she announced to me that she had only recently started "working" in the "business", and she was there to service the prospective bridegroom. I believed her story because she looked like a college girl who was still learning "the ropes", so to speak. I put her in touch with my accountant because I figured she should, at least, properly manage the fruits of her labor.

I kept in touch with her after that first encounter. She went on to service, mainly, a single Wall Street brokerage house. (She was smart enough to specialize). The firm was aptly named "Goodbody and Co." The firm collapsed, eventually, and went out of business. The New York Stock Exchange determined that Mr. Goodbody had not properly looked after his assets and banned him from Wall Street forever. I understood completely.

My young prostitute friend told me that she was paid, many times, in "new issues" by her stockbroker clients, and these financial instruments had proved to be quite profitable for her. The good news about "Goodbody" was that she had serviced so many stockbrokers in the heyday of that firm, that she learned enough to become a stockbroker herself. She got her stockbroker license and eventually moved to San Francisco where she worked for a EF Hutton as a successful financial advisor. Let that be a lesson to us all. Sometimes, "happy endings" are just that. Happy endings.

But what was interesting about her life was that she told me that, in servicing the many men of Wall Street, she had noticed one important thing. When the stock market went up on any given day, so did the penises on Wall Street; and she was always very busy. But when the stock market went down, her clients' cocks went with it. And there was nothing she, nor anyone else, could do to "get it up" again. I found that fascinating and, also, kind of a vindication, for some reason.

She went by the same last name of a famous porn star, and I have often wondered whether that name was the "go-to" moniker for a young "working girl." The good news was that, at least, she had too much class to call herself "Stormy".

* * *

Breaking up is hard to do. Isn't that what we learned in high school? It was happening to me at a fairly advanced age, so I didn't want to sing about it. I wanted to talk about it. Endlessly. What is devastating about rejection is the complete negation of self. Monks or Mother Teresa might pray to achieve that; but, for a mere civilian, it's like death without the death part. No wonder I couldn't stop talking about it. I talked about it because the sound of my voice proved to me I was still alive. Unfortunately, it also proved the same thing to those unlucky enough who had to listen to me.

I was running out of close friends who would hear me out, so I recruited near strangers and service people who weren't as accustomed to hearing my story. Thankfully, at least some of them were getting paid. But soon I ran out of them, too.

It was at that point that I decided I definitely needed to change something. I figured I could either throw myself into something bigger than myself, ---a charity, a daring mission, or, perhaps, a religion. Or, I could go to Ireland.

Ireland was where "The Troubles" were happening. Not only would I be able to leave all mine at home, but

I'd be going to a place where they actually had a name for what I was feeling.

I know why everything is so green in Ireland. It's because so much is buried there, so often. Not just their bodies--- their hopes and dreams as well. Mine along with them. There's something futile about walking on the ashes of the recently departed as if being part of the landscape is the purpose, not the reward.

What was I doing treading this soil so rich with flesh? So green and fertile to the eye, but dead just the same. I had come for the revolution. Or, perhaps, even to be martyred myself, if that's what it took to absolve me of my sins. But, in truth, my purpose was less noble. Men were starving themselves to death, and I wanted to watch.

I wanted to feel the ancestral tug which had, hitherto, only come to me tangentially and without herald. A friend, a turn of phrase, a lilt in the spoken word. Nothing I could hang my hat on. I wanted to be part of it more than I wanted to succeed. I wanted to go back and taste what was supposed to be in my genes and on my lips but was not yet in my heart. So I pretended to join the revolution. Pretended like the true phony I was. Phony through and through--- the only truth was that, at least, I knew it.

The road from Dundalk, the last town in the Republic, into British occupied Northern Ireland was like Vietnam might have been had I gone; but I was deemed too crazy, even then, for the U.S. Army. British helicopters were "wop-wopping" overhead, low and menacing. Suddenly, the six counties of the North were a war zone in a landscape that looked like Connecticut. The Brits were afraid to travel on land for fear of bombs, so they helicoptered everything in and out which just added to the bizarre sense of siege on the *ould sod*. Margaret Thatcher wanted it that way to teach the Catholics a lesson. Intimidate the locals. Checkpoints at every turn. Weapons with their safeties off. Telescopic gun sights employed as deadly, one-eyed binoculars trained on anyone who approached.

There was a huge electrical power line tower outside Dundalk on the road to Crossmaglen across the border. It'd been bombed by the "boys" and still remained hobbled, at an acute angle, next to the road. No one had taken it down nor repaired it. It stood as a monument--- like Jesus overlooking Rio. But this tilted tower reminded me each time I passed it that the war was still going on. The Provo's effort to obliterate the tower had failed, but no one cared enough to fix it. Wires still ran to and from it, but the power was long gone. Or was it? Perhaps it still stood because it was still working--- bent, mangled and tortured--- but carrying the load. I never knew. No one knew. It was nobody's icon.

The urinal in Short's Bar in Crossmaglen was the longest piece of plumbing I had ever seen. Perhaps it had been a feeding trough at one time. Or both. If anyone ever wondered how serious the Irish were about their drink, they need only consider their urinals. They are a testament to the dedication of the Irish to their national pastime.

Paddy Short, the owner of Short's Bar, was a diplomat of a barkeep. He lived above the bar with his wife, Rosaleen, and raised his family there. Rosaleen was always referred to as "Mrs. Short" by all the patrons there, even when she worked "behind the stick". She was never "Rosaleen", which, apparently, would have been an insult had anyone dared to call her that. Paddy was sophisticated beyond his station. A man who knew he was on the cusp of history in this small border town famous for its traders and highwaymen who were usually one in the same.

Crossmaglen was the epicenter of the British occupation in South Armagh. More so than Forkhill, nearby, which produced just as many renegades but was far more cordial in doing it. The Brits didn't have to build a fort in Forkhill. In "Cross", their barracks stuck out like a cancerous growth in a benign landscape, an anomalous bastion fashioned out of random sheets of corrugated steel, cobbled together on top of one another and surrounded by rolls of barbed wire in the middle of this quiet Irish village. The fortified barracks stood not only as the last outpost of the British Empire but also as a monument to the terrorism of its Irish subjects.

I sat and drank Guinness at Short's waiting for something to transform me beyond that of a lovesick hunger strike tourist. The locals viewed me with sidelong glances assuming I was British SAS or "Special Branch". But I spoke too endlessly about the lost girlfriend and simpered on about how I had seen a sign for a town whose name, coincidentally, was the same as the ex-girlfriend's, as if this was news and somehow meaningful to them

Finally, a sympathetic bar mate took me aside and informed me that the Irish are not like Americans.

"The men, here, don't talk of such things when they drink. They complain about their cars or their jobs, but never their women," he told me.

He explained the concept of *"craic"* (pronounced "crack") which is a Gaelic word that means the fun of good talk. Complaints about women did not constitute "good *craic*" in the pubs of Ireland. It probably saved my life. The "boyos" sitting beside me, who could have had me whisked away with but a nod--- never to be seen, nor heard of again--- probably figured no "Special" would ever make such a mistake.

But Paddy recognized me for what I was. Another lost American, a benign dilettante, but diverting enough to befriend. He took me up to his farm in the hills above the town where he kept a small herd of Angus cattle. The grazing cows gave him peace, and he waxed poetic about passing his sunny days there discussing life and literature. The cows came to greet him when we arrived.

It was in those hills that I ran across a red-faced pig farmer who could quote the history of Ireland at the drop of a proper noun. He reported to me on the advance of "Rudy the Red" or some other 12th century marauder as if the blaggard had just been there that afternoon. He pointed to a ridge where the siege had begun as if he were an eye-witness and not a scholar. It made me marvel at the Irish school system that was able to imbue its students with such a vivid sense of history. Either that, or it was just the Irish proclivity for making every battle contemporary.

In the middle of the night, I drove down to Long Kesh, the notorious H-block prison that held the hunger-strikers. I was there when Bobby Sands died. Suddenly, I thought it was beholden upon me to inform the world. But, of course, I had no portfolio. Along with everything else that I wasn't, I wasn't a journalist, either. I had no way of getting the message out, or verifying it. And who the hell was I, anyhow? I tried to explain all this to the distracted CBS News desk assistant who answered the phone in the States but ended up convincing neither him, nor me, exactly who I was and what I was doing outside a maximum prison in Northern Ireland.

But it wasn't over. The hunger-strikes would continue. Young Irishmen would continue to starve themselves to death voluntarily and with the blessings of their fellow prison handlers. I remember listening to young mothers schooling their toddlers on how many days it took Bobby Sands to die (66) at the hands of Margaret Thatcher, as if that was now part of their catechism and a tenet of their Catholic faith. The hunger strike is something quite uniquely Irish---to actually persist in not eating until death. And what exactly was I doing among them? What was I was seeking or solving? Self-starvation is an anguished, wasting death imposed by one's sheer will. There's no lilt in that.

Back at Short's, there was much talk about whether a hunger strike was suicide or martyrdom. Patrons wanted to know if there was any possibility that starving yourself to death was a mortal sin. They wondered if Bobby Sands was in heaven or in hell. The consensus was that it was, indeed, martyrdom; and you would end up in the bosom of Jesus Christ Himself for starving yourself to death as long as it was for a just cause. Several priests were cited as having embraced this interpretation at their Sunday Masses. Kamikaze pilots were different. Those bastards went straight to hell.

I went to Bobby Sands' wake. He was laid out in a prom suit like a sad puppet. He even had a sprig of something floral in his lapel. He was that small and that dead. And that tackily elegant. Outside, I walked around in front of the small house where he lay. I struck up a conversation with a wizened mourner who seemed interested in the fact that I had come all the way from America without any credentials or obvious purpose. As we parted, I happened to say, "So long," which he heard as, "Slainte," an ancient Irish salutation. He thought I was speaking to him in Gaelic, long favored by the IRA, as if by way of some code. He stopped, turned back, and motioned me over to him.

"Do you think you could get any guns where you live, there, in New York City?" He asked.

I was confused and somewhat frightened. "No." I told him. "I don't know anything about that." He turned away dismissively and walked back into the wake.

I moved from my motel in Dundalk to the Europa in Belfast. The Europa had the reputation of being the most bombed-out hotel in Europe. It was across the street from the bar where "The Informer" was supposed to have been filmed, but that didn't help me or give me any added context.

At the Europa, I met a group of international journalists and photographers who were headquartered there for the duration of the hunger strikes. Ted Turner's new CNN thought there was going to be an actual uprising, and they wanted to cut "live" to the revolution. They had at least three camera crews crisscrossing the six counties.

I remember one Magnum photographer from France who was there with his attractive, preppy, American girlfriend whom he took everywhere, as if she were an extra lens. After hearing my story and understanding my complete lack of purpose in Ireland, he told me, "I know all about you. There's always one of you everywhere we go, no matter how remote or dangerous." I did not feel honored.

Another photographer, who would later become famous for his pictures of world strife, was on his very first assignment right out of the Ivy League college he went to. We went out on a few "runs" together, but I could see that he was too oblivious to danger, as most photographers are. He would shoot the street battles by wading into the middle of them as if he were bulletproof and invisible. I couldn't get myself up early enough in the morning to be his "war" buddy, ---he dressed in army fatigues--- and I decided he was probably gay anyway.

I wandered around. I had guns pointed at me by the RUC and British Royal Guards who were stationed there. And once, at an IRA cemetery off the Falls Road, I became aware that the Provos, off to the side, were discussing whether or not to hijack my rented car and set it on fire as a barricade in the neighborhood streets. They decided not to do that for some reason, and I was able to drive away unscathed.

I walked into the Sein Fein headquarters across from the British Welfare Office on Falls Road which happened to be conveniently adjacent to the notorious Divas Flats tenements. The Welfare Office was where the Belfast citizenry, Catholic and Protestant, got their weekly dole. It was never bombed, disturbed, or threatened. It was probably the safest place in all of Northern Ireland.

The Sein Fein office had an elaborate security system built around its entrance, a cage really. The actual office was upstairs on the second floor. I remember seeing the young Sein Feiners in their tweed jackets looking like American university radicals from the 60's. I tried to tell them that, because I had been through the civil rights protests in the States, I could tell them what I thought might work and what wouldn't. They did not want to listen. They couldn't figure out who I was or what I was doing there. That was for sure. So they continued to taunt the RUC and British soldiers and place burned-out cars in the streets, with children behind them throwing rocks at the police for the world to see.

As the evenings grew brighter and with advance of spring, there were daily demonstrations after supper in the neighborhoods for no other reason, it seemed, than to provide local entertainment for the inhabitants. Rocks were thrown and rubber bullets fired all of which were then photographed for public consumption around the world. I had never before been part of an international news story. But what the pictures *didn't* show was that, just outside the frame of the cameras, mothers with perambulators sat on benches and stone walls a few feet away, calmly watching it all as they rocked their children to sleep. It taught me something about the ultimate truth of "the news" on television and about the inevitable, but inherently misleading, camera frame that couldn't help but edit out what it wasn't recording. Consequently, the world, outside of Northern Ireland, never got the full story. The world thought the whole country was aflame, which it was far from being so.

I was over in Derry for another one of the strikers' funerals--- Patsy O'Hara's, I think--- when I decided to drive out into the country. When I did, I came upon a Northern Ireland museum that was supposedly financed by Andrew Carnegie for the express purpose of celebrating the contribution of Irish Protestants in America. The place, in early May, was deserted. I walked around the faux village which was supposed to represent a 19th century Northern Irish settlement. I walked into one of the cabins. I was all alone. On the wall was a framed, linen needlepoint that read, "Lovest Thou Me". But I did not read it as referring to God, or Jesus, in the least; but only as a plea to my ever-present lost girlfriend whom I yearned for even in this God forsaken place. I read it as a petition of love, not a call to worship. There was also a young Irish girl I fancied back home that I thought I might present it to as proof of my Irishness.

Without much deliberation, I removed the ancient fabric from its frame and replaced the empty frame on the wall. I folded the delicate needlepoint tapestry and put it under my coat. I justified all of this because, in the moment, I considered myself an oppressed Catholic in Northern Ireland enduring extreme discrimination and starving myself to death while Margaret Thatcher sipped tea. It didn't make any sense, of course, but it was enough to allow me to steal the artifact from this national museum and leave. I drove directly to the airport and left the country.

In retrospect, I was crazy. I let myself be radicalized in someone else's land. I put myself in jeopardy of causing an international incident. What was I thinking? Was I that desperate for relevance? Was the departed girlfriend that powerful? Would the new one be at all receptive?

When I got home, I looked up a friend who was a paparazzi photographer and war correspondent. He was somewhat of a hotheaded fellow who did both types of photography—war and celebrity. I had a drink with him. Why? Because he knew the girl who had left me, and he had photographed her. I hungered for more information that would connect me to her once again. I wanted to pick the scab one more time. I still needed to talk and explain my "case" to whoever would listen.

In the process, I told him everything I knew about Northern Ireland, and especially about that special Irish village I had found there that was so poignantly named after the ex-girlfriend. And, oh yeah, I also mentioned the hunger strikes which were still going on. In return, he told me what he knew about the girl. But, still, I had difficulty---and with a straight face---in trying to connect my mewling love problem with the spectacle of men, in dank, feces-smeared cells, and "on the blanket", starving themselves to death. But, by God, I did mightily try.

As it turned out, he was leaving for Ireland soon afterward to cover the very same "Troubles" for the Daily News just as I had done as a love-sick tourist. The only difference being that he would actually belong there. Consequently, he was eager to receive any sort of briefing, even from the likes of me. It was why he put up with my self-indulgent ramblings that made me sound like some "true believer" who couldn't stop arguing a lost cause.

When the photographer eventually came back from Northern Ireland and his assignment there, he agreed to meet with me once again to share his experiences. That's when he told me I had saved his life.

It turned out that he had taken my advice and had used Short's Bar as his base of his operations. Then he had fanned out from there to photograph and report on "The Troubles" ---Ireland's, that is, not mine. But being the hothead that he was, he inevitably rubbed the locals the wrong way. He was a small, swarthy Italian and not a bit Irish. At one point, they decided he was, most likely, a foreign provocateur and up to no good, maybe even SAS trying to pass as a photographer. The Provos grabbed him one night and took him out in back of Short's to deal with him there. They produced guns, and were about to shoot him and leave his body by the side of the road, as an example to all quislings and traitors, as they had done many times before.

At the last minute, in desperation, he remembered that I was the one who had told him about Short's, and it had been me who had recommended he go there in the first place. Consequently, as he stood before his executioners, with their guns cocked and pointed at him, he blurted out my name and declared that he knew me. They slowly lowered their guns, but they did it very dubiously with grave suspicion and dismissive of his lame attempt at reprieve.

The Provos thought it was a trick---that somehow he had learned my name from Paddy Short, even if inadvertently. They raised their guns once more and aimed at him point blank.

"Exactly how do you know him?" they asked as they took aim and cocked their Armalites once more. "A lot of people know this fellow. How do we know you're telling us the truth?"

It was then that my hotheaded friend blurted out the words that would save his life. "He just broke up with his girlfriend. And he won't stop talking about it," he told them.

The Provos put their guns down immediately. The embraced him and apologized for trying to execute him. Then they slapped him on the back and invited him back into Short's Bar for a pint a Guinness and some "good *craic*."

I was speechless when I heard the story. On the other hand, I felt that now, at least, my life had *some* meaning after all.

* * *

She was known as "The Sad Page". She worked as a page on a show I was working on. But she was sad. She never smiled. Never. She wasn't pissed or anything; or mean, or mad, or in some kind of trouble. She was just sad. She was very nice when you spoke to her, and she was pleasant enough. But no smile, no laughter. She simply never smiled. Hence, the moniker, "The Sad Page".

I was very attracted to "The Sad Page", and so I spoke to her a lot and got to know her somewhat. We decided to go out on a date. And then we decided to sleep together. But even that didn't cheer her up. I didn't take it personally.

We slept together several times, and it was all very pleasant and jolly (except for the sadness before, during and after). She lived at the top of some building over on the West Side.

I remember, when I first met the producer of our show, there seemed to be something "off" about him. Then I realized it was because he never used contractions when he spoke. His mother had told him that using contractions was a sign of "bad breeding" or something. The result was that he sounded like a robot. The producer, who liked to wear his hair like a Dutch boy on a paint can, had a very special winter parka that was lined with some sort of endangered fur or something. He loved that parka more than his wife.

One day, the producer came to work with cuts and bruises all over his head and face. I think he even had his arm in a sling as well. He reported to the staff that he had been mugged the night before not far from our office. We asked if the police had been called. He said he gave the mugger whatever he wanted, but he hadn't called the police because he didn't want to make a big deal out of it. But it was obvious that he had suffered some pretty dramatic injuries.

The next time I went to The Sad Page's apartment, she asked if I had seen the producer. Since we both worked for him I said, "Yes." I told her that he'd been mugged and had gotten beaten up pretty badly.

She told me the producer hadn't been mugged at all. He had been beaten up by her boyfriend. This gave me pause. I decided *not* to take my pants off. I was not aware The Sad Page even *had* a boyfriend, much less one that was violent. The fact she was sleeping with my boss became a lower priority.

The Sad Page then went on to explain to me that she was, in fact, sleeping with the producer (She may have been "sad", but she was "busy"). She told me that, while having sex with the producer, her boyfriend had walked in on them. He immediately started beating up the guy.

But the funny thing about it, according to The Sad Page, was that the producer wasn't worried so much about his *own* health and well-being. What he was *most* worried about was his expensive fur-lined parka. The Sad Page told me that all he kept saying, while the boyfriend was beating on him, was, "Don't hurt the jacket! Don't hurt the jacket!"

The boyfriend, actually, *did* spare the parka; but, mainly, because he was concentrating more on the producer's face at the time. That's why the producer never called the police. He hadn't been mugged on the street; he'd been beaten up by The Sad Page's boyfriend in her apartment. Married guys get into those kinds of jams.

After our last show, The Sad Page went on to become a newscaster in a small Southwestern town. I guess you could say she finally got happy; or, at least, maybe not so sad anymore.

The producer ended up firing me, of course. I wondered if The Sad Page had anything to do with that. Then I heard he knocked up the good looking girl with perfect breasts who had the office next to me; but, at least, he didn't get beat up again. The good looking girl's father was in jail at the time.

* * *

There was a time when official stationary meant something. Stationary used to be a piece of real, printed letterhead that you couldn't create with just the click of a mouse. You had to get it *printed,* baby. But once you had the right stationary, you had power. You had access. People paid attention to stationary.

Across the street from where I lived, there used to be a commercial stationary store. They were in the business of creating embossed business letterhead for commercial use. Naturally, I got to know them very well because I was a true believer in their product, and I understood the opportunities that were available to anyone who took advantage of their services. This is a partial list of some of the business stationary I had printed up over the years with my address on it.

Catholic Boat Owners of America

Catholic Coalition for Media and the Arts

World Christian Tuba Organization

Alexander M. Sorkin, MD

I also had regular, *personal* stationary, of course, that actually had *my* name on it. That was fancy, *good* stationary that was engraved at Tiffany's with a special font of my own design. But then Tiffany's made the mistake of using my stationary in their sample book. I was shocked, *shocked* when I found out. My friend, the lawyer, immediately sent them a sharp note seeking damages as a result of their blatant invasion of my privacy. Because of their breach, I had been subjected to "ridicule from friends" and "mockery by strangers". We dined out on *that* settlement for a year.

"Doctor M. Sorkin, MD" was always available to write letters on my behalf. It was the only way I could avoid the penalties from the airlines when my stickers didn't work. "Dr. Sorkin's" favorite diagnosis was "Projectile Diarrhea", an explosive disorder which, Sorkin felt, should automatically disqualify me from all air travel. He was right. The airlines never questioned him. The good doctor still practices to this day.

The "World Christian Tuba Organization" was a group I invented who, like the "Catholic Boat Owners of America," just wanted to bring Christ back into the music business. "What would Jesus Play?" I think, was one of our mottos.

But the best of them all was the stationary I created for the "Catholic Coalition for Media and the Arts." It worked the best because my address, printed on the stationary, happened to be directly across the street from St Patrick's Cathedral which gave the letterhead a certain amount of verisimilitude. The Catholic Coalition was on my side no matter what; and, especially, whenever

I tried to get my money back from some "No Refunds" operation or other recalcitrant rascal. Since the Catholic Coalition was identified as representing the "Media and the Arts", few people wanted to mess with a bunch of crazy Catholics bad-mouthing them from the pulpit or on television. It was easier to just give the money back.

Except one.

I had signed up, and paid, for a famous screenwriting seminar in New York City that had cost me $400. But when I attended the seminar, I found the course to be tedious and mostly bullshit, so I left. But then, of course, I wanted my money back despite all the "No Refunds" notices posted to the contrary.

The Catholic Coalition took up my case as did my friend "Joe" (who became a Monsignor for this occasion), and even "Dr. Sorkin" (a recent convert) who took time out of his busy medical practice to get involved.

I wrote to the organization's office in L.A, on Catholic Coalition stationary, and I received a quick response from the vice president of operations who was also in charge of the money.

It turned out that the man I was dealing with at the seminar headquarters freely identified himself as an ex-Catholic who still had, shall we say, a few *issue*s with the Catholic Church. This was on top of the company's strict, and I do mean *strict,* policy of "no refunds". There were signs and notices to that effect prominently displayed at the venues and in the literature.

When I wrote my initial letter, my stated reason for leaving the seminar was that I felt the language used by its famous lecturer and the references he employed had been deeply offensive to me, and I was forced to walk out on religious grounds. That's why I had enlisted the Catholic Coalition to help me get my money back.

The correspondence between the Coalition and the man representing the seminar went on for over a year and a half. By the time it was over, the bank, the credit card company, several "priests" and "brothers", United Catholic Parents, a "Monsignor", "Dr. Sorkin", and myself had all gotten involved in supporting my request for a simple refund.

As president of the Catholic Coalition, I had initially written to ask for the return of my money citing the "offensive language" and "extraneous and offensive personal, moral, and political views" of the speaker as my reasons. What I got back from the company's vice president was a three page letter defending the seminar and its celebrity lecturer while condemning the Catholic Church for all of its current sex scandals. The vice president then identified himself as a former Catholic and the product of a Catholic education. But he said he was now "fed up" with the Church. He listed two full pages of Catholic atrocities over the years. He also vowed that he would *never* refund my money under *any* circumstances.

This prompted a return letter from me repeating my claim. I also stated that there may even have been some sexual *nonsense* at the very seminar I was forced to leave. I told the seminar executive I had referred the whole matter to our Monsignor for his review. At the same time, I suggested that perhaps he would like to *join* our Catholic organization.

Then Dr. Sorkin wrote to inform the vice president that, as head of the Decency Committee of the Catholic Coalition, he was informing him that his screenwriting seminar was in danger of being put on the Coalition's "Condemned" list. I figured this would *really* make smoke come out of the vice president's ears. I was right.

The seminar guy wrote back to the Coalition denying all of my allegations. He said he wished to have nothing to do with the Catholic Coalition. He also reiterated, in all caps, that there would be "NO REFUNDS". He then cast some aspersions on my own sexuality and even my suitability as an attendee of the seminar and also as, even, a man. He hoped his letter would finally put an end to our correspondence and the whole "refund" issue. Little did he know.

After that, every time I wrote to him in various guises, I slightly misspelled his name just to make him crazier. The next letter from me took issue with his graphic rendering of the sex scandals of the Church. The seminar guy then wrote back to "Dr. Sorkin" with his reaction to the possibility being put on the "Condemned" list by the Coalition. He was unconcerned. He also wrote back to me with even *more* personal attacks and repeated his company's steadfast refusal to give refunds of any kind.

The next letter to the seminar vice president was from our "Monsignor" who had, somehow, confused the seminar guy's report of the *Church's* sexual misdeeds with his *own* history of abuse. The Monsignor, in his letter, assumed that it was the *seminar guy*, himself, who had been sexually abused by some priests in Canada. As a result, the "Monsignor" graciously invited the seminar guy to attend our special six week rehab and counseling program on Fire Island provided by the Coalition for victims of ecclesiastical abuse such as him. The "Monsignor" assured him that, "Brother Pat Kelly, the retreat master there, has agreed to waive the usual stipend," He went on to promise that the seminar guy would enjoy our unique facilities at the Coalition's Fire Island retreat house, and he added that "Father Chuck is a great cook and known for great quiche and Tex-Mex platters." At the same time, the "Monsignor" stated he wanted to add the seminar guy's name to the Catholic Coalition's "Pedophile Database". The "Monsignor" had discussed his case with the National Association of Catholic Bishops who felt that the seminar guy had "suffered enough."

I then followed that letter up with one from me saying that the Monsignor might have been slightly confused. I also congratulated him on his decision to alter his screenwriting seminar course to conform to the

Coalition's guidelines in order to avoid further trouble. I reiterated my request for a refund, and I said he could send me a check if he wished to.

He wrote back immediately requesting that the Coalition *not* include his name in the "Pedophile Database." He tried to make it clear that it wasn't *he* who had been abused as an orphan in Canada, so leave him *out* of any "Pedophile Database". He said he didn't want to communicate with the Coalition any further and that there would *be* no refund for "as long as I am still breathing," he wrote. He singled me out as "delusional," and stated that he had no intention of being drawn into my "delusional network".

In the meantime, the credit card company issued me a full refund. I wrote to the seminar guy to inform him of this and expressed my relief that this "nasty little matter" had been resolved. But I told him the Coalition had still not yet decided whether to seek punitive damages against him and the seminar. I also told him that the "Decency Council" had not made their final adjudication; but, in that regard, they *could* use a couple of free passes to the next seminar in New York in order to check it out. The Decency Council also wanted to make a video tape of the entire course. I thanked him again for the refund and, again, recommended the pedophile counseling services of our "Monsignor".

The seminar guy summarily turned down our request for free passes. He also refused any interviews and, especially, any taping of the seminar lectures.

The "Monsignor" then wrote to the seminar guy and included a full release form that the seminar guy should sign in order to have his name included in the "Pedophile Database." It gave the Coalition absolute permission to use his name and address in the database, for all time, as the Coalition saw fit.

Then I wrote a personal note to the seminar vice president expressing my hurt feelings at some of his remarks about me. I felt he was trying to "persecute" me. I told him he should try to put the matter of the refund behind him. I told him that the Coalition had worked to revamp the content of the seminar course and had done so "free of charge". Thus, he should be appreciative. But I *did* thank him for the refund. I said it would be our little secret. Then I told him that he should be happy that the Coalition cleaned up his seminar course. Then I advised him, in no uncertain terms, of our admonition: "Don't work blue!"

There was, then, an urgent letter from the seminar guy to the "Monsignor" and the United Catholic Parents informing him that he, the seminar guy, was *not* an orphan and had *not* been abused, and therefore should *not* be in the "Pedophile Database." He also turned down the "Monsignor's" offer for counseling on Fire Island since he lived in California, and it would be inconvenient.

Then the "Monsignor" wrote back to inform the seminar guy that, sadly, I had been summarily relieved of my duties at the Coalition. I was currently on temporary leave. The "Monsignor" had taken over my duties, and the seminar guy should deal directly with him concerning any refunds. But, the Monsignor advised him to make all checks payable to me, personally, in order to keep the Coalition out of it.

I then sent the seminar guy a letter asking why he had re-opened the refund case with the credit card company. I accused him, again, of persecuting me and the Coalition. I also told him that the early polling of the Decency Committee pointed to a "Condemned" decision, and he should be prepared for the worst.

At that point the seminar guy confirmed that he had re-opened the refund case with the credit card company. He also responded to the "Monsignor's" message that I was on "temporary leave." He suggested that the "Monsignor" "make it permanent" and called me a "fanatic" who had "quite possibly, only one oar in the water."

The next letter was from me to sadly inform him that his seminar, the famous lecturer, and even he, himself, had all been placed on the Coalition's "Condemned" list. It meant that members of the Coalition were forbidden to attend any of his subsequent seminar presentations. I also told him that, in my opinion, his failure to cheerfully refund my money had probably contributed to the Coalition's decision.

The "Monsignor" then wrote to the seminar guy and enclosed a letter of his to me inquiring as to my health and rehabilitation and inquiring if I had ever received the refund. In his letter to the seminar guy, the Monsignor then offered the seminar guy a position on The Board of Directors of the Catholic Coalition. He said that all it would take to achieve his directorship would be his apology to me and, of course, the refund. He was sure the board would approve his appointment.

Next was my letter to the seminar guy announcing that I was back from my "leave" and ready to go to work. I congratulated him on his pending directorship because the Catholic Coalition needed victims of pedophilia on the board. I also thanked him for the bank's subsequent decision to fully refund my money once and for all. I, then, asked for a picture of himself and told him the Board of Directors was preparing an off-site meeting in Maui or Cancun to which he would be invited.

Then there was a break in the correspondence. I wrote to the guy to inquire about his reticence. I told him the Coalition had formed a strong relationship with two competing screenwriting seminars. I told him the Coalition would be happy to set up a meeting with those two competitors so that the seminar guy might learn some important tips from these acknowledged giants in the field on how to conduct a successful screenwriting course.

He wrote back a very terse letter citing three points: 1. Remove his name from all Coalition mailing lists. He called us "fascists." 2. Any refund would be handled by the bank, and that I would *never* receive a check from his company. And 3. Never contact him again, or he would take legal action against me and the Coalition as well as the Archdiocese of New York.

He then followed that directive up with a letter to the "Monsignor" citing his past troubles with me and the Coalition. He included a copy of his "cease and desist" letter to me. He then admitted the final settlement of the refund issue, but he said he was, actually, "glad to be rid of it". Then he got into my offer to have two other experts in the field coach him and his boss on how to run a successful screenwriting seminar. He couldn't believe that I had offered "two of our most bitter rivals" as advisors to him and his company. He said I had also asked him for a donation. He wrote, "The last place we would donate money to is to anything [I] was associated with."

He went on to demand that the Monsignor prevent me or the Catholic Coalition from ever contacting him again, or else he would instruct his lawyer to sue for harassment and include the Archdiocese of New York in his lawsuit. In closing, he wrote, "Either you keep this guy out of my life and business or my lawyer will."

I left it at that.

* * *

I've always wanted the best for myself, but that was before psychotherapy taught me to be more realistic. As it turns out, one of the problems with always wanting the best for oneself, at least when it comes to women, is that the best don't always return the favor. It's sort of a basic error in judgment, not to mention a major affront to reality. But it does persist. Everyone wants the best. That's why some girls got to be "Most Popular", and the rest of us spent too much time trying to go out with them.

In the world of desirable women, there have always been a few of what might be considered, "Supergirls". Those are women who are not just good looking but also smart, funny, plucky, inventive, and original. Their beauty is solid and self-evident but, at the same time, slightly quirky and never studied or obvious. It's what romantic comedies are made of. Not only would you bring these women home to mother, your mother would gladly meet them halfway down the driveway.

In the second half of the 20th Century, at certain colleges in the Northeast, there were a small number of women who were in this legendary category, the "Daisy Buchanans" of the 1950's and 1960's. These "legends" included Rosie Blake at Radcliffe, Ali McGraw at Wellesley, and Pixie Eaves at Smith. These were *uber* women. Supergirls. Universities could not contain them. Men could not have them. Only kings and studio heads were allowed to touch them. There is a reason why Kate Middleton married Prince William instead of you.

But in the fifties and sixties, these were the Supergirls of the Northeast. It didn't matter what they did, because no matter what it was, it was always brilliant and perfect. Just right.

Jackie Bouvier (soon to be Kennedy) was an early version of the mid-century Supergirl. When she finally graduated from George Washington after her Supergirl tours at Vassar and the Sorbonne, Jackie became a photographer. But she didn't just grab a Brownie or even a Leica. Oh no. She had a Speed Graphic, for crissakes. Weegee's camera! Forget about whether she knew how to shoot it or not, it was a 4X5 Speed Graphic, and she looked great carrying it. She was instantly the real McCoy. Because, in the end, it wasn't about being great looking. She was already all that. Now she was great looking *and* could work a piece of equipment!

It probably started with "Rosie the Riveter" in the 40's and that great illustration of Rosie as a babe in a bandanna rolling up her sleeves. These were good looking dames who could get the job done. Their glamour was always an integral part of whatever unglamorous task was at hand. The beauty part was always a "throw-away."

Then there was that period in Hollywood when some of the great beauties of the day chose to play self-effacing nuns. That meant they would show up with only a portion of those glorious faces poking, unadorned, through a tight wimple and black habit. They would be completely oblivious to their innate beauty and sexiness because they had a higher calling. But they would *still* be better than any woman any man had ever known. And smarter, too.

Rosie Blake invented the "Girl in the Raincoat" look. She would look better wearing a raincoat, with its belt tied around her waist like the sash of a bathrobe, than anyone else could wearing a Chanel. Rosie Blake did more for trench coats than rain. There was a rumor that, as a child, she invented an entire language of her own that she then taught to her baby brother who learned it before he learned English, making English the kid's *second* language. For several years Rosie's parents could only communicate with their son through Rosie as an interpreter.

Ali McGraw was such a style icon that, even in college, whatever she happened to pick up that day, or put on, instantly became the fashion of moment. She continued this knack while working as a stylist for Harper's Bazaar and then Bert Stern. She could turn an ordinary photo shoot into a magical event with the addition of just the right accessory she'd found among her New York coterie of shop keepers and junk dealers.

Pixie Eaves was from New Orleans and a Mardi Gras queen. At Smith College, she was famous for always being, and doing, just the right thing. Always. That included even the dorm she lived in. She had survived a car accident while walking on campus that had killed the classmate she was with. But that just added to her legend of imperturbability and class. After she graduated, there was a story that Pixie had a boyfriend who had invented an inflatable rubber beach ball toy called the "Bungee

Ball". You rode it like a bouncing bronco. An angry investor, or so the story goes, actually kidnapped Pixie and held her hostage until the boyfriend did the right thing.

So when I got to be a senior in college, after returning to school after my forced sabbatical, I found myself rooming with the legendary Mike Reily, captain of the football team who was also from New Orleans and a close friend of the fabulous Pixie. Consequently, I immediately started campaigning for a date with her. You can't be that close to greatness and not go for it.

As I said, this was before psychotherapy which would have tailored my quest to something much more realistic and attainable. (The word "quest" always reminds me of "The Impossible Dream". You can't say "quest" without sounding gay.)

It was the fall of 1963. Mike was terminally ill with Hodgkin's disease. I think it must have been the Hodgkin's that weakened him to the point that he actually talked to me because, in truth, I was far below Mike's "Jock Grade" and had joined his graduating class as a returning screw-up from the year before. But since neither of us was playing football that fall ---me, for reasons even more profound than Hodgkin's --- Mike and I struck up a familiarity because we would meet in the common bathroom between our rooms. Him to recover from coughing fits after mustard gas treatment for the cancers, me to check my zits.

I told Mike of my desire to go out with Pixie because I knew they were both from New Orleans, and I had ascertained that they were friends. He agreed that wanting a date with Pixie was, indeed, a very excellent desire. But he also told me that it wasn't going to happen, either. Then he told me to stop saying "New Orleans" like it was part of a song lyric and start saying something that sounded more like, "Nu-Orriens". I never got it right. But I tried. For Pixie's sake.

This went on for most of the fall. Pixie wasn't available. Pixie wasn't interested. Pixie was busy. Pixie was studying. But I had dated Smith girls before, so it all sounded normal to me. I didn't take it as a rejection.

Mike was getting sicker. He never complained. He never bemoaned his fate. He folded all the horrible coughing, pain, and terror of what was happening to him into his daily life as a college student. So much so that the rest of us around him kind of forgot about his illness as well. It became normal to be living with a sick guy. You forgot he was sick. Maybe that's what he was going for.

First, I had to establish that Mike, himself, was not in the running as Pixie's boyfriend. They had grown up together; but, fortunately, probably as part of some sort of Napoleonic Code or something, a relationship between them was off the table. So, then, why not me?

Mike had a way of looking at you in a kind of sideways, squinty-eyed way that was half-way between a look that said you were interrupting him and half-way that he didn't know what you were up to; but whatever it was, he didn't care and didn't want to know. If you weren't wearing a football helmet and pads at the time, a look like that might scare the shit out of you given Mike's size, strength, and legendary ability to throw anything to the ground within twenty yards of him. But I persisted.

Finally, he said I could call her. I think it may have had something to do with the fact that I was a year older than everybody owing to my "sabbatical", or maybe it counted for something Napoleonic code-wise. In any event, after a couple of months of campaigning, I finally got permission to call the legendary Pixie Eaves. Which I did.

She did not sound happy about the call, nor nervous, nor even skittish. After all, groveling males had been calling her all her life. It was about as thrilling for her, and held about as much promise of fun as a dentist's appointment. Pixie being the dentist and me the patient with bad teeth. We set a date and time. It was not a long phone call. In fact, it was excruciatingly short. She definitely had no interest in getting to know me first. She had agreed to see me. Thanks for the appointment, doctor.

It was decided I would drive down to Northampton on a Saturday night and take her out on a date. "Don't bother me anymore," Mike said afterwards. He always called me by my last name which I think was because it perfectly described our relationship and because he probably only knew it anyway because of our proximity in alphabetical seating. But, in the end, the fact still remained that Mike Reily---*the* great Mike Reily--- gave up Pixie Eaves to *me*. Even Jesus hadn't done that for me, and that was in the days when I still believed in the efficacy of prayer.

The date was far enough in advance that I could go into full prep mode for the event. In my mind, I even felt I'd gained a certain amount of campus "cred" just by the fact that I was scheduled to go out with the illustrious Ms. Eaves. Hemingway's Gulf Stream fisherman probably felt the same way after he had hooked *his* "big one." And, although there were no sharks in Northampton, I was just as unsure as the "old man and the sea" was as to whether I could actually "land" this baby or not. But just the reality of the scheduled "hook up" made everything that had happened before worth it, and everything that might happen afterwards deserved.

By the Friday before the appointed Saturday I had finished all my preparations. I had decided on exactly the right unstudied casual clothes; I'd had a session with a sunlamp to give me a healthy "New Orriens" glow; and I even filled my car with gas when I didn't need it as if *that* would make a difference.

Then Lee Harvey Oswald shot the President.

November 22, 1963 is a day that will live forever in infamy. Why? Because November *twenty-third,* 1963, was the day I was to have my date with Pixie Eaves.

I was drinking coffee in the kitchen of the fraternity house after lunch when one of my roommates burst through the door and said, "You won't believe what just happened. They shot the president." Since the roommate was not exactly known for his news bulletins, I immediately assumed it was some sort of prank. But it wasn't.

That began the long, solemn march that weekend over the death of President Kennedy. Non-stop television and carloads of students leaving for Washington for the funeral. I couldn't go. I had a date. A date with Pixie Fucking Eaves, for crissakes.

I was not to be deterred, assassinated president or no assassinated president. While everyone else was carpooling to Washington or glued to their television sets, I was headed down Route 116 to Northampton and Pixie Eaves. I didn't even call to check if the date was still on, given the national tragedy and events of historical proportion. It was safer to merely assume that, as far as Pixie's and my world was concerned, everything was normal.

I picked her up at her fancy dorm, Lamont House---The Beverly Hills of Smith College. Lamont House---where the "elite meet to greet" the unwashed. I didn't go inside. Pixie came out to meet me. Pizza delivery boys have better access. Lamont was the New England equivalent of Kappa Alpha Theta in the Midwest or Tri-Delt anywhere. There were girls crying all over the place. Pixie appeared and looked exactly as I remembered her from her picture. Except for the expression on her face. That was more like, "What the hell are *you* doing here? I can't believe this is happening to me." But, being the good Mardi Gras queen that she was, Pixie was trained to never disappoint. She got her things, and we left.

Note to self: A national tragedy is not a good way to start a meaningful relationship. The President of The United States had just had his head blown off, the world was in disarray, and I was asking Pixie what she got on her college boards. I think we can assume, at this point, that any small talk I was able to produce that evening was positively microscopic.

I tried to put a happy face on the whole thing. "Jack would've wanted us to have a good time tonight," I told her on the way to Rahar's, the firetrap of a bar in the middle of Northampton. The place was deserted. All the television monitors featured the casket in the Capitol rotunda with Jackie hovering nearby and the kids being walked in and out. Marines standing at attention with tears streaming down their faces. As foreplay goes, not exactly the most effective.

But that didn't stop me. The bartender was crying when he gave us our drinks. Pixie was sullen and bored. If she could have, she would have called Mike right then and there and begged his forgiveness for walking out on this little "fix up". But I persisted. I was on a first date, and I was going to be upbeat.

"We have to move on," I heard myself saying. "We mustn't wallow," I advised. "He had a good life." I would have added, "We can't let the assassins win," if that had been in the lexicon at the time

I babbled on. I couldn't talk about any current events given the "elephant" that was so obviously in the *world*, let alone the room. So I was forced to talk about college and my plans after graduation. Pixie was not interested and kept stealing glances of the funeral on the TV sets in the bar.

But, let the record show that, even in national grief, Pixie Eaves was spectacular. She was everything her press had promised. We sat down. There were plenty of empty tables, that's for sure. I continued chattin' away as if the biggest thing happening was Thanksgiving vacation. She endured about as much as she could. But when the staff started sweeping the floors for an early closing out of respect for the assassinated president, she had had enough and suggested that I take her home. She and the other perfectly formed Smithies wanted to mourn, together, in private. I brought her back to her dorm and drove back to my college.

Of course, I reported to Mike that the date had been great, but I'm sure he got a full report from Pixie about this asshole he'd sent down who showed up the night after the president was shot, and wouldn't stop talking about college boards, and who actually thought that a date with her was more important than the assassination of a sitting president. Okay, maybe not *more* important, but certainly *as* important. It probably cost Mike his spot at the Mardi Gras parade.

I never saw Pixie again. Although after graduation, I *did* hear the story about how she'd been kidnapped by the Bungee Ball guy. I always wondered how being held hostage at gunpoint compared to her date with me.

Mike barely lasted through the year, but he made a point of walking across the stage at graduation to get his diploma. I happened to be the last one to see him just as he was leaving to go home. We were alone in the parking lot of the fraternity. He was all packed up and had just gotten into his light blue Jaguar XKE. I realized he was leaving for good and I started to say something, but he waved me off as if to say, "Don't even start..." Then he closed the door and spun out of the driveway. He died a couple of weeks later. In that last year together, we had never discussed my date with Pixie, football, his health, or the death of the president. It had all ended badly.

* * *

A few years ago, all of a sudden it seemed, every time I took a bus or subway, invariably, some old lady would get up and offer me her seat. I didn't care. I gladly took it. I figured, "Fuck it. What do I care?"

But then I started to think about all the ramifications of what was happening to me. So, now, whenever somebody offers me their seat, I yell at them, even if it's an old lady.

"How bad do I look?" I say very loudly. "C'mon. I mean it. How *fuckin'* bad do I look?" And I continue on like that as if I really want an answer. "How bad do I look that makes *you* think you have to get up and give me your seat? C'mon. How bad do I look?"

At that point, especially if it's an old lady, they usually sit down again very quietly and without answering. Then they sorta look the other way as if I'm not on the same bus with them at all. I think that's when most people decide I'm not just old, but demented as well.

Apparently, "standing" is not the problem.

* * *

One of my first jobs after college was working for a guy who ran for governor of our state who had been very successful in business, but he couldn't read. He was probably some sort of undiagnosed dyslexic or something. The guy was an incredibly adept business man and one of the richest people in the state. He told me he got the nomination simply because no one else had wanted it (the sitting governor was extremely popular), and he had gone around the state and bought dinner for each one of the town party chairmen. The next thing you know, he was a Republican nominee who had never held office and never run for anything. Shades of Donald Trump long before Donald Trump.

I became his administrative assistant because I was just out of college, unemployed, and semi-related to him through my father's sister's brother in law or something. In any event, I went to work for the guy in July for his gubernatorial campaign which he ran out of his corporate offices. I think he liked me because I was semi-family, and he was the type of guy who counted on that sort of thing. He was a very private fellow who just happened to want to be governor.

He was a little crazy, of course. He had ten kids or something like that and a very attractive wife. She was beautiful in a non-glamorous "ten kids" kind of way, but he assumed everyone in America wanted to fuck as much as he had, obviously. That was part of his craziness. He wouldn't let her go out of the house alone; and if a workman or a delivery person came to the door, she had to immediately go to the second floor and stay there until they left even though there were hot and cold running servants all over the place.

One-on-one, he was incredibly charismatic and persuasive as many of those self-made business guys are which is why he was so successful. It seemed like he owned half of the state. He just couldn't read, that's all. No one knew about that or would believe it if they did. But he really couldn't. He couldn't read, and he was a recovering alcoholic. So, maybe, because of those two things, he would begin his day at 5:00 in the morning, or something like that. He, really and truly, would schedule meetings for 5:30 in the morning just to bust everyone's chops, I figured, and to prove that he was the early bird. And everyone else he might be meeting with was his worm.

The candidate and I often ate together, just the two of us, at the end of the day. I got to know him pretty well. I liked him. I think he liked me. My actual campaign job was to answer all of his mail which he would, then, sign and send out. There wasn't a speech writer on the staff because he couldn't read, so there was no need to produce copy he couldn't deliver. On the other hand, the candidate could improvise his speeches and do so brilliantly and very compellingly.

Two things happened on that campaign which changed my life and taught me to stay out of politics. Well, actually, three things.

The first was during one of my dinners with the candidate. He was a liberal, progressive Rockefeller Republican in a Democratic state. One night during dinner we got to talking about minority voters, and he schooled me in the political rule of never saying, "You people", because it separates the candidate from whatever minority he might be talking to. I thought that was interesting and very canny. Then, I said something that wasn't original with me, but when I read it or heard it, I thought it made pretty good sense. So I told it to him as if it was my own.

"Actually," I said, "In the end, I suppose the real answer to race relations is that we'll all be a lot happier when we're all coffee-colored," I said as if I had thought of it myself.

I think I remember him dropping his fork in his meatloaf.

"You wouldn't actually *marry* one of those animals, would you?" he snarled.

I distinctly remember how screwed up his face was with distaste when he said it. This was the candidate for governor of our state. The man who just got finished speaking to representatives of Black and Latino voters. This was the man who was presenting himself as the answer to any civil unrest and inequality. I hoped he didn't see the shock on my face after he said that. Of course, being someone who was intent on keeping his job until, at least, *after* Election Day, I immediately backtracked.

"Well, I wouldn't go *that* far," I said, or something like that. But I still thought, theoretically, that he was, basically, on the right side of things. And I still believed that the coffee-colored solution was the smart answer. I circled back.

"But, of course, I mean, *eventually,* I think, intermarriage is the ultimate answer. Right? Don't you think? " I persisted.

"What?" he exploded. "You want to have *sex* with one of those people?

Now, I could see he was outraged at even the very *concept* of it. I immediately backed down and started to scramble like an NFL quarterback who had just stepped out of the pocket.

"Well," I scrambled. "Well, I mean, maybe not. Sure. I mean, whatever," I stuttered. "I just mean, maybe, just. I mean, you know, *generally*. I mean, maybe, you're right. Probably not," I said meekly.

The dinner was over. The exchange had soured the meal and the evening. We were never that close ever again. Something had transpired. I had seen something in him that I hadn't known was there. And he probably knew, on some level, that he had revealed something that neither of us wanted to deal with. So much for politicians as true believers.

The other event happened when a highly problematic letter from a very affluent political club downstate came across my desk, and I decided to answer it without consultation. To tell you the truth, I thought I did an incredibly brilliant job of it and outlined a middle-of-the-road policy that would make all parties happy. It was a question about regional zoning regulations which was a hot button issue in the local wealthy towns that insisted on controlling things such as low income housing projects by themselves. My policy of appeasement and inter-town cooperation did not go down well with the restricted town's wealthy political club. My accommodating solution, which carried the signature of the candidate, ended up as a banner headline on the front page of the wealthy town's newspaper. The headline looked as if a world war had either started or was over.

The finance chairman spoke to me for the first time the day the story broke. He told me that headline, alone, had killed all contributions to the campaign from that particularly wealthy area and that there was no time or way to amend what seemed to be the candidate's definitive statement on the issue. The campaign was fucked, right then and there. I went from being the candidate's most trusted aid to his biggest liability. Fortunately for me, but *unfortunately* for the campaign, it was perilously close to Election Day. The candidate had signed my letter without reading it. It was impossible to take it back. This so-called conservative was in favor of regional zoning.

The candidate ended up as the most soundly defeated candidate of any party in the nation. My political career was over. Although, I might add, we *were* the first ones in the country to call attention to the reality of widespread industrial pollution as an environmental issue even though the opposition made fun of us when ads would appear of the candidate standing next to a dead fish on a riverbank. Those were the days when there was a river in the state that would literally catch on fire in the middle of the city it ran through. The local fire department had to be called to extinguish the fire on the river.

After that first political experience, the closest I got to politics afterwards was when I would stand with my friend, Joe, the Irish contract guy, on election nights in New York City, halfway between the opposing campaign headquarters. Then, when the returns would indicate a probable winner, we would rush over to the apparent winner's side at his headquarters. Joe would, then, embrace him, saying, "We *did* it!"

The only *other* notable milestone achieved while working in politics was that I got my first blow job in the front seat of a car from an anesthesiology nurse after a campaign stop at a healthcare meeting. When she was finished, she immediately opened the car door and vomited profusely onto the pavement. It was not a good omen of things to come.

* * *

An old girlfriend of mine became the girlfriend of the Mayor of New York City. They lived together before, during, and after his three terms as mayor of the city. But all that time, I couldn't help but think, that maybe, if I hadn't broken up with her, *I* could've been mayor of New York.

* * *

My wife announced to me that she wanted me to start treating her more like the husbands in pharmaceutical commercials treated *their* wives. At first, I thought that what she was alerting me to were the dangerous side-effects of marriage (i.e." Do not operate heavy machinery"; "May induce drowsiness"; "Tell your doctor if you have suicidal thoughts"; "Death may occur"). But then I realized that it was really more that she just thought living with me was like getting chemo for a chronic disease.

* * *

I taught high school for a while as a substitute teacher in the inner city. What I learned immediately was that the assistant principal, at least back then, was the *de facto* enforcer of the joint. Specifically, he ruled the basement. The regular principal was in charge of everything above ground. But the basement was where the tough kids resided in the various "shops" located down there. Some of the teachers wouldn't even go down into the basement unescorted, and it was the same for most of the female students.

On my first day, the assistant principal informed me that my primary job, as a substitute teacher, was just to keep the kids in the classroom for however long the period was. Other than that, he didn't care what the hell I did. To facilitate things, he would actually lock me into the metalworking shop classroom at the beginning of the period and, then, open it at the end. In-between, the kids would fire up every single one of the machines, and the boys would threaten me with their elongated, "druggie" fingernails and taunt me to "make a move".

Upstairs, in the more "civilized" classrooms that taught regular subjects, the kids had already checked out my car, a distressed Volkswagen. They then informed me, in the middle of the school day, that if there was anything I ever needed or a piece of equipment that had to be replaced, they could provide it by the end of the school day. I did not ask how they could do this and still be accounted for as being in school, but it could be done, no problem.

Then I taught at an upscale high school in a very affluent, suburban community. There were no offers of automobile accessories to be delivered before the bell. My car was an embarrassment compared to the students' own sports vehicles. The female students all looked like they'd just completed "hair and make-up" for "High School Confidential II". The school year ended mercifully before any scandal had time to erupt.

* * *

I had a friend who lived mostly by himself in California and who was a wonderfully inventive writer, but he was also a hopeless hypochondriac. He was always well-dressed and loved clothes. The height of his hypochondria occurred one Christmas when he was given a beautiful red velour bathrobe as a present. He was overjoyed by it, put the robe on immediately, and wore it throughout the morning during which he had his Christmas Bloody Marys and breakfast with whomever he was living with at the moment. After breakfast, he decided to have his morning bowel movement before, finally, getting dressed for the day.

Everything went well on the commode, and he was able to move his bowels in great fashion and with no problem. But when he looked down into the bowl, he saw that he had in fact hemorrhaged and expelled an elongated section of his lower intestines which, now, lay in the toilet bowl rather than in his stomach.

My friend was horrified and would not move for fear of causing more internal damage. He immediately called his personal physician from his bathroom and told him of the emergency. He insisted that the good doctor make a house call immediately, even though it was Christmas, before he bled to death or expired from shock. The doctor told him not to move. He would be right over.

The doctor arrived and immediately assessed the situation after examining my friend's vital signs and more importantly the results of his calamitous bowel movement. It turned out that what had happened was that when my friend sat down on the toilet while still wearing his brand new red bathrobe, in so doing, the sash of the robe had fallen down behind him and into the toilet bowl. Hence, the sudden appearance of his blood-red intestines as a result of his bowel movement. The doctor swore at my friend and told him to lose his number never call him at home again.

My friend was a loving ladies' man and was married many times and had many long term relationships with wonderful women. As he lay dying in the hospital after a stroke and before a botched carotid artery operation that ultimately killed him, all of his ex-wives and girlfriends gathered around his bed to lovingly minister to his needs. It was quite a scene of shared and mutual love without the slightest hint of rancor or recrimination. Their love for him infused their affection for each other as well. I always thought it was not a bad way to go.

* * *

A group of comedy writers that my California friend used to hang out with in Hollywood had something they called "The Luncheon Club" where, each month, a member was to provide a wonderful and memorable lunch for the other members. There is nothing a comedy writer loves more than lunch.

One legendary comedy writer in the group organized what has never been excelled as the greatest iteration of "The Luncheon Club" known to man or comedy writers.

When it came his turn to host, the writer hired a helicopter to take all the members of the club for a ride around Los Angeles. Inside the helicopter, he had hired two world-class hookers who were stationed there to service the other members (and their members) at certain intervals during the sightseeing flight. The plan was to fly over each man's house in LA or Beverly Hills and wave to their respective wives out of the open door of the chopper while, back in the helicopter itself, the writers would be getting blown by one of the world-class hookers. Now *that's* what I call lunch.

That same legendary comedy writer was once asked to babysit for a recently married young couples' new baby. It was the couple's first night out after the birth of their baby; so, naturally, the young mother was somewhat nervous and apprehensive. But her husband, who was a friend of the legendary writer, assured her that everything would be taken care of, and they would enjoy a wonderful evening out by themselves.

When they came back home at the end of the evening, the legendary comedy writer was watching television and smoking his cigar. The young mother rushed into the house and immediately went into the child's room. But the crib was empty.

"Where's my baby? What did you do with my baby?" she cried hysterically.

"He's in the kitchen," the writer replied.

The young mother then rushed into the kitchen to see her new baby, but the baby wasn't there, either. She called for the writer. The legendary comedy writer, casually walked into the kitchen and opened the oven door on the stove and took out a platter on which was the sleeping baby, lovingly garnished with the vegetables and parsley he had found in the refrigerator.

The legendary comedy writer was never asked to babysit again.

* * *

There was a stand-up comedian who was not very successful but whom everyone in the business loved because he was such a nice guy. He was born and raised in Queens, New York; and he continued to live in his old neighborhood even after he got married. He just never got the right break in show business; or, maybe, he wasn't a good enough stand-up in the first place. But everyone loved the guy. The producers of the Tonight Show and the Sullivan Show used to book him on their shows as a favor when he needed money knowing that they could schedule him at the end of the live show but then "bounce" him for time constraints. Of course, he would get paid the union minimum, anyway.

One of the reasons everyone loved him was because he had a *very* difficult wife who berated him constantly and mercilessly. She was known to his fellow comedians and comedy writers as the meanest women any man could ever be married to. But the comedian was loyal and faithful to her, even though she beat on him continually. His downtrodden tales of woe became an hysterical part of any conversation he had with his friends, but those laughs never got translated into his professional life.

Towards the end of his career, he found work as a comic on cruise ships, and this is where he found a modicum of success and steady employment. Specifically, he worked many of the ships that travelled between New York and Bermuda. It was in the middle of one of those trips, that he suffered a massive heart attack and died very suddenly.

The captain of the ship was, then, obliged to call the comedian's wife on the "ship to shore" radio and give her the bad news. In that difficult and sad conversation, the captain outlined the various options that were available to the new widow.

"Your husband's remains are, right now, being kept respectfully in the ship's morgue. We won't reach Bermuda until tomorrow night," the captain told her. "At that point, if you fly down, you could meet the body after we dock. Or your husband could be placed on a plane after we land and be flown back to New York. And you could meet the body there. Short of that, we could keep your husband in the ship's morgue while we make our return trip which would take three days from the time we depart Bermuda. In that case, you could receive your husband's remains after we dock in New York. It's entirely up to you. I will do whatever you wish and whatever you think is best." Then he added, quite emotionally, "I'm very sorry for your loss. We are all devastated by what has happened. Your husband was beloved by everyone on board and anyone who ever met him."

There was a long pause while the comedian's wife considered all the options that the ship's captain had outlined for her.

"Thank you, Captain," she finally said, "I appreciate your concern."

"Of course," the Captain said.

"But you know," the wife began. "Lenny always wanted to be buried at sea."

Impromptu "burials at sea" are, apparently, not that uncommon on cruise ships. I knew a great and wonderful comedy writer and comedian from Boston, a bachelor who took his Writers Guild pension when he got too old for anyone to hire him and simply retired and lived on cruise ships. He travelled all over the world and would, often, stay on one ship that did nothing but cruise the same route, back and forth, between Los Angeles and Hawaii.

Whenever he was in port, we always had great laughs at lunch when he would regale us with the tales of his travels. He would talk about his life as a permanent cruise customer who had become friendly with the captains and crews of the many ships he lived on. He talked about how widows often traveled with the ashes of their late husband and, then, would go dancing with the urn at night in the ship's ballroom.

He swore he often would spend the evening dancing with some newly-minted widow whose husband had died onboard only a day earlier, on that very trip, and been, promptly, "buried at sea". After which, the widow would feel free to continue their trip as a single woman and start making passes at him. No problem. At that point in life, one doesn't have time to play "the waiting game".

That same writer was an ex-Marine who had enlisted in the Marines, on impulse as a teenager, and then continued his impulsive and hysterical life in comedy afterwards. During the Vietnam War, he had actually booked a flight to Saigon, just to check out the situation there. Apparently, you could do that for a while during that conflict; and girlfriends and comedy writers would simply "show up" on the battlefield like it was a tourist destination.

* * *

I had an Italian friend who was born and raised on Mulberry Street in New York City. He was truly a character without being the least bit self-styled. He was never conscious of the persona he presented or how truly unique he really was. Meeting him was like being introduced to a fictional character in the flesh.

Even though he looked, acted, and talked like a civilian's idea of a *Mafioso,* he was never in the mob, nor even close to being a "made man" of any kind. I don't think he was even ever considered "mobster material" by those that were. But that doesn't mean my friend wasn't "Mafia-adjacent". He was fully conversant with all manner of thieves, lowlifes, gangsters, and mob guys. Someone told me his real-life godfather was the infamous "Fat Tony" Salerno, head of the Genovese family. (or maybe it was "Matty the Horse") But, basically, my dear friend was simply too fun-loving, too kind, and too generous to have ever been "mobbed up". He freely and generously shared his love for Little Italy and his heritage with everyone he met.

Occasionally, film producers would hire him to play mobsters on television or in the movies. He took those acting assignments very seriously. I remember, once, asking him how his recurring role as a mobster in a famous television series was going. The producers of the show had forced him to shave off his moustache, because they said modern mobsters were clean-shaven in order to distinguish themselves from old-style "Pistol Petes".

"Yeah. And if the show runs another year, I got a good chance of bein' made boss," he told me straight-faced. He was hoping to move up in the ranks of his fictional mob family as if he were actually being tested in real life. My friend was a "method" mobster.

When this lovely man suddenly "went to God", his wake looked like something out of a gangster movie just by the sheer number of floral displays in the parish hall where it was held. As might have been expected, a large contingent of shady characters from the neighborhood *did* show up for the event. But if you listened closely to their conversations---whispered behind the backs of their hands---what these modern "wiseguys" were talking about that day had nothing to do with "hits", "whacks", "heists", or "boosts." All of the talk at my friend's wake that night was about "under fives", "dressing room trailers," "agents," "sides," and "lousy scripts".

"My fuckin' agent don't get me no decent auditions, no more. How'm I supposed be somewheres besides a fuckin' extra if I don't get no fuckin' lines, here."

I swear I heard those statements at my friend's "mob" wake. It's what modern *Mafiosi* have become. Nothing but bad actors.

The other reason why I believe my friend's "family" left him out of any of their organized crime enterprises was because he was, basically, too much of a "fuck-up" to be effective. He was too accident-prone to be trusted with anything important. But that trait, alone, probably saved his life. As proof of his dubious gangster "cred", the only job the neighborhood bosses ever gave him was permission to sell illegal fireworks on the 4th of July. That should tell you what the *real* "wiseguys" thought of him. Thank God.

I got to know him through my boxing connections and mutual friends who also cultivated his unique company. One time, we heard he had a beef with the lawyers from the Manhattan D.A.'s office that was headquartered just across Canal Street. Some of the ADA's had started parking all day on Mulberry Street which prevented my friend from parking *his* distressed Cadillac there. (The car never had any gas in it, so my friend's "travel" was always severely limited. Hence, the importance of a parking space) As a remedy, my friend took it upon himself to slash the tires of the Assistant D.A.'s cars in order to send them a message about using Mulberry Street as a parking lot.

Unfortunately, the actual mob boss of the street did not take kindly to this move, jurisprudence-wise. So, in order to teach my friend a lesson of his own about taking matters into his own hands, enforcers were dispatched to his abode who, then, proceeded to throw my friend off the roof of his back porch just to remind him who was in charge of things on Mulberry. *Especially* parking. My friend claimed his ladder broke when he was trying to fix something.

He once fell in love with an underage girl who lived in the neighborhood. But since she was, indeed, underage, and this *was* his own Italian neighborhood, my friend patiently waited however many years it took for the young girl to grow up and become legal. Then, on their first date, (she was still calling him, "Mr.") he decided to take the young woman down to Atlantic City for the weekend. Unfortunately, on their way down the New Jersey Turnpike, my friend proceeded to have a major heart attack and had to pull off to the side of the road. He couldn't continue the trip although he *did* try desperately, despite his severe chest pains and despite the young girlfriend's cries to the contrary. I mean, after all, he *had* waited all this time. As fate would have it, it simply proved impossible to drive a car *and* have a heart attack at the same time. So they never made it to Atlantic City. He ended up in a hospital instead. In the end, the closest my friend ever came to bedding the young woman was when she visited him there. Teenagers don't usually have to deal with myocardial infarctions on first dates.

I had secured a job to write and produce a pilot for a proposed talk show starring a game show host who was trying to move up. Immediately, I enlisted my Italian friend along with a friend of his from Arthur Avenue in the Bronx to appear as guests on the show for the proposed demo tape. I wanted them to come on as authors of something I called "The Mafia Cookbook". It was an idea I had come up with as a pretext for having these two colorful New York characters interviewed on camera. My friend and I discussed the planned interview and the ruse, at length, at his place on Mulberry Street. I even wrote a script for the interview. We talked about how we would claim that the "cookbook" contained actual recipes for "Al Capone's Lasagna" and "Meyer Lansky's Meatballs", etc. Everything was planned and scripted ahead of time.

Since this was just a demo tape, it didn't matter that none of it was real. In the end, I thought it would be a nice payday for my friend, and their appearance would serve as a different kind of talk show interview for the new host. My friend completely understood what we had concocted, and we laughed about our invention and even discussed whether, maybe, we should actually *do* "The Mafia Cookbook".

I flew my friend and his Bronx buddy (whose nickname referred to the meat he served at his Arthur Avenue deli) out to California in order to shoot the pilot. I flew them out First Class, all expenses paid. Everything was in order. Then, the day for the actual taping of the show finally arrived.

With the tape rolling in the studio, and my producing career on the line, the putative talk show host asked his first question which I had dutifully prepared for him.

"So, tell me, fellas, about this 'Mafia Cookbook' you guys have put together," the host asked cheerfully.

My Italian friend and his Bronx buddy both looked absolutely shocked.

"Wha?" they both said almost in unison. "What Mafia? Whatchu talkin' about? Whadda youse gettin' at?

There ain't no such thing as no Mafia here. The Mafia was a 16th century literary society in Italy. We don't know nothin' bout no Mafia. There ain't no such thing."

Little "tilt" signs came up in the eyes of the talk show host who was, really, just a famous game show host trying to pass. (I remember he wouldn't let me touch his "game show" hair) The cameras continued to roll. My friend, whom I had billeted in nothing less than a suite at the Beverly Hills Hotel for a week, went on to disparage, in no uncertain terms, any suggestion that there might be any such thing as the "Mafia." My friend said he had no idea what the host could *possibly* be talking about. Even the large Italian friend from Arthur Avenue frowned and proclaimed complete ignorance as to what the host meant by the term, "Mafia."

"There's nuttin' there," he said. "No such thing," he continued, shaking his head dismissively and turning up his nose as if he'd just been offered an inferior canoli.

It must be remembered that this whole thing was just a presentation tape, not a real show and certainly not "live". This was never going to see the light of day much less a television set. It was a sales pitch. These guys were neither under oath nor under subpoena. But they continued to deny any knowledge of anything that might vaguely be described as "Mafia", the "mob", "gangsters", or bad guys in general. And they *certainly* didn't know "nuttin'" about "certain people we may know" or about what "certain people" might've prepared in their own kitchens or, even, eaten.

Needless to say, the show never got sold. I don't think the presentation was even viewed by anyone other than myself and the tape editor. It was my last job as a producer. After the taping, my Mulberry Street buddy proceeded to hold court at his Beverly Hills suite for ten days. He was having a very lovely time in L.A. But, then, the studio that had financed the project finally pulled the plug and threw them out.

I still thought the basic idea of a "Mafia Cookbook" was a good one. I even pitched it to the most powerful literary agent in new York, whose father had once offered me a $2500 option from Houghton-Mifflin on my yet-to-be-written first novel (I, of course, turned it down because I considered myself unworthy and unprepared. As my father would've said to me, "They'll think you're crazy!"). The powerful agent had said he could absolutely get a huge advance on such a book of famous gangsters' recipes, but only if my friend from Mulberry Street would actually front it. But no, my dear friend, born and raised in Little Italy, claimed I was trying to get him killed. For recipes?

The "dead air" cookbook segment finally came, mercifully, to an end. At that point, my *other* boxing friend, the one who claimed to have been knocked out on every continent but Antarctica came on camera for *his* interview. He did better than my Italian friend and answered all the game show host's prepared questions beautifully. Apparently, being slightly punch drunk makes one much more pliable and agreeable to a producer's needs. At least he followed the script. As the "quintessential opponent", he was used to it.

* * *

The bad news is you have to have your prostate taken out.

The good news is if the surgeon writes you a prescription for Viagra, your insurance will pay for it.

The bad news is you have to take Viagra to masturbate.

* * *

I was introduced to a German filmmaker whose family had made the uniforms for Hitler and the Nazis---a Nazi *garmento,* if you will. He shot primarily ski documentaries, but he had just produced and directed his first independent feature film about the exploits of a fictional secret agent skier. The movie told the story of this inept man who, whenever he heard some "magic" music, suddenly became a world-class ski champion.

The movie had failed miserably. But, in typical German "rule the world" fashion, my new German friend had decided it would be a good idea to turn his existing, secret agent ski adventure into a whacky "Woody

Allen-type" (his description) comedy for the American market. He thought he could do this by, merely, re-cutting the existing failed movie footage and, then, dubbing in funny English dialogue. (Only a German cinematographer would think this was doable.)

Through a connection that involved a major airline, I ultimately got the job to do the comedy re-write, from which the "new" film would be cut and dubbed into English. I got on a plane with my best friend (who was the original contact), and flew to Germany to see if we could pull it off. The cinematographer had already informed me that he had thought "The Godfather" was an awful film and would *definitely* fail at the box office, so I knew I was in trouble even before I got on the plane.

The German guy clearly had a lot of family money. The Nazi uniform business had been very good to his family. He lived in a converted monastery outside of Munich. It was quite a place. Beautiful. He had a full Steenbeck flatbed editing deck in a separate room and large-screen video and projection areas.

The first thing we did was watch the cinematographer's most recent ski footage of an avalanche in Switzerland that had enveloped and killed his young girlfriend who was trying to out-ski the avalanche while her boyfriend filmed her. She didn't make it. There were pictures of the girl all over the house, and she had been quite beautiful. But it was bizarre to be watching this woman's actual demise while her camera-toting boyfriend described the genius of the shot. He was famous for being able to ski backwards while filming and had become somewhat famous for working on a James Bond picture.

But what does one say while viewing footage of a disaster? "Great camera work! I love the way you got the whole avalanche in before your girlfriend even knew it was coming." Apparently, she had thought his waves and shouts of warning were mere encouragement, and she had continued to ski unaware of the avalanche that engulfed her.

This was my introduction to the world of German filmmaking. After the *homage* to the dead girlfriend, my best friend and the filmmaker decided that they wanted to go to his apartment in Munich to spend a few days going to clubs and listening to jazz. I would be left alone with the Steenbeck to fashion a comedy script whose dialogue would fit the existing footage. No problem. I was left alone in the former monastery with only the German housekeeping lady who came in to clean each day.

I tried to make friends with the cleaning lady as a sign of international friendship and to prove I had no hard feelings about the whole war thing. She didn't know any English, so my attempts at this gesture of good will were lost on her. She was a dedicated housekeeper, and she was intent on doing her job for her beloved boss. That's when I decided I would entertain her by doing my imitation of a cockroach in order to break the ice.

(A great entertainer always adjusts for the house---or, in this case, the housekeeper.)

My cockroach imitation was actually a performance piece that attempted to simulate the effect of a light being turned on in a darkened kitchen where cockroaches might be foraging for crumbs. Upon being surprised by the light, in mid-forage, the cockroach (me) would then proceed to immediately scurry behind the refrigerator or under another appliance for cover.

The main thing I learned that first day alone with the housekeeper was that the word for "cockroach" in German is "*kakerlake*" which sounds like, "cockalocka!" when screamed. So, thanks to my extensive training watching Mike Stokey's Pantomime Quiz on television, I was able to convey to her approximately what I was planning to do and what her vital role in our scenario would be.

We went into the living room. I laid face down on the floor and then gave the cleaning lady the signal to "turn on the light." When she did, I immediately sprang into action and scrambled frantically, cockroach-style, on my stomach, in apparent panic to escape the light and hide under the couch. This is when she screamed "Cockalocka!" several times. The couch was a fairly light-weight one, so I was able to partially lift it up and place it on top of myself in my, apparent, cockroach panic to hide underneath. I figured the whole thing was in the cleaning lady's "wheelhouse", and she would enjoy the re-enactment. She did not. She left shortly thereafter never to return again for as long as I (the *kakerlake)* was in residence. She reported everything to the filmmaker *garmento* who then gave me a stern warning about menacing his cleaning lady. I took the warning seriously. It *was* Germany, after all; and I didn't have a helmet.

I *did* venture out into the little town during my sojourn in the monastery. But I must tell you that hearing 100% German spoken in a public place makes a child of the forties feel like he's in a WWII war movie. It was deeply unsettling, and I only went out once.

The rest of the time, I spent at the Steenbeck while my best friend and the German clothier were partying in Munich. I ran the footage backwards and forwards. (Skiing uphill. Now *that's* funny!) I couldn't make any sense, in terms of comedy, out of the dreadfully stupid, secret agent adventure movie that had been shot.

The main problem was the filmmaker's plan to dub English language comedy into the mouths of German actors who were, obviously, speaking German, in Germany. *AND,* at the same time, *make* the resulting movie hilariously funny----"Woody Allen-funny". Well, guess what? Germans aren't funny. Even in German. And German is such a fucked-up language that the German mouth speaking German doesn't look like it's saying anything *remotely* funny, no matter what language is coming out.

On the other hand, the plane tickets were free; and I was getting paid to spend a week in Germany. Under *those* circumstances, the whole enterprise seemed perefectly reasonable.

I tried to write dialogue that would fit roughly into the mouths of the actors, but I quickly decided the safest way to go was with a comic voice-over monologue that would describe whatever was happening on film with a comedic take. The result was pretty clunky and not very funny. And the whole thing made less and less sense as a cohesive story. But I persevered and actually finished a semblance of a new script for my employer's "Magic Music" movie.

When my best friend and the Hitler *garmento* returned from Munich, they were surprised to hear that the cleaning lady had left, but the German guy was encouraged that I actually had pages for him to read. Unfortunately, after reading the script, he was not entirely happy.

"Vhere is da philosophy?" I remember him saying after a few pages. "Dere is no seriousness here, no deep thoughts, no meaning, and no philosophy," he emphasized. He was not laughing. Apparently, you only get "yocks" in Germany when you invade Poland. Now *that's* funny!

I had to keep telling myself that this was a German clothier/cameraman reading an alleged comedy script in *English.* He was concerned that it didn't sound enough like Nietzsche. His original, international playboy *ubermensch* had become very definitely a *schlemiel.* Not only that, my greatest literary sin was that the lead character definitely sounded Jewish. This is not a good thing, even in post-war Germany. I tried to defend my comedic choice by saying that I thought he wanted a "Woody Allen-type" comedy. He agreed that he had originally requested that; but, c'mon, that didn't mean he wanted it "*Jewish!*" I reminded myself to never try to sell jokes in Germany.

A re-write was in order. We all left the monastery and went into Munich together and reconvened at the clothing company's corporate offices where we met his current girlfriend/secretary (don't go skiing with him, honey). My best friend, who is, also, a brilliant lawyer, insisted we get paid, first, before any re-writes. We got our money and, promptly, left the office.

Then, check in hand, we immediately got on the next plane out of Munich which happened to be going to Holland while, at the same time, the German guy and his new girlfriend went over my script and made the changes they wanted.

This was all part of my best friend's and my history of re-creating the Dean Martin and Jerry Lewis films of the fifties. This had been "Dean and Jerry Go To Germany", which, then, immediately became "Dean and Jerry Go To Amsterdam."

Once we got to the hotel in Amsterdam, the first thing my friend wanted to do was to thank me for my literary services which had been responsible for our current "Dean and Jerry". He also wanted to somehow pay me back for the great time he and the German guy had had in Munich. He decided the best thing he could do, as compensation, was to buy me an Amsterdam hooker in the Canal District of that city.

I was still recovering from my Steenbeck table "screen-writing" experience and, although I declined at first, he insisted. So we went down to the canals that night.

The canals were alive with people and action. We walked along the canal-side streets and passed a series of store fronts with half naked girls in the windows. My friend spotted one especially animated black girl, and we went inside. This was not exactly what I had in mind, nor did I think it was what we were looking for. But he quickly made the deal with the woman, gave her some money, and left.

Now it was just me and the prostitute in what seemed like the store front of a knitting shop. She quickly pulled the curtains across the front window in the same way we had seen other storefronts with *their* curtains closed. Now, I knew that this meant that the prostitute inside the storefront was "busy" or "otherwise engaged".

"Okay. Let's go," she said in very American English.

"Huh?" I replied.

"Take your clothes off," she said.

"I don't think so," I said. Now she knew she had a real patsy on her hands.

"Whatchu talkin about?" She said, getting seemingly angry and more "street" at the same time. "I'm busy. I can't waste time."

"Look," I said. "Couldn't you just do a blowjob or something?"

My thinking was that I was in a foreign country, for crissakes. I didn't think it would be smart of me to remove my clothes and actually get in bed or whatever she had in mind. In fact, I didn't want to take my pants off in Holland, period. I just didn't *feel* like it. But this signaled to her that I was a complete piece of shit, and she could fuck with me. It's why hookers insist on getting paid up front.

"What?" She said in mock outrage and shock. "You want me to do *what*?"

I explained to her that, actually, I really wasn't interested in having full-metal sex with her. But since the fee for such had been already paid, a blow job would suffice. Then everyone would be happy.

"A *blowjob*?" She said, loudly. She was getting louder and angrier. Now I was *really* not going to take my pants off. Maybe not even when we got back to the hotel. "You want me to do something like that? What kind of girl do you think I am?" she said. She was really pissed now. "That's disgusting." She kept repeating: "What kind of girl do you think I am?" as if she were a Miss Porter's Debutante instead of an Amsterdam prostitute.

I tried to calm her down. I told her she didn't have to give me the blow job. But then I suggested that, perhaps, in that case she should consider giving me my friend's money back.

"What?" she said again in outrage. "If you want to have sex right now, that's one thing. But what you said you wanted to do I wouldn't even do with my boyfriend," she continued even louder than before, "And he's in the next room right now," she told me and made a feint for the door at the rear of the little shop area we were in. "What kind of girl do you think I am?" she repeated several times again. .

I, then, assured her it was no longer necessary to give me a blowjob *or* give me my money back.

"Keep the money," I said. "All right? *No* blowjob. Okay?"

I just wanted peace. She wouldn't stop laying it on about how I had insulted and demeaned her by asking her to do an unnatural act. She accused me of trying to take advantage of a poor black girl by trying to make her do terrible things. I finally begged off the whole encounter. I told her to keep the money. I was leaving. I opened the door and stepped back out on the street that ran beside the canal.

Once outside, I momentarily felt good that I had decided to keep my pants on, but I felt bad that I had wasted my best friend's money. At that point, my friend came up to me. He wanted to know how it went. I told him about the blowjob request and how the whole thing had gone down badly. At that point, the black prostitute opened the curtains on the front window. She had my friend's money in her hand and was dancing happily for all to see as she waved the cash over her head.

The area around the little store became alive with other prostitutes in *their* windows all waving their congratulations to her. In my mind, it was as if the boats in the canal even blew their horns as well. But, actually, it was just a little private celebration that this particular prostitute had succeeded in getting her money without having to do anything. In whoredom, that, apparently, is a big deal and definitely a cause for celebration. She continued to dance happily in the window while flashing her unearned cash as we skulked away and returned to our hotel.

I was so embarrassed. I don't think I can *ever* show my face in the Amsterdam "Red Light" district again.

We left the country the next day and flew back to New York. I think my best friend understood my reluctance to remove my clothing in a foreign country. He didn't seem mad. He had paid his debt to me, so it didn't matter. But I still think the prostitute could've, at least, done *something* for the money. Shaken my hand or something. Maybe a touch. Or, maybe, taken *her* clothes off. *Anything*. It's not easy being an asshole in Amsterdam. After all, these are the same people who turned in Anne Frank. It made me miss the German housekeeper.

* * *

I owned a monkey for a very brief time in college. I must have been working out some movie fantasy or something where a monkey would be my best friend and constant companion. Complete horseshit, of course, but it was enough to make me go down to see the "Monkey

King" of New York, Henry Trefflich, the man who sold "Cheetah" to Tarzan. It was from Treflich's Pet Shop that I purchased my monkey. The "monkey", actually, turned out to be a "red faced ape", but it still looked like what you would think a monkey should look like. He had an ass that match his red face, and he was a mean fucking animal who didn't like me or anyone else, especially women.

I took him up to college and to my fraternity house where he promptly jumped up onto the chandelier in the front hall and started throwing shit at all the girls in the room who had gathered around to marvel at me and my new friend. I remember realizing that he actually knew how to shit into his hand before he threw it. Then he started masturbating. It was right about then that I decided this monkey was not going to be anything even *close* to my best friend, and my movie fantasy of being a cool guy with a monkey was just that, a fantasy.

I returned him to Trefflich's. I don't think I had him long enough to even give him a name, and I don't remember, either, if I ever got my money back. Whatever happened, it was worth the lesson. To this day I don't know where I got the initial idea, but one thing I *did* find out was that monkeys are no good. They're not cute, and they stink. Even the organ grinder ones are faking it. There's a reason why Johnny Weissmuller used to keep a blackjack with him whenever he did a scene with Cheetah, and he would whack him over the head with it between takes. A chimp recently ate the face off his owner in Connecticut. If I had really wanted to become involved in diapering a disgusting animal, I should've gotten married.

* * *

My phone number in Los Angeles, where I owned a three room cottage in "Bungalowland", was 213 650-6600. I got that number because, when I signed up with the phone company, I told the lady I was blind, and I needed an easy number. It never occurred to her, or to me at the time, that blind or not blind, people don't usually dial their own number, so what difference does it make *how* simple it is. Now, if *all* my friends were blind, then maybe it would've made sense.

* * *

I pissed in Mickey's mouth at Disneyworld one evening and got thrown out of the "Happiest Place on Earth" as a result. But c'mon! It was just a stupid topiary of Mickey with his mouth open; so, at least, it was *partly* eco-friendly. But that wasn't the worst thing that happened that night.

That same evening I happened to have picked up a doll's arm that I had found on the sidewalk. Actually, it was more than a doll's arm. It was a life-size infant mannequin's arm. I carried it around that night and would occasionally stick it in my fly so it looked like an enormous dick. Ah, the comedy! (That was the other reason why I got thrown out). But the interesting thing was that whenever anyone asked me where I got the anatomically correct arm, I would tell them I ripped it off one of the figures in the "Small World" ride because that song drove me nuts, and I hated the attraction anyway. The interesting thing I found out was that everyone I told this to *believed* me. I got a reputation for having dismembered a doll from "It's a Small World", and it persists to this day.

Of course, I never, actually, *denied* it, and I have kept the arm to this day as proof. But the fact is, no one has *ever* disputed my claim; nor have they ever questioned it; nor has anyone even been the least bit *shocked* that I might actually have, violently, ripped the arm off the figure of a child from a foreign land in a Disneyworld attraction. Now, *that* gives me pause.

On that same trip to Disneyworld, they were just about to open "Giftshopland", or whatever they were going to call their mega gift shop that the Disney folks had constructed on an island there. They were just beginning to stock the place when we got there, and we looked around as they were bringing in the Mickey Mouse *tchotchkes* and all manner of Disney-themed apparel to the shop.

I happened to pick up a ceramic rendering of Mickey, as the Sorcerer's Apprentice in "Fantasia". He was depicted cavorting with mops, and pails, and whatever else he danced with in that cartoon in this very handsome and colorful ceramic tableau. But I noticed immediately that, if you looked at the ceramic figure from the side, Mickey clearly was sporting a huge erection. It was probably either his thumb or a mop handle, but there was no mistaking what it looked like. It was so blatant, in fact, that I was convinced the Disney Imagineers had played *another* secret porno trick on old Walt as they had done so many times in the famous Disney feature-length cartoons.

I pointed out the ceramic penis erection to our executive producer who agreed that Mickey definitely had a big hard-on for the dancing mop. But then, he immediately felt compelled to bring it to the attention of the "cast member" manager who was running the store. Of course, we all bought one of the ceramic renderings as the manager took note of the offending Mickey and his engorged mickey.

But when I, then, returned to the store later to buy more copies of "Horny Mickey", there were none to be found, and no one would even acknowledge they had ever been in the store or had ever existed at all. These were all Disney-type people with blonde eyebrows which, for me, always meant trouble. You would see them walking around the park, talking into their sleeves, reporting on anything "dark".

Later, when I finally questioned a Disneyworld executive about the fate of the "Fantasia Mickey", he told me that, rest assured, every single one of the offending ceramic tableaus, including its original mold, had been destroyed beyond recognition by, literally, a steam roller running over them in the parking lot. And it had all been accomplished before the day was out. Like a totalitarian regime destroying history. Gone. As if it never, ever happened at Disneyworld, the happiest place on earth.

* * *

The only sexual harassment I would ever admit to was that, sometimes, in the middle of sex, I would insist that the woman say, "I love you," even though I knew she didn't, and she had only gone to bed with me in the first place just to shut me up. But I didn't care. It made things a whole *lot* nicer.

* * *

I worked for a British comedian on an American television show who loved more than anything, as all Brits do, toilet jokes and jokes about bodily functions, including vomiting. The only way to get him to settle on a script for the show was to write poopoo-kaka lines. That is, until the other writers and I found a book of "Fly in my soup" jokes. The Brit comedian had never heard this joke about a diner in a restaurant informing his waiter that there was a fly in his soup, and the waiter's witty reply.

But once we had that book, the writing job became *a lot* easier. We kept that book under lock and key. The Brit comedian never caught onto our ruse but would always marvel at our inventiveness. He would confess to us that he could not fathom how we were able to constantly come up with so many variations on that, to him, entirely novel premise. I was fired by Christmas time. But the book stayed on and continued to work on the show.

* * *

Where I grew up in Connecticut, there was a small grocery and candy store (it would be called a Bodega today) known as "Jimmy the Greek's", even though the proprietor, as I learned later, was Albanian, not Greek. So much for ethnic accuracy in Connecticut. Jimmy had an interesting niche in the little village in which we lived. He claimed to have never crossed the street in the fifty years he was there, or set foot in any of the other stores in the small village. However, the owners of the competing grocery stores all would cross the street to obtain products and produce from him rather than from each other. It was also the place every kid in our small town went for candy.

Regardless of the apparent disdain for his background, Jimmy understood the upscale community he served better than anyone suspected. He knew exactly what his function was in their minds, and he knew, better than they ever imagined, how to effectively market his services to them.

For instance, he sold apples out in front of his small store. One bushel basket held apples that were priced at $1.00 apiece. The other basket held apples that were priced at $.25 cents apiece. He knew that the upscale community he serviced would never buy cheap apples for themselves and would always prefer the more expensive apples over the cheaper ones. Then, when the expensive $1.00 apiece apples were sold out, he would merely pour the $.25 cents apples into the more expensive basket, making sure to keep some "cheaper" apples in their basket so that his customers could *not* buy the "inferior" produce. But he would keep the same two signs on each basket. In the end, *all* the apples would sell for $1.00 apiece. Everyone was happy.

I worked for a disagreeable woman on a show who did not get along with her neighbors. On top of that, whenever she walked her dog, one of the neighbors she didn't get along with had a dog that would menace her dog when they passed each other on the sidewalk. Apparently, the neighbor's dog would growl and always tried to bite her dog and fight with it. The disagreeable woman's dog became terrified of the neighbor's dog and resisted even being taken for a walk. In New York, this calls for crisis management.

The woman knew that I had an assortment of "dubious" friends, one of whom had gotten her out of jury duty for life. Consequently, she asked me if I could arrange a "hit" on her neighbor's dog. Usually, I didn't get involved in that sort of *nonsense,* but I thought it might be good for job security. So, I took the contract.

The plan that my "friend" and I came up with was that a passerby would stop by to admire the neighbor's dog during its evening walk. At the same time, he would drop a meatball laced with arsenic out of the bottom of his pants. The neighbor's dog would, then, gobble up the meatball while the stranger continued to talk to the neighbor. Fido would barely make it back to his apartment before expiring.

I never "pulled the trigger", so to speak, on the "hit". Even "wise guys" have a soft spot for animals. I kept telling the disagreeable woman we were waiting for just the right time. But in the interim, she moved to a new apartment on the West Side; so the contract and the "hit" became moot.

The disagreeable woman fired me anyway. But not before she inquired, on the morning I was fired, if her jury duty pass that my friend had arranged for her was still good. I assured her it was because it was as if she had died. That was the last conversation I ever had with her. But since then, I have often thought that I should've dropped a meatball on *her*. She was so disagreeable, she would have gobbled it up in a heartbeat.

* * *

The first real job I had was as a beach boy at a country club where my father was a member. It was a *shanda* at the time to have the son of a member working at the club. (I'm sure no one at the club knew what a "*shanda*" was). But it was a good job and paid the minimum wage of $1.25 an hour. (That goes into my litany of things that "cost a nickel" when *I* was a boy.)

I eventually became a lifeguard and a swimming instructor. By that time, the tediousness of the job had set in; and, in an effort to entertain myself, I formed a play group out of the kids who would show up regularly at the club each day. For want of a better word, I came up with the name, "Gringos" for the group, not because of what the word actually meant, but it sounded sort of fun and camp-like.

Then I decided that what we needed was a mascot. For that I chose a water rat, since most of the activities were based around the beach and pool. The kids seemed to like it and adapted the name and the mascot. The problem was that when I tried to get an emblem of a rat for them to sew onto their bathing suits, the closest thing I could come with was an embroidered beaver. So the "Gringos" ended up being an organization comprised of scions and future debutantes, named after a derogatory epithet for North Americans, whose mascot was a rat that bore a striking resemblance to a beaver. The summer flew by.

* * *

The first time I heard the term, "Clear!" barked like an order to nobody in particular, it was shouted by my architect friend out the side window of his Cessna four-seater airplane. He was about to fly my best friend and me from Block Island to New York. No problem. The fact that he was almost certifiably insane in *addition* to being a brilliant architect just made his uncharacteristic seriousness about flying that much more palatable.

"Clear!" He shouted once again and then started the plane's single engine. I asked him what "Clear!" meant, and he explained that it was a regulatory audible warning for all private aviation in order to make sure no one was standing near the propeller. As it turned out, coincidentally, a relative of his had walked into a small plane propeller on that very island and had met a horrible death some years earlier. I agreed it was a good regulation even though I had never heard it implemented before. But as a result, we all started yelling, "Clear!" at random times during that trip, and afterwards as some sort of passenger support, or anytime the conversation might veer into controversial territory.

We took off. The flight was uneventful, but instructive, due to the seriousness with which our, otherwise, wild and whacky friend took his duties as the pilot of an airplane. Everything was done by the book. No jokes. No ribald tales. No pornography. He used the radio like he was in a movie. It was all very impressive.

We were headed to a small landing strip in Flushing that was used occasionally for charter flights to Montauk and beyond. It was nothing more than a simple, single runway in the middle of nowhere for skywriter planes and rogue private aircraft. No control tower, no personnel, just a single strip of cracked asphalt. It's most distinguishing feature was a large, low-income apartment building that had been built, unfortunately, at the end of this short, ad hoc runway. It was obvious, to even a *non*-pilot, that this imposing edifice presented a "Hail Mary" situation for every take-off. In fact, shortly after our visit there, a Piper Cub *did* plow into the upper floors of the building. It signaled the end of the Flushing air strip and, also, sky writing in in the city.

On this particular summer afternoon, we approached the general area of the landing strip as if we were looking for a ball field to play on. I knew approximately where it was in relation to LaGuardia, and our pilot friend was sure he would be able to spot it from the air.

We flew into the Metropolitan area from the East, as if everything was normal and calm. We had traversed the length of Long Island Sound from Montauk to Rye. But once we crossed into the air space of the five boroughs, everything got *real* serious. The dividing line seemed to be the "two bridges"--- the Throgs Neck and the Whitestone. They were clearly visible from the air as we approached at 6000 feet. But that was when the trouble began. Our friend took the plane down below 5000 feet, so he could get a better look at the landing strip. This maneuver put us in the direct take-off and landing pattern of LaGuardia Airport, one of the busiest airports in the nation.

The plane's radio lit up with urgent alerts. The LaGuardia air traffic controller wanted to know what the hell we were doing between the "two bridges" when this was definitely restricted air space for all general aviation. My pilot friend told them we were trying to land at the Flushing air strip. The air traffic controller didn't care and ordered us to leave the area.

At that point, I could see 727's coming up out of LaGuardia like large, silver fish rising from within a deep pond. Suddenly, there were commercial jets all around us and close by, too. It was quite breathtaking but, also, terrifying. Our pilot friend, however, was hell-bent on completing his mission and blithely flew deeper into the LaGuardia air space. Finally, we spotted the Flushing airstrip, and he descended toward it in a desperately steep dive.

As a result of our adventure, our pilot friend was reprimanded severely by the FAA and forced to go through a complete recertification as a pilot. Thanks to him, there is now a hard and fast restriction on all private aircraft entering the area south and west of the Throgs Neck Bridge, and our friend has probably been banned for life from the area as well. I doubt that his name is attached to the FAA directive he inspired, but I think he deserves *some* recognition for his pioneering flight in the service of New York airport safety.

Of course, were we to perform that same maneuver now, under present-day conditions, I'm sure we would be shot out of the sky instantly on orders from Homeland Security and the Strategic Air Command. Times have changed.

* * *

As a favor to a mutual friend, I once agreed to help a woman train for a position as a 1-900 phone sex operator. Although I never actually met the young woman face to face, she *did* get the job.

* * *

At one point in my adult life, I became convinced that one nostril of my nose had grown bigger than the other. After extensive examination and calibration, I finally attributed the physical deformity to my proclivity of picking one side of my nose more than the other. I tried to remedy this situation by consciously becoming an equal-nostril picker; but, finally, I had to admit that the damage had been irreparably done; and I was, thus, consigned to a nasal abnormality of my own making. Then I started to worry that my nostril nonsense was actually quite obvious, and that even my closest friends and family had decided to never mention it to me.

* * *

I have jumped out of an airplane only once in my life. But I did it when skydiving first came out. In 1962, they opened a skydiving center an hour away from where I was going to college. It was in June, and final exams were upon us. I decided that jumping out of a plane with a parachute would be a good test to see if the universe really wanted me to actually pass those exams. I made arrangements to go to the "jump center" in Orange, Massachusetts with a fraternity brother who was a famous football player and notorious for his bold and bizarre behavior. Once we had decided to go, my friend immediately gave us the nicknames of, "Rip" and "Cord". I think I was "Cord."

This same fellow once announced to me that he no longer wore underpants because he liked the feeling of freedom it gave him. He was from Toledo and also said he could always tell if a girlfriend of his was actually pregnant or not by the number of green lights he was able to score while driving down the main drag there. He always had a lot of theories and formulas.

We arrived at the skydiving place early in the morning. Skydiving, back then, was an all-day event. First there was ground training. After a classroom session covering, in theory, what the jump would entail, we were taken outside to jump off a platform to learn how to roll upon impact. This was all part of the landing protocol, apparently, with or *without* a chute. Somehow, I really thought, that if I were to jump off a 17 story building, I could survive by expertly rolling after I landed.

After lunch, we were issued our main parachute as well as our "emergency chute" which we would deploy if the main chute didn't open. This was the part of the lesson that started to worry me. First of all, we were assured that our main chutes had been packed by "professionals". The parachutes would open automatically, thanks to a static cord that would be hooked up inside the plane.

Just like in the WWII movies. No problem. But then the "emergency chute" was a whole other issue altogether.

The instructor, unfortunately, then went through several scenarios of main chute failure. Suddenly, I wasn't too sure about all those unseen "professional" parachute packers. Apparently, sometimes the pesky main chute on your back doesn't open at all. Other times, it *sorta* opens, but it doesn't fill. This is known as a "Roman Candle" in parachute lingo. And then there were other possible mishaps as well. The problem for me, specifically, was that the remedies for main chute malfunctions were harder to learn than the final exams I was trying to avoid.

For instance, should you find yourself under a chute that opens but doesn't fill, you are then supposed to deploy your emergency parachute by simply pulling the release handle and then casually spreading the emergency silk parachute material out in front of you like a tablecloth as you descend at 120 MPH under your non-filling "Roman Candle" chute. I don't think so. But, then, if the main chute doesn't open at *all*, then, as you tumble through space at 120 MPH, you are to locate your trusty emergency chute handle, pull it across your chest, and, *voila,* a parachute that's just as good as the main one opens up. (Then why is one called, "Main", and the other one, "Emergency"; and why is the one that's "just as good" visibly smaller and punier?)

All of this talk of mid-air emergencies was making me long for the blue books of final exams. And the arcane, detailed instructions were beginning to sound like my 8:00AM Geology class. I watched and *tried* to follow the instructions, but my eyes glazed over, just like back at school; and I learned nothing.

Suddenly we got "chuted up" and climbed into a medium-sized single engine plane with its side door removed. We got hooked up and sat in a row while the plane took off and circled up to 5000 feet (our jump altitude) above the skydiving center. Inside the plane, everything was okay. My friend was ahead of me, eager to go. A small amount of spittle had formed in the corners of his mouth. I think there were one or two other jumpers, but I never got to know them. (In Jump School, you purposely don't bother to get to know your fellow jumpers because, well, *you* know, it's *Jump* School. Don't get close to anyone. Just in case)

Suddenly, it was time to jump. We had to jump when they told us to because there was a target (unfortunate terminology) on the ground below, and you were supposed to try and "hit it". (So to speak). We made several passes over the "jump zone" while the other "jumpees" successfully exited the plane, including my fraternity brother. And then, it was my turn.

I positioned myself at the open space on the plane where the door had been, and I thought I might, first, just hang my legs out over the edge just to get used to the whole thing. But what I remember most about that experience was the wind. No one had warned me about, or, even, mentioned the wind during our orientation. I forgot that the plane would be traveling at a rapid rate of speed which would create enough fucking wind to blow you off your feet (oh-oh) or even prevent you from venturing forth out of the aircraft. You certainly couldn't stick your head out of the plane to see where you were supposed to be headed. How was I supposed to jump with all that windage? This was what was going through my head as I squatted in the doorway. Too much wind. I figured I couldn't possibly exit. Besides, the target on the ground, 5000 feet below, not only looked very far away, but menacing as well. And dangerous. Something to be avoided at all costs. I *did* notice, however, that the landscape *did* look like sort of a map. I became singularly struck by the unique perspective the experience had afforded me.

It was at about this time, crouched in the doorway of the plane with the wind blowing, that I remember turning back to the instructor and saying something like, "I don't think so," or words to that effect. The point I was trying to make was that I had decided *not* to jump out of a plane that day. That's when, I believe, the instructor pushed my ass out of the plane because I *know* I would never have left voluntarily. It did not seem to be a good way to die. I had decided, right then and there, to take my chances with "History 301".

But, because I had been pushed out of the plane, I did not exactly jump or assume any sort of skydiving, swan dive-like, pose of any kind. Instead, I went straight down, head first, toward that goddamn target 5000 feet below. The main parachute opened. At least they were right about *that*! I said a prayer of thanks. But, instead of the chute opening off my back like a parachute would if it had been attached to a *normal* jumper, because of my bomb-like trajectory straight down, head first, the parachute opened between my legs.

I knew I was saved. There would be none of that *emergency* nonsense. But my feet were tangled up in the risers of the parachute, and I was upside down. I succeeded in kicking free of the shrouds and, finally, swung beneath my parachute like a normal jumper. I breathed a sigh of semi-relief because, at least, I was finally in the right position. It was incredibly quiet. I think that must be one of the perks of being under a parachute at 5000 feet. It's quiet. You can't hear the plane. There's no wind. Nothing. You are suspended in space.

But, then, *another* problem arose. For a fleeting moment I marveled at the quiet and the tableau of green fields before and below me. But, then, terror seized me like a clenched fist. I was in my "jumpy suit" thing at 5000 feet, I thought. But how do I know this thing will hold me? And will I be able to hold the risers long enough to land if it *did* slip away? I was consumed with the notion that the whole fucking harness of belts and straps between me and the parachute was going to suddenly go, "poof", and fly away like something made out of slipknots.

I remained motionless while I descended. I did not try to steer the parachute by pulling the steering ropes.

Besides, when I tested them, I noticed that steering was achieved by voluntarily collapsing a corner of the parachute. Not a good idea. So I hung there without even *looking* from side to side. And when I landed (thank you, Jesus) there was no rolling, or folding, or crouching, or cool recovery. My feet touched the ground, and I sat down hard. Immediately.

The funny thing was that my jumping companion had been completely energized by the experience. He wanted to go right back up in the plane again. I declined. It was late, and we had to get back to college. After all, good ol' "Cord", now, was alive and had to study for finals.

* * *

For a very brief period, I decided that carrying a cane while traveling was a good idea because, then, strangers would volunteer to help carry your bags. I actually *did* try it once on a trip to Texas, and it worked. Especially in the airport. My fellow travelers were extremely accommodating and helpful. But I quickly abandoned the whole cane bit because walking with enough of a limp to *justify* the cane was more tedious than actually carrying my own luggage. And the cane helpers tend to be assholes just like you were instead of good the looking women you had hoped for.

But I *did* consider the gambit of walking into a men's room and announcing loudly that I was a Vietnam

Veteran who had lost the use of my arms in the war and would any fellow American come to my assistance. Then, I would ask whoever volunteered to unzip me, take out my dick, and hold it while I took a piss. Of course, when I was finished, I would, then, ask the guy to shake my dick (Only once, please. This isn't a social call) and put my cock back in my pants. Then, I'd ask him to zip me up, of course. But *then,* if I *really* had balls, I thought it would be funny if I, then, tried to thank him by shaking his hand. But, on second thought, I'd decline because his hands were dirty, and he hadn't washed them.

I swear I never had the balls to try that. Never. I *swear.*

* * *

I had a friend who was a paraplegic. He had had polio as a teenager; and, as a result, he used crutches for the rest of his life. His legs didn't work at all. He was a terrific guy and great company. Then, I didn't see him for a couple of years. But when I saw him again, he told me he had become a nudist. That meant that when he came and stayed at my apartment in New York, he would strip naked as soon as the door was closed and move around my place on crutches, balls-ass naked. That was okay, I guess, but I didn't like it when he sat on the couch. It was also weird to see what his legs looked like in the braces on them.

Then, on top of that, he turned gay. I don't know. Maybe, he was gay all along. It's hard to tell a person's sexual orientation when they're on crutches 100% of the time. He never, actually, *told* me, outright, that he was gay; but, all of a sudden, he announced that he was not only paraplegic and a nudist, but he had also become a serial hugger, as well. All of a sudden, he wanted to give me a hug all the time. So, now, when he stayed over at my place, I had a gay, paraplegic nudist on my hands who insisted on hugging me as much as he could as a means of communication. That's when I decided the place was too small for all that. So I told him he couldn't stay there anymore. Fortunately, that didn't change our relationship. Except that, after that, when he hugged me; at least he had his clothes on.

The funny thing was that, then, towards the end of his life, I think he decided to give up the homosexual thing, and the hugging, and the nudism and go back, instead, to being just a guy on crutches who like to drink. I think he was happier that way. It's hard to be a gay, nudist, paraplegic *and* an alcoholic. It's too much.

* * *

I tried to run for Congress when our local Congressman suddenly died of AIDS (even though he had had five kids. He always blamed the five kids on my mother's prayers for him and, at one point, told her to stop lighting candles). They had a special election in the middle of August in order to fill his Congressional seat. Then, for some reason, I learned that the number of signatures a person needed to get on the ballot for the regular November election was just one percent of the votes cast in the *last* election. Since the last election, in this case, was the special one in August when nobody bothered to vote, the necessary number of signatures was remarkably low and doable. It was a once in a lifetime opportunity.

The first thing I did was form a political party. I called my party, "The Charter Oak Party" because it was Connecticut, and that sounded respectful and pertinent. Then I went about trying to get the signatures I needed.

My friend, Joe, immediately scammed a printing outfit in Florida to print up a large number of sample bumper stickers and lapel buttons in hopes of being the official supplier to the campaign. Unfortunately, the buttons and bumper stickers had me running for the "Senate", not the "House"; but that was a minor concern. It's in the same building, isn't it?

Of greater concern was my father who was well-known in the community and in the state. He immediately forbade anyone from putting my bumper sticker on their car. Consequently, the only friend and supporter of mine had to stick his bumper sticker to the *inside* of his garage. Not exactly on his car, but close enough.

I thought I had come up with a fairly interesting and attractive platform. Number one was that I would not take any cash contributions. I would only accept contributions "in kind" in the form of meals and services. (i.e.

lodging, rides, etc but no cash). My reasoning was that no one ever gave anyone money for *them* to get a job, so why should I take people's money so *I* could get a job. Then I vowed to legalize all drugs if elected, not because I was a druggie, but because I knew the reality was that anyone who wanted drugs, at any time, could obtain them immediately anyway. So why clog up the police force and judicial system with drug cases. Take a fraction of that money and put it into rehabilitation.

The other plank of my platform was to take all the nuclear weapons and give them away. Make *other* countries have to deal with the nuclear issue and figure out what to do with them. I wanted to get rid of the tri-partite defense system of our military (air, land, and sea), and only keep five fully-armed nuclear submarines that would continually patrol the globe. I figured that was all we needed to keep things in order. The rest of the military was superfluous and redundant.

And that was it. Simple. Elect *me*. Unfortunately, my campaign never got off the ground. (Although I still have the buttons and bumper stickers) I couldn't get the Board of Elections in each town of the state to take me seriously. Nobody wanted to join the "Charter Oak Party". My father didn't have to worry. But it was a once in a lifetime opportunity (because of the election anomaly) to do something new and different. I never understood why more people didn't see it that way. It didn't help that my father had banned my bumper sticker, of course, even though he was once a political leader in

Connecticut. I realized too late that I couldn't count on his endorsement.

* * *

My abortive career as a half-assed prizefighter eventually led to a job writing a movie script about a failed boxer whom we called "Kid Natural", since that's who I was. The story that my writing partner and I ultimately concocted had the fighter stuck, permanently, in Long Beach, California. Naturally, at that point, we decided we needed to go to Paris, France for research.

It was my first trip to Paris. Our hotel was a huge commercial joint on the Champs Élysées, and I had my first experience of paying money to drink water. Perrier had just bubbled into the American consciousness. Suddenly, it seemed like everyone---certainly everyone in France---was drinking Perrier water. How quaint. So we sat and drank expensive water while doing research for the film in Paris.

Our room in the hotel was directly over the hotel kitchen. I remember, one night, we were being kept awake by the incessant clanging of dishes that were either being washed or stacked or both. My writing partner finally called up the front desk and placed an order with room service.

"Send up everything you have," she said, "On a dish." She had figured out that it was, probably, the only way to stop the racket.

The movie starred a famous diva who was also addicted to fast food. While editing her daily publicity stills, she would retouch the inches of flab off her Big Mac belly with a grease pencil while downing her second cheeseburger that, she always insisted, should be served, "R-a-a-are!" She had a way of saying, "R-a-a-are!" as if she were actually devouring the under-cooked burger in one bite as she spoke.

The male star fancied himself an actual prizefighter, and he trained as such for the movie. His stunt double, and sparring partner, was a young man who resembled him but who had just been let out of jail after being convicted for the Frank Sinatra Jr. kidnapping hoax. The poor guy would arrive each day severely beaten about the head and face by our male star in their sparring matches. It would've been unwise, and certainly grounds for unemployment, for him to have returned any punches.

I sparred with the male star only once, and only because the fictional Kid Natural wanted to test himself against the *real* Kid Natural. Fiction won that day, and I was roundly pummeled by the star. It would've been equally unwise for me to have returned any punches, even if I could have.

I remember talking to the actor in the middle of production to inquire how he was faring. He was deep into his part---that of a fighter trying to make a comeback, and he spoke to me with his head bowed in serious self-determination.

"I just gotta get past this next big fight," he told me seriously. "I *gotta* win. Then everything will be okay."

"Hey. I saw the script," I told him, "You win. Really. Guaranteed."

He was not convinced. "I still gotta just get past this guy," he said. "I *gotta* do it. I *gotta* win."

Actors.

* * *

I was an actor in two movies. In one I played The Happy Hooker's first professional trick. I was designated, "Man in a Hurry", in the credits. I was supposed to be a guy who had left his wife at the theater watching a show while he had excused himself in order to go see the woman who was The Happy Hooker. But he had to return before the end of the second act to pick up his unsuspecting wife. There was no sex in our scene. We faded to black right after Ms. Happy said "Then, let's do it."

My second movie appearance was playing a Jewish stockbroker whose partner had become a bicycle messenger. The film was written and directed by an Irish friend of mine which, undoubtedly, was how I got the part. (I beat out Henry Winkler. Yeah!) But the night before shooting was to commence, we were all in a hotel room in San Francisco. The Jewish producer of the movie was concerned that I didn't look the least bit Jewish. I stood in one corner of the room while the producer and the director discussed this issue in the opposite corner accompanied by many inquisitive looks over in my direction. At one point, the producer even walked over to me and stared into my face. I just didn't look Jewish enough as far as he was concerned, and he looked *very* Jewish, so he knew what he was talking about. This was a problem beyond any putative acting skill I might have had.

Finally, it was decided that, maybe, if I wore glasses, *that* might help. I put on glasses, and it did the trick. In other words, In Hollywood, a Jew is just an Irishman wearing glasses. Of course! I put on the glasses, and the producer immediately signed off on my "Jewishness". He certified my transformation as "uncanny". Now *that's* what I call *acting*!

* * *

My father was born in 1903. He reported to us that, when Halley's Comet made its scheduled appearance in the sky above East Hartford in 1910, his father held him up to a window so that he could view the extra-terrestrial visitor. That event and the vision of the comet had remained a vivid memory from his childhood.

When Halley's Comet made its reappearance in the night sky 76 years later, my father was 83 years old and had six adult children. When the comet reappeared on that winter evening in 1986, we all happened to be at home with him. We remembered our father's story about his childhood memory of seeing the comet in 1910, and we excitedly went outside to view its momentous return. As we looked up into the night sky, we urgently called to our father to come out and see this unique event which he was now fortunate enough to be able to witness twice in his own lifetime.

But my father never moved from his customary seat next to the fireplace in the library. He didn't even lower his newspaper. But he *did* answer our calls for him to come outside and view the extraordinary return of Halley's Comet.

"I've *seen* it," he yelled back petulantly. And that was the end of it.

Apparently, when it comes to once-in-a-lifetime events, once is enough.

* * *

The other vivid memory I have of my father is when, as a college student, he asked me what I was planning to do with the rest of my life in order to support myself. I told him that, at that point, I was thinking of going into comedy and, perhaps, even becoming a stand-up comedian. He thought about this for a beat; and then, very seriously, offered me some fatherly advice.

"Good luck to you," he said. "But if that's the case, then let me give you a little piece of advice."

I remember turning to him eagerly and being pleasantly surprised that he was actually acknowledging one of my pursuits and seemed genuinely interested in my plans for the future.

"Yes, sir," I answered.

"Now, let me give you one little piece of advice," he said again, tapping the tip of his little finger as if he were about to enumerate more than one piece of fatherly advice.

"Yes, sir," I repeated, anticipating his cherished counsel. "What is it?

"You're not funny," he said bluntly.

I don't think I reacted to his stark proclamation other than to merely nod my head knowingly and respectfully---as in, "Right. Got it"--- to indicate my appreciation for having received this wisdom of the ages *and* a much needed reality check.

* * *

Once, during my early days in New York, my best friend and I were traveling to Bermuda for yet another, "Dean and Jerry", weekend. At that time, my friend was working as an Assistant DA in Norristown, Pennsylvania. We were flying out of Newark. This was in the late 60's or early 70's when only Cubans were hijacking planes. And *they* all want to go somewhere---on *earth,* that is, not in heaven. Ah, the old days.

I was slightly hyper and excited about the trip because I was out of work and spending most of my days alone. Consequently, I was definitely in a party mood at the airport and the prospect of a couple of days in Bermuda with friends was exciting. When we were at the gate, waiting to board the airplane, for some reason I thought it would be droll to grab my friend's arm and say to him confidentially, "Does you have de bomb?" or words to that effect.

Unfortunately, a fellow passenger overheard me. We boarded the plane and took our economy seats near the rear of the plane. As we were sitting there waiting for them to close the door and taxi out to the runway; suddenly, I saw this very large black man in a suit lumbering down the aisle toward us. He was not happy, and he definitely did not look like he was going to Bermuda. When he got to us, he identified himself as a U.S, Marshal. He, then, grabbed us and told us to follow him off the plane, which we did.

Suddenly, I realized what this was all about. When the federal marshal got us outside the plane and at the gate, he was seething with anger. But it was not because he thought we were going to blow the plane up. We had frightened one of the other passengers. We quickly identified ourselves as upstanding citizens. I don't think the term "terrorist" was in the domestic lexicon then. As further proof of our innocence, my friend announced that he was, currently, an Assistant D.A. in Norristown, Pennsylvania.

"What the hell is John Mitchell gonna say about this when he hears about you? What is John Mitchell gonna think about one of his lawyers doin' something like this?

What's John Mitchell gonna say?" The marshal kept repeating to us.

My friend apologized, and I copped to the fact that it was me who had made the statement, not him, but it had just been a joke to my friend. Of *course*, we didn't have a bomb. We're just on our way to Bermuda for some laughs.

The federal marshal kept repeating my friend's apparent affront to Attorney General John Mitchell and the U.S legal system given that my friend was an Assistant D.A. Of course, this was before John Mitchell, himself, was carted off to jail. Mitchell should have asked *us* for a character reference.

I think only because of my friend's valid I.D. as a lawyer in the D.A.'s office that the marshal let us back on the plane, and we finally took off. I doubt whether the other passengers, except the one who had complained, knew exactly what had transpired. But I *do* remember we had a ball in Bermuda. A lot more fun than if we had gone to jail in New Jersey or been shipped off to Guantanamo. It was a different time back then. Thankfully.

* * *

At a dinner party at my friend's house one evening, I began flirting with an attractive woman guest. After dinner, when we all were sitting around, I suggested that the woman and I go upstairs, exchange clothes, and then come back down again and conduct ourselves as each other for the rest of the evening.

I was, actually, surprised when she agreed. So, we went upstairs to exchange clothes. I remember we went into the same bedroom to exchange our clothes; and, for some reason, I found the entire process very sexually exciting. I don't know why.

When the woman and I came back downstairs, each of us was wearing the clothes that the other one had worn to the party. We proceeded, then, to act out and respond, for the rest of the night, as we thought the other one would. It was great fun and proved to be very funny as well. At the end of the evening, when we went back upstairs to get back into our own clothes again. Once more, I found the woman extremely attractive and sexy. We kissed passionately. I don't think we had sex that night as she was on her way home with the man she had come to the dinner with.

But we *did* have sex once or twice after that. She later was elected to public office or something and became somewhat of a local celebrity. I never saw her again after our brief fling. I have often wondered exactly what the nature of the attraction was for me having a woman cross-dressed in my clothes. What exactly was the turn-on? Should I have been alarmed that I was kissing a woman who was impersonating me? In *my* clothes? If we had had sex that first night, I would have been unbuttoning *my* pants on *her*. And she would have been deftly removing *her* bra on *me*. I have chosen not to explore the phenomenon any further, but it *did* give me pause. Perhaps the actual affair was brief and abortive because we never performed in each other's clothes again. Maybe the thrill was gone when she was dressed only as herself and not as me. Don't tell nobody.

* * *

I was driving my six year-old son up Route 8 in Connecticut one weekend to a father/son camping sleepover sponsored by his school. It was in the early Fall, and both of us were ambivalent about the prospects of camping out. Midway through the trip, the boy announced he was getting carsick, and he thought he might throw up. I immediately pulled off the highway and parked on the broad, grassy median between the two opposing lanes. One of the features of Route 8 is that its median is very wide and irregular. At this particular point, there was a small knoll, and I brought the boy up to the top of it, figuring the air would be fresher up there and that would help his nausea.

My son then sat down on the grass at the top of the little hill, hung his head between his knees, and rested his forehead on his folded arms as he tried to recover from his carsickness. I tried to be compassionate and supportive; and, at one point, stood behind him and lightly massaged his shoulders as a palliative. He didn't move, and it took a while for him to feel better. Eventually, I figured it was best to leave him alone, and so I walked a short distance away from him to give him his space while checking back on his condition and progress.

Apparently, the "supportive father with a carsick son" tableau we were acting out had looked neither "supportive" nor "innocent."

The next thing I knew, an unmarked police car pulled up behind my car with its interior red light flashing on the dashboard. A plainclothes detective got out. He was armed.

"Step away from the boy, please," the detective said to me in his "police" tone.

I was surprised by the order and tried to explain that the boy was feeling carsick, and it was why our car was pulled over to the side of the road.

"You stand over there," he said, now, slightly more insistent.

He waited until I, in fact, moved away from my son. At that point, I think he identified himself as a police officer, but there was no question in my mind what he was, and that he was there in an "official" capacity. I moved away from the child.

The detective then came up to the top of the knoll and went over to my son who was still dealing with his nausea and had not moved or changed his "head-down" sitting position. The detective went up to the boy and rested a fatherly hand on his shoulder. He identified himself as a policeman and asked my son if everything was all right. He wanted to know if I was his father. I think my son nodded and mumbled, "Yes," He confirmed to the detective that he had gotten carsick.

The detective's attitude changed immediately. He straightened up and strode down the hill with a parental smile on his face. He waved to me.

"Everything's okay. Just checking," he said happily as if I should be relieved that he didn't have to shoot me. "He'll be fine. Have a nice day."

"Huh?" I think I said. The detective got back into his unmarked car and spun out of the meridian and back onto the highway. Only *then* did my son stand up and announce that he had recovered. We got back into our car and continued up Route 8 to the campsite.

I wondered about that encounter. What was it that passersby or, even, the detective, himself, had observed that prompted the "Amber Alert" that there was foul play afoot on Route 8? Was it my standing behind the boy as if trying to convince him to get back into the car? Was it his posture of nausea, as he sat alone on the knoll with his head bowed and appeared to be resisting my advances and pleas to get back in the car? Or, maybe, it was *me*---who a) automatically looks like a child abductor and b) looked somewhat pissed that I had to do the school camping bullshit in the first place. There is no way of knowing. But, at least, I wasn't arrested.

The kid *could* have turned me in by saying to the cop, "I don't know who this man is, but he's taking me away in his car to go sleep with him somewhere in a tent."

* * *

I was trying to convince my young family, one day, that I was just as good as Santa Claus. But my youngest son, who is somewhat of a comedian, ended the discussion by saying, (and this is a direct quote) "Dad *thinks* he's like Santa Claus; but, in reality, he has only some of the weight but none of the charisma."

* * *

There used to be a priest's haberdashery store around the corner from where I lived which I always thought was funny in itself. "Would you like that in *black*, father?" The concept killed me. I thought it was like a nun's dress boutique. But, I guess, even Catholic priests have to get their clothes *somewhere.*

With that in mind, I bought a priest's collar and bib ensemble there once. I told them I was in a play. They, of course, rolled their eyes knowing *exactly* what I was up to. I could've just told them the truth. I wanted it for bits.

Things change when you wear a priest's collar. My friend, Joe, always wanted us to take a trip to Ireland together dressed as rogue American priests on holiday who were only interested in women and liquor. We figured it would scandalize the Irish who have a problem with sex anyway.

I like to wear the collar when visiting friends who are in the hospital. Once, when I was seeing a doctor friend who was sick, the Filipino nurse there started confessing her sins to me. I felt conflicted but, in the end, decided not to tell her I wasn't ordained since she was already deep into her confession. But, at the same time, I knew any absolution I gave her was worthless. I could only hope she re-confessed her sins to a *real* priest in a *real* church. Otherwise, I had to hope that God has a sense of humor. Although I doubt it.

* * *

While living alone in New York and in and out of gainful employment, I often experimented with "alternate food". One dish I invented was "paper towel lasagna". For some reason, I thought that paper towels could easily be considered a source of protein. I would pour red spaghetti sauce over sheets of Scott's Paper Towels and serve the dish piping hot. I even tried it on friends.

It didn't work. On any level.

* * *

As Garret Morris would say, "The airlines have been *berry, berry* good to me." I used to fly from New York to Los Angeles like it was "a glass of water" (As they used to say on Broadway). For some reason, I thought it was important for my career for me to be equally present on both coasts. That proved to be an erroneous conclusion, but I made a lot of friends in the airline business along the way.

This was pre 9-11 and pre-terror. You could show up late for a flight and literally knock on the cabin door after it'd been closed and still gain entrance. And if you had balls, and a certain amount of chutzpah, you could simply turn left when you entered the airplane and sit in First Class. No one bothered you.

The advent of the Boeing 747's made flying coast to coast like a party in the air. They even had a piano bar on some of the flights. The stewardesses were into it as well. There were well-known motels in Inglewood, California where the stews would "lay over" (uh-uh), and there were apartments on the Upper East Side where five or six flight attendants shared a two-bedroom flat. Flying was glamorous, sexy, and romantic. And good for *everyone's* career. It doesn't happen now days, but in the 70's and 80's, powerful and successful men fell in love with, and married, stewardesses. (Although few would admit their *provenance* now.) I sat next to George Plimpton once and Warren Beatty another time. Warren actually invited me to call him at his hotel in the city, which I did; but he, obviously, thought better of his "Let's hang out together" invitation by the time he got to Manhattan. He didn't take my call.

The secret was stickers. Stickers were those little adhesive strips with boxes printed on them for flight numbers and departure times that travel agents and reservationists used to change non refundable tickets that had already been printed. I stole an entire pack of them from the American Airlines ticket counter in Rockefeller Center. It instantly made me a travel agent. With my stickers I was able to fly back and forth to Los Angeles on supersavers, at any time, on any schedule. But I *still* didn't get any work.

Besides stickers, the other secret to travel in those days was "Special Services". These were the "magicians" of the airlines who could work miracles, cut red tape, and, best of all, provide free upgrades after the airlines got hip to people like me turning left and sitting in first class.

I *liked* First Class. First Class was "*berry berry*" good to me. Once I sat next to a great looking blonde woman whom I vaguely knew through mutual friends. We were happy to have each other's company for the trip; and, after a sufficient number of drinks, we were also happy to have each other's bodies as well.

The "Mile High Club" was old news even then. Truthfully, I never saw the attraction. I remember, during my initiation into the "club", thinking, "Wait a second. This is where people take a shit."

On the other hand, getting laid in First Class under a blanket. Now *that's* a club. All I remember is that it made the trip from LA to New York go a *lot* faster. I think we declined the in-flight meal. But I *do* remember the Captain, Co-pilot, and Navigator all felt compelled to come out and walk down the aisle past us for reconnaissance and verification. I never dated my flight partner after that experience. She *was* certifiable, after all. Hence, the "shared-blanket" sex. I think she became a life coach or a dating expert or something like that. Whatever she became, I *highly* recommend her if you need help.

* * *

A very attractive Japanese girl moved into an apartment on my floor in a building where I lived for a long time. She was a great dresser and had beautiful, long, black hair. Or, as my friend would say, "You could bench press her hair."

I befriended her because a) she was beautiful and b) she didn't have any furniture. I think I gave her a lamp and, maybe, some other things. We started sleeping with each other. You don't "date" someone in your own building and, especially, someone on the same floor. You sleep with them. And then you both decide not to because the elevator rides become tricky.

I quickly learned about her situation. Her family owned a Japanese restaurant in Queens where she dated the sushi chef. They went out for a while and had gotten engaged to be married, but then my neighbor broke it off because she decided that what the sushi chef *really* wanted was the restaurant. The sushi chef was not happy about the break-up. That's why she had to move to Manhattan.

But the sushi chef followed her into the city. He would stand outside our building and wait for her to come out so he could yell at her and abuse her. He was not a happy man. But he was, also, not a happy man with a collection of knives, as well. Since I was sleeping with his ex-fiancée, that made me somewhat nervous.

I remember deciding that, to a Japanese sushi chef, all westerners must look alike because he never recognized me as the tenant who was sleeping with his ex-fiancée when I passed him as he stood outside our building.

Ours was a perilous relationship, the beautiful neighbor and me. She actually had the faint odor of fresh tuna, but I couldn't tell if this was natural or just an occupational hazard. It was probably what made the sushi guy go crazy. But she was extremely sweet, and very beautiful, and loved to dress in great clothes and wear high heels to work.

I think she liked me, but I couldn't really tell because when we made love, the more passionate she became the more she lapsed into Japanese. It was impossible to tell whether she was saying, "I love you" or, "Get off me". And when she had an orgasm, she sounded like an outtake from "The Seven Samurai." I had never heard Japanese spoken *in extremis.* It was a little unsettling. And it always happened at the most intimate of moments. I never got used to it.

Eventually, the sushi chef got tired of standing outside our front door, and my beautiful Japanese neighbor abruptly moved to Washington State, one day, with her new boyfriend where she went into the travel business.

I never knew exactly what she had been saying in Japanese whenever we made love. But it was probably better I didn't know. To tell you the truth, from the sound of it, it probably *was,* "Get off me!"

* * *

Life is like a roll of toilet paper.

When your roll is fresh and new, it's fat, soft, spotless, and seems like it could go on forever and always be there. You think you now have an endless amount of toilet paper at your disposal. You haven't a care in the world. You use your roll indulgently and spend it freely without concern or conservation.

Even when you're halfway through your roll, you still think it will last forever and never end. No problem. You don't give it another thought. There will always be enough toilet paper.

But then, at some point, you notice that your, once, fresh roll of toilet paper has diminished in size and newness. It has become small, somewhat misshapen, and puny. It even looks dull and grey. Suddenly, almost overnight, your roll is a shadow of its former self. Not only that, this reduced roll now spins faster and faster as you use it up. It seems, suddenly, to be hurtling toward its own inevitable end. You find that you disparage the sight of *any* less than half roll of toilet paper. You would give up your seat on a bus for such an obviously infirmed and inferior specimen.

You finally accept that your roll of toilet paper is going to end someday and be finished because it is, now, so plainly obvious. You can literally see the end of your roll. It's only a matter of time before it will be over. There is no other possible conclusion. Your roll will simply run out of paper, and there will be no more. You know it. But you continue to hope and pray that you can get by just one more day with what is left. You hope that you can get by just one more time without disaster, inconvenience, and the horror of nothingness.

You hope that when the end of your toilet paper comes, it will happen at a convenient time and be painless instead of at the worst possible moment when you least expect it or when you are in the worst possible situation or condition.

But then, it is finally over. Your once glorious new roll of toilet paper is, now, completely gone. It has vanished and is no more. There is nothing left. Only the skeletal core remains, and that must be removed and discarded to make way for a new one.

A New York neighborhood friend of mine was always known, simply, as "The Hat"; or, sometimes, just, "Hat", because he never went anywhere without his porkpie hat. Never. He wore his hat when he was inside and when he was outside; and, probably, he wore it in bed, too. "The Hat" was famous in the neighborhood because he, allegedly, was the only man in the history of the ILA to ever be on full, psychological disability from the union owing to his brief and bizarre career as a longshoreman on the Westside docks.

"The Hat" hated elevators. He would avoid them at all costs even though he lived his entire life in New York City. Specifically, he would never, *ever,* ride an elevator on a Friday, under *any* circumstances. His reasoning for this was because, if you ever got stuck in an elevator on Friday, nobody would come and get you until

Monday. The prospect of three days in an elevator alone, or with God knows who, was too much for "The Hat". Consequently, you would never catch him in an elevator on a Friday. No matter what.

I think he had a point.

* * *

I worked on a network comedy show one summer that was supposed to be a humorous take on the week's news and pop culture. Around the third week of the show, Vikki Morgan, Alfred Bloomingdale's mistress, was brutally beaten to death with a baseball bat under very strange and dubious circumstances. Curiously, the murder happened on Nancy Reagan's birthday. But what made the abrupt removal of Ms. Morgan from this world significant was the fact that, at the time of her demise, she was suing the Bloomingdale estate because Alfred's widow, Betsy Bloomingdale, (Nancy's best friend), had cut her off from her "support for life" which the late Alfred had provided for Vikki to the tune of $18,000 a month.

Vikki had been threatening to go public with her accounts of Hollywood sex parties with Alfred and members of Ronald Reagan's "Kitchen Cabinet". Apparently, according to Ms. Morgan, these upstanding citizens and hugely successful businessmen and, now, presidential advisors were fond of partying together in L.A. with a bevy of hookers and Ms. Morgan. Vikki reported that all manner of sexual hi-jinks were involved, including Alfred's favorite sadomasochistic ritual where he would play "horsey" with the naked hookers and ride them around while he, literally, according to Ms. Morgan, would drool on them. She also said that Alfred had shared many White House secrets and classified briefings with her.

The fact that the murder coincided with Nancy Reagan's birthday struck me as legitimate comedy fodder, especially given that Betsey was Nancy's best friend, and they shared a mutual stake in Ms. Morgan's revelations. Subsequently, I wrote a joke for the show's "Update-style" newscast that went something like this:

"Nancy Reagan had a birthday bash this week that featured the fatal bludgeoning of Vikki Morgan, mistress of the late Alfred Bloomingdale. The birthday bash was Nancy's special favor to her close friend, Betsey Bloomingdale, who said it was 'the best present *ever*'."

The joke made it to the live broadcast, and it was read on air by the comedy newscaster. I think it may even have gotten a laugh.

The next morning, the production of our show was abruptly suspended. The entire run was immediately cancelled, and the show was taken off the air after only three episodes and for no stated reason.

Apparently, Nancy was not amused. I always assumed someone had made a phone call. After all, the network was owned, at that time, by GE.

One might say I got fired from *that* job by my own hand. Either that, or I was an unwitting whistleblower.

* * *

Would I do anything for a laugh? Probably. Why not? Especially, if I knew, in the end, it would actually get a laugh. Basically, life is more palatable if there are a few laughs in it *somewhere*, now and then. William Burroughs in his novel "Naked Lunch", kept repeating the phrase, "Wouldn't you?" over and over to describe the lengths to which a junkie might go in order to get his fix. "Wouldn't you?" he kept saying as a constant refrain. "Wouldn't you?" Yes! Maybe the laughs are *our* drug. Or, maybe, the laughs are just the excuse. I don't know. Run into a wall for a laugh? Wouldn't you?

CALL TO ARMS

Brendan White, who had always considered himself an irreplaceable comedy writer, had recently been told, in no uncertain terms, that the daytime talk show he was working on, "The Ladies Room", was not going to renew his contract. He was told this by the show's buffoonish producer, "Bad Bob" Vapors. But, of course, Beverly Frost, "her reptilian highness" and the *capo di tutti capo* of "The Ladies Room"--- as well as its most revered and senior star---- was the person who *really* made the decisions on the show even though she pretended to have no more power than a P.A.. She had foreshadowed Brendan's abrupt dismissal by mentioning to him, out of the blue and apropos of nothing, that she hoped it would all work out between him and her co-executive producer. A comment like that, coming from Beverly Frost, was not to be taken as pre-show small talk.

Thus, since Beverly had already alluded to his firing weeks before the fact, Brendan figured his first step in trying to undo the decision was to go back and deal directly with her. But he couldn't figure out exactly what the best approach to her on that subject might be. But then, in October, the show traveled to Las Vegas for a week; and Beverly Frost brought herself to him, instead.

Any man worth his dating "jones" knows in the first minute after meeting a woman at the beginning of a date if he is going to get laid at the end of it. Brendan remembered a long ago girlfriend who would signal her readiness by loosening her newly-washed and blown-dried blonde hair, piled luxuriously on top of her head, at the exact moment she opened the door to her apartment. The effect was stunning and always took his breath away as if, suddenly, he had found himself in the middle of a shampoo commercial. The fact that he knew it meant he would soon be having sex with her and could shove that hair up his ass if he wanted to only added to the expression of joy and gratitude on his face which, of course, the girl took merely as the appropriate response for her deigning to open the door for him in the first place.

So it was, when Brendan was suddenly summoned to Beverly Frost's suite at Caesar's Palace because "Beverly needed some lines for a charity roast" that he found himself strangely elated when a uniformed maid answered the door with an overly welcoming smile and graciously ushered him into a sitting room off the foyer of the main suite which was big enough to have hosted an orgy and probably had.

Rather than think he might fuck the agreeable maid, the thought immediately came to Brendan that he was, instead, going to fuck Beverly Frost that night. The suite *smelled* like he was. And Brendan was not opposed. It was the opening he was looking for. Besides, the idea of sticking his dick where Kissinger, Castro, and Geraldo Rivera had already been made him feel that some sort of fame was, at last, going to be thrust upon him. It was like finally getting his star on the Hollywood Walk of Fame.

"Oh, Mr. White. Señora Frost expecting you, yes," the maid said.

One wouldn't think that a perfunctory greeting such as that would indicate the promise (or demand) of sex, but since Beverly had never acknowledged Brendan before as anything other than a mere subject; and given the way the suite had been expensively perfumed for his benefit, the thought of sex with her immediately leapt into his head. On top of that, the place was lit as dim as a church, so he figured something was up.

"I was told Beverly wanted to see me."

"Oh yes!" the maid said.

Beverly Frost was one of those stars who traveled with a decorator---like Prince or Sandy Gallin. A single evening in a hotel or even a dressing room, much less a week, would necessitate a complete overhaul of the premises to accommodate her mood. Thus, the lavish Vegas suite that came replete with spitting dolphins, ceiling mirrors, a wet bar, and wetter hookers had been transformed by Ralphie the set guy into a Pacific Heights mansion. Brendan almost expected to see the Golden Gate Bridge rising majestically in the mist out of the windows instead of the ersatz Eiffel Tower in the hotel parking lot across the strip. Of course, this paroxysm of decorating indulgence was another lie in Beverly's life since she had officially grown up in the Lower Haight District; and closer to the Tenderloin than Pacific Heights or, especially, Woodside. The closest she ever got to a hunting lodge was when she lost her virginity in the back of Bill's Sporting Goods in Oakland where she worked as "Miss Ammo", dressed in a bandolier of shotgun shells, during deer season.

"You sit, no?" the maid said motioning to a table and two chairs that had been set up there. Brendan sat down and dutifully took out a small spiral notebook on which to, supposedly, take notes for whatever Beverly allegedly had in mind.

"You like drink?" the maid said nodding enthusiastically and smiling with wide eyes like she was about to witness an execution.

"Yeah, sure," he said. "That'd be nice."

"What kind?"

"Scotch," he told her. The maid then turned and took a new bottle of "Macallan Single Malt" out of a credenza. It had been bought especially for this occasion and was, thoughtfully, Brendan's brand. She opened it and generously poured out a full highball glass of the liquor without any ice as if it were apple juice.

"Whoa, easy there," he said and tried to stop her, but the maid thought he was just being polite and filled the large glass right to the brim as if she wanted to show him how generous she was.

"For you," she said offering it to him.

"Thank you. That's very nice." Brendan had to take a small sip before putting it down on the table so he wouldn't spill it.

"You want some more, it's right here," she said gesturing grandly toward the liquor bottle like Vanna White toward a vowel.

"Right," Brendan said. "Thank you," Obviously, this was not going to be your average story meeting.

Brendan looked around. There was no sign of Beverly, but he could hear some faint Frank Sinatra playing somewhere in the bowels of the suite. The place did smell great, though. No cheap Airwick "Stick-ups" for Beverly Frost. The place smelled like those wonderful dress shops Brendan's mother had often taken him to as a young boy, with rich old ladies' perfume mixing with laundered linen and the tart ping of undergarments. It was immediately exciting.

It reminded him of the time he gone to one of those lingerie joints on La Cienega with a hot, but unfamiliar, girl where the air inside bristled with static sexual electricity; and the girl, now given license, suddenly began to present herself to him in a parade of garter belts and teddies as if both of them were suddenly allowed to play out their separate sexual fantasies. It's the secret of upscale titty bars. Incredibly beautiful, but very proper looking, young women with clean flowing hair who cheerfully and willingly drop their one piece halter tops to expose their naked breasts without the slightest bit of urging on your part---exactly the way all men wish that all female encounters should be.

"Miss Beverly be right here. You stay." The maid said sweetly.

"Fine," Brendan said raising his hand to indicate that he was perfectly taken care of. She disappeared. There was silence. The room seemed to get dimmer, but Brendan decided he was imagining it. He looked around. Ralphie the set guy had out-done himself this time, he thought. The place was draped in browns and wine-colored reds. Only occasionally did the blare of Las Vegas hustle break through the tasteful, but hasty, re-decoration.

Brendan didn't know quite what to do sitting alone at the table. He took a sip out of the highball of straight Scotch. It was unfamiliarly tepid and harsh, but soothing nonetheless. There was silence except for the faint Sinatra playing non-stop. He looked around, unsure of exactly what he was supposed to do. He stood up momentarily and then sat down again. Then he took another sip of pure Scotch. He felt stupid and out of place.

Suddenly she was there. Beverly had somehow entered the room as if she had simply materialized within it. Her expensive perfume preceded her as she swept around the table, running her fingers along the tops of the lampshades and then turning and sitting down dramatically into a primly seductive pose on the edge of the chair across from Brendan's. It was pure theater, and he was impressed.

Beverly looked great. Forget about her age; her people had put her together in spectacular fashion. She was made up as he had never seen her before. He could imagine her sitting before "Syd Vicious", her make-up team, saying, "Darlings, we're doing *sex*, tonight, not news. Pretend it's Colin Powell." She had a huge crush on the former Five Star General, Chairman of the Joint Chiefs of Staff, and Secretary of State and had openly told friends, "I wish Alma would O.D. on her anti-depressants so I could have him."

Brendan had no idea why she fancied him this particular evening unless it was something that happened to her whenever she went on location, and he hadn't known about it. "Location" does strange things to even the most disciplined players. And, best of all, everyone concerned knows "location doesn't count". Beverly must have picked that up from her first days doing "continuity" for Roger Corman at AIP after graduation. It was a job secured for her by an operative of the West Coast mob as a favor to her father. There had been no horse's head necessary in that transaction. Beverly *was* the horse, and she gave great head.

"How *are* you, darling," she said after sitting down as if Brendan were a long lost friend. He couldn't help recoil slightly and was unable to hide the somewhat shocked look on his face.

"Oh come, now, dear Brendan. Don't get all WASPy on me all of a sudden. We're in Las Vegas!" she said with a flourish.

She waved her hands above her head like a show girl. She wore a tight sleeveless turtleneck with a little extra "turtle" to take care of her ravaged neck. It was an old trick she'd learned from Katherine Hepburn to hide the neck wattles that had been missed in surgery. She'd learned that and to always have your hand at your chin for any portrait past the age of forty-five. And from Pamela Harriman she'd learned to open her mouth slightly for all "candids" at parties, red carpets, and casual meetings. Consequently, all pictures of Beverly Frost looked exactly alike: a slightly surprised, open mouthed smile as if inhaling a mouthful of rarified air, and just a girlish hint of that famous tongue. On anyone else it would've looked daffy.

"This is quite a set up you've got for yourself, Beverly," Brendan said, "It's *good* to be a star."

"Oh, darling, I never think of myself like that. You know me better than that." Then, in her best, faintly southern, coquette, "I'm just a little old townie from Pacific Heights where my daddy runs the liquor store."

"I didn't know your father did that," Brendan said, but of course, he did know. "No wonder you were so popular."

"I was *very* popular," she said with a look. At that point the maid reappeared silently with a glass of white wine on a silver tray. Beverly took it without acknowledging her and swung it over to clink with Brendan's tumbler of Scotch.

"Cheers, darling," she said and took a long, overly eager sip that would have been a gulp by anyone else and then put the glass back down on the table. The sip seemed to trigger a tipsiness that had been lurking just beneath the surface.

"You know something about you, Brendan? She went on, "You *get* it," she said leaning forward and making a grabbing motion in the air with her hand as if she were catching a fly. "You. Get. *It*."

"I try to," Brendan replied making sure he stayed with her suddenly drunken bullshit.

He had never been this close to her face before. Her lips were dry and cracked and slightly ajar exposing the tip of that famous, accommodating tongue. He could see the exquisite make-up job, the eye liner, and the faint outline of the two, small, shoulder pad-shaped implants her plastic surgeon had inserted just beneath her cheek bones to preserve the architecture of her face. During the years that Brendan had worked for her, the sunken recesses at the center of each cheek would deepen when the contents of whatever fix had been injected there would wear off. She would begin to age and dissolve right before the staff's eyes as she made her entrance into the make-up room each morning. The outline of those "pads" in her face would grow more distinct until it was thought she would finally have to admit to the plastic surgery, Botox, or monkey glands she always denied using but eagerly reported in everyone else. Then she would remove herself from the show for a week and return wearing sunglasses for a day or two, and everything would be like the old, or "new", Beverly again. As a result, with all those nooks and crannies so diligently attended to for so many years, Brendan figured her face, at this point, probably had a shelf life of close to 500 years. About the same as a Hostess Twinkie.

"Well, darling, we all must do what we must do," she said. Brendan wondered if that included firing him. "But this is Vegas, and I am determined to have fun in Las Vegas."

"Me, too," he said feeling that he'd just agreed to some heavily coded sexual contract. "Nice shirt." Brendan liked to treat Beverly like the "dame" he knew she was at heart. The slightly rough speech thrilled her.

"Why, thank you. It's just something fun."

She presented herself to him ever so slightly and crossed her legendary legs which looked like they belonged to somebody fifty years younger. If it had been anyone else, Brendan would have leaned over and kissed on the spot and then fucked her right there on the floor.

But he was a long way from being in his element, and the whiff of sexuality made him realize he hadn't dropped any Viagra for this historic occasion. He didn't want Beverly to have gone through all this trouble and then have him show up with a cock that looked like one of her tits. But for this particular occasion, Brendan would probably need a Viagra drip--- maybe even Viagra dialysis. But since neither was available, he reached into his shirt pocket and extracted two of the magic pills he'd saved to jerk off with later and quickly downed 200 milligrams of "Blue" as if they were a couple of aspirin for a headache.

"Are you well, darling?" she asked. Not because she was honestly concerned; but, given what she had in mind, she didn't want to catch anything.

"Yeah, I'm great. Feel good." He took a big sip of the Scotch. "Raring to go. Whaddya need?" He returned to the originally stated purpose of this visit. She stared at him for an extra-long beat.

"Just you. For now," she said smiling and blinked several times in mock naïveté. Then she opened her mouth slightly to moisten her lips with the tip of her tongue and kissed the air sensuously for his benefit without ever taking her eyes off of him. "Work can always wait."

The whole thing would have been ludicrous except that Brendan felt he was being entertained by an obvious pro. Sex with an older icon had always been something he was open to. He had been prepared to bed Zsa Zsa Gabor had she demanded it of him when he worked on the Cavett Show. And walking around New York in the 80's Brendan always thought he would run into Jackie Kennedy and be taken home to 1040 Fifth Avenue by her as had happened once to a friend of his. But Jackie died too soon for the odds to bring her to him. Nevertheless, Brendan loved the fact that Jackie had been embalmed right there at 1040 up in her own kitchen by the Frank Campbell homos in order to specifically frustrate any other post mortem paramours like himself. He was sure that Beverly, upon hearing of Jackie's private in-home embalming, had already set the wheels in motion for her to be similarly accommodated by Forest Lawn despite the laws against it and the affront to her neighbors should they, as they say, get "wind" of it.

As it was, having his face closer than normal to Beverly's made Brendan think about the missed possibility of fucking poor, dead "Jackie O" and whether he would've actually done it if given the chance. The answer was "probably", but whom could he tell about it afterwards? But now, with the corpse of Beverly Frost in front of him for real, his mission was to stall long enough for the Viagra to kick in. Once that happened he hoped that thoughts of immortality and Henry Kissinger would prove sufficiently arousing.

"Have you ever been to England, Brendan, darling?"

"Yeah, once," he said. "When I was working at Forbes. I was there for about twenty-four hours with Mr. Forbes for some meetings about the magazine."

"Did you fuck Malcolm?" she said bluntly, but she really wanted to know. It was the whole sanitary thing again rather than the scandal aspect of it.

"Not as far as I know," Brendan said. "I know you and Bad Bob think I did because Bad Bob's been ragging me about working for him ever since I started on the show. And I know where it came from, too. Gloria. And I don't appreciate him spreading his opinion all over the office. So now I get it from Mugsy, and Marge, and anyone else who wants to call me a 'faggot'." He put his glass down and was about to get up to leave when she placed her hand on his knee.

"This is a very difficult business," she said, "*Very* difficult." He took a beat because he wasn't sure whether he wanted to blow the whole sexual defamation and age discrimination case he was building against them. But Beverly was smart enough to realize that Brendan was loaded for bear on the subject, and it would undoubtedly get back to Bad Bob.

"Sometimes you can't control these things," she said looking at him meaningfully. Brendan didn't know exactly what she was talking about, the rumors or the reality.

"And now your partner's actually fired me, you know," he said without really meaning to.

"Oh, darling, I don't know anything about that. You'll have to take that up with Robert."

Beverly had slipped into her pose, once again, of being at the secretarial level in her own company. She would often retreat behind the fiction that she didn't know anyone's salary or any of the deals or business permutations of PermaFrost Productions---that it was all too, too complicated and/or mundane for her to concern herself with. She really thought she could pull off the conceit that she was just one of the girls with the other co-hosts as well, and she would make statements to that effect on the air so that the audience really thought she worked for someone other than herself. The truth was that she was a micro manager just like her buddy, Chet Young, the head of the network, who would fuss over the hors d'oeuvres being served at the "Up Front" presentations in New York and insist on personally sampling all of them first even though the radiation for his throat cancer had obliterated his taste buds. Everything he put in his mouth tasted like Styrofoam.

"Well, now you know. I'm outta here in a couple of months."

"I am sad to hear of the decision. I'm fond of you and will miss you," she said flatly. Then, brightening, she added cheerfully. "But there must be *something*...The show needs you."

"Apparently not."

"Well, *I* need you." She said trying to lighten things up.

"Then why did he fire me"

"Oh, Brendan, he didn't fire you, I'm sure he was just doing what he thought needed to be done. The network can be just impossible sometimes," she said revealing that, of course, she knew everything.

"So am I fired?"

"Darling, you'll really have to straighten that out with Robert. That's completely between you and him. I stay out of it."

Beverly and Brendan regarded each other. This was not the foreplay she had intended, but she was too far down the road to retreat gracefully now. Brendan could feel the Viagra kicking in. His face was becoming flushed with the side effect of the drug. Beverly, of course, took it as a compliment. She put her hand on his cheek instinctively.

"You're burning up. Are you well?"

"Yes," he said, still slightly combative.

"Is it the liquor? Or is this the way you are all the time?"

"I'm fine," Brendan said.

Then she leaned over and gently kissed him on the cheek. He did not move his head or respond when she did. He thought it very cool that he hadn't.

"Brendan White, you are such a dear, sweet boy."

Brendan didn't know quite how to respond, so he did his best Steve McQueen, thin, stoic smile. Then, after a beat, Beverly stood up abruptly.

"I think I shall retire," she said with a slightly more mid-Atlantic accent than usual.

And then she was gone---like a quick-change artist making an exit through an opening in a curtain. There was no sense of a door or wall. One moment she was standing in front of him, and the next she had disappeared.

Of course, when Beverly Frost says she wants to "retire", Brendan could rest assured she wasn't talking "Social Security". She was headed either for bed or leaving the building. He couldn't tell which. He sat there, having not stood when she left because of the abruptness of the exit. He took a sip of Scotch and waited to see if she would return. Instead, the maid reappeared again. She was carrying a stack of towels and a folded plush terry cloth bathrobe.

"You take shower, yes?"

"No, that's okay," he said shaking her off. But she persisted.

"Shower good for you now," she said benignly.

Brendan really didn't get it. He thought the maid thought that for some reason he had come for a shower, and he couldn't convince her otherwise. But then it dawned on him. This was part of the "Sex with Beverly" ritual. This was the shower phase. The *cleansing*. Beverly required absolute assurances that the men she ordered up, like so much take-out, be lathered and scrubbed clean of any offending odors or trace aromas from their own unfortunate lives. She insisted they smell like her.

"Oh," Brendan said finally getting it. "Thank you. Okay. You want me to take a shower first?"

The maid was overjoyed at his cooperation and led him out of the small dining area, across the grand living room to a small guest bedroom with its own bathroom and shower. He half expected her to get in the shower with him to make sure he washed everything. But instead, she went in and laid the towels and a bathrobe out for him on the bed and then stood at the door smiling at him.

"I come get you," she said. "Twenty minutes."

Brendan took his time in the shower and actually enjoyed the appointments. Talent always got better accommodations than writers. Usually, writers were relegated to bad hotels on the wrong side of the strip, the ones that had "Fat Elvis" appearing in the lounge and rooms decorated with red flocking and sperm. You practically had to grease yourself with Ortho Novo just to lie down in the bed without waking up pregnant or with a bad taste in your mouth.

The shower filled the room with sweet steam and lavender. Brendan even took one of the shampoo vials for later. He dried himself off and put on the lush terry cloth robe. He felt like either a fighter or Fernando Lamas. Then he sat on the bed and waited. There were no magazines around, and he dared not explore. So he waited. Presently, there was a soft knock on the door. It was a different maid. She was very pleased that he had apparently completed his "pre-schtupp mikveh".

"Come with me, now," she said.

But first she looked past him into the room to make sure Brendan's boxer shorts were on the bed where they should be and not on him. They walked down the length of the living room to what he assumed was the master bedroom. She opened the door. The area inside was even darker than the rest of the apartment. Beverly had applied a different "love perfume" for the occasion, and it came wafting out of the actual sleeping area. The maid led Brendan to a little dressing area where there was a small couch next to a make-up table. She motioned for him to sit down there and then left him alone once again.

He looked around at the various dresses hanging there. He tried to peer into the actual bedroom but couldn't see much beyond the door. Brendan smiled to himself at the thought that everyone seemed to know the routine but him. At first he self-consciously crossed his legs, but then he decided that was un-cool, so he uncrossed them and sat there, instead, like a benched football player waiting to go in.

Suddenly from another door, probably the toilet for all he knew, Beverly appeared. She was also in a dressing gown now. It was silk and Chinese looking. The freckled skin of her chest above her tits announced that she was also nude underneath. Brendan's heart started to pound, not out of sexual excitement, but out of the sheer terror that this was actually going to happen.

She sat down beside him on the little couch and purposely jammed her hip into his. Then she turned, and suddenly her face was all over his. He could smell her breath which was sweet and not a bit old as he had feared. The billowing perfume effectively enveloped them in an intoxicating floral cloud as if they were in some magical bower and not in a penthouse suite overlooking the Las Vegas strip.

"I want you to kiss me, darling." She said with her mouth only inches from Brendan's. "Don't be afraid."

He kissed her the way an employee is not supposed to kiss his boss, even when ordered. The whole thing came apart immediately. Her mouth, either because of the surgery, botox, collagen, or all three, had no embouchure. It spread out all over her face. Brendan couldn't contain it. And her tongue, unexpectedly thick and sinewy, filled his mouth like a python trying to extract a tooth. He instantly realized that his job, now, was to work around this unbridled hunger in such a way as to never let her know how unattractive it made her and how ultimately un-sexy she was being. He flashed on how Henry Kissinger, Geraldo, and, probably, even Eubie Blake must have come to the same realization, and he wondered how they dealt with it.

Brendan broke away from the embrace as if overwhelmed by the intensity of her passion when, in fact, he simply had to get her goddamn tongue out of his mouth before he gagged. He pretended to be shy and tentative. Shades of "Tea and Sympathy" or "Summer of 42". He pushed her away and held her at arm's length and looked into her face which was, even now, starting to disassemble like a cubist painting.

"What's the matter?" She asked. "Surprised?"

"By you? Never. I just want to enjoy this moment. I want to savor you."

With that statement, he thought he was going to gag on his *own* tongue. But now it was time for him to kiss *her,* or else she'd think something was up. He moved his lips toward hers very slowly as if they were doing a tight "two shot" in a "coming of age" film. It was the only chance he had of getting the thing under control and back on track.

But as soon as their lips touched, it set her off again; and she started devouring him as she had done the first time around. This time he shoved her tongue back into her mouth with his own tongue and kept a reasonable amount of pressure on her lips. But even so, it was a disaster as far as kissing goes. One good thing about growing up Catholic in the fifties, Brendan thought, was that you learned to be a great kisser since that was all there was going to be---for *hours*--- and you had to make the most of it. In the present case, there was spit all over his face, and Beverly's face was melting before his eyes like something out of "The House of Wax"; but she was totally into it.

There was a real hunger at work here. Brendan couldn't imagine Henry Kissinger handling the situation any better than he was. The Middle East was probably nothing compared to fending off a rampant and rutting Beverly Frost. He tried a few more seconds of tongue control but quickly ascertained that she was not going to learn. It was decidedly un-sexy---for him. *She,* on the other hand, was heaving like a cow being artificially inseminated by a ham-fisted vet. Brendan pulled away once again. Now *she* held him at arm's length but with a wild look in her eye that told him she had found what she was looking for.

"We must..." she began breathlessly, "...We must do something about this."

"I hope so," he replied looking deep into her sad, surgically enhanced eyes.

Brendan didn't want her to think he wasn't into it. Although, by now, the situation was losing its freak appeal; and he knew he was facing what can only be described as: "The Job of Sex."

She continued to hold him, stiff-armed; searching his face for God knows what. Then, abruptly, she stood up and disappeared again but not into the bedroom.

Brendan sat there dutifully in the half light, again not knowing exactly what to do or what was expected of him. After a few beats he heard the tinkling of glasses and a *third* maid appeared with a silver tray and two glasses of champagne. He took one when the tray was offered to him. Then the maid turned and headed into the bedroom.

"This way," she said as if it was a doctor's office, and he was next. He then followed her into the actual bedroom section of the suite.

The bed was freshly made with the bed covers neatly turned down on each side like an envelope. The maid led him over to what he could only assume was his side. He lay down, but the maid didn't move.

"Shall I take your robe, Mr. White?" she asked.

At that point, like a Jewish girl on her third date finally agreeing to have sex, Brendan pulled the covers up to his chin and took the robe off underneath them. Then he bunched the robe up, extracted it from under the covers, and handed it to the maid. She was quite pleased. She then proceeded over to the other side of the bed where she place the other glass of champagne on the bedside table there and left the room carrying his bathrobe.

Brendan eagerly drained his glass of champagne. The combination of the Viagra kicking in with booze on top gave him a comfortable buzz. He actually relaxed for the first time. It was a great bed, he thought. Too bad it was about to be ruined by Beverly Frost getting into it.

At first he thought it was his imagination, but he slowly became aware that the lights in the bedroom were being silently dimmed even lower. It was not unlike a play about to begin. Then, with a rustle somewhat like a turkey crossing an open field, Beverly swept into the room, dropped her peignoir, and got into the bed all in one motion. Then the lights then went down completely. Or perhaps it only seemed that way because Brendan's eyes could not adapt fast enough to the lack of illumination. He was now naked in bed with Beverly Frost. He rolled over on his side to face her.

Beverly, balls-ass naked, was actually much smaller than anyone would have ever thought--- the result of eighty-three years of four inch heels and coiffed hair, no matter what. Brendan made the mistake of cupping one hand around her ass to draw her closer. It was not like any ass he had ever known. It had the consistency of a bean bag that was suffering some serious loss of bean. He deftly moved his hand up to her waist so as not to call attention to it.

"Oh, darling," she breathed into his face. "Take me. Do with me what you will."

She threw her head back dramatically with the back of her hand pressed damsel-like on her forehead as he'd seen her do "on-air" so many times when she was feigning shock or trying to be funny. But it was a good thing because it meant Brendan could kiss her neck and trace the plastic surgery scars there with his tongue. It was much sexier than kissing her on the mouth by a long shot.

"You *know*!" she said as if he were some sort of sexual psychic. "You *know*! You *know*!" she repeated. Brendan couldn't tell whether she thought he was clairvoyant or she just couldn't think of anything else to say and was stalling like an empty-headed schoolgirl.

"I'm going to fuck you, Beverly," Brendan said in his best alpha male, "dom" growl.

It was such a porno lick that it even turned *him* on. He said it with full dramatic and cinematic import as if, arms akimbo, he was standing astride her while she groveled on the floor. Brendan had learned from bedding feminists during the 70's that successful business women all wanted to be dominated in the sack in the most abject way possible as if to make up for the balls they broke during the day at the office. Secretaries and wardrobe girls, on the other hand, were to be treated like spoiled princesses.

"Yes, *yes.* I'm just a little girl," she whimpered. This coming from an eighty-three year old diva/mogul pulling in thirty million a year who considered herself nothing less than the long-lost cousin of the British Royal family. At that moment Brendan had just enough of a hard-on for his cock to be serviceable. Nothing like the old days, of course, when it would get hard enough to drive a nail with, but it was sufficiently aroused out of some sense memory so that, highly confused at the moment; it at least *looked* like a hard-on even if it definitely wasn't the stiffest thing in the room.

"You are so hot," he said to her figuring that spoken passion would do them both a world of good. He moved his lower body over on top of hers and held the upper part of himself up at arm's length so that he could look at her. Big mistake. She was deteriorating rapidly like a decomposing corpse. Her face had fallen, and the creases in it had become so pronounced that he could now see the actual outline of her cheek implants, and the deep depression in the center of each cheek was cavernous. She suddenly looked like one of those God-awful, villainous witches that Disney trots out for their animated features. In addition, her overly red lipstick had smeared so disastrously across her mouth that she looked like a *drunken* Disney villainous witch.

Resting on top of her, Brendan became aware that her body felt as if it was all bones. It was as if there was no actual flesh on her at all. He could feel her ample bush against his belly; and he was grateful for that, if for no other reason, than to use it as a bookmark for where he was headed. Brendan closed his eyes as if in a swoon of passion; but, in truth, it was more like averting his gaze at the scene of an accident or coming upon someone deformed on the street. Something was not right.

She looked up at him again with a wild, frightened look as if she thought he was going to hit her. Then he noticed that one of her false eyelashes had come loose and was stuck on her cheek like a centipede. He reached down with one hand and gently flicked it away. She took it as a sign of affection rather than an act of emergency grooming. Then he reached down and grabbed his semi-hard cock and squeezed it tight in order get it into her before it, too, collapsed like her face.

"Please, darling. Just one moment." She spoke very matter-of-factly. It was the tone a woman sixty years younger might use when reaching for birth control. He rolled back off her. She reached over to the bedside table and picked up a small plastic bottle.

"Astroglide, darling. It's the secret of life." She took a beat and then explained further. "Lubrication is *so* important at times like this."

"Oh," Brendan said, "Right. That's great. I love that stuff. I'll take a little myself," and he held out his hand to show how perfectly down he was with the whole thing.

"Lubrication," she said again. "Always remember." He figured that she must have momentarily thought she was back on television doing a segment on marital aids.

The small plastic bottle disappeared beneath the covers, and there was a little "bottle fart" sound from her pussy area as she applied the juice. It meant that, obviously, it had not been a full bottle. This wasn't the first time she'd used it. Brendan flashed on "Henry the K" again and wondered how he liked Beverly's little "jet assist", compliments of Astroglide, when he had fucked her.

"There," she said with finality, very satisfied and relaxed as if, now fully lubricated, she had just gotten a tune-up and wheel alignment as well. Brendan had this vision of Beverly Frost up on a car rack with men in overalls underneath working on her with grease guns and pneumatic wrenches

"There," she said again, "I'm all yours, darling,"

By this time Brendan had lost his hard-on and knew that, unfortunately, the "moment of strange" that all men have, when they could fuck a stump if they had to, had passed. Of course, sometimes that "moment of strange" can last a lifetime, and that's called a happy marriage. But when you are trying to answer a booty call from an eighty-three year old pain in the ass, it is as fleeting as a whiff of grilled meat from a fast food exhaust fan: the anticipation of something tasty is spontaneously triggered within you even though, intellectually, you know its source is disgusting and inedible.

"You're going to have to help me, Beverly," Brendan said rolling over on his back. He threw back the covers to expose his cock lying limp in his lap--- perfectly formed, but dead as a doornail, like one of those British guardsmen who faint in the reviewing line. Not scary or dire, just useless and sad.

"I'm *very* good at that, darling. Leave it to me." She moved down and took a position next to his crotch as if she were going to do a little sewing. She picked up his cock with those perfectly manicured nails (the same color as Paris Hilton's whom she'd interviewed after her sex tape) and placed the head of it on her tongue as if it were a lozenge.

"Oh, yeah." Brendan moaned trying to punch it up by adding a porn sound track. "Oh, *yeah*." (He'd always wanted to write a porno flick called "Oh, Yeah" where that was the only dialogue.)

Beverly then moved the head of his cock off her tongue and looked at it as if she were going to admonish it. Brendan watched her not knowing exactly what she was up to. Then she shook her finger at the cock and touched its head.

"You be good!" she said to it as if she were talking to "Rémy", her dog.

It suddenly occurred to Brendan that maybe she had no idea what to do with a cock but was afraid to tell him. He was about to take it away from her and try something else when she took the entire penis into her mouth so completely that her lips threatened to swallow his balls as well.

"Whoa!" he shouted and arched impulsively. He looked down at her mouth with no cock showing and realized that if, in fact, he had actually *had* a righteous hard-on; he would have choked her to death on the spot or at least pierced her lungs. Not because his cock was that big, of course, but because she had inhaled the thing as opposed to swallowing it. She then began sucking it in a manner unlike any way Brendan had ever been sucked before. She was sucking it with her throat, or tonsils, or uvula, or something other than whatever is in a woman's mouth that she's supposed to suck a cock with. Needless to say, it was exciting, and best of all Brendan only had to look at the top of her head. But then he saw the join where a hair piece had been laced into whatever natural hair she had left. He made a mental note to not grab it if he came, or else she might think she was getting fucked at Little Bighorn.

Brendan decided it was time to seize the moment and his erection. He tried to gently lift her head off his cock while she knelt on the bed. She would not let go. But at least now she was moving up and down the shaft like a normal person. He slipped his feet off of the bed and onto the floor while still attached to her so that he could stand while she knelt on the bed and sucked him.

"Show me your eyes," he said standing over her. Brendan had learned that line from the cock-sucking clips on PornHub, and, also, from a famous Stallone story; so he figured it was probably demeaning enough to excite her. He was right. She obliged, and he watched as this creature, looking like something out of "Clockwork Orange", gazed up at him with her Cocker Spaniel eyes---and only one eyelash---while she continued to suck his cock.

The deterioration of her make-up was moving as inexorably as the shadow of an eclipse across her face. Brendan realized he had to proceed sooner than later, or else there would be nothing left to fuck. He grabbed his cock on one of her up strokes and lifted her mouth off the head. There was an audible slurping sound when the contact was broken. The expression on her face looked like she had just been punished. He gently pushed her back down on the bed, and sprung her legs out from under her. Then he slid her torso toward him so that he had one of her legs under each arm and her pussy at the edge of the mattress. She bit the back of her bony knuckle in wild expectation like a child fearfully anticipating another thunder-clap from a storm, a look of mild terror on her face.

Brendan couldn't get over how much slighter Beverly seemed than he would've thought. On top of that, her desiccated body indicated that she was well past her "fuck by" date. Calling Beverly nothing but skin and bones would've been a compliment. He started to slide his cock into what he assumed was her vagina.

"Oh, *GOD*!" She blurted out in a smoky growl. The trouble was he couldn't tell if he was in or not. It wasn't that her vagina was big; it was the complete lack of muscle tone within it that Brendan was unaccustomed to. She had a flabby pussy that was devoid of any articulation. He withdrew and looked down to reconnoiter the lay of the land (so to speak). Her vagina looked not unlike her mouth, but without the lipstick. He could feel his hard-on receding, so he turned her over with about as much ceremony as a butcher flipping a side of beef.

She went completely limp when this happened as if she had given up any hope or desire of being an active partner in this enterprise. She lay on her stomach with her face buried in the bed covers. He easily bent her legs up underneath her to make her present her ass to him. It was a mess. Brendan entered her from behind this time, and it felt much better. She made little whiny sounds into the covers with each thrust. He had to work hard and fast in order to trick his cock into thinking it was actually somewhere where it wanted to be. His mission, now, was to cum and be finished with it. Of course, given that she *was* a senior citizen, it would've been helpful if there'd been a "grab bar" or two on her ass; but, instead, Brendan had to bunch up some loose skin from around her waist in order to have something to hold on to.

There was Astroglide squirting out all over the place as he doubled up on his rhythm in order to get where he had to be as quickly as possible. This ship was going to land come hell or high water. He went deep, in hopes of touching even just a hint of new pussy

"Oh, my God! You *know*!" she shouted when she came up for air.

"Say you love me!" he demanded incongruously in a low, throaty voice.

Despite the strangeness of the request, Beverly responded as if she knew it was coming.

"I love you," she said almost tearfully. He fucked her harder. "I *adore*you," she added gratuitously. "My. . .*Champion!*"

Giving it up like that made her swoon again. Her eyes rolled back in her head, and she went dramatically limp. What had started as a gambit of domination on Brendan's part had touched her deeper than the sex she had ordered up from him. He was momentarily embarrassed he had pushed her into that secret place.

Her pussy suddenly took shape and formed around his cock. And, as he thrust deeper, his cock grew harder and meaner. The wimpy sounds from Beverly became guttural groans and then full-throated shouts of ecstasy. He was surprised at the transformation, and easily came in her with a final thrust that went as deep as he could drive it. Brendan's cock was still throbbing, and it glistened in whatever stray light had entered the room when he withdrew it from her. It was only then that he realized that he'd been fucking her in the ass most of the time, having inadvertently made the switch in mid-stroke. The abundance of Astroglide had facilitated the anal sex;

and, apparently, she was no stranger to it. But it had not been what he had in mind.

"Oh-oh" Brendan said as if, by apologizing, he could take back the violation. "I think we just had anal sex. I'm sorry. That's not what..."

"But, you *knew,*" she said in a little voice with her head still flat on the bed and her ass in the air. There was Astroglide, and sweat, and cum all over the place.

"No, I didn't," he told her. "I don't know what to say."

"Say, 'Thank you, Beverly,'" she said regaining some of her customary dismissiveness. Then she rolled over on her side and drew her legs up into a fetal position. Her eyes were closed. Brendan assumed cuddling was not called for in this situation. He stood there catching his breath while she cuddled with herself. Then she sighed a very self-satisfied sigh signaling that she was comfortable, and he had become superfluous. She didn't move or attempt to acknowledge him, so he merely turned and walked into the dressing room to find his robe.

"Your things are in the other room, darling," she called to him without ever raising her head from where it had ended up on the bed. He took this to mean that, perhaps, this was not the right time to continue their discussion about his employment.

Brendan put the bathrobe on and walked alone through the darkened suite to the small bedroom where his clothes had been neatly laid out as if they'd just been laundered. He put them on and let himself out. The maids were nowhere to be seen or heard. He imagined them silently descending upon Beverly and attending to her as she lay curled up on the master bed awash in lubricant and sex.

The next day Brendan saw Beverly getting mic'd just before they were about to start the show. She walked right past him with that singularly motivated, obliterating gaze while trying to get the attention of a PA who had worked intimately with her on a daily basis for 15 years.

"Person!" she called to the P.A. even though the girl was standing only a few feet away but with her back turned, "Oh, Person! Hello! *Hel-lo*!" She had no idea what the girl's name was. "Excuse me. Person. I said, *Person*!"

Brendan knew then that everything was the same. Beverly had risen from her own hauled ashes. He also knew that their little "encounter" would change nothing. He was still fired.

1972--- THE DAWN OF CIVILIZATION

It was 1972 in New York. I was young, and employed, and had a rent controlled apartment. So how bad could it be? I was talking to Carol Buckingham who was doing an admirable job of playing "Betty" to my "Archie". We were talking about "Veronica, natch, who in this case was none other than the legendary Penny Lutrell. I say "legendary" only because I think Penny would want it that way. I don't know any other girl who tried quite so hard to carve out a legend for herself. No other girl had ever parried my initial advances by announcing, "Gee, you should have been here *last* summer. Last summer, I slept with *everybody.*"

I remember gulping, in character, and saying ingenuously and with appropriate hesitation, "You mean there were....others?"

"Others?" she said, tossing her head so that her hair covered her face and then fell back over her shoulders. "Hell, I'm in double figures."

I made a mental note to forego any more passes at college girls for whom the sexual revolution on campus was just an updated version of counting beers. Totaling up drinks consumed at one sitting in *my* day was our relatively innocent way of measuring our manhood. What did *we* know? We grew up in that miasma between Asian conflicts and were completely unaware of body counts, be them military or sexual.

"W-e-l-l," Carol said. There was a long pause. There was always a long pause after one of Carol's "W-e-l-l"s. Some people say Carol's affected. I disagree. I think she's stupid. In reality, she simply can't remember which word comes next in the sentence. It is true that her jaw gives one the impression that it was wired shut at birth, but she is certainly not a snob. After all, I've seen her drink water out of a kitchen tap several times. Her drawn-out manner of speaking *does*, however, tend to gather your attention. It all attests to the fact that Carol has made a lifestyle out of playing "Betty".

"W-l-l-l," Carol groaned again. I continued to look through a pile of pink phone messages that were on my coffee table. I had grabbed them off my desk at campaign headquarters that morning just before I'd abandoned the office for my apartment. The coffee table was now beginning to resemble the top of my desk which was why I had abandoned the office in the first place.

"W-e-l-l."

"For crissakes, Carol," I said. "Will you stop it? From now on, when you talk to me, just start every sentence with the second word."

"Oh, how exciting," she said.

"It'll be our secret code. None of your friends will understand us. Now, come on. Just give me the bottom line on Penny. Was she sorry she had to leave and go back to school?"

"W-e-l-l."

"That's four," I said.

"I'm sure she really likes you, Phil. I mean, you two were so perfect together."

"That's not what I asked. I want to know if she was sorry. Was there remorse? Did she cry? Was she torn?"

"I don't know. She doesn't talk to me."

"Nobody talks to you," I said, "They haven't got the patience I have. But you're her best friend, so you must know *something*."

"Well, after all, she *did* have to think about her situation at Yale."

"You mean, she actually *wanted* to go back to that college-punk boyfriend of hers?"

"He *does* live in the same dorm."

"So do pigeons."

I remember Penny telling me that she had decided she should stop sleeping around in the new Co-ed dorms at Yale one morning when she was brushing her teeth in the communal bathroom on her floor. She had looked in the mirror and realized that she had slept with all four men standing with their backs to her in from of the urinals. I think that's called a revelatory experience in a true liberal arts education. You on one end of the log, and Mark Hopkins and all of your lovers on the other.

I was half-dressed. I was trying to get the information I wanted from Carol without having to direct my full attention to her. It's not that I'm callous; it's just that a thirty-two year old speech writer should not be overly concerned about the vagaries of a nineteen-year-old college girl and why she dumped me out of a summer romance instead of the other way around.

The candidate---which is what Congressman Sinclair Bingham liked to be called---was due at the Knights of Columbus Gridiron Lunch in one hour. I think he liked being called "candidate" because it sounded vaguely like "Kennedy", whose style he secretly coveted. I think that's also why he liked having me write for him. He thought I could graft a sense of humor onto his stuffed shirt. That task, alone, would be comparable to lending cheer to a tepid bowel of farina. Nevertheless, the "candidate" had visions pf a book called "The Bingham Wit". It would be a volume only slightly thinner than his congressional record. He was the only man I ever knew who could read the punch line of one joke with the straight line of the following one and not understand why there was no laugh when he stopped.

His purpose, or more correctly, my task, at the luncheon was to demonstrate that he was not just "all politics" but a hale fellow, to boot, who liked a good joke as much as any of us. Under the circumstances, it might also be helpful if he could give the impression that he was up for a conversion to Catholicism. What I needed, I figured, was a good supply of "rabbi, minister, and priest" jokes where the priest always had the punch line. We already had some of these from the Jewish War Veterans Dinner, but only an act of God would enable the candidate to remember that, in front of Catholics, the rabbi doesn't get the laugh. Anyway, it was these good-natured remarks and tri-partite jokes that were my responsibility, and they had yet to spring from my head and onto the blue 5X7 cards that I would hand to the candidate as he speared his green peas on the dais.

The confluence, in my brain, of good government and my sex life was proving fortuitous while I searched, at the same time, for some clean socks and more information from Carol. (To wit: "Democracy is like sex. When it's good, it's fantastic; and when it's bad--- it's *still* pretty good." That line was nothing new, but its arrival on the scene at the right moment was what I was being paid for. It was interesting how it covered the two subjects currently on my mind. The line could just as well have been used at a luncheon honoring Penny Lutrell--- attended by guests numbering in double figures, no doubt. "Gentlemen, I'll say this about good ol' Penny. When she's good, she's fantastic; and when she's bad, she's *really* good.")

"Phil, do you really want to hear about this or not?" Carol was saying, "I can't *stand* it when your attention is divided."

"I'm paying attention," I said. "I want to know everything."

"Well, don't you think it's a little morbid?"

"Morbid?" I said. I liked the sound of that word and wrote down "morbid" on the cardboard from a laundered shirt. (Appearing at one of these luncheons in the middle of a campaign is a little morbid. It's sort of like attending a wake where they've misplaced the corpse." I'd have to work on that. Maybe, "Like attending a wake when nobody died." Closer, but still not rght.)

"Yes, morbid, Carol said. "I think you should just chalk it up to experience. Your pride is hurt, that's all."

"Pride? Me? Pride?" I said. "My pride has nothing to do with this. So what if she, a callow school girl, was being entertained by the likes of one of the city's greatest political phrase makers and failed to see the importance of such a relationship. So what? You think that hurts my pride, do you?"

My face had ended up about three inches from Carol's face. She quickly took out a cigarette without changing her expression or averting her eyes. Carol's veins are filled with well-chilled Champagne.

"Be serious, Phil. Because I am. You didn't really care about her anyhow. So why are we even talking about it? Tell me about Sinclair Bingham," she said shifting her bottom expectantly. "Do you really think he'll be re-elected?"

"I don't want to talk about that. I don't trust anyone whose first name sounds like a last name. There must be something in that, I thought. ("Do you think it's easy running for office with a name like Sinclair Bingham? The polls show that half the people are voting for Sinclair so they can get Bingham out of office.")

"Listen to me, Carol," I said, "I want you to tell me what her thinking was. She's an allegedly smart girl, and I want to know how she made her decision."

"I don't think there ever *was* a decision, Phil. You knew all along that he was very involved with Barry Stempian, and you knew that she planned to stay that way. At least until after she graduates, anyway."

"Then what's that make me, a summer hobby? Like a lanyard she made at camp? There was *always* a decision to be made. Every moment of our lives is a decision. Do I have to get existential to make my point?"

"Spare me."

"So tell me what tipped the scales?" I asked like a defense attorney. "That last day you spent with her before she went back to school, did she say anything about me then?"

"I've *told* you. I've told you everything she said."

"But what was the quality? I mean, what was the texture of how she acted when my name was brought up?"

"You're crazy."

That was Carol's standard response when her circuits have become overloaded with too many thoughts or sexual advances.

I put ballpoint to shirt cardboard again. (Anyone crazy enough to try and explain American politics to a foreigner is crazy enough to try and explain Transubstantiation to a cannibal." Blasphemous and too egghead.)

I bore down on Carol as if she were a hostile witness in a Perry Mason re-run. "Carol I have to go out now, so you're going to have to leave my apartment. But I'm not finished. I know there is something you're not telling me, and I have a right to know."

I went back to the cardboard before she answered. ("Regarding the 'right to know' debate, I use the same guidelines I did in deciding what should be told to my son about the facts of life. When I realized that he had already experienced more than I was telling him, I decided, right then and there, that he had a 'right to know'. In other words, when it comes to government secrets *or* sex secrets, if someone is getting screwed, they have a right to know.")

Carol watched me silently as I wrote this down. The cardboard was filled, and I folded it and put it into my back pocket. I would transcribe these gems when I got to the Knights of Columbus Hall; or, maybe, I would even hand him the cardboards themselves. ("A few thoughts occurred to me as I was buttoning my shirt this morning, and I took the liberty of jotting them down." He would never do it. Sinclair Bingham doesn't want people to know he *ever* takes his shirt off.)

"She said she would stick with Barry because she had more in common with him. And he offered her more security."

That stopped me. Carol had been saving that one.

"So that's it? More in common? And security? Terrific. Phillip Marcovicci up against a two-bit college punk who's never had a job in his life; and she says that we have nothing in common, and I don't offer her any security."

"I knew I shouldn't have told you. Are you mad?"

"Mad? I'm not mad. I just might have to slap her the next time I see her, that's all." I could feel myself rising to the attack.

"I knew it would get you mad, Phil."

"You want to know what I really think about Penny? And you can tell her this. She hasn't got half the brain she thinks she has, and she never did. I gave her the best two weeks of her life *and* the funniest two weeks of mine. I mean, I let it all out for her. My best shot. The 'A' material. I didn't hold anything back.

And if she thinks that I don't stack up against some slack-jawed academic asshole who hasn't worked a day in his life and whom she's turned into a cuckold, she's got a lot to learn."

I stopped. I was breathing heavy. My finger was raised high in the air. What was I doing to myself? Why was I getting so excited?

"He was in the war, Phil," Carol said reverently.

"He was a supply corporal in the quartermaster corps," I said quietly. "The closest he ever got to a gun was a box of puffed rice. Come on. Let's go."

I pulled Carol out of the apartment and closed the door.

Do I have to. tell you that the "candidate" was the most soundly defeated aspirant to congress that year? He went back to his law practice, and I went back to freelance copywriting for some of the Madison Avenue greats. It amounted to having lunch at P.J. Clarke's more times than I would ever care to. With the demise of the New York-based talk shows, the anecdote addicts at the advertising agencies seemed to be running their own little talk shows at lunch. Whereas before, a talk show personality might make the rounds of Cavett, Carson, Griffin, and Frost; now he did the same material over lunch at Clarke's, Michael's Pub, Charlie O's, or Manny Wolf's. And if he was *really* good, he might even get a guest shot for dinner at Ratazzi's.

Anyway, I found that my repertoire for the N.Y. ad biggies was growing professionally tight out of my necessity to hustle work as well as laughs out of them. As the fall progressed, the biggest story I had was the one about my brief, but abortive, affair with a junior co-ed at Yale. It went something like this.

"Listen I gotta tell you guys about this chick I had a run-in with this summer. It was out at my brother's place in Connecticut where I was suckin' up some country club sun and booze. Now, are you ready for this? She was a junior at Yale? I mean, a heterosexual one. But it's the liberation now. Half the student body in New Haven is wearing pantyhose and high heels. And the *girls* are dressed pretty strange, too. They ever let women into Mory's. It's all changed up there. Remember the Yale Bull Dog? Now it's the Yale "Bull-Dyke". What can I tell you? The Yale mascot's a bitch. Literally. I swear. Really.

"So I take up with this broad for two weeks this summer, and get this. Are you ready for this? Nineteen years old. One-nine. And with a body that looks like it's been sheet-wrapped since puberty. Doesn't know the meaning or the word "bra".

"All right. So now, all of a sudden, for me, it's fifteen years ago; and here I am out necking in all my old spots again. The beach, the dead-end roads, the driveways, the back seats, the porch, the living room couch. We even got caught by the cops, and the cop turns out to be a guy I went to school with. He's got a wife and three on the floor now. And here I am with my pants down, and he's got his flashlight on me. Lemme tell you how young this girl is. She'd never heard anyone call a cop by his first name before. Well, I called him more than that. I say, 'Frank, you son of a bitch, get out of here with the flashlight, will ya? It's me. Marcovicci.' And he says, 'Hey, how you doin', Phil?' And I say, 'I was doin' a hell of a lot better before you showed up.' So he says, 'When're you gonna come by and see us?' And I say, 'As soon as I get my pants on, you dumb bastard.' Then he whips out a picture of the wife and kids to show me with the flashlight while Penny is on her hands and knees looking for her panties.

"Well, that's when the trouble started because the girl, Penny, felt she had been demeaned by me and the cop. I mean, this girl is hotter than a pistol, but she's also majoring in Women's Lib at Yale. Really. It's a full-credit major up there now. Of course, most of the girls end up writing their senior thesis from a maternity ward in Scarsdale. But that's the funny thing about these college liberation types. Most of them can talk a pretty good game over dinner and drinks which, of course, they insist on paying half of; but it's 1972 only in their brains. From the neck down, it's 1959 all the way. Sure the call you names and tell you what a pig you are, and how oppressed they are, and how they're going to change the world. But once you get their feet off the ground, once you get them horizontal, it's all, 'Take me, take me, do with me what you will.' And when I'd ask her about that afterwards, she'd only say it merely proved she was a victim of her sexist conditioning as a child. Some conditioning!

"Anyway, she refuses to go to a motel because a motel has connotations of male supremacy. That's because she knows I would be the one signing us in, and I would register us as 'Mr. and *Mrs.* Marcovicci', not 'Mr. and Ms'. My car is out because of the police; my brother's place is no good because she refuses to take her clothes off in any house that's violated zero population growth. What that *really* means is that she knows that, with more than two kids in the place, her chances of being caught <u>in flagrante</u>---and *very*---<u>delicto</u> are definitely not in her favor.

"So, you know where we end up having our affair? In the goddam kids' tent in the back yard. She liked that. I tell my brother about it, and he says he doesn't mind as long as we check-in after the kids go to bed because they like to play there. He also tells me to keep it clean because he doesn't want the kids to catch anything.

"You don't know what living is until you've had an affair with a liberated college girl. First of all, they're demanding as hell because they never had to go very far for what they wanted. I mean, when *we* were in college, we had to drive fifty miles over bad road to get even a sniff of what we were after. These kids are all living together in their dormitories. So, now, sex doesn't give them that sense of accomplishment it gave us. The work ethic is finished. It's different when all you have to do is go into the next room to borrow a cup of sex, or a book, or whatever. I mean, in our day, a liberated woman was a girl who got into the back seat without being asked. These girls are something else. In the first place, you're not allowed to call them 'girls'. You have to say 'women'. I mean, how does it sound if I fall in love, and I have to tell people I have the most wonderful 'womanfriend' in the world. Christ, it sounds like I'm dating Mamie Eisenhower.

"So, anyway, at the end of the two weeks I'm really suckin' wind because the campaign is heating up, and so is she. She wants to camp out every night and all day on the weekends. So I end up commuting between the goddam tent in Connecticut and campaign headquarters in town. Then, fortunately, she has to leave to join her erstwhile boyfriend. I tell her, 'Why don't you call him your 'manfriend' and see how far that gets you?' He happens to be kyacking in New Hampshire. That's another thing, guys. I think these college kids are so busy backpacking into the environment and collecting ecology that the chicks have to get their rocks off with workin' stiffs like us.

"So there's this big scene the night before she leaves, and she places one hand meaningfully on my shoulder and says, 'I have a boyfriend in college whom I'm going back to, and I don't want to hurt you.' So I tell her, 'Go ahead. Hurt me.' I say, 'Don't worry sweetheart, I'll manage somehow.' Then she says, after a long thought, 'Would it be all right if I called you when I came home on vacation?' Can you imagine that? These girls want everything we have, *including* our old lines. So I say, 'Sure. You can call me. But only if you're nice.' She liked that."

So much for P.J. Clarke's at lunch. Stories about insatiable nymphets always score big in the backroom there. But all of a sudden, it's November, and I can't help noticing that the city is filling up with college urchins. Am I really thinking what I am thinking? Is the anticipation of an appearance by Penny Lutrell actually swimming into the lobe of my brain that normally plays host to thoughts of women in the many service industries of our great nation?

In the interim between August and November, I had begun to date her friend, Carol, with a certain vengeance. Not with any luck, mind you, just with a certain vengeance. Carol's genitalia are hermitically sealed in one of those boxes that wrist corsages usually come in. Not the consistency of metaphor. A box within a box. Actually, I imagined that her family took her downtown one day when she was fourteen and had her private parts sealed in clear plastic with one of those machines that usually do licenses. I actually have seen Carol's most delicate gear; and, believe me; it is intact, to be sure. I have even touched it, but I have never disturbed it. That is one document that will never become dog-eared.

There was no reason for me to take Carol out, of course, but I think I did it to show Lutrell just who was liberated and who wasn't. There was something unsatisfying there. I was angry at myself for playing school girl games just because I'd been turned around by a school girl.

The Wednesday before Thanksgiving went by, and I found myself staying in the city when I should have left early to spend the holiday with my brother in the country. I got on the train Thanksgiving morning while thinking that, maybe, she was still up at Yale with a lot of work. I remembered the strange affinity that college girls had for the "libes", as they called it; and that, by prowling the stacks of any women's college library, you could find an untold wealth of talent at any given hour, day or night. It used to be one of my specialties. At one time, I could quote the floor plan of ten women's college libraries the way some motel make-out artists could quote the Gideon Bible. Familiarity breeds a certain amount of temporal knowledge.

On the other hand, I thought, as I watched the grimy brick of the city turn into trees along the railroad tracks, maybe she had come home with her college honey and was being held incommunicado by her own romantic circumstances. That would mean she might even be seen gamboling on her front lawn, tossing a diaphragm-shaped Frisbee back and forth with her fumbling college boyfriend. There was poetry in the vision of that scene. Officially, I was not thinking about it.

Thanksgiving dinner with my brother and his family was the usual circus. He had married a saint of a woman who had attached a career-like fervor to the task of raising their five children. Housekeeping was not part of that career, and so their home always looked comfortably lived-in since no attempt was ever made to erase the humanity that ran over it. The talk at the dinner table was filled with business-type metaphors ("I'll take a purchase order on some of that white meat") and references to my confrontation with the realities of hyperactive children. ("This is the best birth control in the world, hey Phil? Hell, you won't be able to get it up for two weeks after *this* meal.") The truth of the matter was that I enjoyed it thoroughly. The wash of life over me was soothingly nostalgic.

My brother's toast towards the end of the meal was not so soothing. He raised his glass to the memory of the tent in the back yard and the many hours of pleasure that were had beneath its canvas. Only the weight of wet leaves had forced him to decommission this monument to his younger brother's ingenuity, pluck, and love of the wild. Necessity was the mother of housing, he said. It was good for a lot of laughs. They wanted to know if I had seen Penny, and I said, "No." They wanted to know if I was going to, and I said I hadn't planned on it.

This news cheered them. The loyalty of my brother and his wife far surpassed their voyeurism, and they were glad to hear that I was not waiting on the whim of a rutting prom queen.

I was back in the city Thanksgiving night wondering why I was back in the city Thanksgiving night. Then the call came in. It turned out I'd been waiting.

Penny has a strange voice. There is an official quality to it that sounds as if it belongs to the phone company itself. In a courtroom, her voice would belong to the foreman of the jury. In business, it would belong to a career secretary who had been on the job longer than her boss. In sports, it would belong to a baseball announcer in the second game of a double header. In short, there isn't a lot of energy there. I didn't recognize it. The trouble with Penny is that she doesn't exactly sound like someone you've been longing to hear from.

"Phill?" she said.

"Yes. This is me," I said

"Hi, it's Penny."

"Well, whaddya know?" I said launching into a bit. "Yale's very own lonesome end calling me on the telephone. The *vera* exciting, the *vera* wonderful, the *vera, vera* Pen-E-Lu-Trell. What a show, ladies and gentlemen. What a show! How 'bout that?"

"Oh Phil, stop it," she giggled. "I'm home." Then, when I didn't break in with a lot of 'huzzah's, she added, "I'm sorry I didn't call sooner."

"So am I," I said.

"Oh," she said. There was a pause. This was turning into a soap opera-paced conversation. I savored the phony dramatics of it all, so I waited.

"I'd love to see you, Phil." I had flushed her out like a Golden Retriever putting up a covey of quail. I could proceed more recklessly now that she had broken cover.

"What did you say?" I said. One thing I have never denied are accusations that I am not a nice person. I tease helpless children, I make jokes about cripples, and I am unkind to women who make the mistake of giving me an advantage.

"I said, I'd love to see you. Were you out in the country today?"

"Don't mix your tenses," I said. "Yeah, I was out there."

"Why didn't you stay around?"

I was tired of handling this thing poorly. It was time to show her whom she was talking to. Time to show her what messing around with someone in the real world was like. No more college love games. No more scarves, and mums, and all that Yale Bowl bullshit. It was time to let her know who was in charge here.

"I'm sorry," I said, "I didn't know you were home. Maybe I could get on a train and come back out there tonight. If you're free, that is," I sniveled.

"No, don't do that, Phil. It's too late," she said. "I have to come into the city tomorrow for some doctor appointments. I could see you then."

"Great. Why don't you schedule a visit to good old Doctor Feelgood while you're at it."

"It *would* be fun to see you." She sounded now like she was thinking about it lasciviously and smiling.

"Fun?" I said. "*Fun* to see me? Hey, Penny, it's *me.* Remember? August? The tent? You're talking to Philly-babes, not some pipe smoker in a vest from Skull and Bones. This is your New York action. What the hell do you think I am, the Statue of Liberty? *Fun to see me?*

"Can't you ever be serious?" Frost was beginning to form on the receiver in my hand.

"Listen, Penny, dear. Get in here and see your doctors, and then call me when you're through. And we'll see what happens. Okay?"

"I can't spend the night, Phil. My parents can't deal with that."

"Yeah, I know. They can only deal with it when they're paying tuition. Why is it that you're up there in New Haven all year long bumping your brains out with that apple-cheeked, cardiganned Turk of yours; but when you come home, all of a sudden, I have to pay *his* dues to your parents?"

"Phil," she interrupted, "Phil, you're making me upset. Please. I can't deal with you when you're like this."

"And how about striking all that 'dealing' horseshit from our vocabulary for a start?"

"I'm hanging up."

"Don't hang up. Penny. Please." Don't be too proud to beg, I said to myself. "I'm sorry. Please call me tomorrow. It works better face to face. *You* know that."

"I suppose you're right," she said. She promised she would call me before noon the next day, and then she hung up.

I felt a surge of exultation. It was an unaccustomed feeling. I won't say that seven years in New York had made me jaded when it came to relations with the opposite sex, but I *had* given up on going out on what, traditionally, would be called "dates" five years ago. And, now, here I was looking over my wardrobe wondering if I had any jeans that could pass for "college hip".

I can't believe that I spent the next twelve hours preparing for a luncheon date with a college girl. Rather than making me feel young again, it made me feel old, very old---roughly in the "codger" category. As I cinched myself up for my encounter with this sweet young thing, even the Palm Court at the Plaza flashed through my mind as a suitable place for our meeting. And believe me, that's codger heaven. I discarded the Palm Court, however, because I figured it would be just my luck to run into some faggot wedding reception there, and I thought I should avoid even a passing knowledge of that milieu. I needed something more butch, my own turf. Some place where I could show this little honk o' hair and piece o' bone what the real world was all about. I had to show her that she was dealing with a two-fisted, big-time, New Yorker, now. So when she called the next day, I told her to meet me at P.J. Clarke's.

Clarkes is a good bar. That's number one. But, of course, like any other place in New York, you have to know when to go. It's like a municipal swimming pool where five times a day they clear everybody out and bring in a new crowd. The front part of the place is good for juicing up your date before getting down to some serious propositioning at the tables in the back,. The only problem is that, in the front, you have to climb over a certain number of method New York Irish and grey-flannelled pimps before you can establish a beachhead at the bar. But if you plant the girl at the right place at the bar, by looking in the mirror, she can watch the pimps and Irishmen relieving themselves on huge blocks of ice in the giant 19th century urinals when the door to the men's room opens directly behind her. It's not even a men's *room,* it's a men's *partition,* but it'll make her feel like an insider, and she'll forget to notice that Five Dollar Frankie, the maitre d', is ignoring you and won't give you a table in the back. There is one good table in the middle room in an alcove behind the bar that you can opt for in a pinch, but the lighting there is bad; and then you have to watch all the raccooned women trying to squeeze into the only stand up ladies' room in New York. That tends to take your mind of the girl you're paying for at the table.

But Clarke's is an important move to have in your bag of tricks because it has the ambiance of "our place". Even though it is probably the most famous bar in New York, it gives you the feeling that you're discovering it every time you go in. Unfortunately, this feeling is usually dispelled shortly after you get in the door when you see that half of New York is *also* discovering it for the first time, too. The main thing is that Clarke's takes the onus off of any sort of "date-type" occasion. You ask a girl who's made the rounds in New York, and she will tell you how many first dates she's had sucking fondue at the old Good Table, or messing with ice cream at Serendipity III, or listening to jive Spanish waiters at El Parador. There used to be a place called Soerabaja that was useful because it was the only bar in the city with a trellis in front. That trellis, alone, was worth three drinks as far as loosening up a new girl was concerned. But then it turned out that the trellis had the same effect on hairdressers and chorus boys, and the pace went gay about two years ago. The point of all this is to say that Clarke's remains the best all-around place to go. And no matter how berserk your date is, the most expensive thing on the menu is still six bucks. it is better to go to a place famous for hamburger than to a place noted for its choice center cut.

The day that Penny and I were meeting was the Friday after Thanksgiving. It occurred to me that Friday was usually my day for lunch at Clarke's with the New York ad biggies sitting around re-telling stories.

Big Ed was usually the master of ceremonies and would always introduce someone's anecdote with a question. "Say Harry, didn't you once barricade your kitchen door on the wrong side while you were putting the make on your neighbor's daughter during a cocktail party? And then your wife walked in for some ice?" Everyone would laugh, and the Harry would start the story over again as if no one either knew it or hadn't just heard the intro. "Oh yeah. You won't believe this," he would begin, hunching over the center of the table and leaning on every word. "You see, I forgot that the door between the kitchen and dining room opened *out* instead of in."

Homeric singers of epic tales, sitting in their caves, had nothing on us in the darkened back room of P.J. Clarke's. But even though it was Friday, I figured they would all be taking *this* Friday off.

I was wrong.

I said hello to short and frank Five Dollar Frankie and asked for a table.

"You *have* a table," he said looking past me in his inimitable, warm, friendly way.

"Frankie," I said, "You flatter me, which is very pleasant in front of this young lady of indeterminate age. But what are you talking about?"

"Bagger and the others are already eating in the back, near the slot, " he said. Frankie had still had not looked at me directly. With Frankie, eye contact costs you five dollars in the palm.

My heart sank. I mean it *really* sank. I could feel it dropping like a stone through my diaphragm. I hadn't figured on coming up against the Madison Avenue merrymakers at this point in my relationship with Penny.

"Are you meeting someone else, Phil?" Penny asked.

"No. It's a mistake," I said while I fished a Five Dollar bill out of my pocket. I placed my hand in Frankie's, and he looked at me straight in the eye. The slight look of love that came over his face attested to the fact that Frankie could read Braille when it comes to deciphering the denomination of paper money." Frank, I'll just take a table for two, please," I said.

Penny had moved in close to my other side. Being known at a New York bar is impressive to the uninitiated. Despite her academic quest for independence and sexual parity, Penny Lutrell was glad to be under my wing and not lined up against the wall like the six or seven unfortunates who were waiting for a table like it was a bus at the Port Authority. Penny may *think* she's liberated, but she *knows* she's an elitist. I used to think it was important to be known by waiters and maitre d's all over town until a jazz musician friend of mine informed me that *he* considered it an insult if someone that low on the social scale ever called him by name. I guess there are two ways of looking at it.

Meanwhile, Frankie was looking at that folded envelope he always carried to write down his reservations on. Of course, to preserve your ego, it was best never to actually watch him write your name. I wouldn't be surprised if Frankie only knew how to spell his *own* name. Aristotle Onassis would come in and ask for a table for fifteen, and Five Dollar Frankie would still only jot down what looked like "Frank" with no number.

Frankie looked from his envelope to over the top of everyone's head about three times and then pointed to the only open table. I moved Penny out into the middle of the room before I realized exactly where the table was.

Are you ready for this? The table was right next to the table I was trying to avoid. They were all there. Big Ed, Bagger, Harry, the Dodge Boys from Grey, Feiny-the illiterate copywriter, and Wally from the editing house. All of them were halfway through their bacon Cheeseburgers and three quarters of the way through their quota of "silver bullets." That is, their martinis.

Well, well, well, if it isn't Phil Marcovicci, the greatest Italian of them all, " Big Ed said with both hands outstretched in salutation. "Come join us at our humble table where comedy is king and hilarity will ensue."

"Is that a friend of yours?" Penny asked.

"New York advertising types. Juiceheads," I said, "Don't pay no attention." I headed her directly for our table.

"Pull up a chair, Phil, and bring that person of immense loveliness with you," Feiny said. Feiny suffered as the house Jew at a WASP agency and was assigned to a "red neck" textile client who thought he was Italian. Feiny was known as the only illiterate copywriter in the business because he had made a career out of one-word print campaigns (which he'd recently reduced to only punctuation marks like "&") and was acknowledged as the best in the business at it. He was also the nicest and straightest man on the street.

"Hello, boys," I said sounding cheerful. "Can't do it today. Gotta service the account. Know what I mean? This young lady's just home from college for the day."

I looked at Penny as she sat down. She was bored. Her attention span outside the rack was about 90 seconds. She didn't understand this scene. that was for sure. What do smart-ass college girls know about the woof and warp of Madison Avenue comradery, anyway? At least these guys at the next table had a modicum of civility. She was lucky they weren't "garmentos" from the rag trade.

"Right on, fella" Wally said. "By the way, how's the wife?"

"Yeah. Saw your oldest boy the other day. He's gettin' real big, Phil," Bagger added.

They all laughed at this. Penny knew I was single, of course, but the humor of the guys was lost on her. I found it pretty funny, actually. By the time she had settled her purse and coat, she was scowling. I couldn't understand why she was angry instead of impressed. It isn't everyone who can walk into Clarke's and turn it into their living room.

"What's the matter?" I asked her finally.

"Nothing," she said. "It's just that you're always joking. I can't deal with that."

I was still in pretty good humor. I knew one of her problems was that she both exploited the fact that she was good looking and, at the same time, resented anyone who responded to her that way. One is a natural, feminine perk. The other is an acquired, feminine cause.

"Whaddya mean? I said. "And will you stop always 'dealing' with things? You keep talking about 'dealing' or '*not* dealing'. You think too much about it. Why not just sit back, and live, and stop trying to treat life like one of your courses at Yale."

"You just can't deal with an educated, articulate woman. That's all."

"You're not so articulate once you get your pants off, Sweetie. And do you want to know what I think? I think it's just like Vonnegut said. Education, for a woman, is like honey poured into a fine Swiss watch. It just gums up the works."

"He didn't say that. A character of his said it."

"Then, *I* say it. Okay?"

"I don't think that's funny," she said.

"It wasn't supposed to be funny. I'm just trying to help you out. Stop being Joan of Arc. Enjoy yourself."

"I don't need to be helped out. Order me a drink."

I smiled.

"Right. A drink. What'll it be? Brandy Alexander? Whiskey sour? Banana Daiquiri?"

Her eyes narrowed. She was really beginning to burn. She *was* like Joan of Arc.

"Forget it," she said. I waved to the waiter.

"A gin and tonic and a Guinness," I told him.

"Thank you," she said quietly.

There was silence at our table. Meanwhile, next to us, Big Ed and Harry were making faces trying to decipher which girl she was. There was wild gesturing and pointing. Feiny was merely shaking his head and sucking wind thorough his pursed lips. He *knew* who she was.

"Would you rather be over there with your friends?" she asked without looking up from the drink that had just been placed in front of her.

"Of course not," I told her. "I want to be right here with you. I want to talk. I want to have all those intellectual conversations we were too busy to have this summer. Go on, ask me a cogent question. Something that will take us across the epistemological gulf and into the realm of reality," I said quoting a standard college thesis bullshit line.

"If you really want to know what's wrong between us, that's it," she said.

"What?"

"I think you hate women." She took a drink on that one, but she still didn't look at me.

"You're probably right," I said. "Why else would I be so attracted to you?" This didn't produce the explosion I had expected.

"You can't be serious with me. You're always doing material." She was reacting to the rhythm of my remark, not the content.

"Call it survival," I said. "God help me if I should ever get serious with you. *You're* the one who's opted for the convenience of a college lover. What do you expect me to do?"

"That's why we have to talk. I've become closer to Barry."

"I should hope so," I said. "After all, you both share the same sop dish."

"Phil."

"It must be nice to be sleeping with your roommate at college. Think of all the money you save on gas.

"And I don't have the same relationship I had with you before."

"*Now,* you tell me. How about all the plans we made? I thought I was going to be your Independent Study Program."

"But I would still like to see you," she continued as if I hadn't been speaking at all. I think she had either practiced this or had said the same thing to someone else before. "It's just that we can't sleep together right now. I can't deal with that and still be close to Barry." The boys at the next table were catching everything. They started humming the Yale football song. I didn't need that.

"What does Barry think of all this?" I asked her.

"You *know* I could never tell him about you. He's not like you. He'd leave me immediately."

"Oh," I said. "Didn't he ask you why you came back to school all hot and sweaty? He doesn't think you're <u>that</u> close to your parents, does he?"

"I told you, Phil. He's not like you. He would never ask. He's a man of his honor."

"Oh," I said again.

"Let's go," she said. I think she had just recognized the song they were humming.

"No. Wait. Don't pay any attention to them. They do that all the time."

I couldn't help shooting the Dodge Boys a look and a quick smile. Then I reached across the table as she was gathering her coat and grabbed her forearm just like art directors do when they tell you you're the best in the business.

"I don't understand your reasoning in all this," I said. "I mean, look. I don't want to get involved or do anything that would tie you down, but if it was all right this summer, why isn't it all right now?"

"I still feel the same way about you as I did this summer," she said, "But it's very hard to go back to Barry after one of our 'sessions'."

By this time the group at the next table was well into their holiday round of drinks, and they were singing "Tenting Tonight." Fortunately, Penny was not catching the reference to our canvas boudoir.

"Then you feel something for me," I said. "You like me better than a vibrator."

"Of course. I'm human," she said.

"Well, if you're so goddam human, why do you turn your alleged boyfriend into a cuckold. At least, with me, you're semi-honest."

"It's not like that," she said.

"Of course not. Because you're liberated. Listen, Penny, you can do whatever you want as far as I'm concerned. But you don't want love; you just want something that's handy. And you don't know the difference. You're just waiting for the day when you can change your name from Ms. Lutrell to Mrs. Stempian."

"I don't want to get married. I can't deal with that right now."

"You don't exactly want to go out on your own, either. The trouble with you so-called liberated college women is that you don't really have a case. You're all on the take from those good old male chauvinist fathers of yours. All you really want to do is adopt all the worst traits of the men you're supposed to be freeing yourself from. And do you want to know something, Penny? You've made it. You're a real prick. And you can take *that* back to your Social Psychology class and discuss it."

The ad boys at the next table cheered and so did several others. My finger had risen into the air along with my voice, and it was in this frozen pose that I watched Penny stand up from the table. First her napkin hit me, and then the gin and tonic. Even in her wrath, her logic was inverted. I stood up without drying my face and started to go after her, but the valley of turned heads between me and the door stopped me. I instantly mused over the fact that, yet again, *another* one of my dates had stormed out of a restaurant and left me to pay the bill. Then I sat down.

As I landed heavily on the seat of the chair, the waiter laid down a double Scotch in front of me. I picked it up and drank it. Big Ed and Bagger got up and stepped over beside me. They picked up my chair and carried me over to their table. At once, I was back among old familiar faces, and I came to.

"Don't worry," Bagger said, "We've all lost accounts like that. I remember the time Sid Gravert stood up and pissed all over my art work after laying it out on the client's carpet. He was a man of few words.

"Yeah, you were superb, Phil. Take it from a guy who's had three wives go bad on him," one of the Dodge Boys said while the other one nodded.

"Never come down to their level," Feiny chimed in, "Always show them that you have more options open than they have charge accounts---whatever that means. Did I ever tell you about the time I picked up a female impersonator at the Giants game at the stadium? Danced with her all night before I found out. And do you know what? He was the best date I ever had. Didn't regret a minute of it. Wish I could get fooled like that again."

"Yeah," I said. "You're right. I wish I could be fooled like that again. Listen. That was *college* action, fellas. Can you beat that? This broad just walked out on *me*. She couldn't understand why I was never serious. 'Serious?'

I told her, 'I can be just as serious as the next guy.' And then I make the mistake of looking over at Bagger, here; and see him wearing an orange peel like buck teeth; and Big Ed's doing his napkin-folded-like-a-bra schtick. I'm telling you, no more nineteen year olds for me. From now on eighteen is tops. I'm gonna start hanging out at Baskins and Robbins or FAO Schwartz where you can meet some *real* women. These old college age troopers are too crusty for me. You know what I want? I want a young nymphomaniac---but from a good family. Am I right? A nymphomaniac who's a shut-in; a slut who's leads a sheltered life. I want a nympho virgin, see, because I'm very strict about those things.

I spent most of the afternoon there at Clarke's with the guys. It was Friday, and there was nothing else to do No one wanted to go back to work so late, or go home so early. What can I tell you ? We've all wasted better days.

BRIGHT LIGHTS, SELF-PITY

You're walking around New York like a total idiot. Nothing satisfies you. You satisfy nothing. You sound like Holden Caulfield turned private dick. Sort of a smart-ass with a hangover. You do everything but wash. No one seems to care. No one seems to notice that your style smacks of Anne Beattie on Quaaludes. No one cares. Not even you. Hell, you don't even know if the "you" you use is singular or plural. That's the goddam beauty of the piece.

The depression is coming. You decide that what is needed is some drugs. You decide to drop some good, old-fashioned acetylsalicylic acid and let those A's run amok in your bloodstream while you try to figure out if you'll be ready when the depression actually arrives.

The sludge off Atlantic Beach will be landing any day now. It was created by dumping all the filth they could find in New York into the same six square miles of ocean off New Jersey for the last fifty years. Now it is coming back. People are worried. Will the sludge be able to adjust to life in the big city?

If you look where you spray as you apply your "Sure" deodorant, you'll get lung cancer. They're sure. In fact, aerosols alone are effectively ending life as we know it on this planet. Not with a bang or a whimper, but with a p-s-s-s-t.

A young derelict lurches toward you at the corner of Broadway and 72nd Street. He asks you for neither your money nor your life.

"Could you recommend any colleges that might be right for me?" he says. You tell him that you cannot think of one. You avoid him gingerly by walking sideways like a spider. But all the time you cock a weather eye at him. He poses the same question to the truncated man behind a newsstand. The man inquires as to the level of the derelict's SAT's.

You return to your apartment. You contemplate the sludge and the ps-s-s-s-t Will they reach you even in the safety of your de-controlled hole in the wall? Next door there is a bomb scare.

The bomb scare occurs in a building that once housed a priests' haberdasher that went out of business after Vatican II and the advent of the "what's happenin'" liturgy. Now the building houses the embassy of an emerging nation, but it still looks like a store, an empty store. You can look through the window and see a well-swept embassy. There is never anything or anyone there except for a janitor (a holdover from the haberdasher days) who sits and stares out of the widow. His legs and hands similarly crossed. He looks not unlike one of those wax museum loss leader items; the kind outside on the sidewalk with a heaving chest to simulate breathing.

After the bomb scare, two policemen from Midtown North are assigned to the embassy around the clock in order to ward off an international incident. All the policemen of Midtown North look like the old Oakland A's dressed in blue, but the moustache look has turned gay now, only they don't know it. A carload of short FBI men arrive in an unmarked car. The car is so unmarked that even the Midtown North boys don't recognize it. The FBI men pile out of their car wearing dirty raincoats and short blond hair. --- like fraternity brothers at the end of a road trip. The FBI men are mostly interested in the whereabouts of an all-night coffee shop. The agent who rides shotgun keeps his hands in his pockets and approaches one of the uniformed policemen.

"Loose packed black powder, right?" he says.

"That's what it was,' the cop says.

"Figures," the FBI agent says. He gets back in the car with the others, and they drive off. The cop turns to you.

"They know what the story is," he says.

"What's the story?"

"The country what runs this here embassy ain't got a pot to piss in. Let's face it. So they go and set their own bomb, see? Then they discover it themselves and call it in. Now they got two uniformed cops outside their establishment twenty-four hours a day. Makes their chickenshit country look like a threat. Makes them look busy. You get my drift? And what's it cost them? A couple of cents for some black powder and a shoebox. And what's it cost you and me? Plenty.

"I never thought of it that way," you say.

"You *got* to think of it that way," the cop says. "These days you gotta offset everything. Even someone like a country is looking to cut a few corners."

You nod and scuff the pavement with your shoe. The younger of the two cops does the same. "Yeah, you're right," you say.

"What's this guy like inside the restaurant here? Think he'd give us any coffee?" the cop says. "Or maybe a bun in the morning?"

"I don't know," you say. "Maybe the FBI will bring some back."

The next morning a telephone repair man comes to fix your phone.'

"This here is your battered phone syndrome," he says.

"Why would you say a thing like that?" you say

"Your bell housing has been beaten about the dial and cradle in a senseless manner. And it was done with a semi-blunt instrument.

"Like the handy receiver, for instance?" you say.

"Could be," he says, holding the phone and the receiver as if he was making a call. "After all, one is attached to the other with your standard self-coiling cord." He studies the damage for a few more moments. "Is this a business or a residence?"

"Residence."

"You live alone or with another party?" he says.

"Neither."

"Because that's normally a reason for this type of malfunction. That is to say when one party rips the phone out of the wall as a conversational gambit and throws it across the room at another party to underline a particular point. Or worse." he says.

"Yeah. Or worse. Like *not* ripping the phone out of the wall and trying to call Information."

"Why would you say a thing like that," the phone man says.

It is my contention that the phone company hires the most obtuse people available from the labor pool to man, or, shall we say, 'person' the Information lines."

"Fully half our operators are assigned to the information board as it is," he says.

Consider this," I say, "The number of information calls handled is a direct function of the number of operators available times the square of their intelligence as reflected in the formula, $C=OS^2$ where "C" is the number of calls, "O" is the number of available operators, and "S" is their smarts. Thus, by increasing the brain power of your operators by a factor of 2, you can reduce the number of needed operators by four or increase the number of calls handled to the second power. *Cabish?*"

"True, the phone man says, performing a dialoplasty and bellectomy on the instrument. "But let us investigate that further. Your equation is well taken. The point here is that an arithmetic increase in operator intelligence will produce a geometric increase in the number of information calls. Since Information is now a revenue producing service of the phone company, it is to our advantage that we maintain the lowest possible efficiency level while still providing a service that can still be identified as "Information. To wit: The company is thinking of phasing out the trainables who now answer the phones, and installing two, three, and four-year- olds in their place and charging daycare fees to the parents. Thus, when you call Information, it will be not unlike calling your brother's house on a Sunday morning and having his young daughter knock the receiver off the hook and then proceed to say the word "stink" twenty-seven times in a row.

"And for this they are charging us?" you say.

"Most certainly," the telephone man says addressing the transmitter innards with his snub-nose pliers. "Because there is a charge, there is a revenue stream incentive. Consequently, the company will subject the daycare kids to early retirement and hire muti-lingual graduate students from Barnard. Then, as your question indicates, the number of revenue producing calls will rise to the geometric power of the simple increase in operator intelligence. We will have revenue up the ass. It's all been figured. The phone company has an actuary department.

You wonder about all the products housed in aerosol cans. Do any replenish the soul? Is Silly String worth the destruction of the lifesaving Ozone high above your head? And Cheez-It, and Reddi-wip, and Fix-a-Flat, and spray paint for graffiti? Are ultra-violet rays cooking your brain so that, now, you cannot even think of what it is that might be killing you? Is Easy-Off the Warfarin of the human race?

A Puerto Rican gentleman arrives to paint your apartment.

"Can you do the molding, too?" you ask.

"Das extra," he says.

"Oh."

You try to make friends with him to demonstrate that you are a good fellow, hoping this will inspire him to put pride in his work and a second coat on the doors.

"The doors could use a second coat," you say.

"Das extra," he says.

He picks up everything you own and moves it once. When he pauses momentarily over your latest copy of "*Gleanings in Bee Culture,* you say, "I subscribe to that because I thought it was some sort of sex thing. You know what I mean? I thought it was code for something freaky."

He laughs inappropriately.

Then he says, pointing to a picture of a stern beekeeper in pith helmet and veil, 'You keep de bees right here?" He waves a finger around your semi-painted, two-room apartment.

"Oh, no," you assure him. "It was a mistake. See? No bees. No bees"

"Si," he says, and tosses the magazine on top of the others. Even so, you think you have made some sort of connection.

"Will you help me put the books back on the bookshelves? you ask.

"Das extra," he says and frowns philosophically, as if somewhere it is written, and he is powerless to alter or amend it.

Your father calls on the telephone. You stand as if summoned, saluting an imaginary colonel with the receiver.

"Here's our plan," he says. You hear him thumbing through the tiny appointment book he carries in his billfold. "This is the weekend we're going up to Block Island with the Cardinal and two monsignors."

I heard about that. Do you think they'll like it?"

"Oh listen. It'll be great," your father says. "These guys like to get away to some place where they can relax. We're doing it for them. But you're invited if you want to come up. There's plenty of room."

"My apartment's being painted," you say. "I'd better stay here." You look over at the Puerto Rican gentleman who smiles and waves to you with the paintbrush. He splatters his face with latex acne.

"What color?" your father asks.

"Land O' Lakes," you say hoping it will pass. You don't want to explain to him that you had to produce a quarter pound of butter for the Puerto Rican man to mix and match with.

"Great!" you father says with energy. "Who's paying for it?"

"The landlord is. He owes it to me."

"Fine," he says. "What else?"

"Not much. I started collecting unemployment today."

"You ought to be careful about that. It's against the law, you know. I don't think someone like you is eligible."

"I may not be eligible, but I deserve it. Anyway, nothing will happen," you say.

"Two things will happen," he says. "First you'll go to jail. And then you 'll go to hell."

"Actually, I just *filed* today. I haven't collected anything. I just went down to see if I had enough weeks."

"You make too much money."

"Just trying to keep body and soul together, Dad."

"Well, cheerio," your father says and hangs up without letting you say goodbye. You put the phone down and stand at ease.

"Would you like lunch or something?" you say to the painter.

"Yes," he says.

"Like, maybe, a hamburger from the joint downstairs?"

"Yes," he says.

"Or a cheeseburger?"

"Si."

"You want both a hamburger *and* a cheeseburger?"

"Das right," he says, expertly rolling on the paint.

"And to drink? Do you want a beer, milk, or coke?"

"Dat would be nice," he says.

"Everything?" you say.

"Okay."

"You want a beer, a milk, and a Coke," you say carefully.

"Si. Das it."

You go downstairs and get a hamburger, a cheeseburger, a beer, a milk, and a Coke. You spend $42. 47 and buy nothing for yourself because it is too expensive. You come upstairs and give the Puerto Rican man his food and watch him unwrap it with the certainty of a man who eats like this often.

"You turn on de *telebision*?" he asks.

"Sure thing," you say jumping half-way to the set before he has finished his request.

"I watch my story."

"Your story?"

"On de *telebision*. Das the one," he says as the picture comes up on a soap opera. Everything seems to happen at the right time for this man as if my haphazard offers are part of some omniscient schedule of his.

You call your mother.

"I wish you'd come up to the island and give us a hand with these priests and the Cardinal."

"My apartment is being painted. I'll come if it gets finished in time.

"Bring a jacket and nice pants and some shoes. Please. For me.

"What?" you ask.

"For the Cardinal," she whispers.

"Your mother wants you to bring a shirt to wear for the Cardinal," your father says from another extension. He hangs up.

"On Block Island?" you ask.

"I know," your mother says. "But after all."

"Is the Cardinal there right now?" you ask.

"That's right," she says cheerfully. "We're just about to leave. We'd love you to come."

"You're really going all out for these priests, aren't you?" you say

"Well, your mother says, "Why not? It isn't every day."

"I never thought the old man would make a move like this for anyone."

"Oh, he's very excited. Really. He's tickled pink."

"Neat," you say and hang up.

The Puerto Rican gentleman finishes panting the small bedroom. You begin to move everything from the living room back into the bedroom.

"Do you know anyone who could come in and clean this up for me?" you ask.

"My wife, and her sister, and her friend clean de whole place for you," he says.

"How much?" you ask.

"They clean here and the other room, and it cost you, maybe, seventy-five dollars," he says.

"Will they clean the bathroom?"

"Das extra."

"How about "100 dollars and they clean everything," you say

"Sounds okay to me," he says. "I paint. They clean."

"Why don't you have them come and start on this room tomorrow and then finish up the rest when you do?"

"He points to the phone. "I call," he says. He speaks in Spanish for a long time and then hangs up.

"Eight o'clock. Everyone right here," he says, pointing to where he is standing on the drop cloth.

You call your friends who live on Park Avenue. The thrift sale they are running in their co-op has been cancelled because they are having trouble meeting the electric bill. A divorcee and her daughter have moved in with them after the break-up of the divorcee's latest affair. They ask you to help her move. It takes one trip. She brings two suitcases and four paper bags full of remnants of a vigorous four moths' siege of LI-FO kitchen cupboard inventory. Red Cross Salt, a box of A & P book matches, several half bottles of catsup, Knox gelatin, Worcestershire sauce, Cup –a-Soup, lunch box size Bumblebee tuna, olive oil, and two bottles of champagne.

The divorcee's daughter has a new pet. Her old pet, a small, unattractive dog, was dissolved along with her mother's latest relationship. Her new pet is called "Guatti." It is the perfect pet for its time.

"It has two heads so it doesn't need any paper," the little girl says. "It doesn't have any legs so you don't have to walk it.

"You just take him for a drag three times a day," you say.

"And he smells nice," she continues. "Guatti doesn't make any noise, and he's so soft and cuddly that you can play with him in bed when the lights are out."

Guatti is a six inch wad of cotton that was born out of the top of a new Flintstones Chewables" vitamin bottle.

You walk down to Bradley's Restaurant. Jimmy Rowles, there, tells you that Lester Young spoke in a strange tongue that was fully understood by no one but him.

"Give me an example," you say.

"Hello ma, I went again," Jimmy says. "It means a total bust, a failure, a washout. You know, 'Hello ma, I went again.'"

Jimmy shrugs and goes back to his chopped steak. After a few bites he continues. "It happened in Chicago. Prez and I were waiting in Prez's dressing room when the janitor came in and said that someone had stolen his mop and bucket. 'Hello ma, I went again.' That's how Prez described it when the janitor left shaking his head."

You leave Bradley's shaking your head.

You walk over to the West Side. You meet a psychologist at the Four Brothers' restaurant who is looking for some work on the side.

"My practice is down," he says. "It's just not generating the kind of cash I can depend on. So I was thinking of maybe something like dance instruction or massage. I've been told that I'm good at both. But only on the side. After all, I can't take too much time away from my patients."

You tell him that depression, either economic or psychic, is supposed to be good for the headshrinking business. You try to quote him a variation of your Information Operator Intelligence Equation. You try to establish a technical index of leading indicators. He looks at you blankly. He is too depressed to bank on elf talk.

You ask him why he has called you. You and the, now, psychologist had not seen each other for more than 20 years.

"Two memories came to me," he says. "One was when we were having an underwater swimming race, and you brushed by my leg after I had come up for air. The other was when we were sitting in a pile of leaves in th backyard watching the clouds, and my brother frightened us from behind."

You tell him what you know of the freelance dance and massage businesses, and you part. As he walks up Broadway, you notice he is wearing a matching tam-o'-shanter and muffler ensemble. It makes him look top-heavy.

You turn in the opposite direction and walk downtown. You think of all the group therapy sessions in progress at that moment on the West Side. You think of the brooding old buildings filled with Jewish psychologists and their wives, and the mustachioed film makers getting it together with comic versions of their mothers. You stop for the light. The traffic sign on the corner flashes "Ask/Don't Ask." Hello ma, I went again.

The next morning, Saturday, the Puerto Rican gentleman, his wife, her sister, and their friend all arrive at eight o'clock sharp. The doorbell rings many times before you realize that you must wake up, get out of bed, and let them in. More acetylsalicylic acid.

When you open the door the three women giggle at your boxer shorts. The Puerto Rican gentleman beams as if he had just produced three women for a night of high-jinx. They all move past you into the apartment. The man speaks quick, but authoritative, Spanish to the women.

"Would you like some coffee or toast or...?" You open the icebox, "....Or eggs?" you say.

"Yes," they say. You remember the luncheon order of the day before. You decide that guests do not deserve a menu.

"Eggs any style?" you ask, with the attitude of an Assistant D.A. unleashing an entrapping conundrum for a hostile witness. Your eyes close slightly.

"Das nice," they all say. You've caught them now. You decide to make only the most perfunctory of scrambled eggs using half 'n' half instead of heavy cream and round off the meal with raison bran. If they want English they must ask for it. You pick up your Peugot Freres coffee grinder with its clear plastic cover. It looks like a chalice. You carefully measure, grind, and spoon the grounds into the filter. Then you quietly pour the hot water through. Coffee miraculously appears in the bottom half of the hourglass.

You do a walk-through with the ladies in the apartment while the man prepares his paint. The apartment is not big deal: two 9' X 12' rooms in a Brownstown that houses twelve apartments and a hamburger stand. Your kitchen is in one of the closets; your clothes are in the other. But the Puerto Rican ladies assume a posture and mien reserved for entering the nave of St Peter's. They stand in the middle of the living room still touching one another.

"Eeet's so big," one of them, says.

"Not really," you say. "Just two rooms. See?" You open the door to an identical room where you were, of late, sleeping.

"You live here alone?" one of them says. He hands are folded across her stomach. She looks up from under her humbled brow. You are embarrassed. They are acting like peasants brought into a palace. You wonder if they are serious.

"All alone," you say cheerfully. "Just me. Knocking around here like a marble in a bathtub."

You all walk into the bedroom. They all catch sight of the king-size bed at once. A triple inhale occurs.

"Oh, *mira*," one of them says reverently in a very un-subway–like tone. You sleep here?" she says.

"That's right."

"Eeets just for you?" she says.

"Sure," you say. Suddenly the bed looks decadently large to you. The Puerto Rican lady relays this information to her friends who are taking it all in like the Three Magi. They work it over in Spanish.

"All alone," one of them repeats.

"Eeets so big."

"I guess so," you say. "It *is* big. But, what the hell?"

Then they spot the small single bed up against the other wall.

"You sleep there, too?"

"No, That's for my brother."

Now they nod. It is the first indication of real comprehension all morning.

"Si. Your brother," they all say. Then one of them breaks off to attend to the bed.

"*Eeeets* so big," she says. "Just for your brother."

You are convinced they are up to something. You turn back to the other room, the one where the Puerto Rican gentleman is painting. You look back to see the women standing around the single bed, now, as if it were a fallen hero to be dressed. Then you think that, perhaps, you are jaded. Perhaps the bedroom resembles a marina of beds, or, at least, a flat top and a destroyer escort. Maybe.

You get right to the eggs and raison bran. The man yells at the ladies in short bursts of Spanish, and they seem to move a little faster.

While they are eating you call Block Island to see how things are going.

"Well," your mother says, "I guess we've caused quite a stir. The planes couldn't fly us across from Westerly so the Coast Guard took us across.

"The Coast Guard?"

"Listen, dearie, your father was in a state. We drove down to point Judith, and he was going to charter a fishing boat when he spotted the Coast Guard. He asked them if they would like to do a favor for an old Cardinal; and, to tell you the truth, I think they thought it was going to be Stan Musial. I don't think the Coast Guard is supposed to make that much fuss over Catholics. Then, when the Cardinal stepped on board, he dropped his ring in the water.

"The one you kiss?"

"You said it. Well, of course, then the commander, or whatever he was, felt responsible for these clerics. So, first he got some frogmen to get right on it, and then he took us over to Block Island though the pea soup. It was a large cutter and turned out to be a nice boat ride. But I thought your father was going to lay down right there on the dock and, God forbid, never get up when that ring went over the side. The frogmen found it about four hours later and flew it over in a PBY. They were still in their wet suits when they landed.

As your mother speaks, you have a vision of the Cardinal flanked by the two *monsignori,* all in full skirts and red caps, standing on the prow of a United States Coast Guard cutter, braced against the wind.

"Your husband, my father, is taking all this pretty seriously," you say.

"Honey, after all, it *is* the Cardinal. It's quite special."

"How's Dad's health?"

"The nitroglycerine is disappearing like M&M's. I think his pacemaker must be feeding off the Niagara Grid and Big Allis by now. God help us if we have a brownout. There's an awful lot of claptrap involved in this sort of thing, and your father is lugging all of it. Sometimes four trips to and fro."

Don't they help? I mean, at least the monsignors? What are you calling each other anyway?"

"I'm sure that they *would* help, but dear, they don't know what to *do.* These three men between them don't even know how to mix a drink. If it isn't water and wine, honey, forget it. Although they did fall on that case of Laffite your father brought up here like a fumble, but God, don't ask them to make a scotch sour.

"You know, your father never speaks to me civilly anymore, so it's about the same between us. Although

I think now he's calling me by whatever I have on. Like 'Hey Halston.' or 'For God's sake, Lacoste, will you bring me my tea?' He threw his arm around the Cardinal and said, 'Look, we're going to be up on this island for three days together. What should I call you?' 'Call me You Eminence,' the Cardinal said. It was a big disappointment for your father. I think he thought he could call the Cardinal, 'Red,' or something. After all, they've known each other for twenty-five years at least. I thought the whole thing was a little arch, if you ask me. Even the monsignors wouldn't back down. We call them 'Father.' And I've been calling your father, 'Father' recently. So I guess with Your Eminence calling himself, 'His Eminence,' it makes things a little less confusing. But not much."

"Are you happy?" you ask.

"Your father is in seventh heaven," she says. "I think he feels that he's captured the bird of paradise and is getting a leg up on the rest of the faithful. We're all very happy. I wish you were here. But on second thought, it's just as well you're not. You wouldn't wear a coat and tie, would you?"

"Not hardly," you say. "Not on Block Island."

"I thought so," your mother says. You hang up

"Why not paint the windows semi-gloss and the walls flat?" you say to the Puerto Rican man.

"Das extra," he says without taking the half cigarette out of his mouth.

"Did the landlord tell you that when he contracted you or did your boss? Which is it?" you ask.

Now the cigarette comes out of his mouth. He flicks the two-inch ash into his trouser cuff. He appears to be really trying to help. "Sometimes the boss," he says. He is speaking in Zen koans.

You go outside. It is a fine Saturday so you walk downtown to the "Divine Flame Rest." on Park Avenue South for something grilled and holy. After the counterman hands you your Divine Deluxe with a side of fries, he whispers, "Have you ever performed a totally self-sacrificing act?"

Your mouth is full of sesame bun. You look at him with wide eyes over the top of the hamburger. You shake your head, "no." You notice that when you hold your Divineburger with two hands, it looks like a meaty host in the hands of a consecrating priest. You wonder about the look of transubstantiation. If you could see with the eyes of St Francis, would the host actually become a Big Whopper between the fingers of the priest as he whispers the right words over the bread?

You walk from the Divine Flame to Bobby Gleason's Gym. Bobby is there along with another man who looks enough like Bobby so that his main function appears to be telling people that he's *not* Bobby Gleason and then pointing to the man who is. You pay your ten dollars at the door because there are no exceptions to the rule. "Everyone pays," the sign says.

Twins are sparring in the front ring. One twin has a process and the other has a natch'l 'fro. Otherwise, you could not tell them apart. They have identical deep ridges where their identical twin noses join their identical foreheads. If you were to meet them singularly, you would think that the ridge was a boxing wound. However, when you see them together, you understand that the ridge is a feature.

Each of the Twins is called "The Twin" on the boxing cards, such as Freddie "The Twin" Ramos and Miguel "The Twin" Ramos. Everything about them is the same except for their hair and their overcoats. Miguel, "The Twin" is partial to a fur collar offsetting his dandy konk job. Only Bobby Gleason himself knows that one twin is a light heavyweight and the other is a heavy middleweight, which is a difference that can be negotiated when setting up a match at the Felt Forum.

The automatic timer is on. Every three minutes the bell sounds. Then there is a fifty second wait. Then a warning buzzer; and then, ten seconds later, the bell rings again. All the boxers working out seem to welcome this arbitrary division of their day. The all punch the heavy bag for a round and then walk in circles snorting for air during the rest period.

Presently, Bobby throws someone out of the gym for giving advice to a fighter at ringside. It is a clear violation of the rules on the wall. "No Advice," the sign says. Nobody argues the decision.

A large white kid with mammoth legs gets in the ring with Jeff "Jersey Slim" Johnson. Johnson is a welterweight. The white kid is an overweight heavyweight. They are practicing knocking each other out and falling down on the mark. "Jersey Slim" is a serious fighter. He fakes about five of these dives and then clocks the heavyweight a good one upside the head.

The kid goes down without moving his feet, his arms outstretched. His gloves clenched around an imaginary nail driven through the "Everlast" on each cuff. He lifts his head only once to view himself pinned to the canvas, to see his dead belly heaving rhythmically. "Jersey Slim" walks around and around the white kid. The bell rings again.

You walk over to Clamente's to get a haircut. Clamente is of the old school. First he puts a tissue paper collar around our neck. Then a white towel bib. And then, with a Roman flourish, he settles the pinstriped barber vestment over your mufti. You don't really need a haircut, but he cleans it up a little and makes it nice. Then he removes the vestments one by one and offers his hand as you step down from the chair. You are ordained, clipped, and defrocked inside of twenty minutes. Clamente follows you to the door holding a mirror to the back of your head until you pay him.

You can smell the paint in the elevator on the way up to your apartment. When you walk in, the Puerto Rican gentleman is standing there in a row with his wife, her sister, and her friend. Both rooms look painted and cleaned.

"Eeets all finished" he says. The ladies giggle and each one covers her mouth with her hand.

You look into the bathroom, and it has been "Comet-ized" until it is gritty and shiny. Even the tub. You wonder if the women got into the tub to clean it since the sliding doors around it make it impossible to scour with any sort of dignity.

"Looks great. You did a good job. Good cleaning and good painting," you say. "How much do I owe you?"

"One hundred dollars," one of the ladies says.

"Right you are," you say. "A hundred it is." You take five twenties out of your wallet, and then an extra ten. You give the ladies their money. "And here's something for you," you say as you fold the ten and backhand it to the man.

"Gracias," they all say.

Then you turn and see that the little stove and sink in the closet kitchen have not been touched. "What about the kitchen?" you say. "You didn't clean the kitchen."

"They clean it a little," the man says. The three ladies nod. You walk over to the sink. The sink has been wiped by a Handy Wipe that now shrouds the spigot, but the stove still has Chunky Soup spattered all over it.

"What about the stove?" you say.

"Das extra," the Puerto Rican man says somewhat truculently for the first time. He does not look at you but concentrates on mating the ten you just gave him with a large wad of mother bills. "De stove is an extra thing, man," he adds.

"Howe much extra?" you say.

The man and the three women talk briefly in Spanish. "Twenty dollars now or ten dollars tomorrow," he says.

You are unable to follow the logic, but you catch the meaning. They must know that you would prefer to not have to confront them again in the morning. Twenty dollars comes out of your pocket.

"And the icebox and everything," you say, to prove that you know what you're doing.

"We do a top job. Da whole enchilada," he says. Now you know that they are up to something. You give him the extra twenty, and the women begin immediately while he carries out the paint. Only one of the women can fit into the closet kitchen at a time. They take turns as if they were tag-team maids.

You call Block Island to check in. Your father answers.

"How do you feel?" you say

"Great. His Eminence is a great walker. We just did five miles."

"You must have had to go around the island twice." you say

"Well, we make out the best we can."

"Which one of you is older? you say.

"His Eminence. But, at our age, it doesn't make any difference."

"That's the first time I've ever heard you discount your age," you say.

"Well, you know, to a true believer in Holy Mother the Church, other things are important. It matters not. Life passes. It is but a wink in the eye of God. But we're having a fine time. Very relaxed. Here's your mother. I have to go turn over the butterflied lamb in the Weber cooker. I marinated it myself, you know, in my briefcase on the way up. Here's your mother.

"Your father is wired," she says *sotto voce.* "There isn't enough L-dopa in Minnesota to get him through what he's going through.

"True," you say.

"This weekend is the limit. I want to tell you. It is not to be believed.

"It sounds that way. How're the Cardinal and the *monsignori?*"

"They're having the time of their lives. Really."

"But are *you* going to make it?" you ask.

"Oh sure. We met a nice couple. The McGloons. He's an undertaker from Pawtucket."

"McGloon, the Undertaker?" you say.

"I know. Can you stand it?" she says. "Anyway she's a nifty gal, and he's going to fly us back in his own plane."

"Nice," you say.

"They've been a great help."

"I'll call you later," you say.

The Puerto Rican gentleman is bearing down on you with two mason jars of paint the color of a quarter pound of "Land O' Lakes butter.

"You keep theses for touch-up," he says. You are actually "touched-up" already at the thought. He unscrews the cap of each jar. Then he sticks a finger into one and smears a line of paint on the cap.

"This one flat," he says. Then he wipes his finger and dips it into the other jar. Then he smears another line of paint on the other cap. "This one semi—gloss," he says. They look the same to you.

"But you didn't paint with semi-gloss," you say.

"Si. Das extra. But you can do it if you want."

"Touch-up?" you say. "What am I going to touch-up if you didn't paint semi-gloss in the first place?"

"You paint around it, man," he says.

"Oh," you say, looking at the two jars of paint in your hands. They are heavy and strangely warm. This is a joke on you, you decide. Like the year the Massachusetts Prison inmates urinated in thc license plate paint, and the Bay State plates rusted out before they expired. "Thanks," you say and put the jars down on your wormwood writing desk. You consider washing your hands.

The ladies have finished the kitchen. One of them keeps going back for just one more wipe at the stove for a final burnish. Like a shoeshine man fixing the right gleam on the toe of a cordovan.

The Puerto Rican gentleman waves grandly, describing a large circle above his head.

"Eees all yours," he says.

"Thank you very much. It looks good. It really does. Honest to God," you say.

They back out of the door with small Chinese shuffle steps. You follow them into the hall; and when the elevator door opens, it is full of equipment. You smile and wave at them after they line up rather formally inside the elevator. The closing automatic door wipes them from your view.

As the elevator descends you hear them all speaking Spanish faster than you have heard them speaking before. You go to the elevator and listen with your ear pressed to the elevator doors. They talk that way until they reach ground floor, and you can hear them as they unload. Then they all laugh. They have never laughed before as a group. The elevator door on the ground floor finally closes all the way, and you hear nothing.

You remain there with your hands and ear flat against the elevator door. Silence. Then, from behind you, you hear the click of your neighbor's peephole. You walk back to your apartment pretending you didn't hear it, pretending you don't know he's watching you. You are carefully nonchalant.

At eleven that evening, your mother calls.

"It's marvelous," she says. "They're going to concelebrate a midnight mass right here in the living room. In front of the fireplace. They're using the butcher block from the kitchen for an altar. It's the only thing in the house that's the right height. The monsignors are going to concelebrate with the Cardinal, and the whole island is coming over for drinks afterward. And eggs, I guess. I don't know. What do you serve after a midnight mass in your own winterized summer house? We are, after all, fifteen miles at seas, so I don't suppose it has to be too fancy.

"I'm going crazy as you can probably tell. I have to do everything. I've been running around here like a chicken with its head cut off cleaning up after everybody. But you know me. I can do more in a room with a piece of toilet paper in my hand than the entire ServiceMaster division of ITT. But I'm not as whacko as your father. He has enough nitroglycerin in him now to blow us all to kingdom come. I'm telling you.

"The islanders turn out for this sort of things in diamonds and Cadillacs, you know. God knows where they get them from. As Tony the gardener would say, it'll be a 'mir-ackle' if we get through this. A 'mir-ackle.' I wish you were here, but I'm glad you're not."

She hangs up. You walk around the apartment and check to see if the Puerto Rican gentlemen and his three ladies have stolen anything. You decide that they must have known that you were going to walk around and check up on them because, not only have they not stolen anything, but they had judiciously preserved every piece of dirt and debris they cleaned up. Bits of paper are stacked neatly on top of other bits of paper, and these little monuments are all over the apartment. Even the garbage itself has been taken out of its can and neatly repacked in a Hefty Bag. Nothing has been lost, only rearranged. Your universe is stable.

The art director for Landlubber pre-washed jeans tells you that while the jeans themselves are manufactured on small, foreign, tropical islands; the actual pre-washing is done right here in the United States. The art director says that people are more apt to buy new jeans that have already been pre-washed.

"It adds about a dollar to the cost of the jeans," she says. "But that's the way people are." The young man who is modeling the Landlubbers is a singles restaurant tycoon. The girl with him is a cherubic blonde, apple-cheeked girl from Oregon. The blonde used to live with the tycoon's brother, but gave it up because she was tired of being a slave.

"I don't clean my bathtub as a safety measure." the tycoon model tells the photographer. The strobe lights pop. "That way I won't slip."

"Then why is you toilet dirty, too?" the blonde says without spoiling her pose.

On the window of the African tourist office there is a neatly taped message written on St. Patrick's Cathedral stationary. The African tourist office is decorated with a stuffed, rampant lion, a photograph of the Nairobi Hilton, some native artifacts, and a model of the Salt Lick

Lodge. The message says, "This is not the St. Patrick's Parish House. The St. Patrick's Parish House is across the street." You look across the street. The St Patrick's Parish House is a newly hollowed-out catacomb beneath the nave of the cathedral. It took workmen six months to fashion the fancy stonework and glass door so that it would look as if there was nothing new about the old St. Patrick's.

You contemplate the sludge. You follow your three year-old nephew into the bathroom to urge him to produce a bowel movement. He requires company. You wonder what the purity of his body has to do with the sludge off Atlantic Beach. Does his labor make him an accomplice? If the sludge came through the door now and encased you both, Pompeii-like, would future archeologists be able to come up with an explanation?

"Look ma, I went again," the child says, pulling up his pants. You point out to him that you are not his mother.

You have become friendly with the exterminator. He has begun arriving earlier and earlier so that now he arrives bi-weekly in the middle of the night. You are the only one in the building who will let him in. You sign the card while he turns on the lights in the bathroom and the kitchen to squirt the poison. He moves like a roach. The poison brings tears to your eyes, but he doesn't notice this.

"Why twice a week all of a sudden? And why the middle of the night?" you ask him.

"The early bird gets the worm," he says. "Only the quick and the strong in the exterminating industry will survive the times we live in."

You have begun to notice that the janitor wears, on the following day, whatever you throw out today. He is forcing an "I-Thou" relationship. You ignore him. You stop throwing anything out. Then a letter arrives from your cousin in Kansas City who is in the garbage business. It is a picture of his wife and three children in front of their incinerator. The postage meter message on the envelope reads, "Your trash is our bread and butter."

You step over the Collier Brothers assemblage that is growing in your apartment. Do they know about the sludge in Kansas City? Will it reach them, too? Why not put ozone in the hair spray to offset the aerosol?

At four o'clock in the morning the phone rings. It is your mother again.

"Are you sitting down or lying down?" she says.

"Lying down." you tell her.

"Are you alone or with others?"

"I'm alone."

"I have bad news for you then," she says. "Your father bought the farm."

"What are you trying to tell me?" you say

"Your father is dead. Myocardial infarction. There is no other way I can say it.

"Heart attack," you say.

"I hope we all go like that. He would have wanted it that way, believe me." she says.

The phone floats in your hand. You are watching yourself receive the call from across the room.

"The Cardinal and the two monsignors con-anointed him as he went out. I held the candles. He died with chrism on his senses and a smile on his lips. What can I tell you? It's not a time for mourning. He was so relaxed. It's the first moment of peace he's had all weekend. If he doesn't make it to heaven, none of us will. Believe me. There was no pain. He was happy as a clam.

"I'll drive up there to meet you," You say

"No. Don't bother," she says. McGloon has arranged everything. He's flying your father, the Cardinal, the two monsignors and me to Flushing this morning. Thank God he has a Beech 18. Think of it. It's as if it was all planned ahead of time.

"Are you all right?" you say

"I'm fine. State of shock. Can't feel a thing, either. I'm telling you. Dying with a Cardinal and two monsignors right there at your side with the Extreme Unction is a once in a lifetime. Or maybe it's one in a million. Whatever. It was very impressive. We should be thankful. Say your prayers."

"Mother," you say, "What about the body? How're you going to handle it?"

"McGloon's taken care of everything. I don't know what we would have done without him. Really. You won't believe this, but he carries a convenience in the plane for just this sort of thing. It couldn't have worked out better."

"What do you mean, 'a convenience'? you ask.

"A cover thing for the body. A bag, I guess. Nothing fancy. You'd think it was from LL Bean to look at it." she says.

"What about the casket?" Shouldn't he be in a casket?" you say.

"That's extra," she says, "McGloon says that's extra."

"Oh."

Christmas comes. The top rated show on Christmas Eve is a three hour broadcast of a log burning in a fireplace. You place your hand on top of the television set. It's warm, but not *that* warm. You stop worrying about the carpet.

You go to the bathroom and look into the mirror. The drink you mixed in front of the fire is still in your hand. You try to make the two sides of your face match.

BEVERLY FROST HAS A PROBLEM

Beverly Frost never met an underling she didn't snub. She'd been on television for so long she thought reality was just a commercial break. She'd had had her hair and make-up attended to by someone else longer than most women are alive. Everything in her world as the nation's most respected news diva was under control and kept safely at bay. That included death, hers and others.

"Death is something other people do, darling," she would say. She meant, especially, rival anchors. It was a good day whenever one of them died.

Her interviews were always about herself; and her "gets", no matter how austere, impossible, or vaunted never rose beyond the level of drop-ins to the penumbra of Beverly's own celebrity.

But Beverly had a problem. Her personal manicurist, maid, and confident had been just diagnosed with terminal cancer. The dear woman had been with Beverly for twenty-five years and was closer to her than even Chewy, her dog. Well, almost closer.

Beverly had originally taken the woman on as a favor to the Shah of Iran who had been fucking her royally even though she was a Saudi, and he was gay. She was that adorable. But just before the Shah got sick, the Shahness, or whatever they called Mrs. Shah, got wind of the affair; and the Peacock Throne was forced to reach out to someone who really knew how to make a deal. In return for the "get" of having the last interview with the Shah before he was overthrown and sent into exile and, ultimately, to his death, Beverly agreed to take his highness' girlfriend off his hands and bring her to America. For Beverly, it was perfect fit. The girl knew how to serve unconditionally and knew only a minimal amount of English.

Sasha (that wasn't her real name but one Beverly gave her because she couldn't remember her Saudi one) had daily manicured Beverly's nails and massaged her hands and feet adoringly like a devoted saint during the twenty-five years she'd been in service. It was an indulgence Beverly allowed herself because it reminded her of her father who would buy his mistresses expensive manicures at The Plaza the same way some other producers would buy their various girlfriends expensive handbags at Gucci. Manicures were harder to trace.

When Sasha got sick, Beverly felt she had to intercede and do <u>something</u> for the poor, dying woman. After all, she was practically part of the family. So Beverly decided to send Sasha back to Saudi Arabia to die among her people. And, best of all, because once in Saudi Arabia, as a woman, she would never be allowed to publish her memoirs. What Beverly had forgotten or, perhaps, remembered only too well, was that "Sasha" had been married to a prominent ambassador in the Saudi foreign ministry while she was wildly fucking the Shah; and, as such, would be executed as an adulteress when she returned home. But Beverly insisted. She ordered Janet, her stylist, to go on a <u>special</u> re-gifting tour of the <u>best</u> Manhattan shops and <u>specifically</u> told her to demand cash this time when she returned the lovely but useless gifts that had been lavished on Beverly during the year by her high-toned friends.

Then she told Lawrence, her manservant, to buy a one-way ticket to Saudi Arabia with the accumulated cash. When she presented the ticket to the, now, failing Sasha; the woman was all the more appreciative because she herself had been the one who had located all the foolish Scully & Scully green leather desk sets, still in their tissues and boxes, and discarded pashimas from Bendels.

Part of Sasha's tears of gratitude were because she had originally feared Beverly would merely direct an anonymous PA to purchase $100.00 worth of CD's as her parting gift as Beverly had thoughtfully done when her personal secretary was rendered a quadriplegic in a car accident. The CD's had arrived, useless, at the hospital while the girl was still in the Bellevue emergency room sans insurance. At least the non-stop coach seat to Ryddai for Sasha came with a meal.

Unfortunately, the cash payment for a one way ticket to the Middle East flagged the dying Sasha as a terrorist, and Sasha was all but water-boarded at JFK before she gave up the name of her former employer and re-gifter. Sasha had been afraid, not for herself, of course, but for the revelation that Beverly had returned so many of her fancy friend's gifts for the cash to get Sasha's cancerous Arab ass out of town. The matter was cleared up by Lawrence on the spot, with the help of Henry Kissinger and Mayor Bloomberg; and Sasha was finally sent on her way out of the country. More importantly, a pending Post headline reading, "Beverly Frost Returns Gifts for Cash!" was summarily quashed.

Upon Sasha's arrival in Saudi Arabia, she was immediately arrested for her thirty year old crime of adultery and condemned to a worse death than the one she was already facing with the cancer. She was sentenced to be beheaded by order of the strict Muslim high court with an additional 200 lashes to be administered beforehand just to teach her a lesson. The only mercy shown was that the Royal Saudi whipper would hold a copy of the Koran under his lashing arm to restrict the severity of the lashes and guard against any rotator cuff injury of his own in the process.

On her way to the chopping block at half-time during a soccer match, Sasha proudly wore an Hermes scarf with Beverly Frost's initials embroidered on it along with Michael Douglas' and Catherine Zeta-Jones' birthday wishes that had been personally given to Sasha by Beverly when Bendel's had absolutely refused to take it back. The Douglas/Zeta-Joneses probably never imagined in their wildest dreams that their carefully thought-out birthday gift would one day end up 10,000 miles away on an executioner's chopping block in a soccer stadium in Saudi Arabia, carefully spread to the side, as the manicurist of their friend, Beverly Frost, daintily laid her head down to be severed. But then, to add insult to that indignity, when the assistant executioner jabbed his pointed stick into Sasha's side in order to make her neck involuntarily extend and stiffen, thus thrusting her head forward to facilitate a nice clean swipe, the sword that followed the poke tore a hole in the scarf and ruined the perfectly good Hermes scarf beyond repair. It was a small price to pay for justice.

Beverly was devastated when she heard the news. The Saudi's, of course, assumed Sasha had stolen the scarf from her esteemed (in Saudi Arabia) former employer because they couldn't believe that anyone would have given away such an expensive item of obvious personal and celebrity value. And so, Sasha died an adulteress and a thief.

The only redeeming news for Beverly upon hearing and devouring every detail from King Abdullah himself was that, fortunately, Beverly could be comforted in the knowledge that dead manicurists write no "tell-alls".

RUMFORD

She placed two glasses of Scotch in a floral handbag she incongruously carried this evening, even in August, for the express purpose of getting her Dewer's upstairs without being seen by her husband who sat, still, at the dining room table.

"I've had it!" she declared when she rose from the table in disgust and final resignation after fifty years of intellectual isolation and one-upsmanship.

Did he notice? Did he realize she was gone? Gone upstairs. To bed? To drink? Did he know she was no longer there? Anymore. He resumed his mantis-like manipulation of a grandson who had inexplicably chosen to live with them rather than brave the siren song of New York below 14th Street.

Upstairs, in her dressing room, the guest room where she had set up shop as a permanent guest in her own house, she carefully unpacked the Scotch, one glass at a time, careful not to spill any of the light brown liquid into the handbag. It was still about detection, not care. With the two Old Fashioned glasses safely on the bedside table, she tossed the purple and white purse unceremoniously on the upholstered chaise lounge in the corner. Then she sat on the edge of the bed and took a small sip of her treasure. The warm liquor burned down her throat and spread through her body. She smiled for the first time that night. This, alone, was hers.

"It's time for bed!" he proclaimed with the certainty of a despot. Then he stood up from the dining room table, and by so doing, signaled an end to the meal and his games. There was almost an audible, "All rise", when he did so. The grandson silently cleared the dishes.

Something had happened at the dinner table, but it was not clear what. To anyone. Some event, a passage, a major shift in the landscape, a sea change, a choice. Something. Nothing would be the same again--- even though it had been the same for so many years, so many lifetimes. Had she really "had it"? Had what? Enough? Just enough? Did she win? Had she finally cleansed herself of her sin? Was she now exonerated? Was it over?

Without transgression there can be no dominance. Isn't that what God is all about? And kings and queens? So, too, with the husband who had stayed, newly married to her. Not because he loved her but because he needed her to serve him, as God needed man to remind Him that He was, indeed, God. It was an unholy relationship.

But the adulterous act had produced a son, a beloved boy, his dead best friend re-incarnated, springing up in their very midst to flower and befriend him once again. Together. As if by some gift from on high. It was as if, by that breach of marriage vows---an exception he would have freely granted had he known of their desire---his lost friend was returned from the dead. But this magic, this magic blessing that only he could give and, by so doing, save everyone in the process, this accommodation that he had easily granted had made him what he was this night: father, primogenitor, sole survivor, imprimatur, grand provider. A force to be guarded, coddled, worshiped and reckoned with for all his beneficence. And, yet, she had "had it".

Now, alone upstairs, finally, with her friend, she finally felt free.

"Your next!" he used to say randomly, referring to nothing. I always took it literally, as if I was next for whatever. I would wait. But nothing happened next. I was certainly next, but for what? Nothing. Just next. Eternally waiting. Summoned but never engaged. Called but not needed. Just next. I was next. But not for anything good. I wasn't next for a reward or an opportunity. I was next for an unknown obligation. Something difficult and distasteful, no doubt. A punishment, perhaps, or a chore. Eternally next in line for some debt to be paid. But for what, I did not know.

"You're next!" he would say. Just to keep us on our toes. But now, it seemed, *she* was next. And then him.

And then the rest of us. I wondered if he ever included himself as being next. I came to find out we're all next, aren't we? Waiting in line for what, even God doesn't know. Just next. It's part of being human. Animals don't have any sense of next as they wait patiently in the slaughterhouse line. They know nothing of next and don't want to know. Only us. I wanted to know what I was next for but was never told. But I felt I must always be ready, however, because I was, most certainly, next, and I knew it. Forever.

But on this night, she was next; and, perhaps, she knew it and had gone upstairs to *be* next. To get her shit together for everything that was coming next.

"You must tread the winepresses of doubt alone." That was his universal advice when he had none to offer. It was his extra judicial way of saying, "Fuck you and good luck." I used to think there was some hidden truth within those words, some message to be deciphered and applied. But I finally realized that there was none. There was nothing. It solved nothing. You could substitute "treadmill" or "hamster wheel" for "winepresses" and be more on the mark.

She was treading her own winepress of doubt alone upstairs. All alone. She drank her Scotch, without ice tonight because she thought it too prissy to go back downstairs to get some after she had successfully managed her secret transport in the first place. She felt like a heroine in a bad movie where everyone pours brown liquor and drinks it straight from tumblers. Warm booze was had in movies when someone was distraught or a really bad apple.

Strange that the two things I remember as quotes from my father are, "You're next!" and "You must tread the winepresses of doubt alone." We look for truths from our fathers. Words to teach us. Words to show us the way. Words as hand-holds for safety and guidance. "If I fall, I'm finished" he would proclaim later in life. But I don't know, now, whether he was talking about physically losing his balance or, perhaps, a moral lapse, a mortal sin. He would know about that.

The secret died with him, of course, and with her. The secret of the pregnancy in their disjointed life as a townie married to an intellectual on the cusp of a lucrative career. And that secret and that blood would run in the family forever without revelation. It probably had something to do with why he would whistle lightly through his teeth, on the way home from Sunday Mass, "Oh Lord, I Am Not Worthy" while she dutifully drove home the back way from the church to our house. Whistling through his teeth, "Oh Lord, I Am Not Worthy" while reading the Sunday Journal American that he had pulled into the car on his way for that very purpose. The only solace being that the funnies also came with the Journal, and we got them in the back seat and spent our time pondering Mark Trail, Prince Valiant, The Katzenjammer Kids and Blondie while he, in the front, whistled about not being worthy and read the news, folding the paper as he did.

He would be taken daily to the post office for the mail and would read it silently on the way home. Then he would exit the car leaving the torn envelopes and junk mail in the well of the front seat for her to pick up after the screen door on the back porch had slammed shut with a loud, "Thwack", announcing his exit from the scene.

We called her by a corruption of her first name that had been passed down from the oldest son, the one he had rescued her for. The origin of the name knowable only after fifty years of living with them and hearing his constant calls to her--- like an armchair codger in a private club summoning a waiter. So, only because the baby boy heard his mother's name called so often, and with such urgency and insistence, demanding her presence, did the toddler equate the word---her first name---with the stuff of survival and comfort usually associated with, "Mother".

She was never a wife, but always a hand-maiden, and he treated her that way right up until the night she exited up the stairs with the two Scotches in her purse. She had had it. She had had waiting on him hand and foot, the more so as they grew older. But she, in his mind, had always remained eternally nimble and young enough to do his bidding.

She was not as besotted with the oldest son as he was. Namely, because he was the symbol of her sin. Whereas, for him, the son was living proof of his generosity, the consideration for the contract, and the reincarnation of his best friend. Magic had trumped betrayal. But her redemption had enslaved her as much as it had delivered her.

When the son became sick with a bad heart, inherited from the boy's bloodline---further marking him as the rare gift he was--- he declared that the boy lived under "The Sword of Damocles" because the doctor had said this beloved son, now a man, would most certainly face an early death. But it was he, more than his son, who felt the approaching edge. We were all under the sword, and that sword was threatening to split the charade wide open. Everyone has their own "sword" to deal with in the end.

In the inevitable eulogy, one brother extolled the favored son for his distinctiveness, his otherness, and his uniqueness as a way of honoring his brother as if those differences that separated him from the rest of the family were of the boy's own making and not the result of the sainted mother's sin.

But this night she sat on the edge of the guest bed not yet ready to go to her own in the next room. Another sip of Scotch. This one soothing and warm with none of the harshness of the first. Like the caress of a warm hand along the length of her body. She felt tired and spent. She had nothing left to give. The endless march of things to do had finally stopped with nothing left to do.

Death pricked her ear, "I'm coming."

It didn't disturb her or alter her nightly routine in the least. A final thing to do. The nightly routine. Creams, wash, scour, medicate. Why? For what? Must one brush for the grave? Be presentable for the maw of eternity? It was her pride to be so at all times. No matter what.

Ah, the sleep that night, the rest. Her bed as her refuge. The covers drawn shroud-like around her. Peace. It didn't matter that she never finished the Scotch. Her bed had delivered more of the sweet tranquility she sought. Her bed was the friend that never disappointed or betrayed her. Never. Once in her bed, the bed did the driving. Finally.

As she lay waiting for the shadow of sleep to silently sweep over her like a swift, wind-blown cloud, she thought of her children, all of them. Happy that her secret would almost die with her. This relaxed her beyond anything she'd felt since the early days. He came in and went to his bed, content in his primacy. They slept, as if in adjoining plots.

Secrets have a way of rearing their heads like long-buried bones eroding into the sunlight---unexpected but rarely surprising. Perhaps, memory comes to you *after* you die. Perhaps, memory is not for the living but for the dead---the memory of one's life and the lives around you. That is what endures. And much longer than the fleeting memory of those left behind. She longed for the feeling of her memory wrapping around her like a cocoon of thoughts. She wondered what she would remember; and, more significantly, what she would forget after she was dead. Was it worth it? Yes. No one would know, but *she* would remember. Forever.

The next morning came with its customary call to duty. She arose in pain, but not enough to stop her. It was a familiar ailment throughout her entire body---an old friend. A cranky traveling companion that had accompanied her doggedly, but faithfully, for years---a friend that greeted her each morning with a nudge like the snout of a persistent pet.

She was embarrassed only by the fact that she had been born in Rumford, Maine. That embarrassed her. The name, like the place, held no romance, no caché, no hope. It was the same with the County Roscommon in Ireland from whence her ancestors had come. "Nothing good ever came out of Roscommon," she would say as if to include herself. She, no doubt, felt she embodied her low opinion of Rumford and the legacy of Roscommon. It was a heritage she embraced, even if awkwardly.

The morning routine was more complicated than the evening one. Getting started trickier than finishing. She got out of bed and went into the guest room to begin. Again. Alone in the half light of the bathroom, she looked into the mirror, blotched with time, before turning on the lights. She thought she saw a ghost. Or something. Or someone standing behind her. She turned around, but there was nothing there breaking through the morning gloom but the ancient pink paint peeling off the bathroom wall.

A hot bath would expel the demons inside her body. The water came tumbling out of the spigot like a rumble of fraternity boys falling out of a car. The tub seemed to fill with water all at once. And when she dropped her nightgown, un-customarily, on the mat where she stood with no effort or thought of ever hanging it up, she slipped effortlessly beneath the warm water's embrace and felt, for a moment, as if she were back in her beloved bed.

She exhaled audibly and smiled at her own indulgence. This would cure everything---at least, for the moment. But it made her mind race instead. Thoughts. She thought about the lover who had produced her first child---long dead and forgotten, even by his own patrician family who, at first, were shocked that the lost scion's sole legacy was now residing, unceremoniously, inside her womb. She thought about his quick laugh and quicker temper. The curly hair and rich boy's teeth. He was tall. It was worth it. Look at all it had wrought.

Her brother, lost in the war. Forever smiling and jaunty. The good looking one. The hope of all of them. Foolishly dead and thrown into a ditch in the South Pacific. All that goodness gone. All that hope lost. She thought of his wallet, the one they sent home instead of his body. It was in the house, somewhere, as she lay soaking in the tub. She remembered fingering it privately, endlessly, taking the small papers and coins out of the pockets and putting them back in again. Perhaps he was alive somewhere, still smiling, eyes squinted, confident in the future he deserved.

She remembered growing up in Maine and the summers on Little Ossipee Lake. And the camps, which is what the family cabins that circled the lake there were called. It was a time when she was endlessly fetching---posing in shorts and a white blouse against a tall pine tree, as straight and defiant as she was, her hands clasped behind her back looking confident, but distant, at the camera.

Rising out of the bath, she reached for something to hold onto. "Don't get old," she would say. And at other times, she would describe something of note as being, "Beyond the beyond." But unlike his bathroom, where all precaution had been taken, there was nothing near for her to grasp except the sink, if she could reach it. She pulled a towel off the rack---modesty before safety---and stepped out of the tub as best she could. A robe was nearby. She wrapped that around herself while still wet.

Perhaps, the dead *do* dream. Perhaps, they dream wonderful tapestries woven from their lives and the lives of the people they loved. She thought about what her dead dreams would be like and if she would be content with them.

Then, suddenly, without warning, something broke apart deep within herself. A silent, catastrophic rupture of an internal vessel that brought her to her knees as if she had never stood or walked before. In an instant, she knew everything; not just about what was happening to her, but about what had happened in her life and the bargains she had made. The choices. The sacrifices. She had "had it," and she knew it. Her body had "had it". The house, their house, the one she had correctly identified as a "wife killer" when they first bought it, was suddenly and irrevocably triumphant around her.

There would be no standing. She had to gather all her strength just to remain stricken and humbled on her hands and knees as if in abject supplication. She stayed there on the bathroom floor, feeling her life gush out of her with every heartbeat, until she could catch her breath. Finally, she turned like a dog catching a scent, but when she did, she completely collapsed. She could no longer hold herself up. Her cheek pressed against the cold, checkered tile of the bathroom floor.

But in turning before she had collapsed under the dead weight of her body, she ended up splayed toward the open door of the bathroom and the possibility of the guest room bed close by. No longer able to raise her body off the floor, she forced herself to drag herself on her stomach, her belly filling with blood, out of the bathroom and toward the bed next to the open door. When she got beneath the bed, she grabbed the bedspread she had so lovingly smoothed the day before when she had made it, just as she had made every other bed in the house in order to be in constant readiness for hospitality. She pulled herself up and onto the bed and rolled over on her back, exhausted. She had done it.

He was still in his own bathroom, and the door to their bedroom was closed, so she knew that she would have to wait until he decided to go downstairs to breakfast, the breakfast she was supposed to have made by then---with all its utensils and dishes so strategically placed on the tray each morning he could have eaten his tea and toast blindfolded.

She would wait. Wait as she lay dying on the guest room bed.

She thought about her family, her dead brother, her lover who had died suddenly after swimming in Chesapeake Bay without ever knowing about the pregnancy. And the child who grew uncommonly tall with black curly-hair and looked so much like him that it was as if he were still alive and still young. It was why it had all worked out. Everything. All of it. But now it was her turn to complete the saga.

On the bureau there was an enameled portrait of the Virgin and Child, illuminated in full blue radiance, looking down on her. She glanced at it briefly but did not pray. Then she closed her eyes momentarily and saw nothing but fire as her abdomen filled with blood and began to distend as if she were pregnant again. She was ending as she had begun. Only, this time, death was in her belly instead of the child of his best friend. She would often say, "I didn't hold the lamp" when asked about some scandalous report to indicate her knowledge was, at best, second hand. But in that long ago moment when she lay with her husband's friend, she *was* the lamp; illuminated by the embrace that changed her life. And if anyone had asked her if her firstborn was, in fact, their best friend's child, she would have had to say, "Yes." And, this time, she absolutely *did* hold the lamp.

She waited. What else could she do? She had waited for him, and on him, their entire married life. He never drove. But she did; and upon their engagement, he gave her a car instead of a ring but never followed that up with a diamond. She could drive; but, strangely, she couldn't ride a bike. A large red bicycle with balloon tires that he bought for her during the war, and on which we all learned to ride, would remain, unused, in the garage for years as a reminder of her inability. But, from the beginning, his commitment to her was such a leveraged contract that on their belated honeymoon, a cruise taken years after their marriage and the birth of the child, fellow passengers on the ship thought she was his nurse, not his wife. An ancient Irish aunt would say, "He got the jump on her," and she never recovered.

She waited for him to finish his morning routine and finally open the door to their bedroom to go downstairs for the breakfast she would have lovingly laid out for him. But not this morning.

When he finally emerged and walked past the door of the room where she lay, almost comatose now; she called to him. But no words came from her parched lips. No sound. She desperately called out again. Nothing. He walked past the door and disappeared from sight. She was not surprised. She was resigned to dying alone upstairs while he cursed her absence in the kitchen.

But something had caught his eye. Some anomaly had disturbed his peripheral vision as he passed the door. Something was different. Something was not right. He turned back and then suddenly reappeared, framed in the doorway like a portrait.

She turned her head and gazed at him silently for a beat. His cloudy blue eyes looked at her as he had looked at her when she told him her secret so many years ago. Silence. She needed him to rescue her one more time.

"I think I'm going to die," she said. He knew without knowing and turned immediately and went back into their bedroom to call the ambulance. She could faintly hear him ordering it through the open bedroom door.

She could feel the inconvenience of her impending demise. The disruption. The usurption of his daily routine. He returned after making the phone call and, this time, sat down on the side of the bed with her in a rare gesture of affection and care. Usually, it was she who had forever attended to him.

"Help me," she said.

"I've called the ambulance. I don't know what to do, who else to call, what doctor?"

"Help me," she said again and tightened her grip on his forearm.

"I've done everything," he said.

"Help me get up," she said, now being more specific about the meaning of her request, "Before the ambulance."

Talking exhausted her. She slumped back on the pillow. But then she pulled on his arm again, more desperate this time. He had no choice but to bring her up into a sitting position.

"I must get ready," she said. For fifty years she would dress, with full hair and make-up, in order to drive him two blocks to the train because he was above walking, and she refused to appear at the station in a bathrobe and curlers like some cigarette-dangling housewife who had just rolled out of bed.

But now she chose, for the millionth time, to once again ignore the commonplace and defy custom. She insisted on being presentable even though this time *she* was the one being driven, not him. She would dress for the ambulance.

"Get me up," she asked of her husband. Unaccustomed to providing any sort of physical assistance, he clumsily swept the lower half of her body to the edge of the bed. Then, with his arm around her torso, they stood up together as a joined couple. It was the most contact they'd had in decades.

Once standing, he held on to her and then limped across the room with her as if delivering a clumsy and unfamiliar package. When they reached the bathroom, she became more animated as if in familiar territory and friendlier surroundings.

As the blood continued to pulse into her abdominal cavity, she feebly brushed some rouge across her cheek.

Then, after carefully unscrewing her lipstick, she applied it perfectly in two sure swipes. Then, the wig.

"I need my wig," she said. The wig was a skull cap of hair she had resorted to in order to amplify her thinning locks and cover a nagging bald spot that had plagued her for years like the tonsure of a monk. But when he turned to locate her cherished *accoutrement,* as she would say, he briefly let go of her shoulder. Her one pretense was a fondness for using random French words in conversation as a vague indication that she had a special affinity with the finer things in life. Thus, words like *soupcon, accoutrement,* and *fini,* among others, were sprinkled freely throughout her speech regardless of their incongruity.

But, by momentarily turning away to retrieve her wig and releasing his grip on her shoulder, she immediately began to tilt dangerously away from him like an unstable grenadier. When he turned back, she was close to falling over completely, but he quickly grabbed her and set her upright in front of the mirror, thus saving her from a devastating fall. Now, it was all she could do to set the wig on her head. In fact, she would have said that the effort required for her to get dressed this morning was definitely, "Beyond the beyond."

"I think I have to lie down again," she said which signaled a return trek back to the bed to wait for the ambulance

She was slipping in and out of a coma by the time the ambulance arrived. Then, as she was being loaded into the vehicle, the attendant randomly asked how she was doing. All she could manage was a shrug. That was her goodbye to the world. A shrug. One palm up, eyebrows arched, her mouth flattened into a half smirk of bemused resignation and acceptance. Thus, did she silently comment on the life she'd led and all that she had tried to do. Neither with a bang nor a whimper, but a shrug. As if to say, I did my best. The beds are made. The house is clean. His breakfast tray is set out with its precise placement of essentials. What more could you ask of me?

"She was a bleeder!" the old man would announce at the dinner table the day after she died, as if absolving himself of all guilt and responsibility. He made it sound as if she had had some secret, but voluntary, disorder that he was forced to live with during their life together. He was right, of course. She *was* a bleeder; but not in the way he meant it.

The car was in the garage where she had parked it when I got into it the next day without any anticipation or foreboding. But I was immediately greeted by the familiar, too-far-forward, and cramped position of the driver's seat. Her customary setting. Suddenly, I was flooded with her presence. Her animus was where it had always been, behind the wheel.

I wept as I pressed the lever and moved the seat back for the last time.

THE RING

I would have asked her long ago except that she always got very excited whenever I hinted that it might be a possibility. And if she didn't get nervous, she got mad and thought I didn't respect her. Like the time I said, "Francie, sometimes when I see you, you fire me up so much that I want to get right down and lick the ground.

As far as I'm concerned, I like her. But now that we finally got engaged over this ring, I'm afraid I'll miss something, like the next payment to the First National Trust; and then she'll probably end up marrying the bank.

When I was in the Navy, I learned to type, so that now I can write down a few things that are going on between Francie and me. And if I don't write it all down I'll forget it, and if I forget what it's like at this stage in the game, I sure as hell am not going to remember what it's like when things cool off in fifty-six years. I think too many people forget what a kick getting married is; after payments, kids, and general change of life set in.

Well, it all begins very quietly and usually among friends, or in a lot of little things which have nothing to do with what Francie calls "concubinal bliss." For instance, today Francie and I went downtown a little to buy some underpants for her father. We have been doing things like that for months, things that should be done by her mother, or by Francie in her lunch hour or on the way home from work. When you start making a big deal out of every little thing that has to be done,, like spending all day one good Saturday buying her old man underpants, then it's time you either got in and got out, because you're already in it up to your elbows.

When the engagement happened to me, we weren't buying underpants, but we might as well have been. We were buying ball-point pens for a party between Francie and me, and Frank and Marge, and George and some pig form Portland who was always climbing in the phone booth with him.

Francie is big on games, and for this one she needed six ball-point pens or else she couldn't put it over. Everything is production for Francie when it comes to throwing a party. Like, after dinner she'll only fill the cups halfway with coffee because she hasn't got any of the doll cups especially made for it.

"Look," I say, "Why does it have to be pens? What's this game called, Signing Checks?"

"It's called Battleship, and pens are better," she says.

"But I know a caddy master who'll give me a thousand pencils for free," I say. "You could use a different one for each word."

"Do you want to appear like a bum in front of your brother?" she says.

"I've appeared like worse in front of him, and I don't see why I should start buying ball-point pens for Frank now," I say.

"You don't seem to understand that pens are better for a game you play after dinner," she says.

"I know a better game," I say

"What's that?" she says.

"Dessert," I say, "And all you need is a spoon." We are arguing in the middle of Alfie's stationary sore, and the clientele is taking it for a big laugh.

"Why do you embarrass me every time we go out of the house>" she says.

"I'm not embarrassing you," I say. "I'm trying to educate you."

"Well, don't educate me; just buy these pens," she says.

I pick up six ball-point pens and walk over to the cashier.

"Battleship," I say. "Sounds like a great game. Will it ever replace night baseball, Francie? Do you remember in the old days when all we did was neck?"

This last line I deliver to the cashier, who gives me a look with his eyebrows. Meanwhile, Francie is still shopping around.

"Will that be all?" he says.

"Would you buy me this book?" she says

"What book?" I say.

"This *Sex and the Single Girl,*" she says.

"No," I say.

"Why?" she says

"Because there's no such thing," I say. "It's folklore."

"What do you know about it?" she says.

"In your case, plenty," I say.

"Like what, for instance," she says

"Like, for instance, you're not the single girl you used to be," I say. "And you never were."

So while I pay the man and watch him fumble through eighty paper bags trying to find the right one for pens, Francie storms out to the side walk and stands facing a telephone pole with her arms folded.

When I come out, I can see that she is really fuming, so I 2walk up behind her and put my hands out her belt.

"Don't lock your jaws on me, Francie," I say. "Come on, I'll buy you an ice cream."

"Maybe you'd like to do everything yourself," she says.

"Not a chance, Francie," I say. "You know I'm not that kind of guy, and besides, it's against my religion. But there's nothing that says we can't plan on getting married. We'll announce it here on the telephone pole like everyone else."

Unfortunately, there were a few other things announced on the telephone pole besides love, which didn't make my intentions spear any too honorable. But it was enough for Francie, and I could see her whole body relax. She put her hand behind her neck and smiled like somebody had just taken off her shoes.

"Now what made you say a thing like that, Art?" she says.

"Well, as a matter of fact, "I say, "I said it to keep you off the street. Now let's go home."

"See, I knew you were kidding me," she says, and her mouth turns upside down like I just took a lollipop out of it.

"Who says I'm kidding?" I say. "I'll marry you right here on route two if that'll make you happy."

"Well, do you mean it or not?" Marriage is not for laughs," she says.

"Yeah, I know," I say. "It's forever. Wait a second."

So I walk up to 5he drugstore to think it over and happen to look in the window, and there's a diaper rash display looking back at me. My stomach pops at that for a few seconds, and I turn back down the street. Just before I reach Francie, I reach the department store where they are dressing and undressing the models in the window. Now this appeals to me more than the diaper rash, and I stand there and soak it up a little while I'm trying to decide exactly what to do.

Well, Francie decides it for me, because she comes up and starts rocking back and forth on her shoes. And every time she rocks she gives me s nudge, and every time she nudges I nudge her back, so that in no time at all we're pushing and shoving and leaning up against one another like two kids. Francie gets laughing out loud, and everybody else on the street is getting their kicks watching us. It was very jolly there on the sidewalk.

"OK," I say, "Let's go buy an anklet or a photo-I.D. bracelet."

"That's the nicest thing I've heard in six months," she says, and starts blowing her nose.

Switzer's Jewelry happened to be unfortunately close by, so Francie drugged me around the corner with one hand while she was crying with the other hand.

"Try this girl on for a ring," I say.

"Are you and the young lady interested in an engagement ring?" the jeweler says.

"Not exactly," I say. "But we'd like to buy one." Francie is still crying, but she manages to navigate over to the diamond rack. Looking over her shoulder, all I can see is zeros.

"That one," she says, pointing.

"Which one?" I say.

"If you are interested in a fine stone, perhaps you would like something from our private collection?" the jeweler says going into the back.

"What did you point at?" I say.

"Just the medium-small one on the left," she says, taking a long sniff and then crying it up again. The jeweler comes in with a tray of boxes.

"Perhaps this will suit the young lady, "he says and opens one of the boxes.

There was one of the loudest silences I had ever heard. Francie stopped blowing her nose. What caught us by surprise was that instead of diamond, there was red. And the red spilled out over the box and onto the counter and into her face. Francie reached for it ever so slightly, and the jeweler had it on her finger in a second. Naturally, it was a perfect fit.

It's a ruby," she says. "I love it."

"Put it back," I say.

"How much is it," she says

"Put it back," I say.

"Fourteen hundred and fifty dollars," the jeweler says.

"Put it back," I say, getting pale.

"Oh Art," Francie says. "You can buy it."

"Sure, I can. Then we'll go buy the Taj Mahal so you won't clash," I say.

"If you buy this for me now, you can wait as long as you want before the wedding," she says.

"When I get married," I say, "I want to get married. And not just cash in.

"We can do both," she says.

"I don't make that much money, you now' I say.

"I know," she says; "But then again you're not having that much fun, either."

"We can do both," I say.

I figure it this was. You only live once, and basically it's like buying a Volkswagon, where the only thing that depreciates in the driver. And Francie's good for a few thousand miles in the next forty years.

So that the way it happened. Nothing's changed really. Except that this week we bought underpants instead or ball-point pens. I'm fourteen hundred dollars in the hole; Francie says "we" about eleven time as much as she used to; and everybody things what a sport I am for going for a ruby ring. And they're right, because if I had to do it all over again, I'd be a sport and do it all over again.

THE FEELING IS MUTUAL

Yesterday turned out to be May Day. Now, I've found out that the first of any month, like the first star or the first robin, really turns Francie on. As a matter of fact, she's big on lasts, too, like the last leaves of the fall, or the last words of dead people. She even breaks up over the caboose on a train, and he told me once that on her tenth birthday she cried for three days because she would never have just one number in her age again. I hope she doesn't live to be a hundred.

So bright and early she's over at my house to tell me it's may Day.

"I suppose you want me to run around a pole with as stick of crepe paper in my hand," I say.

"Don't be silly," she says, "But we have to do something in the country. I crave a picnic.

"I crave to go back to sleep," I say.

Another thing about Francie is that the names she five to things are not what they really are. Like when she says, "picnic" she doesn't mean picnic like everybody else in the world does, she means taking the lunch for a walk in the woods. For instance, last fall I went on one with her, and after a reasonable time I would say, "He looks like a nice spot." And she would say, "Oh, let's not stop yet. Besides, it's much prettier over there." So we'd walk around a little more through every bramble bush she could find, and I'd say, "Here is where 'there' was about half an hour ago." And she's say, "But there is so much to see and it's so beautiful out." And I'd say, "What's so beautiful out? If I don't eat soon, I'll go blind." But we'd go on walking in brambles and wading in rivers or climbing up clay cliffs. And the basket starts feeling like she made stone sandwiches. And the more she walked the more she got excited and the countryside. And the more I exercised the hungrier my stomach got. On the way home in the car, when I finally opened the lunch, she was still talking about what a great picnic it was. So I slapped a we cucumber sandwich in her hand to show her how great.

But to get back to the situation. There I am in bed.

"Come on," she says. "It's May Day.

Big deal," I say.

"But it's May Day and we must do something in the country," she says.

"Not with you," I say. "Anyhow Frank and George are taking me to go shooting with them.

"Then we will all go together, and I will make some lunch," she says.

"To eat?" I ask

"Of course," she says.

"Fat chance," I say

"Oh, don't be silly, there'll be plenty for everybody," she says.

"Right," I say. "That's fine. Now may I brush my teeth?"

"Not before I kiss you," she says.

"It's your funeral," I say.

"what do you mean?" she says.

"My mouth has been taking inventory of my stomach all night," I say.

"Prove it," she says. So we start loving it up, and after a while I tell her that she'd better go downstairs and pack the lunch because I am right out to here with all the kissing and can't get out of bed until she leaves the room. That makes her laugh out loud, but she stands up. Then we begin talking a little, and I tell her the ring looks good on her finger. That makes her sit down on the bed and kiss me again. And I'm right back where we started from.

Finally she had a phone call, or I would have never gotten dressed. Breakfast like that in bed is not bad, I think to myself as I am putting on my shorts. No crumbs.

When I come downstairs, Moma is hung up in the kitchen with a cake.

Francie's gone home to make sandwiches," she says. "You're to call Frank and George and tell them what is up."

"What're you doing this fine May Day, Mama?" I say.

I am going for a drive with Mrs. Sitch in the country," she says. "And do not mention May Day to me. To the Russians it's the Fourth of July.

"And to the Turks it's probably the 31st of February," I say

"Do not be smart to your mother," she says, "And give me ten dollars. We're going to stop in some shops on Route Seven."

"What's the matter with you, Moma?" I say. "You got a twenty pound knick-knack on your back?"

"What's a knock-knick?" she says.

"Here," I say. "You buy whatever you wants, Mama."

"That's my Artie," she says. You have such a good heart."

On my way over to Francie's house, I am wondering what will happened to Mama when I get married. Perhaps we will all move in together, Francie and me. Or better, perhaps Mama should move in with Francie's parents so they won't feel the loss so much. It will be a problem.

George is already over at Frank's house, and when I get there, everything is turned on. The dogs are barking, and the kids are crying, and Marge is sweating on her upper lip the way she does when she gets pressed.

"Hi, Uncle Art," the kids say. "Where's Francie?"

"She's coming," I say

"Mama called," Frank says, "And she wants you to remind Francie not to wear her ring in the forest, she says."

"You don't mind?" I say.

"No," Frank says. "I got a red jacket and that's all we need.

"I mean about Francie coming along," I say. "She's bringing some lunch for us."

"That's great, pal," Frank says, "Now take a look at this gun George got for you. It's a twenty-two semi-automatic.

George is very serious about his out-of-doors. While all this commotion is going on he is picking up each of the three guns and aiming them at imaginary birds. I have seen him do this in the sporting goods store. Sometimes he pretends like he is caught off guard or just walking along when he snaps into position and stats wheeling around at the ceiling.

"What're we going after, George?" I say.

"Rabbits," he says, still moving around like anti-aircraft.

"Oh," I say. "For s second there I thought it would be red-winged blackbirds." George stops and puts the gun down.

"Red-winged blackbirds are not game," George says.

"I wouldn't be game either if I had you shooting at me," I say.

Then Francie drives up in time to add to the confusion.

"Hi, Francie," the kids say.

"Your lip is sweating, Marge, "I say.

"Oh, shut up, Art," Marge says.

"Good, we're all set to go," Frank says. "Francie, you take the dogs in yor car."

"I'll take the munch in my car," I say

"There's no use in taking three cars," George says

"Aren't you going to play with us, Francie?" the kids say

The dogs start barking at each other.

"What's in the lunch?" I say.

"Frank, are you going to leave me with all these kids?" Marge says, "And without a car?"

"We'll play when we come back," Francie says

"You take the dogs and the lunch and Art in one car," George says, "And Frank and I will go in the other."

"Why don't you take them to the Dogwood Bazaar?" Frank says.

"There's some oyster spread for you," Francie says

"You've got a lot of good ideas," Marge says

"Wow, the Bazaar," the kids say. "Why don't you come with us, Francie?"

"Thirty days has September, April, May, June and November," I say.

"O.K., everybody in. Let's go," George says.

"I can't. I have to go with your father," Francie says. "What's the matter, Art?"

"We can't take the lunch and the dogs in the same car." Frank says.

"The oysters, " I say. "If it is not the right month we will all catch some kind of sickness."

"Art, you don't know what you are talking about," Marge says

"Marge," I say, "Your lip is sweating"

Finally we get going with the dogs, Francie, me, and lunch in my car., Francie drives while I run int4rference for the syster sandwiches, The dogs end up licking the windows.

So pretty soon we're walking around with the guns looking for some skinny rabbit who probably hasn't has a square meal since the day he was born. All of a sudden, George just about steps on one and then almost blows his foot off shooting at it.

"Let's go back a little, " I say to Francie.

"Why?" she says. "George has just killed a rabbit."

"I know. And this is getting liker the Korean War," I say.

"We're going back and start lunch," Francie says. "You two come back when you're ready."

"What's the matter, Art?" George says. "Am I spoiling your appetite?"

"Not much," I say. "Only sometimes."

"Well, Frank and I will have plenty of rabbits for a good stew before we leave," he says.

On the way back to the car Francie is grabbing wild flowers again and keeps testing me for butter under the chin.

"I thought you liked butter," she says.

"I do like butter, every day," I say

"The buttercups say not," she says

"When we the last time you buttered your bread with flowers, "I say

She looked at me with squinty eyes smiling in the corners and threw all the buttercups on my head.

"If you can't eat them, wear them," she says.

Francie's not satisfied with the flower pickings in front of us so we jog over to a quarry where a river is still running.

"Why did you come all the way out here to go hunting and then not go hunting?" she says.

"Because it's the wrong time for hunting, "I say

"What do you mean?" Francie says.

"When you kill a rabbit in the fall you're probably doing him a favor," I say. "But in the spring, it's a different story. Spring is a hell of a time to get cut down."

"I didn't know you felt like that, Art," she says

"It just occurred to me," I say.

After lunch is eaten, and Frank and George go after rabbits some more, Francie and I start lying around on the rocks in the sun.

"I feel like a dog," I say.

"The sun is nice," she says.

"Hey," I say, "Get a load of the smell in this rock.

"Mmmmm," she says.

That tone of "Mmmmm" tells me that Francie is halfway asleep and is not going to roll over and smell the rock. So there I am on my stomach watching her sleep for about twenty minutes. The sun is coming right in at my face and catches her body so that the shadow of her chest is almost in my mouth. She is looking very good lying in the sun, I think to myself, and one knee is bent so that it makes her look as if she is posing.

I am lying there like that for about five minutes when she really starts to snooze. She brings her hand from the rock and rests it on her stomach,. Right away the ring lights up like a little Lionel Train Stet switch. The sun is shining through the stone and slopping out all over the ring so that it looks bigger than I think it is. I am watching the light change in the ruby every time she breathes when I remember that Mama did not want her to wear it. So I pull myself over to her and start taking off the ring.

"You might lose this in the country," I say. "I'll keep it for you."

"Mmmmmm," she says. Her hand is hot from being on the stone, and she;'s all loosey goosey from lying in the sun. So I bend her arm at the elbow an put the palm of her hand over her nose.

"That's what the rock smells like from the sun," I say.

"Mmmmmm," she says. I put the ring in my pocket and then, before I put her hand back, I pick up her shirt and kiss her square on the belly

"Mmmmmm," she says and puts her hand up on the back of my head. I stay like that biting her stomach in different places and smelling her body for a while, and then I slip out and leave her alone so she can finish her nap.

While I am waiting for Francie to wake up so we can hunt up Frank and George and go home, I take out the ring and take a hard look at what has gone between she and me. The ruby itself is set up on the ring so that the light can shine through it. It's really a very simple thing, and I can see that I am paying for the jewel and not the hardware, which should be a comforting thought I try and put it on my little finger, but it won't fit, so I put it in my mouth like I used to do with my marbles, but the silver in the ring and the silver in my cavities keeps sending volts of electricity up into my sinuses. In the end I am lying on my back with the stone stuffed in my eye like a monocle and taking in all the country and Francie also in Technicolor.

I am entertaining myself like that for about half an hour, and all the while I cannot get out of my head the song which goes, "I'm looking at the world through rose colored glasses." And I hum the first line over and over again as I look at the trees and the birds and Francie, her face, her chest, her legs, and her body. Everything is red, and I think of all the things that are red in the world and how they compared to the jewel. Lips, Valentines, Barns, Christmas, Fire Crackers, Strawberries.

I write this down because this is what it is like to be with Francie. Even though she does not say much, or even spend her time the way I do, she is still more than anyone I know. And I would rather take a day shopping for underpants with Francie than shouldering around in some bar with the guys.

<u>AH AM HONGRAY!</u>

Moonie Brown's humongous fat ass hung over her toilet like the top of a giant bran muffin. In fact, if you didn't know there was a toilet somewhere beneath her, you might think she was sitting, suspended, in mid-air, in her Louis Armstrong memorial bathroom in her Trump Plaza Apartment. But she had a problem. This time, when she had shifted her gargantuan ass-cheeks to open the gates of hell over the toilet---which, in her case, was like a blind man trying to aim a catapult----she had unseated a crucial joint in the plumbing beneath. As a result, a persistent trickle of toilet flush was now oozing out from the base of the commode and onto her genuine ermine fur shag rug she'd had had specially installed, compliments of Jacob the Rug maker.

Of course, there was no way Moonie could actually <u>see</u> where the water was coming from, so she could only assume that it was coming from the bottom of the toilet. But she knew enough about over-stressed plumbing to know that she was now trapped because, were she to release the pressure on her plumbing by standing up, her bathroom would look like Yellowstone Park in geyser season. Her only hope of preserving her hard-schnorred goods and not incurring the further wrath of the white people living underneath her was to stay put.

Moonie reached for the phone. Beverly Frost would know what to do in a situation like this. She'd covered Mount St. Helens.

"Really, darling, I don't know what you're going to do," Beverly said when she finally picked up the phone. "What time is it?"

"11:30, 'BF'. I figured you would know some plumbers who were used to this sort of thing."

"Used to what, darling?"

"Well," Moonie began slowly. The sustained weight of her ass on the toilet seat was now causing her pain. She was sure the resulting welt was making her ass look like one of those imitation "cowboy" wallets with an embossed horseshoe on it. "What I mean is, what with your connections and seein' how you is the co-hostess with the co-mostess, that you might know of some, how shall I say, discreet plumber who is used to this sort of delicate celebrity work."

"Darling, I'm entertaining Princess Monique and Alan Greenspan at Le Cirque in thirty minutes. I don't know if I can help you. Call Bobbie Sue." Bobby Sue was the assistant to all the anchors on "The News Room" except Beverly who had two of her own.

"Bobbie Sue don't know shit 'bout discretion the way we know it, 'BF'." Moonie was getting extra ghetto now, and it was driving Beverly nuts. Here was this black woman, claiming to be a full blooded Indian, who had bootstrapped her way through medical school, and then given up medicine to become a network television personality suddenly talking like Stepinfetchit. Beverly was not amused.

"Ah needs somebody wif da intuition to be sensitive to mah situation," Moonie continued, "Yunerstan' where ah'm comin' from, girl? Ah needs a Saturday mornin' plumber who can keep his mouth shut and his eyes open just squinty enough to fix dis ol' pipe dats done bursted on me. Otherwise, my sorry ass gonna be on Page Six agin, and da show gonna be gwine down da ribbah with the unwanted publicity."

Beverly thought she was going to be ill. But, at the same time, Moonie had managed to hit a nerve. Beverly owned 100 percent of the show, and she needed the immense revenues she extracted yearly from its run to try and make her net worth more than Mike Wallace's and sufficient to gain access to the British Royals she so lusted after, and finally, to be beyond the social reach of Delores Whitcomb, her arch enemy in life and at work, who tried to do the same thing by marrying Harvey Weinstein.

"Darling, look in the yellow pages. I really have to go."

"Dis ain't no yellow pages job. Dis a white pages job, 'BF'; and dats why I have done called you."

Beverly paused for a moment. Was Moonie actually playing the race card just for a plumbing issue?

"Don't you know anyone who is, perhaps, legally blind, Darling, and good with his hands? Like Melanie's husband, but not him.

"It's got to be someone I don't know. Sheee-it. If only Josephine the Plumber was real. I will die on this here crapper if you don't git me someone, "BF". Is that what you want? Me, like a female black Elvis, on the bathroom floor, and my apartment lookin' like the Superdome during Katrina for all the world and the New York Post to see? You da man, Beverly. Only, this here Brownie is in extremis, and you ain't offerin' me shit for solutions. The phone records gonna show dat you the last person I called, just like Marilyn and the Kennedys. Dat what you want your legacy to be, Ms. Beverly Frost?"

Moonie had gone all the way to the wall on that one. Beverly could hear footsteps on the warning track of life. No one but Moonie would ever dare talk to the queen of New York and television "gets" like that. But Moonie knew where her leverage lay. She did go through medical school as an affirmative action neurosurgeon, so she did know a thing or two about the way the brain worked, especially a white, female, Jewish one. Moonie knew that Beverly had put herself over a velvet barrel the moment she'd hired her, and Moonie was not above rolling it.

"Call Robert. He's used to staring ugly pussy in the face and living to tell about it. And I think he has a wrench." Beverly said finally.

There were times when Beverly would drop the pretension of being "to the manor born" and come out with a line directly from her mobbed-up beginnings. Born into the Jewish/Italian/Irish underworld cauldron of New York before her father took the family on the lam to Massachusetts, the borscht ran thick in her blood. But in making a Memphis redneck roadhouse operator like Bad Bob Vapors her partner, she'd brought a semblance of heartland heterosexuality into her camp and had also found someone who was probably more anti-Semitic than she was.

"Why didn't I think of that?" Moonie said. "This is a man's job. And Bad Bob is just about big enough to handle it." She hung up and pushed the speed dial on her phone. She actually had thought of her executive producer originally, but Moonie never missed an opportunity to call Beverly over the weekend on Beverly's secret private number---the one only her man servant, Lawrence, had, and the one her private hair and make-up team thought they had. Not even any of her surrogate-carried triplets had that number. It was reserved for those who were closest to Beverly and those who could make her money. Edwardo, the groomer of Chewy, her beloved Scharpei, had the number; but that was only because Chewy couldn't use a phone himself, yet.

Of course, the fact that "Mother" held her dog in higher esteem than her own three "so-called" flesh and blood daughters was not lost on the Frost triplets who ran a chain of aerobic studios in Minot, North Dakota. "So-called" because when Beverly had decided to have a child she opted for not only a sperm donor but donor eggs from a WASP clinic in Vermont, and then a surrogate mother to carry them all. It was the surrogate mother who had caused the triplets when she refused to allow any of the embryos to be culled from her womb and because Beverly then decided it was "such a bargain" and besides "the girl's getting paid, darling. It's the highpoint of her life".

Years later, Moonie would asked her if she had ever wished her daughters were genetically Jewish instead of only the byproduct of some borrowed WASP DNA.

"Yes," Beverly had said. "They'd be smarter,"

Bad Bob arrived at Moonie's apartment building with rollers still in his hair from the perm and dye job he had been getting at The Plaza. (Bad Bob had once seen Ned Tannen, then head of Universal, forlornly getting the same procedure in the window of a Brentwood salon, so he figured it was okay) Bad Bob always considered a call from one of Beverly's employees equivalent to a call from her, which it usually was, since it usually came when she didn't want to deal with a situation any longer.

Moonie had provided Bad Bob with a running account of her situation during his trip across town from the Plaza. Thus, when he finally arrived at her building on Freedom Place, he was more up to date than he needed to be. He was able to get himself past the doorman and upstairs to Moonie's penthouse door without much trouble. Such is the power of being 6' 6" and dropping Beverly Frost's name as part of your own. But once at the door to the apartment he could go no further without alerting the building to the predicament and exposing Moonie Brown, literally, as full of shit and definitely fatter than anyone had ever imagined. Their cell phone connection had been cut off by the elevator ride, so he called her again while leaning against her door for privacy.

"Moonie?" Bad Bob said. "I'm here."

"Shit, you ain't," Moonie shot back. "If you were here you'd be helping me wif mah problem"

Bad Bob winced. There had been times, when he used to try to imagine exactly how the prodigious Moonie Brown ever wiped herself after a bowel movement. Now he was close to finding out. He had hoped that the dirty deed was not performed by one of Moonie's revolving personal assistants. On the other hand, it would explain why most of them didn't last past the second movement. He suddenly became afraid that he might be asked to be the next in that long line of first time wipers of the dark side of Moonie Brown.

"I'm outside your door," Bad Bob said quietly into his bullshit cell phone that he had either scored from an advertiser, stolen out of an audience giveaway, or gotten with a subscription to Sports Illustrated. Since the phone actually looked like a phone instead of a football, he'd probably scored it as swag after approving a giveaway on the show.

"Dat don't do me no good," Moonie said, "I'm stuck in here on my potty with my hemorrhoid gettin' 'bout as big as a shepherd's pie."

For that image, Bad Bob had to put the phone down against his thigh and take a deep breath. He knew she was being absolutely literal, and it made him feel sorry for all her assistants and interns for the first time since the start of the show. He even thought that, perhaps, a labor union would be in order even though he hated all unions and the liberal Jews that organized them. But if there were a union for assistants, maybe they wouldn't be required to fall on Moonie's hemorrhoid like a fumble every time she took a shit.

"Listen, Moonbeam," Bad Bob said, using her given "Passamaquoddy" name, "Lemme tell you what I think we ought to do here. I understand the precariousness of your situation and the delicacy of the solution."

"An' don't forget my white ermine bath rug from Jacob the Rug Maker in appreciation of my image as a fine, round, brown, full-bodied lady who appreciates style in the bathroom."

"Oh, right. That ermine bath rug. I'll tell props and sales we found it. But listen up. What I think you should do is come off the toilet and let the water take its course. Then quickly grab a robe and open the door. Then I'll come in and turn the water off. Or, if that's not possible, then I'll take your place on the toilet to stop the water while you go for help."

"Why can't I turn the goddamn water off and cut out the middle man? Moonie asked.

Bad Bob knew in his heart that this was an impossibility. If Moonie's girth was such that it prevented her from wiping herself, then any contortion necessary to reach the cut-off valve was out of the question. But he wasn't about to tell her that. Part of his strategy of working with Moonie Brown was to always treat her as if she were thin as a rail. He learned that from President Clinton and the way he'd treated Monica Lewinsky---the difference being that all Bad Bob got in return was a show to produce, instead of a blow job.

"Okay," he said slowly. "Tell you what. There ought to be a faucet somewhere in the bathroom that turns the water off in the toilet and everything else." Bob could picture Moonie swiveling her head from side to side like a giant robotic Buddha.

"Nu-huh. They ain't nothin' here that I can see. And if there's a faucet in my commode, it better have a gold dolphin on it like I was promised. Moonie was beyond ghetto now. Even a rapper would have trouble understanding her, and she was sinking fast.

Bad Bob was now talking half into his cell phone and half through the crack of the closed door of the apartment. "I don't know if the shut-off valve would be that fancy. Look for something down near the tub or the sink," he said only slightly pleading.

"I see somethin'," Moonie said. "But there's no way in God's Heaven that I can reach it. Unless I......." There was silence. Bob held his breath which was good training for what he was soon going to have to face. Suddenly, there came a roar from the phone and from the apartment itself.

"Whoooooooooaaaaaaaaah!" Bad Bob heard Moonie shout.

There was a thud and then the unmistakable sound of rushing water. A column of sewage had erupted from under the ruptured toilet. The next sound that Bad Bob heard was that of a wounded water buffalo stampeding across the apartment floor, and Bad Bob didn't have to put his ear to the ground, Tonto-style, to know the pounding hoof beats were heading his way.

The front door to Moonie's apartment burst open. There, in front of Bad Bob, was the fat, semi-black, but full-blooded Passamaquoddy, co-host of "The News Room" on her hands and knees, balls-ass naked, and looking up at him like a manatee caught in an oil slick with a shit tsunami right behind her.

"Help," Moonie said in a tiny, meek voice. Bob quickly stepped inside like an action hero and shut the door to stop the wave of shit from escaping into the hall.

"You okay?" Bad Bob said, strangely enjoying his role as the go-to guy for the minority obese in distress.

"The ermine rug," Moonie said without moving but with an intensity in her eyes usually reserved for a bag of White Castle burgers. Bad Bob swung into action, although getting around Moonie without calling attention to either her nudity or her size proved pretty much impossible. Thus, after several attempts to circumnavigate her and proceed upstream, he finally had to simply stop trying.

"Would you excuse me?" he said finally and matter-of-factly.

With that, Moonie rolled over on her back to let him pass. When she did, she automatically squeegeed the water from the shag carpet beneath her and made a "slushing" sound like that of a load of wet laundry hitting the pavement. The water was rising rapidly in the living room, and Moonie was now lying naked on her back in her own shit. Her tits had flopped to either side of her chest, and they looked like two large brown hovercrafts lashed to the side of a Forestall Class aircraft carrier. She had now completely given up the ghost of any acquired gentility.

"Get mah muthahfuckin' er-mine rug off da fuckin' flo and out o' da fuckin' waddah!" She screamed at the top of her lungs while wiggling her hands and legs in the air like a monster Japanese beetle turned on its back. For some reason, Bob remained in his "Rescue Hero" mode which--- because it was, after all, only him--- came off about as heroic as a Con Ed "Blue Truck".

"On it!" He said proving that he had neither balls nor originality. Bad Bob stepped gingerly around Moonie being careful not to soil the laceless bowling shoes he was wearing and headed for the bathroom as if he had a pistol in his hand. He even held his hands together next to his chest like he had seen cops on TV do. But the "pistol-ready" pantomime actually had the opposite effect on the out-sized Bad Bob and made him look, instead, like a big queen pirouetting across the floor in a performance piece.

Moonie's bathroom was easy to find. Just follow the yellow brick river of Native American shit. The toilet was on its side, and there was water and shit everywhere. Bob could not immediately locate the shut-off valve, so he decided to try and stem the tide by righting the toilet and re-setting it on the waste pipe and intake valve. This was accomplished in one motion, but the water pressure threatened to blow the thing over again, so he had no choice but to sit on it himself to keep it in place and slow the flow.

Suddenly, there was a semblance of peace in the apartment. In fact, Bad Bob almost felt like grabbing a magazine and settling in. But there, in front of him, was the aforementioned ermine bath rug. It was no longer fluffy and definitely no longer white. Bob looked around, located the shut-off valve, and turned it off. The flow of water subsided.

By now, Moonie had rolled back on to her stomach and been able to get up to her hands and knees again without the help of a crane. She crawled back to the bathroom and looked up, like a gargantuan St Bernard, at Bad Bob now sitting where she had sat only moments ago.

"Thank you," she said calmly.

Bad Bob picked up the soaked ermine bath rug by the least offensive corner and showed it to Moonie.

"I'm afraid it's ruined," he said.

"Fuck it, baby," Moonie said, "I'll just return it and get another. Maybe <u>two</u>. One for my sister, Bernice, in Atlanta." With that, Moonie reached out and wrapped her fat hand around an industrial strength grab-bar and hauled herself upright. At the same time, she reached around to the back of the bathroom door for a luxurious double-wide terry cloth robe with "Peninsula Hotel" embroidered on it. By the time she had closed the robe around her belly and breasts---a feat that rivaled Christo trying to wrap the Black Hills of South Dakota for its sheer audacity and awe-inspiring grandeur,---Moonbeam P. Brown, co-host and lapsed neurosurgeon, had returned to her lofty, diva self.

"You're a good man, Bad Bob," she said, "We can talk about this on the show Monday. I'll lead."

With that, she turned and swept into her bedroom like a fat-bellied Black Widow spider settling down for a meal at the center of her web. Then she closed the door with just enough certainty that Bad Bob knew he should let himself out when he heard the click of the latch.

UNCENSORED

Jeanie Murphy loved being a network censor, not only because of the power she had to intervene and interdict SBS programming with a "beep" that would replace something she'd instantly decided was inappropriate; she loved it because of the endless march of salacious material that was laid at her feet each day for her consideration. She loved smut but could tell no one of her delight. Her life was one of quiet fascination with the lewd, dirty, outrageous, libelous, and nasty side of life.

Jeanie lived that staple of primetime television known as the "frustrated fuck". Her life was a litany of frustrated fucks, of others yearning for the unattainable, of men getting close but never achieving what they relentlessly sought. But she longed to be, just once, that which she censored. This war of ying and yang within her, this yearning for climax in the face of restraint, gave her an appeal to men and women that went far beyond her classic good looks and unassuming demeanor. She was "The One". She was the sweetheart that everyone wanted to embrace, protect, and fuck at the same time. It was why writers didn't really mind when she would, pre-emptively, reject a turn of phrase or premise; and producers willingly accepted her alteration of an intricately crafted segment. Jeanie Murphy was that nice. She looked and acted like a Daytime version of an idealized sitcom star---straight, long back, adorable bangs, and winning, toothy smile

Thus, Jeanie's whole life was one of making men ache. It was the only real, personal power she'd ever achieved; and she was a master at it. She had identified Bad Bob as a lover long before he, himself, ever realized he was in play. Even while he was having his affair with Mugsy in the early days of the show, Jeanie had earmarked him for herself. Bad Bob was everything she wanted in a man: straight, older, successful, powerful, married, and, most importantly, fertile. He had five kids, and contrary to what one might expect, this turned women squishy at the thought of all that potent sperm swimming around inside of him. She wanted him because she wanted a baby more. She had once, half-jokingly, even begged Brendan for his sperm after Zeke was born. Brendan had declined. He would have enjoyed the deposit but not the interest.

It really was no secret that Jeanie had singled out Bad Bob at practically the first meeting of the production staff. Even the stage crew knew what she was up to since they had worked with her on other shows and had seen her in action. The way gay men liked to boast about their conquests of unattainable straight men, Jeanie was proud that she could make any man desire her to the point of obsession without ever consummating it. It was her own private genius. She was the perfect girl that no one could have.

In the early days of "The Ladies Room", Jeanie insisted that she be at all rehearsals with Bad Bob. Then she would deliberately ignore him while endlessly conferring with stage managers at home base, standing in heels in profile, leaning on the table as if in deep discussion with her ass deliciously raised and presented to him while the stage hands set up a food demo. Those were the days when Bad Bob was still seeing Mugsy. But that didn't deter nor distress Jeanie in the least. She knew what she wanted, and she knew her customers.

Of course, everyone on the studio floor knew exactly what was going on from the start. There was a pool run by Sean, the outside prop man, on how long the seduction would take. And in typical fashion, Bad Bob was the last to figure it out. He vaguely knew of Jeanie's reputation as the Holy Grail of women, but his southern formalism prevented him from ever thinking he might be the object of her interest. Before he became aware of his seduction, the crew would smile knowingly behind him as they readied shots and moved furniture. But then, once Jeanie's chaste vamping became too obvious for even an oaf like Bad Bob to ignore, the fun went out of it for the crew. Now they were forced to ignore it and pretend to concentrate on their work while the two circled each other like zoo animals. The only good news was that their sex dance (suddenly tedious rather than titillating) usually added an extra hour, and sometimes more, to the time sheet. And since Swann had imperiously switched the entire crew of "The Ladies Room" from "staff" to "freelance" in order to avoid paying health benefits, that wasn't an entirely bad thing. But leave it to Bad Bob to make a public display of forbidden sex actually boring to behold. The problem was that the crew knew Jeanie was an unattainable tease even though Bad Bob suddenly thought he actually had a shot. So the whole thing had become tedious and a nonstarter for years.

"That's a wrap, guys," Bradley, the stage manager, said with a good ol' boy clap on Bad Bob's shoulder. The loving couple hardly noticed him as they sat murmuring to each other on the show couch. Jeanie had fixed her prey with a long stare of adorableness designed to undress his will before she, supposedly, would undress herself. "We're going home. Lock up when you're finished." Bradley continued into Bad Bob's deaf ears.

Bradley didn't wait for an answer, nor did he want one. He turned immediately and walked off the set whistling a Beatles tune as the lights were "killed" with a heavy, muffled "thump", leaving only several work lights and safety lamps illuminating the cavernous studio.

"Thanks, Brad. Nice show today, man." Bad Bob called after him with a manly wave and an upraised clenched fist. Bob remained transfixed, his hard-on filling his pants. Jeanie feigned being deeply concerned with the script in her hand just to intensify his passion.

Bradley knew better than to answer. He kept walking toward the exit acknowledging the couple with only a half wave without looking back. The rest of the crew had already tip-toed out when the inevitable had become obvious: The "inevitable" being Bad Bob actually making an overt sexual move only to be left twisting in the wind when Jeanie drew back in innocent, chaste horror.

There was silence. Jeanie returned her gaze to Bad Bob, and smiled slyly at him as if she were a child and he was playfully withholding a present for her. Her mouth opened slightly and her jaw skewed as she ran the tip of her tongue around the back of her teeth as if she were thinking about something. Even merely opening her mouth was enough to drive a man wild. Bad Bob felt more like Elvis, at that moment, than any impersonator he'd ever showcased in his Memphis roadhouse.

Finally, the door to the studio thudded shut when Bradley left.

"I'll be right back," Bob said unnecessarily. He got up from his chair without realizing the full extent of the erection he'd produced during their little *tête-à-tête*. He was suddenly overcome with a Tennessee gentleman's modesty that white folk in Memphis liked to affect in order to differentiate themselves from the freed slaves. Unlike the black man, Bad Bob preferred to hide his erection rather than parade it around like a symbol of emancipation.

He turned away from Jeanie and went quickly to the main door of the studio and slid the top grey bolt across, locking it. Then he proceeded to the back entrance, by the green room, and bolted that one shut as well. Secure in his privacy, he turned back toward the set where Jeanie sat with the script. She'd even put her glasses on to reinforce her bona fides as the nicest girl in the world. Bad Bob moved more slowly now and unzipped his fly as he approached the riser that held the table and chairs on the set. Jeanie's back was to him so he could reach inside his pants and feel his heavy cock for reassurance. He had done this before with all of his conquests. It gave him confidence.

"There," he said as he sat down beside her. "You were saying?"

Jeanie pouted slightly and tucked her perfect chin on her chest because she knew it accentuated her eyes. She looked at him pleadingly, a look that was, at once, innocent but knowing. She had practiced that look in bedroom mirrors since she was ten and repeated it automatically whenever she was in public and in the company of men.

Jeanie's attractiveness was an idealized beauty that had the gestalt of being the most desirable woman in the world. She was one of those iconic women who seem to have it all in just the right proportions. Like Ali McGraw and Natalie Wood in their day or Jackie Kennedy, Grace Kelly, Kate Middleton, or Jennifer Lawrence. Men could never get enough of them, or of Jeanie. She was truly attractive but in an imperfect and accessible way, but that wasn't all. She represented a promise. A promise that any man who might possess her would be complete. She would fulfill all his yearnings for greatness for all time. Her real power rested in the fact that she knew it. And this was the dance she'd done with men all her life. She was the ever-retreating Fitzgeraldian heroine. Powerful in all that she embodied but impossible in her attainability. The fact that she worked as an unassuming network censor just added to her mystique. It inspired men to discover her and be one to uncover her beauty, intelligence, and sweetness. They wanted to be the one to remove her glasses and reveal her swan-like perfection and desirability. It appealed to their egos that they, alone, would be the one to realize the gifts that even she had seemingly overlooked. But what men didn't know was that Jeanie Murphy was way ahead of them. They forgot that her job was saying "no". That is, until she said "yes".

Jeanie knew what she wanted this afternoon. And she had decided that the way to get it was to do what Mugsy would do and undoubtedly had. Unaccustomed as she was of actually realizing any of her seductions, today she relied, instead, on channeling the supervising producer even as tawdry as she knew Mugsy was. She reached up and removed the elastic band that kept her hair tied back in a ponytail in the semblance of a work mode. Her hair tumbled down to her shoulders. She shook it once and lifted it off the back of her collar. Then she flipped it entirely over to one side exposing her neck and shoulder, exactly the way she'd watched Mugsy do a hundred times a day for 15 years. The Censor had suddenly become uncensored.

"You don't really want to discuss the cold open, do you?" she said looking straight at Bad Bob.

"No, I don't." Bob said trying to match her apparent coolness.

"Well then..." she said, "Ain't nobody here but us chipmunks." It didn't matter that what she said made no sense. What mattered was that Bad Bob took it as an invitation. But it was also obvious that---even though the button on her blouse had now mysteriously come undone, and the milky curve and fullness of her left breast was clearly visible---she was not going to make the first move.

Bad Bob could feel himself being transported. His head filled with as much blood as his cock, the vein on his forehead began to throb pleasantly in time with his engorged penis. Was this finally going to be it? After all the months of cock teasing and masturbation in his office?

"I..." Suddenly, his tongue was in her mouth and her breast in his hand. Jeanie's delicately manicured fingers reached inside his pants and removed his cock. She kissed it once, but only once. Then she stood up abruptly, walked around the back of his chair while drawing her hand past his neck and face like a silk scarf. She lost her jeans effortlessly, revealing that she wore no panties. She was that confident of the shape her butt was in. Then she turned around and bent over, with her forearms resting on "The Ladies Room" table so that her incredibly tight bare ass was in his face. She turned her head back to him and smiled sweetly. The sudden sighting of the network censor's asshole and swollen pussy at the same time was like an observance of a double eclipse.

Bad Bob scrambled up from his chair and came around behind her. His cock entered her seamlessly in one liquid motion. He couldn't believe she was as wet as she was without the obligatory 45 minutes of foreplay necessary to get his wife to even audibly inhale.

His wife's breathing problems were such that Bad Bob had come to view her inhaler as a sex toy. He would work on her lifeless body until she reached over to the bedside table for her inhaler. Then he knew he was getting somewhere, and she was actually feeling something. The whistle-wheeze of the inhaler was Pavlovian for Bad Bob, and it would always make him cum. Mrs. Vapors never had the heart to tell him that it was just cat dander that made her wheeze and not the passion. Often, in-between his passionate kisses, she would move her mouth to the side and take a hit off the inhaler, but, fortunately, he always took it as a compliment about his technique. Only she and the cat knew the truth.

The sex continued from behind longer than Bad Bob had ever imagined it would, mainly because Jeanie was able to see herself in the grey glass of the teleprompter mounted on Camera Three. In fact, she was quite comfortable resting on her forearms while he pounded away behind her, her eyes glued to her own image as if watching late night porn.

"Oh, baby," she moaned and felt him engorge even more. She "Kegelled" him once but then stopped because she didn't want him to cum before she'd drawn all of his sperm up from the depths of his balls. Jeanie saw her ass as a deep water drilling platform designed specifically for the extraction of that sweet crude laying deep within a man that no one had been able to reach or exploit before. His cock was her cock now; she was probing *him* not the other way around; deeper and deeper she went as he fucked her.

"Oh, baby....Oh, baby... Oh, *baby*," she repeated. Her shadowy face in the teleprompter glass was contorted by the sex, and she was fascinated by her ability to observe herself being licentious. She thrashed her head forward so that her hair covered her face and then back again knowing that it would fall in wanton curls on either side of her head, framing her face just so. She pouted at herself and cocked her head slightly askance, as if checking out another angle in a store window rather than being fucked from behind by her boss. And she very much liked what she saw.

"Oh, baby; oh, baby; oh, baby," she repeated like a mantra. And then, "OH, BABY!" She screamed, confident that she was, after all, on a sound stage and no one could hear

But only Jeanie knew that she wasn't speaking figuratively. "Oh, baby" wasn't just a random expression, it was a mission statement.

Bad Bob hadn't felt this good since his gang banging days with the University of Tennessee football team. He mistakenly thought that Jeanie's moans and shouts had something to do with his technique when, in fact, what sounded like unbridled passion was merely her single-minded intent. And when she finally let him cum by milking his cock like the teat of a cow with the muscles of her pussy, he thought he would explode right through the top her head.

"Oh, sweet Jesus!" he shouted and slapped her ass as if he were breaking a horse. Bad Bob had never cum like that, and he kept·cumming longer than he thought a man was capable of; the way blood spurts out of the neck of a chicken after its head has been chopped off---in descending jerks until it falls over dead. The image of himself as a boy with an axe on a Tennessee farm flashed in Bad Bob's mind.

Jeanie had watched her expression go from that of a pouty tramp to a cold-blooded hit man as she felt Bad Bob's cock stiffen within her, with its head engorging in expectation. Then, when his warm sperm had risen from his depths and finally exploded into the well of her vagina, only then did she relax her grip on his cock and smile sweetly into the monitor.

She got what she came for.

Bob withdrew himself and sat down heavily on a chair next to the couch. Fortunately, it was Moonie's "column of concrete" chair, so it could take the sudden weight. His wet cock still quivered happily in his lap like a fish that had been freshly landed. He'd broken a sweat, and his face was as flushed as when he lied in public.

It was then that Jeanie finally noticed the red light on Camera Two.

They were live. Or, at least, "live to tape". The first thing Jeanie thought of was the "kill" button that would excise what had just happened before it could be sent out over the airwaves. But then, still in her "Mugsy mode" she checked herself again in the teleprompter glass on Camera Three to make sure her hair was right. Then, instead of outrage at the horror of being violated, she smiled ever so slightly at the knowledge that she, too, would have an uncensored sex tape just like Paris Hilton or Kim Kardashian. She turned and knelt beside Bad

Bob and took his semi hard cock into her mouth, being careful to remain in profile and on her good side which meant that she had to suck it over his thigh which proved slightly uncomfortable. The blow job confirmed to Bad Bob that he had done the right thing, and he turned in his seat to face her and make it easier for both of them. Now he, too, was in profile to the hot camera.

Jeanie could taste herself as well as his cum on his dick. She wondered if she was good enough to get him hard again as she had done so often on her knees in his office. Bad Bob's unbridled amazement at her oral dexterity was the only blowjob review she'd ever gotten. She flipped her hair over to the upstage side of her head so as to not obscure her face by the camera angle.

"Oh baby, you're so hot," she said woodenly as she sucked him and screwed her hand up and down his cock.

She was happy that, as luck would have it, the best hand for the shot, the furthest from the camera, was her right hand; and she was right-handed.

"I've wanted you so badly." Jeanie was careful to be grammatically correct even though it sounded unnatural in the context. Her innate knowledge of camera angles made her more self-conscious about never finishing college than the fact that she was being recorded as an adulteress. She wanted her sex tape to be hot not stupid.

"Go easy, mama." Bad Bob moaned like an Elvis Impersonator. "You're sweet, but it's tender as hell down there."

"Mmmmmmmmmmmmmm," Jeanie responded, her mouth full of him. She was able to get him firm but not hard enough to fuck, and she didn't want to be seen trying to stuff his malleable cock back into her pussy on her sex tape. She might have been able to do it by sitting on him face to face, but then the camera would be looking at the unfortunate display of moles on her back. She thought of doing a "reverse cowgirl", which was the preferred porno position, but there was no way she would have gotten his cock inside her from that angle. It just wasn't stiff enough. She reverted instead to a vigorous hand job while watching his face intently. She knew he wasn't going to come again, but the fact that she had been able to give him enough of a re-erection to make it a possibility was exciting enough.

"Oh, mama. Y'all could raise the dead," Bad Bob said, still doing Elvis. "But mah well's done gone dry."

Jeanie didn't answer him but responded by doubling her stroke and jerking him even more emphatically just to make the point that she was hotter than he was. She was able to face the camera now and pout sweetly as she abused his cock mercilessly. Finally, he stopped her with both his hands and rolled away from her.

"Can't take it, mama. Have mercy." He said.

"You okay, Sweetie?" she said as if they were a long married couple just getting up in the morning.

"Yeah, I'm better'n I've ever been." Bad Bob said trying to calm his cock down.

Jeanie, still playing to the camera, put her jeans back on in deliberately slow, incremental stages as if she were doing some sort of reverse striptease. The red light on Camera Two had never wavered nor blinked, and she was momentarily disappointed at the possibility that, perhaps, there *hadn't* been any tape rolling, that nothing had been recorded, and it was just a random camera left "hot" by mistake. She looked the camera full in the lens as if she could tell by doing so if it was being manned in the control room. The notion that the apparent recording might be completely innocent and not happening at all made her even more reckless and blatant. She smiled at the camera and even winked before turning back to Bad Bob. She was indulging herself in the possibility that she was being watched even though, now, in her heart, she had decided that it had all been a voyeuristic fantasy.

She was wrong.

The tape had been rolling and the reel was an instant treasure, more highly regarded than even the Moonie yoga fart tape. It would be years, after the show had been canceled and no one could be hurt by its production that Jeanie ever saw it. At that point she was proud that her body and sexuality had been preserved electronically in order for her, then, teenage daughter to know, and witness, her provenance.

Bad Bob had fallen silent. When Jeanie finished buttoning her jeans, and his own fly was zipped, and the cum stains blotted dry; he slipped an arm around her waist and they walked silently off the set.

Three weeks later, Jeanie knew she was pregnant. She made her doctor try to pick up a heartbeat at six weeks, and he lied when he said he did. That's when she told Bad Bob she was keeping the baby.

Eight weeks later she began to show, such was the intensity of her desire to have the baby. It was around that time that Bad Bob hastily called a special staff meeting to announce that Jeanie Murphy was pregnant and going to have a baby. Everyone cheered. Jeanie looked suitably demur but proud.

"It's her baby, and it's her business," Bad Bob felt compelled to add since there was really nothing more to say about the soon-to-be unwed mother who had miraculously become "with child" without the apparent benefit of a husband, a boyfriend (Jeanie had never, in fifteen years, been seen with as much as a date), or even a visit to a sperm bank.

"And if anyone asks you who the father is, you are to leave the room… immediately," Bad Bob said pointing a finger menacingly at the assembled, "Just walk out, without another word." St Joseph must have made the same speech just before Bethlehem. In this case, censorship was in the family.

No one left the room. Everyone knew. The eagle had landed.